P9-DMR-817

ROBINSON CRUSOE

Daniel Defoe

COLLINS
CLASSICS

Harper Press
An imprint of HarperCollins*Publishers*
1 London Bridge Street
London SE1 9GF

This edition published 2013

A catalogue record for this book is available from the British Library

ISBN-13: 978-0-00-735084-1

Printed and bound by CPI Group (UK) Ltd, Croydon, CR0 4YY

MIX
Paper from
responsible sources
FSC® C007454

FSC™ is a non-profit international organisation established to promote
the responsible management of the world's forests. Products carrying the
FSC label are independently certified to assure consumers that they come
from forests that are managed to meet the social, economic and
ecological needs of present and future generations,
and other controlled sources.

Find out more about HarperCollins and the environment at
www.harpercollins.co.uk/green

Life & Times section © HarperCollins*Publishers* Ltd
Gerard Cheshire asserts his moral rights as author of the Life & Times section
Classic Literature: Words and Phrases adapted from
Collins English Dictionary
Typesetting in Kalix by Palimpsest Book Production Limited,
Falkirk, Stirlingshire

History of Collins

In 1819, Millworker William Collins from Glasgow, Scotland, set up a company for printing and publishing pamphlets, sermons, hymn books and prayer books. That company was Collins and was to mark the birth of HarperCollins Publishers as we know it today. The long tradition of Collins dictionary publishing can be traced back to the first dictionary William published in 1824, *Greek and English Lexicon*. Indeed, from 1840 onwards, he began to produce illustrated dictionaries and even obtained a licence to print and publish the Bible.

Soon after, William published the first Collins novel, *Ready Reckoner*, however it was the time of the Long Depression, where harvests were poor, prices were high, potato crops had failed and violence was erupting in Europe. As a result, many factories across the country were forced to close down and William chose to retire in 1846, partly due to the hardships he was facing.

Aged 30, William's son, William II took over the business. A keen humanitarian with a warm heart and a generous spirit, William II was truly 'Victorian' in his outlook. He introduced new, up-to-date steam presses and published affordable editions of Shakespeare's works and *Pilgrim's Progress*, making them available to the masses for the first time. A new demand for educational books meant that success came with the publication of travel books, scientific books, encyclopaedias and dictionaries. This demand to be educated led to the later publication of atlases and Collins also held the monopoly on scripture writing at the time.

In the 1860s Collins began to expand and diversify and the idea of 'books for the millions' was developed. Affordable editions of classical literature were published and in 1903 Collins introduced 10 titles in their Collins Handy Illustrated Pocket Novels. These proved so popular that a few years later this had increased to an output of 50 volumes, selling nearly half a million in their year of publication. In the same year, The Everyman's Library was also instituted, with the idea of publishing an affordable library of the most important classical works, biographies, religious and philosophical treatments, plays, poems, travel and adventure. This series eclipsed all competition at the time and the introduction of paperback books in the 1950s helped to open that market and marked a high point in the industry.

HarperCollins is and has always been a champion of the classics and the current Collins Classics series follows in this tradition – publishing classical literature that is affordable and available to all. Beautifully packaged, highly collectible and intended to be reread and enjoyed at every opportunity.

Life & Times

About the Author

Daniel Defoe was born at the beginning of a period of history known as the English Restoration, so-named because it was when King Charles II restored the monarchy to England following the English Civil War and the brief dictatorship of Oliver Cromwell. Defoe's contemporaries included Isaac Newton and Samuel Pepys.

Defoe was born in London and during his formative years was witness to the Great Plague (1665-6) and the Great Fire (1666), both of which had considerable effect on the neighbourhood he lived in. In addition to these disasters, the English were at war with the Dutch between 1665 and 1667, which saw many privateer ships involved in attacking the Dutch fleet as Charles had insufficient money to fund the war. Privateers essentially paid themselves with the booty they acquired from the enemy ships, which included trade vessels as well as men'o'war. In turn this led to the evolution of piracy in times of peace. It is undoubtedly this roguish activity on the high seas that inspired Defoe to write his famous novel *Robinson Crusoe*.

Defoe's original surname was simply 'Foe' and his family were humble traders, but he added the prefix to make himself sound more continental and sophisticated. Defoe became interested in social reform and used his first efforts at writing to promote ideas for improving social and economic conditions in London. He was arrested for his activities but had caught the attentions of Robert Harley, 1st Earl of Oxford, who made him an agent for gathering intelligence about his political rivals.

His literary journey began soon after this when Britain was struck by a full scale hurricane in 1703, which travelled across the Atlantic Ocean and ravaged the southern British Isles for two whole days. The storm killed thousands of people, felled millions of trees and damaged every building in its path. Defoe was inspired to record many first-hand accounts of the hurricane, which he published the following year in *The Storm*.

DANIEL DEFOE

For the next fifteen years Defoe was very active politically, writing hundreds of documents for the Tory party, a party which had emerged as a political wing of the Cavaliers following the English Civil War. They were essentially royalists with deeply held conservative views. There had been many stories of pirate adventures in exotic places and a Scotsman named Alexander Selkirk had been rescued in 1709 after four years castaway on Juan Fernández, a tropical island in the south Pacific, off the coast of Chile. Clearly Defoe had been inspired by these tales of danger and derring-do. In 1719, Defoe published his masterpiece, *Robinson Crusoe*, which is widely considered to be the first English novel.

The novel was an instant success, seemingly because there was a great appetite in England for yarns about intrepid explorers who survived against the odds in far flung corners. Added to that, there was a certain innate appeal about the idea of fending for one's self in isolation – building one's own shelter, making clothes, finding food and water, staying alive. It seemed to resonate with a primal desire in people that had lain dormant since time immemorial – the reawakening of the hunter gatherer instinct.

This reaction to *Robinson Crusoe* was perhaps an expression of the way developing society was making people feel trapped by circumstance. The British Agricultural Revolution was beginning, soon to be followed by the Industrial Revolution, and these events were compartmentalizing society, so that people had defined jobs to do rather than being required to put their hands to a number of tasks. The psychological effect was to divorce people from their fundamental sense of self worth and independence. Crusoe's ordeal may have been tough and isolating but it was also life affirming and character building. Most of all, Crusoe had his own kingdom to reign over, when most English men, women and children couldn't call any patch of land their own.

The psychological freedom delivered to Crusoe seemed worth all of the hardship he endured over his 28 years waiting to be rescued. There must have been many a reader who would have gladly swapped their life for his, so Crusoe became a kind of folk hero even though he lived only in the world of fiction.

Despite its attraction as an escapist fantasy, *Robinson Crusoe* also reminds the reader that they are essentially social animals and that loneliness is the enemy of most humans. Crusoe fears that he may never see another person again and die alone, but then he sees a footprint in the sand. It is the moment of his reconnection with humanity. Although he doesn't know whether the footprint belongs to a potential friend or enemy he is compelled to seek out that person whatever the outcome.

This is why the book is considered the first novel, because it says something between the lines, about the human condition. It contains allegory and makes the reader think beyond the plot. The reader becomes the intimate voyeur, feeling Crusoe's emotions, frustrations and revelations as he learns to cope with his surroundings. Ultimately he turns the wilderness into his home because he comes to realize that we all come from the wilderness, but we have forgotten our prehistory.

Robinson Crusoe

At the time that Daniel Defoe wrote *Robinson Crusoe* many European countries were conquering new lands around the globe and enterprising men were making their fortunes through trade of goods and slavery. Defoe used this world as the backdrop for his story.

When Crusoe first sets out into the world he is shipwrecked and captured by pirates who make him their slave. He then escapes and manages to make his own fortune by establishing a sugar plantation. The tables are then turned again, when he is shipwrecked a second time and has to survive by his wits on an island. Defoe cleverly allows Crusoe to acquire the life experience to make his story of survival believable. He probably recognized that a European gentleman would not have faired very well had he been stranded on a maiden voyage.

After a number of years alone Crusoe discovers that other people visit the island from time to time. He is alarmed to discover that they practice cannibalism, but then realizes that their culture is so different from his own that he has no moral right to condemn their actions. This shows considerable wisdom on the part of Defoe, because he is acknowledging that the ethics of what is right and wrong depends on social context. Nevertheless, Crusoe still decides to rescue a captive about to be ritually slaughtered and in doing so finds himself a devoted companion in the form of a native he calls Friday. As unlikely as it may seem, Crusoe has managed to keep an accurate calendar and knows which day of the week the rescue took place.

As the book was intended for an English market, Defoe has Crusoe teach Friday to speak the king's tongue and convert to Christianity. There are then various further twists and turns to the plot that see Crusoe and Friday eventually arrive in England. What is more, Crusoe is able to claim back the wealth from his sugar plantation and live the rest of his life a wealthy man.

There is a forgotten sequel to *Robinson Crusoe*, titled *The Farther Adventures of Robinson Crusoe*. Crusoe decides to revisit his island, establishing a civilized colony there, but Friday is killed by attacking cannibals. Crusoe then embarks on a series of adventures around the world, including Madagascar and Asia. Defoe published this sequel later in the same year, 1719.

The story of Crusoe, in particular his time spent alone on his island, has remained an inspiration for many writers ever since. As well as inventing the novel, Defoe also invented the survival genre, so that any similar story is automatically seen to allude to *Robinson Crusoe*, even when it happens to be a true story. There is an enduring attraction to the idea that humans can, when given no choice, manage to find ways to cope. Common sense, resourcefulness and self reliance are qualities we admire in others and in ourselves, because they reassure us that it is possible to get by without the trappings of the modern world.

ROBINSON CRUSOE

CONTENTS

CHAPTER 1

My Birth and Parentage – At Nineteen
elope with a Schoolfellow, and go to Sea –
Ship founders – Crew saved and landed
near Yarmouth

I was born in the year 1632, in the city of York, of a good family,
though not of that country, my father being a foreigner of Bremen,
who settled first at Hull. He got a good estate by merchandise, and,
leaving off his trade, lived afterwards at York; from whence he had
married my mother, whose relations were named *Robinson*, a very
good family in that country, and from whom I was called *Robinson
Kreutznaer*; but, by the usual corruption of words in England, we
are now called, nay, we call ourselves, and write our name, *Crusoe*;
and so my companions always called me.

I had two elder brothers, one of which was lieutenant colonel
to an English regiment of foot in Flanders, formerly commanded by
the famous Colonel Lockhart, and was killed at the battle near
Dunkirk against the Spaniards. What became of my second brother
I never knew, any more than my father and mother did know what
was become of me.

Being the third son of the family, and not bred to any trade,
my head began to be filled very early with rambling thoughts. My
father, who was very ancient, had given me a competent share of
learning, as far as house-education and a country free school generally go, and designed me for the law; but I would be satisfied with
nothing but going to sea; and my inclination to this led me so
strongly against the will, nay, the commands of my father, and
against all the entreaties and persuasions of my mother and
other friends, that there seemed to be something fatal in that

propensity of nature, tending directly to the life of misery which was to befall me.

My father, a wise and grave man, gave me serious and excellent counsel against what he foresaw was my design. He called me one morning into his chamber, where he was confined by the gout, and expostulated very warmly with me upon this subject. He asked me what reasons, more than a mere wandering inclination, I had for leaving my father's house and my native country; where I might be well introduced, and had a prospect of raising my fortune by application and industry, with a life of ease and pleasure. He told me it was only men of desperate fortunes on the one hand, or of aspiring superior fortunes on the other, who went abroad upon adventures, to rise by enterprise, and make themselves famous in undertakings of a nature out of the common road; that these things were all either too far above me, or too far below me; and that mine was the middle state, or what might be called the upper station of *low life*, which he had found, by long experience, was the best state in the world the most suited to human happiness, not exposed to the miseries and hardships, the labour and sufferings of the mechanic part of mankind, and not embarrassed with the pride, luxury ambition, and envy of the upper part of mankind. He told me I might judge of the happiness of this state by this one thing, viz., that this was the state of life which all other people envied; that kings had frequently lamented the miserable consequences of being born to great things, and wished they had been placed in the middle of the two extremes, between the mean and the great; that the Wise Man gave his testimony to this, as the just standard of true felicity, when he prayed to have neither poverty nor riches.

He bade me observe it, and I should always find, that the calamities of life were shared among the upper and lower part of mankind; but that the middle station had the fewest disasters, and was not exposed to so many vicissitudes as the higher or lower part of mankind: nay, they were not subjected to so many distempers and uneasiness, either of body or mind, as those were, who, by vicious living, luxury, and extravagances on one hand, or by hard labour, want of necessaries, and mean and insufficient diet, on the other hand, bring distempers upon themselves by the natural consequences of their way of living; that the middle station of life was calculated for all kind of virtues, and all kind of enjoyments; that peace and plenty were the handmaids of a middle fortune; that temperance, moderation, quietness, health, society, all agreeable diversions, and all desirable pleasures, were the blessings attending the middle station of life; that this way men went silently and smoothly through the world, and comfortably out of it; not embarrassed with the labours of the hands or of the head; not sold to a life of slavery for daily bread, or harassed with perplexed circumstances, which rob the soul of peace and the body of rest; not enraged with the passion of envy, or the secret burning lust of ambition for great things – but in easy circumstances sliding gently through the world, and sensibly tasting the sweets of living without the bitter; feeling that they are happy, and learning, by every day's experience, to know it more sensibly.

After this he pressed me earnestly, and in the most affectionate manner, not to play the young man, or to precipitate myself into miseries, which nature, and the station of life I was born in, seemed to have provided against – that I was under no necessity of seeking my bread – that he would do well for me, and endeavour to enter me fairly into the station of life which he had been just recommending to me; and that if I was not very easy and happy in the world it must be my mere fate, or fault, that must hinder it; and that he should have nothing to answer for, having thus discharged his duty, in warning me against measures which he knew would be to my hurt. In a word, that as he would do very kind things for me, if I would stay and settle at home as he directed, so he would not have so much hand in my misfortunes as to give me any encouragement to go away – and, to close all, he told me, I had my elder brother for my example, to whom he had used the same earnest persuasions to keep him from going into the Low Country wars, but could not prevail, his young desires prompting him to run into the army, where he was killed – and though he said he would not cease to pray for me, yet he would venture to say to me, that if I did take this foolish step, God would not bless me – and I would have leisure hereafter to reflect upon having neglected his counsel, when there might be none to assist in my recovery.

I observed, in this last part of his discourse, which was truly prophetic, though I suppose my father did not know it to be so himself – I say, I observed the tears run down his face very plentifully, especially when he spoke of my brother who was killed; and that when he spoke of my having leisure to repent, and none to assist me, he was so moved that he broke off the discourse, and told me his heart was so full he could say no more to me.

I was sincerely afflicted with this discourse – as, indeed, who

3

could be otherwise? – and I resolved not to think of going abroad any more, but to settle at home according to my father's desire. But, alas! a few days wore it all off; and, in short, to prevent any of my father's further importunities, in a few weeks after, I resolved to run quite away from him. However, I did not act so hastily neither, as the first heat of my resolution prompted, but I took my mother at a time when I thought her a little pleasanter than ordinary, and told her that my thoughts were so entirely bent upon seeing the world, that I should never settle to anything with resolution enough to go through with it, and my father had better give me his consent, than force me to go without it – that I was now eighteen years old, which was too late to go apprentice to a trade, or clerk to an attorney, that I was sure if I did, I should never serve out my time, but I should certainly run away from my master before my time was out and go to sea – and if she would speak to my father to let me go one voyage abroad, if I came home again, and did not like it, I would go no more, and I would promise, by double diligence, to recover the time I had lost.

This put my mother into a great passion; she told me she knew it would be to no purpose to speak to my father upon any such subject – that he knew too well what was my interest, to give his consent to any such thing so much for my hurt – and that she wondered how I could think of any such thing, after the discourse I had had with my father, and such kind and tender expressions as she knew my father had used to me – and that, in short, if I would ruin myself, there was no help for me; but I might depend I should never have their consent to it – that, for her part, she would not have so much hand in my destruction – and I should never have it to say, that my mother was willing when my father was not.

Though my mother refused to move it to my father, yet I heard afterwards, that she reported all the discourse to him; and that my father, after showing a great concern at it, said to her, with a sigh, "That boy might be happy if he would stay at home; but if he goes abroad, he will be the most miserable wretch that ever was born – I can give no consent to it."

It was not till almost a year after this that I broke loose, though in the meantime I continued obstinately deaf to all proposals of settling to business, and frequently expostulating with my father and mother about their being so positively determined against what they knew my inclinations prompted me to. But being one day at Hull, whither I went casually, and without any purpose of making an elopement that time – but, I say, being there, and one of my companions being going by sea to London, in his father's ship, and prompting me to go with him, with the common allurement of a seafaring man, that it should cost me nothing for my passage, I consulted neither father nor mother any more, nor so much as sent them word of it; but leaving them to hear of it as they might, without asking God's blessing or my father's, without any consideration of circumstances of consequences, and in an ill hour, God knows, on the 1st of September, 1651, I went on board a ship bound for London. Never any young adventurer's misfortunes, I believe, began sooner, or continued longer, than mine. The ship was no sooner got out of the Humber, than the wind began to blow, and the sea to rise in a most frightful manner; and as I had never been at sea before, I was most inexpressibly sick in body, and terrified in mind. I began now seriously to reflect upon what I had done, and how justly I was overtaken by the judgment of Heaven for my wicked leaving my father's house, and abandoning my duty; all the good counsel of my parents, my father's tears, and my mother's entreaties, came now fresh into my mind; and my conscience, which was not yet come to the pitch of hardness to which it has been since, reproached me with the contempt of advice, and the breach of my duty to God and my father.

All this while the storm increased, and the sea went very high, though nothing like what I have seen many times since – no, nor what I saw a few days after: but it was enough to affect me then, who was but a young sailor, and had never known anything of the matter. I expected every wave would have swallowed us up, and that every time the ship fell down, as I thought it did in the trough or hollow of the sea, we should never rise more. In this agony of mind, I made many vows and resolutions, that if it would please God to spare my life in this one voyage, if ever I got once my foot upon dry land again, I would go directly home to my father, and never set it into a ship again while I lived; but I would take his advice, and never run myself into such miseries as these any more. Now I saw plainly the goodness of his observations about the middle station of life, how easy, how comfortable he had lived all his days, and never had been exposed to tempests at sea, nor trouble on shore; and, in short, I resolved that I would, like a true repenting prodigal, go home to my father.

These wise and sober thoughts continued all the while the storm continued, and indeed some time after; but the next day the

DANIEL DEFOE

wind was abated, and the sea calmer, and I began to be a little
inured to it. However, I was very grave for all that day, being also
a little sea-sick still; but towards night the weather cleared up, the
wind was quite over, and a charming fine evening followed; the sun
went down perfectly clear, and rose so the next morning; and having
little or no wind, and a smooth sea, the sun shining upon it, the
sight was, as I thought, the most delightful that ever I saw.

I had slept well in the night, and was now no more sea-sick,
but very cheerful – looking with wonder upon the sea that was so
rough and terrible the day before, and could be so calm and so
pleasant in so little a time after: and now, lest my good resolutions
should continue, my companion, who had indeed enticed me away,
comes to me. "Well, Bob," says he, clapping me upon the shoulder,
"How do you do after it? I warrant you were frightened, weren't
you, last night, when it blew but a capful of wind?" "A' capful d'ye
call it?" said I, "'twas a terrible storm." "A storm, you fool you!"
replies he, "do you call that a storm? why it was nothing at all; give
us but a good ship and sea-room, and we think nothing of such a
squall of wind as that; but you're but a fresh-water sailor, Bob; come,
let us make a bowl of punch, and we'll forget all that: d'ye see what
charming weather 'tis now?" To make short this sad part of my story,
we went the way of all sailors; the punch was made, and I was made
half drunk with it, and in that one night's wickedness I drowned all
my repentance, all my reflections upon my past conduct, all my
resolutions for the future. In a word, as the sea was returned to its
smoothness of surface, and settled calmness, by the abatement of that
storm, so, the hurry of my thoughts being over, my fears and apprehensions of being swallowed up by the sea being forgotten, and the
current of my former desires returned, I entirely forgot the vows and
promises that I made in my distress. I found, indeed, some intervals
of reflection; and the serious thoughts did, as it were, endeavour to
return again sometimes; but I shook them off, and roused myself from
them, as it were from a distemper; and, applying myself to drinking
and company, soon mastered the return of those fits (for so I called
them); and I had, in five or six days, got a complete victory over my
conscience, as any young fellow that resolved not to be troubled with
it could desire. But I was to have another trial for it still; and
Providence, as in such cases generally it does, resolved to leave me
entirely without excuse; for if I would not take this for a deliverance,
the next was to be such an one, as the worst and most hardened
wretch among us would confess both the danger and the mercy.

The sixth day of our being at sea, we came into Yarmouth Roads; the wind having been contrary and the weather calm, we had made but little way since the storm. Here we were obliged to come to an anchor, and here we lay, the wind continuing contrary, namely, at south-west, for seven or eight days; during which time a great many ships from Newcastle came in to the same roads, as the common harbour where the ships might wait for a wind for the river.

We had not, however, rid here so long but we should have tided it up the river, but that the wind blew too fresh; and after we had lain four or five days, blew very hard. However, the roads being reckoned as good as a harbour, the anchorage good, and our ground tackle very strong, our men were unconcerned, and not in the least apprehensive of danger, but spent the time in rest and mirth, after the manner of the sea; but the eighth day, in the morning, the wind increased, and we had all hands at work to strike our top-masts, and make everything snug and close, that the ship might ride as easy as possible. By noon, the sea went very high indeed, and our ship rid forecastle in, shipped several seas, and we thought once or twice our anchor had come home; upon which our master ordered out the sheet-anchor; so that we rode with two anchors ahead, and the cables veered out to the better end.

By this time it blew a terrible storm indeed; and now I began to see terror and amazement in the faces even of the seamen themselves. The master, though vigilant in the business of preserving the ship, yet, as he went in and out of the cabin by me, I could hear him, softly to himself, say several times, "Lord, be merciful to us! we shall be all lost – we shall be all undone!" and the like. During these first hurries, I was stupid, lying still in my cabin, which was in the steerage, and cannot describe my temper. I could ill resume the first penitence which I had so apparently trampled upon, and hardened myself against: I thought the bitterness of death had been past; and that this would be nothing, too, like the first. But when the master himself came by me, as I said just now, and said we should all be lost, I was dreadfully frighted: I got up out of my cabin, and looked out; but such a dismal sight I never saw: the sea went mountains high, and broke upon us every three or four minutes; when I could look about, I could see nothing but distress round us. Two ships that rid near us, we found, had cut their masts by the board, being deep laden; and our men cried out that a ship, which rid about a mile ahead of us, was foundered. Two more ships, being driven from their anchors, were run out of the roads to sea, at all adventures, and that with not a mast standing. The light ships fared the best, as not so much labouring in the sea; but two or three of them drove, and came close by us, running away with only their sprit sail out before the wind.

Towards the evening, the mate and boatswain begged the master of our ship to let them cut away the foremast, which he was very unwilling to do; but the boatswain protesting to him, that if he did not the ship would founder, he consented; and when they had cut away the foremast, the mainmast stood so loose, and shook the ship so much, they were obliged to cut it away also, and make a clear deck.

Any one must judge what a condition I must be in at all this, who was but a young sailor, and who had been in such a fright before at but a little. But if I can express at this distance the thoughts I had about me at that time, I was in tenfold more horror of mind upon account of my former convictions, and the having returned from them to the resolutions I had wickedly taken at first, than I was at death itself; and these, added to the terror of the storm, put me into such a condition, that I can by no words describe it. But the worst was not come yet; the storm continued with such fury that the seamen themselves acknowledged they had never seen a worse. We had a good ship, but she was deep-laden, and wallowed in the sea, that the seamen every now and then cried out she would founder. It was my advantage, in one respect, that I did not know what they meant by founder, till I inquired. However, the storm was so violent, that I saw, what is not often seen, the master, the boatswain and some others more sensible than the rest, at their prayers, and expecting every moment when the ship would go to the bottom. In the middle of the night, and under all the rest of our distresses, one of the men that had been down on purpose to see, cried out we had sprung a leak; another said there was four feet water in the hold. Then all hands were called to the pump. At that very word, my heart, as I thought, died within me; and I fell backwards upon the side of my bed where I sat, into the cabin, However the men roused me, and told me, that I, that was able to do nothing before, was as well able to pump as another; at which I stirred up, and went to the pump and worked very heartily. While this was doing, the master, seeing some light colliers who, not able to ride out the storm, were obliged to slip and run away to the sea, and would come near us, ordered to fire a gun as a signal of distress.

I, who knew nothing what that meant, was so surprised, that I thought the ship had broke, or some dreadful thing happened. In a word, I was so surprised that I fell down in a swoon. As this was a time when everybody had his own life to think of, nobody minded me, or what was become of me; but another man stepped up to the pump, and thrusting me aside with his foot, let me lie, thinking I had been dead; and it was a great while before I came to myself.

We worked on, but the water increasing in the hold, it was apparent that the ship would founder; and though the storm began to abate a little, yet as it was not possible she could swim till we might run into a port, so the master continued firing guns for help; and a light ship, who had rid it out just ahead of us, ventured a boat out to help us. It was with the utmost hazard the boat came near us; but it was impossible for us to get on board, or for the boat to lie near the ship's side, till at last the men rowing very heartily, and venturing their lives to save ours, our men cast them a rope over the stern with a buoy to it, and then veered it out a great length, which they, after much labour and hazard, took hold of, and we hauled them close under our stern, and got all into their boat. It was to no purpose for them or us, after we were in the boat, to think of reaching to their own ship; so we all agreed to let her drive, and only to pull her in towards shore as much as we could; and our master promised them, that if the boat was staved upon shore, he would make it good to their master; so, partly rowing, and partly driving, our boat went away to the northward, sloping towards the shore, almost as far as Winterton Ness.

We were not much more than a quarter of an hour out of our ship, but we saw her sink; and then I understood, for the first time, what was meant by a ship foundering in the sea. I must acknowledge I had hardly eyes to look up, when the seamen told me she was sinking; for from that moment they rather put me into the boat, than that I might be said to go in, my heart was, as it were, dead within me, partly with fright, partly with horror of mind, and the thoughts of what was yet before me.

While we were in this condition, the men yet labouring at the oar to bring the boat nearer the shore, we could see (when our boat mounting the waves, we were able to see the shore) a great many people running along the shore to assist us, when we should come near; but we made but slow way toward the shore, nor were we able to reach the shore, till being past the lighthouse at Winterton, the shore falls off to the westward towards Cromer, and so the land broke off a little the violence of the wind. Here we got in, and though not without much difficulty, got all safe on shore, and walked afterwards on foot to Yarmouth, where, as unfortunate men, we were used with great humanity, as well by the magistrates of the town, who assigned us good quarters, as by particular merchants and owners of ships, and had money given us sufficient to carry us either to London, or back to Hull, as we thought fit.

Had I now had the sense to have gone back to Hull, and have gone home, I had been happy, and my father, an emblem of our blessed Saviour's parable, had even killed the fatted calf for me; for, hearing the ship I went in was cast away in Yarmouth Roads, it was a great while before he had any assurance that I was not drowned.

But my ill fate pushed me on now with an obstinacy that nothing could resist; and though I had several times loud calls from my reason and my more composed judgment to go home, yet I had no power to do it. I know not what to call this, nor will I urge that it is a secret, overruling decree, that hurries us on to be the instruments of our own destruction, even though it be before us, and that we push upon it with our eyes open. Certainly, nothing but some such decreed unavoidable misery attending, and which it was impossible for me to escape, could have pushed me forward against the calm reasonings and persuasions of my most retired thoughts, and against two such visible instructions as I had met with in my first attempt.

My comrade, who had helped to harden me before, and who was the master's son, was now less forward than I. The first time he spoke to me after we were at Yarmouth, which was not till two or three days, for we were separated in the town to several quarters – I say, the first time he saw me, it appeared his tone was altered; and looking very melancholy, and shaking his head, asked me how I did; and telling his father who I was, and how I had come this voyage only for a trial, in order to go farther abroad, his father, turning to me with a very grave and concerned tone, "Young man," says he, "you ought never to go to sea any more; you ought to take this for a plain and visible token, that you are not to be a seafaring man." "Why, sir," said I, "will you go to sea no more?" "That is another case," said he, "it is my calling, and therefore my duty; but as you made this voyage for a trial, you see what a taste Heaven has given you of what you are to expect, if you persist: perhaps all this has befallen us on your account, like Jonah in the ship of Tarshish. Pray," continues he, "what are you? and on what account did you go to sea?" Upon that I told him some of my story; at the end of which he burst out with a strange kind of passion: "What had I done," says he, "that such an unhappy wretch should come into my ship? I would not set my foot in the same ship with thee again for a thousand pounds." This indeed was, as I said, an excursion of the spirits, which were yet agitated by the sense of his loss, and was farther than he could have authority to go. However, he afterwards talked very gravely to me, exhorted me to go back to my father and not tempt Providence to my ruin; told me, I might see a visible hand of Heaven against me: "And, young man," said he, "depend upon it, if you do not go back, wherever you go, you will meet with nothing but disasters and disappointments, till your father's words are fulfilled upon you."

We parted soon after; for I made him little answer, and I saw him no more: which way he went I know not. As for me, having some money in my pocket, I travelled to London by land; and there, as well as on the road, had many struggles with myself, what course of life I should take, and whether I should go home or go to sea.

As to going home, shame opposed the best motions that offered to my thoughts; and it immediately occurred to me how I should be laughed at among the neighbours, and should be ashamed to see, not my father and mother only, but even everybody else; from whence I have since often observed, how incongruous and irrational the common temper of mankind is, especially of youth, to that reason which ought to guide them in such cases, namely, that they are not ashamed to sin, and yet are ashamed to repent; nor ashamed of the action for which they ought justly to be esteemed fools, but are ashamed of the returning which only can make them be esteemed wise men.

In this state of life, however, I remained some time, uncertain what measures to take, and what course of life to lead. An irresistible reluctance continued to going home; and as I stayed a while, the remembrance of the distress I had been in wore off; and, as that abated, the little motion I had in my desires to a return wore off with it, till at last I quite laid aside the thoughts of it, and looked out for a voyage.

That evil influence which carried me first away from my father's house, that hurried me into the wild and indigested notion of raising my fortune, and that impressed those conceits so forcibly upon me, as to make me deaf to all good advice, and to the entreaties and even the command of my father – I say, the same influence, whatever it was, presented the most unfortunate of all enterprises to my view; and I went on board a vessel bound to the coast of Africa; or, as our sailors vulgarly call it, a voyage to Guinea.

It was my great misfortune, that in all these adventures I did not ship myself as a sailor; whereby, though I might indeed have worked a little harder than ordinary, yet, at the same time, I had learned the duty and office of a fore-mast man, and in time might have qualified myself for a mate or lieutenant, if not for a master. But as it was always my fate to choose for the worst, so I did here; for, having money in my pocket, and good clothes upon my back, I would always go on board in the habit of a gentleman; and so I neither had any business in the ship, nor learned to do any.

CHAPTER 2

Make a successful voyage to Guinea –
Taken by Sallee Rover – Escape with a
Moresco boy

It was my lot, first of all, to fall into pretty good company in London, which does not always happen to such loose and unguided young fellows as I then was, the devil generally not omitting to lay some snare for them very early; but it was not so with me. I first fell acquainted with the master of a ship who had been on the coast of Guinea; and who, having had very good success there, was resolved to go again; and who, taking a fancy to my conversation, which was not at all disagreeable at that time, hearing me say I had a mind to see the world, told me, if I would go the voyage with him I should be at no expense – I should be his mess-mate and his companion; and if I could carry anything with me, I should have all the advantage of it that the trade would permit; and, perhaps, I might meet with some encouragement.

I embraced the offer; and, entering into a strict friendship with this captain, who was an honest and plain-dealing man, I went the voyage with him, and carried a small adventure with me, which, by the disinterested honesty of my friend, the captain, I increased very considerably; for I carried about forty pounds in such toys and trifles as the captain directed me to buy. This forty pounds I had mustered together by the assistance of some of my relations, whom I corresponded with, and who, I believe, got my father, or at least my mother, to contribute so much as that to my first adventure.

This was the only voyage which I may say was successful in all my adventures, and which I owe to the integrity and honesty of my friend, the captain; under whom also I got a competent knowledge of the mathematics, and the rules of navigation – learned how to keep an account of the ship's course, take an observation, and, in short, to understand some things that were needful to be understood by a sailor; for, as he took delight to instruct me, I took delight to learn; and, in a word, this voyage made me both a sailor and a merchant; for I brought home five pounds nine ounces of gold dust for my adventure, which yielded me in London, at my return, almost three hundred pounds; and this filled me with those aspiring thoughts which have since so completed my ruin.

Yet, even in this voyage, I had my misfortunes too, particularly that I was continually sick, being thrown into a violent calenture by the excessive heat of the climate – our principal trading being upon the coast, from the latitude of fifteen degrees north, even to the Line itself.

I was now set up for a Guinea trader; and my friend, to my great misfortune, dying soon after his arrival, I resolved to go the same voyage again; and I embarked in the same vessel with one who was his mate in the former voyage, and had now got the command of the ship. This was the unhappiest voyage that ever man made; for though I did not carry quite £100 of my new gained wealth, so that I had £200 left, and which I lodged with my friend's widow, who was very just to me, yet I fell into terrible misfortunes in this voyage; and the first was this – namely, our ship, making her course towards the Canary Islands, or rather between those islands and the African shore, was surprised, in the gray of the morning, by a Moorish rover of Sallee, who gave chase to us with all the sail she could make. We crowded also as much canvas as our yards would spread, or our masts carry, to have got clear; but finding the pirate gained upon us, and would certainly come up with us in a few hours, we prepared to fight, our ship having twelve guns, and the rover eighteen. About three in the afternoon he came up with us, and bringing to, by mistake, just athwart our quarter, instead of athwart our stern, as he intended, we brought eight of our guns to bear on that side, and poured in a broadside upon him, which made him sheer off again after returning our fire, and pouring in also his small shot from near two hundred men which he had on board. However, we had not a man touched, all our men keeping close. He prepared to attack us again, and we to defend ourselves; but laying us on board the next time upon our other quarter, he entered sixty men upon our decks, who immediately fell to cutting and hacking the decks and rigging. We plied them with small shot, half-pikes, powder-chests, and such like, and cleared our deck of them twice. However, to cut short this melancholy part of our story, our ship being disabled, and three of our men killed, and eight wounded, we were obliged to yield, and were carried all prisoners into Sallee, a port belonging to the Moors.

The usage I had there was not so dreadful as at first I apprehended: nor was I carried up the country to the emperor's court, as the rest of our men were, but was kept by the captain of the rover, as his proper prize, and made his slave, being young and nimble, and fit for his business. At this surprising change of my circumstances, from a merchant to a miserable slave, I was perfectly overwhelmed; and now I looked back upon my father's prophetic discourse to me, that I should be miserable, and have none to relieve me; which I thought was now so effectually brought to pass, that I could not be worse – that now the hand of Heaven had overtaken me, and I was undone without redemption. But, alas! this was but a taste of the misery I was to go through, as will appear in the sequel of the story.

As my new patron or master had taken me home to his house, so I was in hopes that he would take me with him when he went to sea again, believing that it would be some time or other his fate to be taken by a Spanish or Portugal man-of-war, and that then I should be set at liberty. But this hope of mine was soon taken away; for when he went to sea, he left me on shore to look after his little garden and do the common drudgery of slaves about his house; and when he came home again from his cruise, he ordered me to lie in the cabin to look after the ship.

Here I meditated nothing but my escape, and what method I might take to affect it; but found no way that had the least probability in it. Nothing presented to make the supposition of it rational; for I had nobody to communicate it to that would embark with me – no fellow-slave, no Englishman, Irishman, or Scotsman there, but myself; so that for two years, though I often pleased myself with the imagination, yet I never had the least encouraging prospect of putting it in practice.

After about two years, an odd circumstance presented itself which put the whole thought of making some attempt for my liberty again in my head: my patron lying at home longer than usual, without fitting out his ship, which, as I heard, was for want of money, he used constantly, once or twice a week, sometimes oftener, if the weather was fair, to take the ship's pinnace, and go out into the road a fishing; and as he always took me and a young Moresco with him to row the boat, we made him very merry, and I proved very dexterous in catching fish; insomuch that sometimes he would send me with a Moor, one of his kinsmen, and the youth, the Moresco, as they called him, to catch a dish of fish for him.

It happened one time that going a-fishing with him in a calm morning, a fog rose so thick, that though we were not half a league from the shore, we lost sight of it; and rowing, we knew not whither, or which way, we laboured all day and all the next night; and when the morning came, we found we had pulled off to sea, instead of pulling in for the shore, and that we were at least two leagues from the land: however, we got well in again, though with a great deal of labour, and some danger, for the wind began to blow pretty fresh in the morning: but, particularly, we were all very hungry.

But our patron, warned by this disaster, resolved to take more care of himself in the future; and having lying by him the long-boat of our English ship which he had taken, he resolved he would not go a-fishing any more without a compass and some provision; so he ordered the carpenter of his ship, who also was an English slave, to build a little state-room or cabin in the middle of the long-boat, like that of a barge, with a place to stand behind it to steer, and haul home the mainsheet; and room before for a hand or two to stand and work the sails. She sailed with what we call a shoulder-of-mutton sail; and the boom jibbed over the top of the cabin, which lay very snug and low, and had in it room for him to lie, with a slave or two, and a table to eat on, with some small lockers to put in some bottles of such liquor as he thought fit to drink, particularly his bread, rice, and coffee.

We were frequently out with this boat a-fishing; and as I was most dexterous to catch fish for him, he never went without me. It happened one day, that he had appointed to go out in this boat, either for pleasure or for fish, with two or three Moors of some distinction, and for whom he had provided extraordinary; and had therefore sent on board the boat over night a larger store of provisions than usual, and had ordered me to get ready three fusils with powder and shot, which were on board his ship; for that they designed some sport of fowling as well as fishing.

I got all things ready as he had directed and waited the next morning with the boat washed clean, her ancient and pendants out, and everything to accommodate his guests; when by-and-by my patron came on board alone, and told me his guests had put off going, upon some business that fell out, and ordered me, with the man and boy, as usual, to go out with the boat, and catch them some fish, for that his friends were to sup at his house; he commanded me, too, that as soon as I had got some fish, I should bring it home to his house: all which I prepared to do.

This moment my former notions of deliverance darted into my thoughts, for now I found I was like to have a little ship at my command; and my master being gone, I prepared to furnish myself, not for fishing business, but for a voyage, though I knew not, neither did I so much as consider, whither I would steer; for anywhere to get out of that place was my way.

My first contrivance was to make a pretence to speak to this Moor, to get something for our subsistence on board; for I told him we must not presume to eat of our patron's bread. He said that was true; so he brought a large basket of rusk, or biscuit of their kind, and three jars with fresh water into the boat. I knew where my patron's case of bottles stood, which it was evident by the make were taken out of some English prize, and I conveyed them into the boat while the Moor was on shore, as if they had been there before for our master: I conveyed also a great lump of bees'-wax into the boat which weighed above half a hundredweight, with a parcel of twine or thread, a hatchet, a saw, and a hammer, all which were of great use to us afterwards, especially the wax to make candles. Another trick I tried upon him, which he innocently came into also. His name was Ishmael, whom they called Muly or Moley; so I called to him: "Moley," said I, "our patron's guns are on board the boat; can you not get a little powder and shot? It may be we may kill some alcamies (a fowl like our curlews) for ourselves, for I know he keeps the gunner's stores in the ship." "Yes," says he, "I'll bring some;" and accordingly he brought a great leather pouch which held about a pound and a half of powder or rather more, and another with shot, that had five or six pounds, with some bullets, and put all into the boat; at the same time I had found some powder of my master's in the great cabin, with which I filled one of the large bottles in the case, which was almost empty, pouring what was in it into another; and thus furnished with everything needful, we sailed out of the port to fish. The castle, which is at the entrance of the port, knew who we were, and took no notice of us; and we were not above a mile out of the port before we hauled in our sail, and set us down to fish. The wind blew from the north north-east, which was contrary to my desire; for had it blown southerly, I had been sure to have made the coast of Spain, and at least reached the bay of Cadiz; but my resolutions were, blow which way it would, I would be gone from that horrid place where I was, and leave the rest to fate.

After we had fished some time, and catched nothing – for when I had fish on my hook I would not pull them up, that he might not see them – I said to the Moor, "This will not do – our master will not be thus served – we must stand farther off." He, thinking no harm, agreed, and being in the head of the boat, set the sails; and as I had the helm, I ran the boat out near a league farther, and then brought her to, as if I would fish; when, giving the boy the helm, I stepped forward to where the Moor was, and making as if I stooped for something behind him, I took him by surprise with my arm under his waist, and tossed him clear overboard into the sea: he rose immediately, for he swam like a cork, and called to me, begged to be taken in, told me he would go all over the world with me. He swam so strong after the boat, that he would have reached me very quickly, there being but little wind; upon which I stepped into the cabin, and fetching one of the fowling-pieces, I presented it at him, and told him, I had done him no hurt, and if he would be quiet I would do him none – "But," said I, "you swim well enough to reach the shore, and the sea is calm – make the best of your way to shore, and I will do you no harm; but if you come near the boat, I'll shoot you through the head, for I am resolved to have my liberty," – so he turned himself about, and swam for the shore, and I make no doubt but he reached it with ease, for he was an excellent swimmer.

I could have been content to have taken this Moor with me and have drowned the boy, but there was no venturing to trust him. When he was gone, I turned to the boy, whom they called Xury, and said to him: "Xury, if you will be faithful to me, I'll make you a great man; but if you will not stroke your face to be true to me (that is, swear by Mahomet and his father's beard), I must throw you into the sea, too." The boy smiled in my face, and spoke so innocently, that I could not mistrust him; and swore to be faithful to me, and go all over the world with me.

While I was in view of the Moor that was swimming, I stood out directly to sea with the boat, rather stretching to windward, that they might think me gone towards the Straits' mouth, as indeed any one that had been in their wits must have been supposed to do; for who would have supposed we were sailed on to the southward, to the truly barbarian coast, where whole nations of negroes were sure to surround us with their canoes, and destroy us; where we could never once go on shore, but we should be devoured by savage beasts, or more merciless savages of human kind?

But as soon as it grew dusk in the evening, I changed my course, and steered directly south and by east, bending my course a little toward the east, that I might keep in with the shore; and having a fair fresh gale of wind, and a smooth quiet sea, I made such sail, that I believe, by the next day at three o'clock in the afternoon, when I first made the land, I could not be less than one hundred and fifty miles south of Sallee, quite beyond the Emperor of Morocco's dominions, or, indeed, of any other king thereabouts, for we saw no people.

Yet such was the fright I had taken at the Moors, and the dreadful apprehensions I had of falling into their hands, that I would not stop, or go on shore, or come to an anchor, the wind continuing fair, till I had sailed in that manner five days; and then the wind shifting to the southward, I concluded also that if any of our vessels were in chase of me, they also would now give over; so I ventured to make to the coast, and come to an anchor in the mouth of a little river, I knew not what or where – neither what latitude, what country, what nation, nor what river: I neither saw, nor desired to see any people – the principal thing I wanted was fresh water. We came into this creek in the evening, resolving to swim on shore as soon as it was dark, and discover the country; but as soon as it was quite dark, we heard such dreadful noises of the barking, roaring, and howling of wild creatures, of we knew not what kinds, that the poor boy was ready to die with fear, and begged of me not to go on shore till day. "Well, Xury," said I, "then I won't; but it may be we may see men by day, who will be as bad to us as those lions." "Then we give them the shoot gun," says Xury, laughing, "make them run away." Such English Xury spoke by conversing among us slaves. However, I was glad to see the boy so cheerful, and I gave him a dram, out of our patron's case of bottles, to cheer him up. After all, Xury's advice was good, and I took it; we dropped our little anchor and lay still all night – I say still, for we slept none – for in two or three hours we saw vast great creatures (we knew not what to call them) of many sorts, come down to the seashore, and run into the water, wallowing and washing themselves for the pleasure of cooling themselves; and they made such hideous howlings and yellings, that I never indeed heard the like.

DANIEL DEFOE

Xury was dreadfully frighted, and indeed so was I too; but we were both more frighted when we heard one of those mighty creatures come swimming towards our boat. We could not see him, but we might hear him by his blowing, to be a monstrous, huge, and furious beast; Xury said it was a lion, and it might be so for aught I know. Poor Xury cried to me to weigh the anchor, and row away. "No," says I, "Xury, we can slip our cable with a buoy to it, and go to sea; they cannot follow us far." I had no sooner said so, but I perceived the creature (whatever it was) within two oars' length, which something surprised me; however, I immediately stepped to the cabin door, and taking up my gun, fired at him. upon which he immediately turned about, and swam to the shore again.

But it was not possible to describe the horrible noises, and hideous cries and howlings, that were raised, as well upon the edge of the shore, as higher within the country, upon the noise or report of a gun – a thing I have some reason to believe those creatures had never heard before. This convinced me that there was no going on shore for us in the night upon that coast; and how to venture on shore in the day, was another question too; for to have fallen into the hands of any of the savages, had been as bad as to have fallen into the paws of lions and tigers; at least, we were equally apprehensive of the danger of it.

Be that as it would, we were obliged to go on shore somewhere or other for water, for we had not a pint left in the boat; when or where to get it was the point. Xury said if I would let him go on shore with one of the jars, he would find if there was any water, and bring some to me. I asked him why he would go? why I should not go, and he stay in the boat? The boy answered with so much affection, that made me love him ever after. Says he: "If wild mans come, they eat me, you go way." "Well, Xury," said I, "we will both go, and if the wild mans come, we will kill them; they shall eat neither of us." So I gave Xury a piece of rusk bread to eat, and a dram out of our patron's case of bottles, which I mentioned before; and we hauled the boat in as near the shore as we thought was proper, and waded on shore, carrying nothing but our arms, and two jars for water.

I did not care to go out of sight of the boat, fearing the coming of canoes with savages down the river: but the boy, seeing a low place about a mile up the country, rambled to it; and by-and-by I saw him come running towards me. I thought he was pursued by some savage, or frighted with some wild beast, and I ran forward towards him to help him; but when I came nearer to him, I saw something hanging over his shoulders, which was a creature that he had shot, like a hare, but different in colour, and longer legs; however, we were very glad of it, and it was very good meat; but the great joy that poor Xury came with, was to tell me he had found good water, and seen no wild mans.

But we found afterwards that we need not take such pains for water, for a little higher up the creek where we were, we found the water fresh when the tide was out, which flows but a little way up; so we filled our jars and feasted on the hare we had killed, and prepared to go on our way, having seen no footsteps of any human creature in that part of the country.

As I had been one voyage to the coast before, I knew very well that the islands of the Canaries, and the Cape de Verde Islands also, lay not far off from the coast. But as I had no instruments to take an observation to know what latitude we were in, and did not exactly know, or at least not remember, what latitude they were in, and knew not where to look for them, or when to stand off to sea towards them: otherwise I might now easily have found some of these islands. But my hope was, that if I stood along this coast till I came to that part where the English traded, I should find some of their vessels upon their usual design of trade, that would relieve and take us in.

By the best of my calculation, that place where I now was must be that country which, lying between the Emperor of Morocco's dominions and the negroes, lies waste and uninhabited, except by wild beasts; the negroes having abandoned it, and gone farther south for fear of the Moors; and the Moors not thinking it worth inhabiting, by reason of its barrenness – and, indeed, both forsaking it because of the prodigious number of tigers, lions, leopards, and other furious creatures, which harbour there; so that the Moors use it for their hunting only, where they go like an army, two or three thousand men at a time – and, indeed, for near an hundred miles together upon this coast, we saw nothing but a waste uninhabited country by day, and heard nothing but howlings and roarings of wild beasts by night.

Once or twice in the daytime I thought I saw the Pico of Teneriffe, being the high top of the mountain Teneriffe in the Canaries, and had a great mind to venture out, in hopes of reaching thither; but having tried twice, I was forced in again by contrary winds, the sea also going too high for my little vessel; so I resolved to pursue my first design, and keep along the shore.

DANIEL DEFOE

Several times I was obliged to land for fresh water, after we had left this place; and once, in particular, being early in the morning, we came to an anchor under a little point of land which was pretty high; and the tide beginning to flow, we lay still to go farther in. Xury, whose eyes were more about him than it seems mine were, calls softly to me, and tells me, that we had best go farther off the shore: "For," says he, "look – yonder lies a dreadful monster, on the side of that hillock, fast asleep." I looked where he pointed and saw a dreadful monster indeed, for it was a terrible great lion that lay on the side of the shore under the shade of a piece of the hill that hung, as it were, a little over him. "Xury," says I, "you shall go on shore and kill him." Xury looked frighted, and said, "Me kill! he eat me at one mouth!" – one mouthful he meant: however, I said no more to the boy, but bade him lie still, and I took our biggest gun, which was almost musket-bore, and loaded it with a good charge of powder, and with two slugs, and laid it down; then I loaded another gun with two bullets; and the third – for we had three pieces – I loaded with five smaller bullets. I took the best aim I could with the first piece to have shot him into the head, but he lay so with his leg raised a little above his nose, that the slugs hit his leg about the knee and broke the bone. He started up, growling at first, but finding his leg broke, fell down again, and then got up upon three legs, and gave the most hideous roar that ever I heard. I was a little surprised that I had not hit him on the head; however, I took up the second piece immediately, and, though he began to move off, fired again, and shot him into the head, and had the pleasure to see him drop, and make but little noise, but lie struggling for life. Then Xury took heart, and would have me let him go on shore. "Well, go," said I; so the boy jumped into the water, and taking a little gun in one hand, swam to shore with the other hand, and coming close to the creature, put the muzzle of the piece to his ear, and shot him into the head again, which despatched him quite.

This was game indeed to us, but this was no food; and I was very sorry to lose three charges of powder and shot upon a creature that was good for nothing to us. However, Xury said he would have some of him; so he comes on board, and asked me to give him the hatchet. "For what, Xury?" said I. "Me cut off his head," said he. However, Xury could not cut off his head, but he cut off a foot, and brought it with him, and it was a monstrous great one.

I bethought myself, however, that perhaps the skin of him

might, one way or other, be of some value to us; and I resolved to take off his skin if I could. So Xury and I went to work with him; but Xury was much the better workman at it, for I knew very ill how to do it. Indeed, it took us both up the whole day, but at last we got off the hide of him, and, spreading it on the top of our cabin, the sun effectually dried it in two days' time, and it afterwards served me to lie upon.

CHAPTER 3

Voyage South – See Savages – Shoot Leopard
– Arrive at the Brazils, and settle as a Planter
– Voyage to Guinea – Ship wrecked off a
desolate island – All lost but myself

After this stop, we made on to the southward continually for ten
or twelve days, living very sparingly on our provisions, which began
to abate very much, and going no oftener into the shore than we
were obliged to do for fresh water: my design in this was, to make
the River Gambia or Senegal, that is to say, anywhere about the
Cape de Verde, where I was in hopes to meet with some European
ship; and if I did not, I knew not what course I had to take, but to
seek for the islands, or perish there among the negroes. I knew that
all the ships from Europe, which sailed either to the coast of Guinea
or to Brazil, or to the East Indies, made this Cape, or those islands;
and, in a word, I put the whole of my fortune upon this single point,
either that I must meet with some ship or must perish.

When I had pursued this resolution about ten days longer, as
I have said, I began to see that the land was inhabited; and in two
or three places, as we sailed by, we saw people stand upon the shore
to look at us: we could also perceive they were quite black, and
stark naked. I was once inclined to go on shore to them; but Xury
was my better counsellor, and said to me: "No go, no go." However,
I hauled in nearer the shore that I might talk to them, and I found
they ran along the shore by me a good way: I observed they had no
weapons in their hands except one, who had a long slender stick,
which Xury said was a lance, and that they would throw them a
good way with great aim; so I kept at a distance, but talked with
them by signs as well as I could, and particularly made signs for

something to eat; they beckoned to me to stop my boat, and they would fetch me some meat. Upon this, I lowered the top of my sail, and lay by, and two of them ran up into the country, and in less than half an hour came back, and brought with them two pieces of dry flesh and some corn, such as is the produce of their country; but we neither knew what the one nor the other was; however, we were willing to accept it. But how to come at it was our next dispute, for I was not for venturing on shore to them, and they were as much afraid of us; but they took a safe way for all, for they brought it to the shore and laid it down, and went and stood a great way off till we fetched it on board, and then came close to us again.

We made signs of thanks to them, for we had nothing to make them amends; but an opportunity offered that very instant to oblige them wonderfully; for while we were lying by the shore, came two mighty creatures, one pursuing the other (as we took it) with great fury from the mountains towards the sea; whether it was the male pursuing the female, or whether they were in sport or in rage, we could not tell, any more than we could tell whether it was usual or strange, but I believe it was the latter; because, in the first place, those ravenous creatures seldom appear but in the night; and, in the second place, we found the people terribly frighted, especially the women. The man that had the lance or dart did not fly from them, but the rest did; however, as the two creatures ran directly into the water, they did not seem to offer to fall upon any of the negroes, but plunged themselves into the sea, and swam about as if they had come for their diversion. At last one of them began to come nearer our boat than at first I expected; but I lay ready for him, for I had loaded my gun with all possible expedition, and bade Xury load both the others. As soon as he came fairly within my reach, I fired and shot him directly into the head: immediately he sank down into the water, but rose instantly, and plunged up and down as if he was struggling for life, and so indeed he was; he immediately made to the shore; but between the wound, which was his mortal hurt, and the strangling of the water, he died just before he reached the shore.

It is impossible to express the astonishment of these poor creatures at the noise and the fire of my gun; some of them were even ready to die for fear, and fell down as dead with the very terror. But when they saw the creature dead, and sunk in the water, and that I made signs to them to come to the shore, they took heart, and came to the shore, and began to search for the creature. I found him by his blood staining the water, and by the help of a rope, which I slung round him, and gave the negroes to haul, they dragged him on shore, and found that it was a most curious leopard, spotted, and fine to an admirable degree, and the negroes held up their hands with admiration to think what it was I had killed him with.

The other creature, frighted with the flash of fire and the noise of the gun, swam on shore, and ran up directly to the mountains from whence they came, nor could I at that distance know what it was. I found quickly the negroes were for eating the flesh of this creature, so I was willing to have them take it as a favour from me, which when I made signs to them. that they might take him, they were very thankful for. Immediately they fell to work with him, and though they had no knife, yet, with a sharpened piece of wood, they took off his skin as readily, and much more readily, than we could have done with a knife. They offered me some of the flesh, which I declined, making as if I would give it them, but made signs for the skin, which they gave me very freely, and brought me a great deal more of their provision, which, though I did not understand, yet I accepted; then I made signs to them for some water, and held out one of my jars to them, turning it bottom upward, to show that it was empty, and that I wanted to have it filled. They called immediately to some of their friends, and there came two women, and brought a great vessel made of earth, and burned, as I suppose, in the sun; this they set down for me, as before, and I sent Xury on shore with my jars, and filled them all three. The woman were as stark naked as the men.

I was now furnished with roots and corn, such as it was, and water; and, leaving my friendly negroes, I made forward for about eleven days more, without offering to go near the shore, till I saw the land run out a great length into the sea, at about the distance of four or five leagues before me; and the sea being very calm, I kept a large offing to make this point; at length, doubling the point, at about two leagues from the land, I saw plainly land on the other side to sea-ward; then I concluded, as it was most certain, indeed, that this was the Cape de Verde, and those thee islands, called from thence Cape de Verde Islands. However, they were at a great distance, and I could not tell what I had best to do; for, if I should be taken with a fresh of wind, I might neither reach one nor the other.

In this dilemma, as I was very pensive, I stepped into the cabin and sat me down, Xury having the helm, when, on a sudden, the boy cried out: "Master, master, a ship with a sail!" and the foolish boy was frighted out of his wits, thinking it must needs be some of his master's ships sent to pursue us, when I knew we were gotten far enough out of their reach. I jumped out of the cabin, and immediately saw, not only the ship, but what she was, namely, that it was a Portuguese ship, and, as I thought, was bound to the coast of Guinea for negroes. But when I observed the course she steered, I was soon convinced they were bound some other way, and did not design to come any nearer to the shore; upon which I stretched out to sea as much as I could, resolving to speak with them if possible.

With all the sail I could make, I found I should not be able to come in their way, but that they would be gone by before I could make any signal to them; but after I had crowded to the utmost, and began to despair, they, it seems, saw me by the help of their perspective glasses, and that it was some European boat, which, as they supposed, must belong to some ship that was lost; so they shortened sail to let me come up. I was encouraged with this; and as I had my patron's ancient on board, I made a waft of it to them for a signal of distress, and fired a gun, both which they saw, for they told me they saw the smoke, though they did not hear the gun. Upon these signals they very kindly brought to, and lay by for me, and, in about three hours' time, I came up with them.

They asked me what I was, in Portuguese, and in Spanish, and in French; but I understood none of them: but, at last, a Scots sailor, who was on board, called to me, and I answered him, and told him I was an Englishman – that I had made my escape out of slavery from the Moors at Sallee. They bade me come on board, and very kindly took me in, and all my goods.

It was inexpressible joy to me, as any one would believe, that I was thus delivered, as I esteemed it, from such a miserable and almost hopeless condition as I was in, and immediately offered all I had to the captain of the ship, as a return for my deliverance; but he generously told me he would take nothing from me, but that all I had should be delivered safe to me when I came to the Brazils. "For," says he, "I have saved your life on no other terms than I would be glad to be saved myself; and it may one time or other be my lot to be taken up in the same condition: besides," said he, "when I carry you to the Brazils, so great a way from your own country, if I should take from you what you have, you will be starved there, and then I only take away that life I have given. No, no, Seignor Inglese," says he, "Mr. Englishman, I will carry you thither

DANIEL DEFOE

in charity, and those things will help you to buy your subsistence there, and your passage home again.

As he was charitable in his proposal, so he was just in the performance to a tittle; for he ordered the seamen, that none should offer to touch anything I had: then he took everything into his own possession, and gave me back an exact inventory of them, that I might have them; even so much as my earthern jars.

As to my boat, it was a very good one, and that he saw, and told me he would buy it of me for the ship's use, and asked me what I would have for it? I told him he had been so generous in everything, that I could not offer to make any price of the boat, but left it entirely to him; upon which he told me, he would give me a note of his hand to pay me eighty pieces of eight for it at Brazil, and when it came there, if any one offered to give more, he would make it up: he offered me also sixty pieces of eight more for my boy Xury, which I was loath to take; not that I was not willing to let the captain have him, but I was very loath to sell the poor boy's liberty, who had assisted me so faithfully in procuring my own. However, when I let him know my reason, he owned it to be just, and offered me this medium, that he would give the boy an obligation to set him free in ten years, if he turned Christian. Upon this, and Xury saying he was willing to go to him, I let the captain have him.

We had a very good voyage to the Brazils, and arrived in the Bay de Todos los Santos, or All Saints' Bay, in about twenty-two days after. And now I was once more delivered from the most miserable of all conditions of life; and what to do next with myself I was now to consider.

The generous treatment the captain gave me, I can never enough remember. He would take nothing off me for my passage – gave me twenty ducats for the leopard's skin, and forty for the lion's skin, which I had in my boat, and caused everything I had in the ship to be punctually delivered me; and what I was willing to sell he bought, such as the case of bottles, two of my guns, and a piece of the lump of bees'-wax, for I had made candles of the rest – in a word, I made, about two hundred and twenty pieces of eight of all my cargo; and with this stock I went on shore in the Brazils.

I had not been long here, but being recommended to the house of a good honest man like himself, who had an *ingeino*, as they call it – that is, a plantation and a sugar-house – I lived with him some time, and acquainted myself by that means with the manner of their planting and making of sugar; and seeing how well the planters lived, and how they grew rich suddenly, I resolved, if I could get licence to settle there, I would turn planter among them; resolving, in the meantime, to find out some way to get my money, which I had left in London, remitted to me. To this purpose, getting a kind of a letter of naturalisation, I purchased as much land that was uncured as my money would reach, and formed a plan for my plantation and settlement, and such a one as might be suitable to the stock which I proposed to myself to receive from England.

I had a neighbour, a Portuguese of Lisbon, but born of English parents, whose name was Wells, and in much such circumstances as I was. I call him neighbour, because his plantation lay next to mine, and we went on very sociably together. My stock was but low, as well as his: and we rather planted for food, than anything else, for about two years. However, we began to increase, and our land began to come into order; so that the third year we planted some tobacco, and made each of us a large piece of ground ready for planting canes in the year to come; but we both wanted help: and now I found more than before, I had done wrong in parting with my boy Xury.

But, alas! for me to do wrong, that never did right, was no great wonder. I had no remedy but to go on – I was gotten into an employment quite remote from my genius, and directly contrary to the life I delighted in, and for which I forsook my father's house, and broke through all his good advice – nay, I was coming into the very middle station, or upper degree of low life, which my father advised me to before; and which, if I resolved to go on with, I might as well have stayed at home, and never have fatigued myself in the world as I had done; and I used often to say to myself, I could have done this as well in England among my friends, as have gone five thousand miles off to do it among strangers and savages in a wilderness, and at such distance as never to hear from any part of the world that had the least knowledge of me.

In this manner I used to look upon my condition with the utmost regret. I had nobody to converse with, but now and then this neighbour – no work to be done but by the labour of my hands; and I used to say, I lived just like a man cast away upon some desolate island, that had nobody there but himself. But how just has it been, and how shall all men reflect, that, when they compare their present conditions with others that are worse, Heaven may oblige them to make the exchange, and be convinced of their former felicity,

DANIEL DEFOE

by their experience – I say, how just has it been, that the truly
solitary life I reflected on in an island of mere desolation should be
my lot, who had so often unjustly compared it with the life which
I then led, in which, had I continued, I had, in all probability, been
exceeding prosperous and rich.

I was, in some degree, settled in my measures for carrying on
the plantation, before my kind friend, the captain of the ship that
took me up at sea, went back; for the ship remained there, in
providing his loading, and preparing for his voyage, near three
months; when, telling him what little stock I had left behind me
in London, he gave me this friendly and sincere advice: "Seignor
Inglese," says he, for so he always called me, "if you will give me
letters, and a procuration here in form to me, with orders to the
person who has your money in London, to send your effects to
Lisbon, to such persons as I shall direct, and in such goods as are
proper for this country, I will bring you the produce of them, God
willing, at my return; but, since human affairs are all subject to
changes and disasters, I would have you give orders but for one
hundred pounds sterling, which, you say, is half your stock, and let
the hazard be run for the first; so that, if it comes safe, you may
order the rest the same way, and if it miscarry, you may have the
other half to have recourse to for your supply."

This was so wholesome advice, and looked so friendly, that I
could not but be convinced it was the best course I could take; so
I accordingly prepared letters to the gentlewoman with whom I had
left my money, and a procuration to the Portuguese captain, as he
desired.

I wrote the English captain's widow a full account of all my
adventures, my slavery, escape, and how I had met with the Portugal
captain at sea, the humanity of his behaviour, and what condition
I was now in, with all other necessary directions for my supply; and
when this honest captain came to Lisbon, he found means, by some
of the English merchants there, to send over, not the order only,
but a full account of my story, to a merchant at London, who represented it effectually to her; whereupon, she not only delivered the
money, but, out of her own pocket, sent the Portugal captain a very
handsome present for his humanity and charity to me.

The merchant in London vesting this hundred pounds in
English goods, such as the captain had writ for, sent them directly
to him at Lisbon, and he brought them all safe to me to the Brazils;
among which, without my direction (for I was too young in my busi-

ness to think of them), he had taken care to have all sorts of tools, iron-work, and utensils, necessary for my plantation, and which were of great use to me.

When this cargo arrived, I thought my fortune made, for I was surprised with joy of it; and my good steward, the captain, had laid out the five pounds which my friend had sent him for a present for himself, to purchase, and bring me over a servant under bond for six years' service, and would not accept of any consideration, except a little tobacco, which I would have him accept, being of my own produce.

Neither was this all; but my goods being all English manufactures, such as cloth, stuffs, baize, and things particularly valuable and desirable in the country, I found means to sell them to a very great advantage; so that I may say I had more than four times the value of my first cargo, and was now infinitely beyond my poor neighbour, I mean in the advancement of my plantation; for the first thing I did, I bought me a negro slave, and an European servant also – I mean another besides that which the captain brought me from Lisbon.

But as abused prosperity is oftentimes made the means of our greatest adversity, so was it with me. I went on the next year with great success in my plantation. I raised fifty great rolls of tobacco on my own ground, more than I had disposed of for necessaries among my neighbours; and these fifty rolls being each of above a hundredweight, were well cured and laid by against the return of the fleet from Lisbon. And now, increasing in business and in wealth, my head began to be full of projects and undertakings beyond my reach; such as are, indeed, often the ruin of the best heads in business.

Had I continued in the station I was now in, I had room for all the happy things to have yet befallen me, for which my father so earnestly recommended a quiet retired life, and of which he had so sensibly described the middle station of life to be full; but other things attended me, and I was still to be the wilful agent of all my own miseries; and particularly to increase my fault, and double the reflections upon myself, which in my future sorrows I should have leisure to make, all these miscarriages were procured by my apparent obstinate adhering to my foolish inclination of wandering abroad, and pursuing that inclination, in contradiction to the dearest views of doing myself good in a fair and plain pursuit of those prospects and those measures of life, which Nature and Providence concurred to present me with, and to make my duty.

As I had done thus in my breaking away from my parents, so I could not be content now, but I must go and leave the happy view I had of being a rich and thriving man in my new plantation, only to pursue a rash and immoderate desire of rising faster than the nature of the thing admitted; and thus I cast myself down again into the deepest gulf of human misery that ever man fell into, or perhaps could be consistent with life and a state of health in the world.

To come, then, by just degrees, to the particulars of this part of my story: you may suppose, that, having now lived almost four years in the Brazils, and beginning to prosper and thrive very well upon my plantation, I had not only learnt the language, but had contracted acquaintance and friendship among my fellow-planters, as well as among the merchants at St. Salvadore, which was our port; and that in my discourse among them, I had frequently given them an account of my two voyages to the coast of Guinea, the manner of trading with the negroes there, and how easy it was to purchase upon the coast for trifles – such as beads, toys, knives, scissors, hatchets, bits of glass, and the like – not only gold dust, Guinea grains, elephants' teeth, etc., but negroes for the service of the Brazils in great numbers.

They listened always very attentively to my discourses on these heads, but especially to that part which related to buying negroes, which was a trade at that time not only not far entered into, but, as far as it was, had been carried on by the *assientos*, or permission, of the kings of Spain and Portugal, and engrossed in the public, so that few negroes were bought, and those excessively dear.

It happened, being in company with some merchants and planters of my acquaintance, and talking of those things very earnestly, three of them came to me the next morning, and told me they had been musing very much upon what I had discoursed with them of the last night, and they came to make a secret proposal to me; and, after enjoining me secrecy, they told me that they had a mind to fit out a ship to go to Guinea; that they had all plantations as well as I, and were straitened for nothing so much as servants; that as it was a trade that could not be carried on, because they could not publicly sell the negroes when they came home, so they desired to make but one voyage, to bring the negroes on shore privately, and divide them among their own plantations; and, in a word, the question was, whether I would go their supercargo in the ship, to manage the trading part upon the coast of Guinea? and they offered me, that I should have my equal share of the negroes, without providing any part of the stock.

This was a fair proposal, it must be confessed, had it been made to any one that had not had a settlement and plantation of his own to look after, which was in a fair way of coming to be very considerable, and with a good stock upon it. But for me, that was thus entered and established, and had nothing to do but go on as I had begun for three or four years more, and to have sent for the other hundred pounds from England, and who, in that time and with that little addition, could scarce have failed of being worth three or four thousand pounds sterling, and that increasing too – for me to think of such a voyage, was the most preposterous thing that ever man in such circumstances could be guilty of.

But I, that was born to be my own destroyer, could no more resist the offer than I could restrain my first rambling designs, when my father's good counsel was lost upon me. In a word, I told them I would go with all my heart if they would undertake to look after my plantation in my absence, and would dispose of it to such as I should direct, if I miscarried. This they all engaged to do, and entered into writings, or covenants, to do so; and I made a formal will, disposing of my plantation and effects in case of my death, making the captain of the ship that had saved my life as before, my universal heir, but obliging him to dispose of my effects as I had directed in my will, one half of the produce being to himself, and the other to be shipped to England.

In short, I took all possible caution to preserve my effects, and keep up my plantation; had I used half as much prudence to have looked into my own interest, and have made a judgment of what I ought to have done, and not to have done, I had certainly never gone away from so prosperous an undertaking, leaving all the probable views of a thriving circumstance, and gone upon a voyage to sea, attended with all its common hazards; to say nothing of the reasons I had to expect particular misfortunes to myself.

But I was hurried on, and obeyed blindly the dictates of my fancy, rather than my reason: and accordingly, the ship being fitted out, and the cargo furnished, and all things done as by agreement by my partners in the voyage, I went on board in an evil our again, the 1st of September, 1659, being the same day eight years that I went from my father and mother at Hull in order to act the rebel to their authority, and the fool to my own interest.

Our ship was about one hundred and twenty tons burden, carried six guns, and fourteen men, besides the master, his boy, and myself; we had on board no large cargo of goods, except of such toys as were fit for our trade with the negroes, such as beads, bits of glass, shells, and odd trifles, especially little looking-glasses, knives, scissors, hatchets, and the like.

The same day I went on board we set sail, standing away to the northward upon our own coast, with design to stretch over for the African coast, when they came about ten or twelve degrees of northern latitude, which, it seems, was the manner of their course in those days. We had very good weather, only excessively hot, all the way upon our own coast, till we came to the height of Cape St. Augustino, from whence, keeping farther off at sea, we lost sight of land, and steered as if we were bound for the isle Fernand de Noronha, holding our course north-east by north, and leaving those isles on the east. In this course we passed the Line in about twelve days' time, and were, by our last observation, in seven degrees, twenty-two minutes, northern latitude, when a violent tornado, or hurricane, took us quite out of our knowledge: it began from the south-east, came about to the northwest; from whence it blew in such a terrible manner, that for twelve days together we could do nothing but drive, and, scudding away before it, let it carry us whither ever fate and the fury of the winds directed; and during those twelve days, I need not say that I expected every day to be swallowed up, nor indeed, did any in the ship expect to save their lives.

In this distress, we had, besides the terror of the storm, one of our men dead of the calenture, and one man and the boy washed overboard. About the twelfth day, the weather abating a little, the master made an observation as well as he could, and found that he was in about twenty-two degrees of longitude difference west from Cape St. Augustino; so that he found he was gotten upon the coast of Guinea, or the north part of Brazil, beyond the river Amazons, towards that of the river Oroonoque, commonly called the Great River, and began to consult with me what course he should take; for the ship was leaky, and very much disabled, and he was going directly back to the coast of Brazil.

I was positively against that, and, looking over the charts of the sea coasts of America with him, we concluded, there was no inhabited country for us to have recourse to, till we came within the circle of the Caribbee Islands; and therefore resolved to stand away for Barbadoes, which, by keeping off at sea, to avoid the indraft of the bay or gulf of Mexico, we might easily perform, as we hoped, in about fifteen days' sail: whereas we could not possibly make our voyage to the coast of Africa, without some assistance, both to our ship and ourselves.

With this design we changed our course, and steered away north-west by west, in order to reach some of our English islands, where I hoped for relief: but our voyage was otherwise determined; for, being in the latitude of twelve degrees, eighteen minutes, a second storm came upon us, which carried us away with the same impetuosity westward, and drove us so out of the very way of all human commerce, that, had all our lives been saved as to the sea, we were rather in danger of being devoured by savages than ever returning to our own country.

In this distress, the wind still blowing very hard, one of our men, early in the morning, cried out: "Land!" and we had no sooner run out of the cabin to look out, in hopes of seeing whereabouts in the world we were, but the ship struck upon a sand, and, in a moment, her motion being so stopped, the sea broke over her in such a manner that we expected we should all have perished immediately; and we were immediately driven into our close quarters, to shelter us from the very foam and spray of the sea.

It is not easy for any one, who has not been in the like condition, to describe or conceive the consternation of men in such circumstances: we knew nothing where we were, or upon what land it was we were driven – whether an island or the main, whether inhabited or not inhabited; and as the rage of the wind was still great, though rather less than at first, we could not so much as hope to have the ship hold many minutes without breaking in pieces, unless the winds, by a kind of miracle, should turn immediately about. In a word, we sat looking one upon another, and expecting death every moment, and every man acting accordingly, as preparing for another world; for there was little or nothing more for us to do in this; that which was our present comfort, and all the comfort we had, was, that, contrary to our expectation, the ship did not break yet, and that the master said the wind began to abate.

Now, though we thought that the wind did a little abate, yet, the ship having thus struck upon the sand, and sticking too fast for us to expect her getting off, we were in a dreadful condition indeed, and had nothing to do but to think of saving our lives as well as we could. We had a boat at our stern, just before the storm;

but she was first staved by dashing against the ship's rudder, and, in the next place, she broke away, and either sunk or was driven off to sea; so there was no hope from her. We had another boat on board, but how to get her off into the sea was a doubtful thing; however, there was no reason to debate, for we fancied the ship would break in pieces every minute, and some told us she was actually broken already.

In this distress, the mate of our vessel lays hold of the boat, and, with the help of the rest of the men, they got her slung over the ship's side, and getting all into her, let go, and committed ourselves, being eleven in number, to God's mercy and the wild sea; for though the storm was abated considerably, yet the sea went dreadfully high upon the shore, and might well be called *den wild zee*, as the Dutch call the sea in a storm.

And now our case was very dismal indeed; for we all saw plainly that the sea went so high that the boat could not live, and that we should be inevitably drowned. As to making sail, we had none, nor, if we had, could we have done anything with it; so we worked at the oar towards the land, though with heavy hearts, like men going to execution; for we all knew, that when the boat came nearer the shore, she would be dashed in a thousand pieces by the breach of the sea. However, we committed our souls to God in the most earnest manner; and the wind driving us towards the shore, we hastened our destruction with our own hands, pulling as well as we could towards land.

What the shore was, whether rock or sand, whether steep or shoal, we knew not; the only hope that could rationally give us the least shadow of expectation was if we might happen into some bay or gulf, or the mouth of some river, where by great chance we might have run our boat in, or got under the lee of the land, and perhaps made smooth water. But there was nothing of this appeared; but, as we made nearer and nearer the shore, the land looked more frightful than the sea.

After we had rowed, or rather driven, about a league and a half, as we reckoned it, a raging wave, mountain-like, came rolling astern of us, and plainly bade us expect a watery grave. In a word, it took us with such a fury, that it overset the boat at once; and separating us as well from the boat as from one another, gave us not time hardly to say: "O God!" for we were all swallowed up in a moment.

Nothing can describe the confusion of thought which I felt

when I sank into the water; for though I swam very well, yet I could not deliver myself from the waves so as to draw breath, till that wave having driven me, or rather carried me, a vast way on towards the shore, and having spent itself, went back, and left me upon the land almost dry, but half dead with the water I took in. I had so much presence of mind, as well as breath left, that, seeing myself nearer the mainland than I expected, I got upon my feet and endeavoured to walk on towards the land as fast as I could before another wave should return and take me up again. But I soon found it was impossible to avoid it; for I saw the sea come after me as high as a great hill, and as furious as an enemy, which I had no means or strength to contend with – my business was to hold my breath and raise myself upon the water, if I could; and so, by swimming, to preserve my breathing, and pilot myself towards the shore, if possible – my greatest concern now being, that the sea, as it would carry me a great way towards the shore when it came on, might not carry me back again with it when it gave back towards the sea.

The wave that came upon me again buried me at once twenty or thirty feet deep in its own body; and I could feel myself carried with a mighty force and swiftness towards the shore a very great way; but I held my breath, and assisted myself to swim still forward with all my might. I was ready to burst with holding my breath, when, as I felt myself rising up, so, to my immediate relief, I found my head and hands shoot out above the surface of the water; and though it was not two seconds of time that I could keep myself so, yet it relieved me greatly, gave me breath and new courage. I was covered again with water a good while, but not so long, but I held it out; and, finding the water had spent itself and began to return, I struck forward against the return of the waves and felt ground again with my feet. I stood still a few moments to recover breath, and till the water went from me, and then took to my heels, and ran with what strength I had farther towards the shore. But neither would this deliver me from the fury of the sea, which came pouring in after me again; and twice more I was lifted up by the waves and carried forwards as before, the shore being very flat.

The last time of those two had well near been fatal to me; for the sea, having hurried me along as before, landed me, or rather dashed me, against a piece of rock, and that with such force as it left me senseless, and indeed helpless, as to my own deliverance; for the blow taking my side and breast, beat the breath, as it were, quite out of my body, and had it returned again immediately, I must have been strangled in the water; but I recovered a little before the return of the waves, and, seeing I should be covered again with the water, I resolved to hold fast by a piece of the rock, and so to hold my breath, if possible, till the wave went back. Now, as the waves were not so high as at first, being near land, I held my hold till the wave abated, and then fetched another run, which brought me so near the shore, that the next wave, though it went over me, yet did not so swallow me up as to carry me away; and the next run I took I got to the mainland, where, to my great comfort, I clambered up the cliffs of the shore, and sat me down upon the grass, free from danger, and quite out of the reach of the water.

I was now landed and safe on shore, and began to look up and thank God that my life was saved, in a case wherein there was, some minutes before, scarce any room to hope. I believe it is impossible to express to the life what the ecstasies and transports of the soul are when it is so saved, as I may say, out of the very grave; and I do not wonder now at that custom, namely, that when a malefactor, who has the halter about his neck, is tied up, and just going to be turned off, and has a reprieve brought to him – I say, I do not wonder that they bring a surgeon with it, to let him blood that very moment they tell him of it, that the surprise may not drive the animal spirits from the heart, and overwhelm him:

'For sudden joys, like griefs, confound at first.'

I walked about on the shore, lifting up my hands, and my whole being, as I may say, rapt up in the contemplation of my deliverance, making a thousand gestures and motions which I cannot describe – reflecting upon all my comrades that were drowned, and that there should not be one soul saved but myself – for, as for them, I never saw them afterwards, or any sign of them, except three of their hats, one cap, and two shoes that were not fellows.

I cast my eyes to the stranded vessel, when the breach and froth of the sea being so big, I could hardly see it, it lay so far off, and considered, Lord! how was it possible I could get on shore?

After I had solaced my mind with the comfortable part of my condition, I began to look round me, to see what kind of place I was in, and what was next to be done; and I soon found my comforts abate, and that, in a word, I had a dreadful deliverance: for I was wet, had no clothes to shift me, nor anything either to eat or drink to comfort me; neither did I see any prospect before me but that of perishing with hunger, or being devoured by wild beasts; and that which was particularly afflicting to me was that I had no weapon either to hunt and kill any creature for my sustenance, or to defend myself against any other creature that might desire to kill me for theirs – in a word, I had nothing about me but a knife, a tobacco pipe, and a little tobacco in a box; this was all my provision, and this threw me into terrible agonies of mind, that, for a while, I ran about like a madman. Night coming upon me, I began with a heavy heart to consider what would be my lot if there were any ravenous beasts in that country, seeing at night they always come abroad for their prey.

All the remedy that offered to my thoughts at that time was to get up into a thick bushy tree like a fir, but thorny, which grew near me, and where I resolved to sit all night, and consider the next day what death I should die, for as yet I saw no prospect of life. I walked about a furlong from the shore to see if I could find any fresh water to drink, which I did, to my great joy; and having drank and put a little tobacco in my mouth to prevent hunger, I went to the tree, and getting up into it, endeavoured to place myself so as that if I should sleep I might not fall; and having cut me a short stick like a truncheon for my defence, I took up my lodging; and having been excessively fatigued, I fell fast asleep, and slept as comfortably as I believe few could have done in my condition, and found myself the most refreshed with it that I think I ever was on such an occasion.

CHAPTER 4

Swim to the Wreck, and get a quantity of
Stores – Moralise upon my situation – The
Ship totally lost

When I waked it was broad day, the weather clear, and the storm
abated, so that the sea did not rage and swell as before; but that
which surprised me most was, that the ship was lifted off in the
night from the sand where she lay, by the swelling of the tide, and
was driven up almost as far as the rock which I first mentioned,
where I had been so bruised by the dashing me against it; this being
within about a mile from the shore where I was, and the ship seeming
to stand upright still, I wished myself on board, that, at least, I
might save some necessary things for my use.

When I came down from my apartment in the tree, I looked
about me again, and the first thing I found was the boat, which lay
as the wind and the sea had tossed her up upon the land, about two
miles on my right hand. I walked as far as I could upon the shore
to have got to her, but found a neck, or inlet of water, between me
and the boat, which was about half a mile broad: so I came back
for the present, being more intent upon getting at the ship, where
I hoped to find something for my present subsistence.

A little after noon, I found the sea very calm, and the tide
ebbed so far out, that I could come within a quarter of a mile of
the ship; and here I found a fresh renewing of my grief: for I saw
evidently, that if we had kept on board, we had been all safe, – that
is to say, we had all got safe on shore, and I had not been so miserable as to be left entirely destitute of all comfort and company as I
now was. This forced tears from my eyes again; but as there was
little relief in that, I resolved, if possible, to get to the ship – so I

pulled off my clothes, for the weather was hot to extremity, and took the water. But when I came to the ship, my difficulty was still greater to know how to get on board; for as she lay aground and high out of the water, there was nothing within my reach to lay hold of. I swam round her twice, and the second time I spied a small piece of a rope, which I wondered I did not see at first, hang down by the fore-chains, so low as that with great difficulty I got hold of it, and, by the help of that rope, got up into the forecastle of the ship. Here I found that the ship was bulged, and had a great deal of water in her hold, but that she lay so on the side of a bank of hard sand, or rather earth, and her stern lay lifted up upon the bank, and her head, low almost to the water; by this means all her quarter was free, and all that was in that part was dry; for you may be sure my first work was to search and see what was spoiled, and what was free; and first I found that all the ship's provisions were dry and untouched by the water; and being very well disposed to eat, I went to the bread-room and filled my pockets with biscuit, and ate it as I went about other things, for I had no time to lose. I also found some rum in the great cabin, of which I took a large dram, and which I had indeed need enough of to spirit me for what was before me. Now I wanted nothing but a boat, to furnish myself with many things which I foresaw would be very necessary to me.

It was in vain to sit still and wish for what was not to be had; and this extremity roused my application. We had several spare yards, and two or three large spars of wood, and a spare topmast or two in the ship; I resolved to fall to work with these, and flung as many of them overboard as I could manage of their weight, tying every one with a rope, that they might not drive away. When this was done, I went down to the ship's side, and pulling them to me, I tied four of them fast together at both ends as well as I could, in the form of a raft, and laying two or three short pieces of plank upon them crossways, I found I could walk upon it very well, but that it was not able to bear any great weight, the pieces being too light; so I went to work, and, with the carpenter's saw, I cut a spare topmast into three lengths, and added them to my raft, with a great deal of labour and pains; but hope of furnishing myself with necessaries, encouraged me to go beyond what I should have been able to have done upon another occasion.

My raft was now strong enough to bear any reasonable weight; my next care was what to load it with, and how to preserve what I laid on it from the surf of the sea; but I was not long considering this. I first laid all the planks or boards upon it that I could get, and having considered well what I most wanted, I first got three of the seamen's chests, which I had broken open and emptied, and lowered them down upon my raft. The first of these I filled with provisions, namely, bread, rice, three Dutch cheeses, five pieces of dried goats' flesh, which we lived much upon, and a little remainder of European corn, which had been laid by for some fowls which we brought to sea with us, but the fowls were killed. There had been some barley and wheat together, but, to my great disappointment, I found afterwards that the rats had eaten or spoiled it all. As for liquors, I found several cases of bottles belonging to our skipper, in which were some cordial waters, and, in all, above five or six gallons of rack: these I stowed by themselves, there being no need to put them into the chest, nor no room for them. While I was doing this, I found the tide began to flow, though very, calm, and I had the mortification to see my coat, shirt, and waistcoat, which I had left on shore upon the sand, swim away; as for my breeches, which were only linen, and open-kneed, I swam on board in them and my stockings: however, this put me upon rummaging for clothes, of which I found enough, but took no more than I wanted for present use, for I had other things which my eye was more upon: as, first, tools to work with on shore; and it was after long searching that I found out the carpenter's chest, which was indeed a very useful prize to me, and much more valuable than a shipload of gold would have been at that time. I got it down to my raft, even whole as it was, without losing time to look into it, for I knew in general what it contained.

My next care was for some ammunition and arms. There were two very good fowling-pieces in the great cabin, and two pistols: these I secured first, with some powder-horns, and a small bag of shot, and two old rusty swords. I knew there were three barrels of powder in the ship, but knew not where our gunner had stowed them; but with much search I found them, two of them dry and good, the third had taken water; those two I got to my raft, with the arms. And now I thought myself pretty well freighted, and began to think how I should get to shore with them, having neither sail, oar, nor rudder, and the least capful of wind would have overset all my navigation.

I had three encouragements: 1, A smooth, calm sea; 2, The tide rising, and setting in to the shore; 3, What little wind there was blew me toward the land; and thus, having found two or three broken oars belonging to the boat, and, besides the tools which were in the chest, I found two saws, an axe, and a hammer; and with this cargo I put to sea. For a mile, or thereabouts, my raft went very well, only that I found it drive a little distant from the place where I had landed before; by which I perceived that there was some indraft of the water, and, consequently, I hoped to find some creek or river there which I might make use of as a port to get to land with my cargo.

As I imagined, so it was; there appeared before me a little opening of the land, and I found a strong current of the tide set into it, so I guided my raft as well as I could to keep in the middle of the stream; but here I had like to have suffered a second ship-wreck, which, if I had, I think verily would have broke my heart; for, knowing nothing of the coast, my raft ran aground at one end of it upon a shoal, and, not being aground at the other end, it wanted but a little that all my cargo had slipped off towards that end that was afloat, and so fallen into the water. I did my utmost, by setting my back against the chests, to keep them in their places, but could not thrust off the raft with all my strength; neither durst I stir from the posture I was in, but, holding up the chests with all my might, stood in that manner near half an hour, in which time the rising of the water brought me a little more upon a level; and, a little after, the water still rising, my raft floated again, and I thrust her off with the oar I had into the channel; and then, driving up higher, I at length found myself in the mouth of a little river, with land on both sides, and a strong current, or tide, running up. I looked on both sides for a proper place to get to shore; for I was not willing to be driven too high up the river, hoping in time to see some ship at sea, and there-fore resolved to place myself as near the coast as I could.

At length I spied a little cove on the right shore of the creek, to which, with great pain and difficulty, I guided my raft, and at last got so near as that, reaching ground with my oar, I could thrust her directly in; but here I had like to have dipped all my cargo in the sea again; for that shore lying pretty steep, that is to say, sloping, there was no place to land, but where one end of the float, if it ran on shore, would lie so high, and the other sink lower as before, that it would endanger my cargo again: all that I could do, was to wait till the tide was at the highest, keeping the raft with my oar like an anchor to hold the side of it fast to the shore, near a flat piece of ground, which I expected the water would flow over: and so it did. As soon as I found water enough – for my raft drew about a foot of water – I thrust her on upon that flat piece of ground, and there fastened, or moored her, by sticking my two broken oars into the ground – one on one side, near one end, and one on the other side, near the other end; and thus I lay till the water ebbed away, and left my raft and all my cargo safe on shore.

My next work was to view the country, and to seek a proper place for my habitation, and where to stow my goods, to secure them from whatever might happen. Where I was, I yet knew not; whether on the continent or on an island – whether inhabited or not inhabited – whether in danger of wild beasts or not. There was a hill, not above a mile from me, which rose up very steep and high, and which seemed to overtop some other hills which lay as in a ridge from it northward. I took out one of the fowling-pieces, and one of the pistols, and a horn of powder; and thus armed, I travelled for discovery up to the top of that hill, where, after I had with great labour and difficulty got to the top, I saw my fate, to my great affliction, namely, that I was in an island, environed every way with the sea – no land to be seen, except some rocks which lay a great way off, and two small islands less than this, which lay about three leagues to the west.

I found also, that the island I was in was barren, and, as I saw good reason to believe, uninhabited, except by wild beasts, of which, however, I saw none; yet I saw abundance of fowls, but knew not their kinds, neither, when I killed them, could I tell what was fit for food, and what not. At my coming back, I shot at a great bird, which I saw sitting upon a tree on the side of a great wood: I believe it was the first gun that had been fired there since the creation of the world. I had no sooner fired, but, from all parts of the wood, there arose an innumerable number of fowls of many sorts, making a confused screaming and crying, every one according to his usual note; but not one of them of any kind that I knew. As for the creature that I killed, I took it to be a kind of hawk, its colour and beak resembling it, but had no talons or claws, more than common; its flesh was carrion, and fit for nothing.

Contented with this discovery, I came back to my raft, and fell to work to bring my cargo on shore, which took me up the rest of that day: and what to do with myself at night I knew not, nor indeed where to rest; for I was afraid to lie down on the ground, not knowing but some wild beast might devour me; though, as I afterwards found, there was really no need for those fears.

However, as well as I could, I barricaded myself round with the chests and boards that I had brought on shore, and made a kind of a hut for that night's lodging. As for food, I yet saw not which way to supply myself, except that I had seen two or three creatures like hares run out of the wood where I shot the fowl.

I now began to consider that I might yet get a great many things out of the ship, which would be useful to me, and particularly some of the rigging and sails, and such other things as might come to land, and I resolved to make another voyage on board the vessel, if possible; and as I knew that the first storm that blew must necessarily break her all in pieces, I resolved to set all other things apart, till I got everything out of the ship that I could get. Then I called a council (that is to say in my thoughts), whether I should take back the raft; but this appeared impracticable; so I resolved to go as before, when the tide was down, and I did so, only that I stripped before I went from my hut, having nothing on but a checked shirt and a pair of linen trousers, and a pair of pumps on my feet.

I got aboard the ship as before, and prepared a second raft; and having had experience of the first, I neither made this so unwieldy, nor loaded it so hard, but yet I brought away several things very useful to me; as first, in the carpenter's stores, I found two or three bags full of nails and spikes, a great screw-jack, a dozen or two of hatchets, and, above all, that most useful thing called a grindstone: all these I secured, together with several things belonging to the gunner, particularly two or three iron crows, and two barrels of musket-bullets, seven muskets, and another fowling-piece, with some small quantity of powder more; a large bag full of small shot, and a great roll of sheet lead; but this last was so heavy I could not hoist it up to get it over the ship's side.

Besides these things, I took all the men's clothes that I could find, and a spare fore-top-sail, hammock, and some bedding; and with this I loaded my second raft, and brought them all safe on shore, to my very great comfort.

I was under some apprehensions during my absence from the land, that at least my provisions might be devoured on shore; but, when I came back, I found no sign of any visitor, only there sat a creature, like a wild cat, upon one of the chests, which, when I came towards it, ran away a little distance, and then stood still: she sat very composed and unconcerned, and looked full in my face, as if she had a mind to be acquainted with me. I presented my gun at her, but as she did not understand it, she was perfectly unconcerned at it, nor did she offer to stir away; upon which I tossed her a bit of biscuit, though by the way, I was not very free of it, for my store was not great: however, I spared her a bit, I say, and she went to it, smelled of it, and ate it, and looked, as pleased, for more; but I thanked her, and could spare no more – so she marched off.

Having got my second cargo on shore, though I was fain to open the barrels of powder, and bring them by parcels – for they were too heavy, being large casks – I went to work to make me a little tent, with the sail and some poles which I cut for that purpose; and into this tent I brought everything that I knew would spoil either with rain or sun; and piled all the empty chests and casks up in a circle round the tent, to fortify it from any sudden attempt, either from man or beast.

When I had done this, I blocked up the door of the tent with some boards within, and an empty chest set up on end without, and, spreading one of the beds upon the ground, laying my two pistols just at my head, and my gun at length by me, I went to bed for the first time, and slept very quietly all night, for I was very weary and heavy; as the night before I had slept little, and had laboured very hard all day, as well to fetch all those things from the ship as to get them on shore.

I had the biggest magazine of all kinds now that ever was laid up, I believe, for one man, but I was not satisfied still: for, while the ship sat upright in that posture, I thought I ought to get everything out of her that I could: so every day, at low water, I went on board and brought away something or other, but particularly the third time I went, I brought away as much of the rigging as I could, as also all the small ropes and rope-twine I could get, with a piece of spare canvas, which was to mend the sails upon occasion, and the barrel of wet gunpowder; in a word, I brought away all the sails first and last, only that I was fain to cut them in pieces, and bring as much at a time as I could; for they were no more useful to be sails, but as mere canvas only.

But that which comforted me more still, was, that last of all, after I had made five or six such voyages as these, and thought I had nothing more to expect from the ship that was worth my meddling with – I say, after all this, I found a great hogshead of bread, and three large runlets of rum or spirits, and a box of sugar, and a barrel of fine flour; this was surprising to me, because I had given over expecting any more provisions, except what was spoiled by the water. I soon emptied the hogshead of that bread, and wrapped it up, parcel by parcel, in pieces of the sails, which I cut out; and, in a word, I got all this safe on shore also.

The next day I made another voyage; and now, having plundered the ship of what was portable and fit to hand out, I began with the cables; and cutting the great cable into pieces, such as I could move, I got two cables and a howser on shore, with all the iron-work I could get; and having cut down the sprit-sail-yard, and the mizzen-yard, and everything I could, to make a large raft, I loaded it with all those heavy goods, and came away: but my good luck began now to leave me; for this raft was so unwieldy and over-laden, that, after I had entered the little cove, where I had landed the rest of my goods, not being able to guide it handily so as I did the others, it overset, and threw me and all my cargo into the water. As for myself, it was no great harm, for I was near the shore; but as to my cargo, it was, great part of it, lost, especially the iron, which I expected would have been of great use to me; however, when the tide was out, I got most of the pieces of cable ashore, and some of the iron, though with infinite labour; for I was fain to dip for it into the water, a work which fatigued me very much. After this I went every day on board, and brought away what I could get.

I had been now thirteen days on shore, and had been eleven times on board the ship; in which time I had brought away all that one pair of hands could well be supposed capable to bring, though I believe verily, had the calm held, I should have brought away the whole ship, piece by piece: but, preparing the twelfth time to go on board, I found the wind began to rise; however, at low water, I went on board, and though I had rummaged the cabin so effectually as that nothing more could be found, yet I discovered a locker with drawers in it, in one of which I found two or three razors, and one pair of large scissors, with some ten or a dozen of good knives and forks; in another I found about thirty-six pounds value in money, some European coin, some Brazil, some pieces of eight, some gold, some silver.

I smiled to myself at the sight of this money. "O drug!" said I, aloud, "what art thou good for? thou art not worth to me – no, not the taking off of the ground; one of those knives is worth all this heap; I have no manner of use for thee; even remain where thou art, and go to the bottom as a creature whose life is not worth saving." However, upon second thoughts, I took it away, and wrapping all this in a piece of canvas, I began to think of making another raft; but, while I was preparing this, I found the sky overcast, and the wind began to rise, and in a quarter of an hour it blew a fresh gale from the shore. It presently occurred to me, that it was in vain to pretend to make a raft with the wind off-shore, and that it was my business to be gone before the tide of flood began, otherwise I might not be able to reach the shore at all; accordingly, I let myself down into the water, and swam across the channel which lay between the ship and the sands, and even that with difficulty enough, partly with the weight of things I had about me, and partly the roughness of the water, for the wind rose very hastily, and, before it was quite high water, it blew a storm.

But I was gotten home to my little tent, where I lay with all my wealth about me very secure. It blew very hard all that night, and in the morning when I looked out, behold no more ship was to be seen! I was a little surprised, but recovered myself with this satisfactory reflection, namely, that I had lost no time, nor abated no diligence, to get everything out of her that could be useful to me, and that, indeed, there was little left in her that I was able to bring away, if I had had more time.

I now gave over any more thoughts of the ship, or of anything out of her, except what might drive on shore from the wreck, as indeed divers pieces of her afterwards did; but those things were of small use to me.

My thoughts were now wholly employed about securing myself against either savages, if any should appear, or wild beasts, if any were on the island; and I had many thoughts of the method how to do this, and what kind of dwelling to make – whether I should make me a cave in the earth, or a tent upon the earth; and, in short, I resolved upon both, the manner and description of which it may not be improper to give an account of.

I soon found the place I was in was not for my settlement, particularly because it was upon a low moorish ground near the sea, and I believe would not be wholesome, and more particularly because there was no fresh water near it; so I resolved to find a more healthy and more convenient spot of ground.

I consulted several things in my situation which I found would be proper for me: First, Health and fresh water I just now mentioned; second, Shelter from the heat of the sun; third, Security from ravenous creatures, whether man or beast; fourth, A view to the sea, that, if God send any ship in sight, I might not lose any advantage for my deliverance, of which I was not willing to banish all my expectation yet.

In search of a place proper for this, I found a little plain on the side of a rising hill, whose front towards this little plain was steep as a house-side, so that nothing could come down upon me from the top: on the side of this rock there was a hollow place worn a little way in, like the entrance or door of a cave, but there was not really any cave or way into the rock at all.

On the flat of the green, just below this hollow place, I resolved to pitch my tent: this plain was not above an hundred yards broad, and about twice as long, and lay like a green before my door, and at the end of it descended irregularly every way down into the low grounds by the sea-side. It was on the north-north-west side of the hill, so that I was sheltered from the heat every day, till it came to a west-and-by-south sun, or thereabouts, which in those countries is near the setting.

Before I set up my tent, I drew a half circle before the hollow place which took in about ten yards in its semi-diameter, from the rock, and twenty yards in its diameter from its beginning and ending.

In this half circle I pitched two rows of strong stakes, driving them into the ground till they stood very firm, like piles, the biggest end being out of the ground about five feet and a half, and sharpened on the top: the two rows did not stand above six inches from one another.

Then I took the pieces of cable which I had cut in the ship, and laid them in rows, one upon another, within the circle between these two rows of stakes up to the top, placing other stakes in the inside, leaning against them, about two feet and a half high, like a spur to a post; and this fence was so strong that neither man nor beast could get into it, or over it: this cost me a great deal of time and labour, especially to cut the piles in the woods, bring them to the place, and drive them into the earth.

The entrance into this place I made to be, not by a door, but by a short ladder, to go over the top; which ladder, when I was in, I lifted over after me: and so I was completely fenced in, and forti-fied, as I thought, from all the world, and consequently slept secure in the night, which otherwise I could not have done; though, as it appeared afterwards, there was no need of all this caution from the enemies that I apprehended danger from.

Into this fence, or fortress, with infinite labour, I carried all my riches, all my provisions, ammunition, and stores, of which you have the account above; and I made me a large tent, which, to preserve me from the rains, that in one part of the year are very violent there, I made double, namely, one smaller tent within, and

DANIEL DEFOE

one larger tent above it, and covered the uppermost with a large tarpaulin, which I had saved among the sails.

And now I lay no more, for a while, in the bed which I had brought on shore, but in a hammock, which was, indeed, a very good one, and belonged to the mate of the ship.

Into this tent I brought all my provisions, and everything that would spoil by the wet; and having thus enclosed all my goods, I made up the entrance, which, till now, I had left open, and so passed and repassed, as I said by a short ladder.

When I had done this, I began to work my way into the rock, and, bringing all the earth and stones that I dug down, out through my tent, I laid them up within my fence in the nature of a terrace, that so it raised the ground within about a foot and a half; and thus I made me a cave just behind my tent, which served me like a cellar to my house.

It cost me much labour and many days before all these things were brought to perfection: and, therefore, I must go back to some other things which took up some of my thoughts. At the same time, it happened, after I had laid my scheme for the settings of my tent, and making the cave, that a storm of rain falling from a thick dark cloud, a sudden flash of lightning happened, and after that a great clap of thunder, as is naturally the effect of it. I was not so much surprised with the lightning as I was with a thought which darted into my mind, as swift as the lightning itself: Oh, my powder! my very heart sank within me, when I thought that, at one blast, all my powder might be destroyed, on which, not my defence only, but the providing me food, as I thought, entirely depended; I was nothing near so anxious about my own danger, though, had the powder took fire, I had never known who had hurt me.

Such impression did this make upon me, that after the storm was over, I laid aside all my works, my building and fortifying, and applied myself to make bags and boxes, to separate the powder, and to keep it a little and a little in a parcel, in hope that, whatever might come, it might not all take fire at once, and to keep it so apart, that it should not be possible to make one part fire another. I finished this work in about a fortnight; and I think my powder, which, in all, was about two hundred and forty pounds weight, was divided in not less than a hundred parcels. As to the barrel that had been wet, I did not apprehend any danger from that, so I placed it in my new cave, which, in my fancy, I called my kitchen; and the rest I hid up and down in holes among the rocks, so that no wet might come to it, marking very carefully where I laid it.

In the interval of time, while this was doing, I went out once at least every day with my gun, as well to divert myself as to see if I could kill anything fit for food, and, as near as I could, to acquaint myself with what the island produced. The first time I went out, I presently discovered that there were goats in the island, which was a great satisfaction to me; but then, it was attended with this misfortune to me, namely, that they were so shy, so subtle, and so swift of foot, that it was the most difficult thing in the world to come at them. But I was not discouraged at this, not doubting but I might now and then shoot one, as it soon happened; for, after I had found their haunts a little, I laid wait in this manner for them. I observed, if they saw me in the valleys, though they were upon the rocks, they would run away as in a terrible fright; but if they were feeding in the valleys, and I was upon the rocks, they took no notice of me; from whence I concluded, that, by the position of their optics, their sight was so directed downwards that they did not readily see objects that were above them: so afterwards I took this method: I always climbed the rocks first, to get above them, and then had frequently a fair mark. The first shot I made among these creatures I killed a she-goat, which had a little kid by her which she gave suck to, which grieved me heartily; but when the old one fell, the kid stood stock still by her till I came and took her up; and not only so, but, when I carried the old one with me upon my shoulders, the kid followed me quite to my enclosure; upon which I laid down the dam, and took the kid in my arms, and carried it over my pale, in hopes to have bred it up tame; but it would not eat, so I was forced to kill it, and eat it myself. These two supplied me with flesh a great while, for I ate sparingly, and saved my provisions (my bread especially) as much as possibly I could.

Having now fixed my habitation, I found it absolutely necessary to provide a place to make a fire in, and fuel to burn; and what I did that for, as also how I enlarged my cave, and what conveniences I made, I shall give a full account of in its place; but I must first give some little account of myself, and of my thoughts about living, which, it may well be supposed were not a few.

I had a dismal prospect of my condition; for, as I was not cast away upon that island without being driven, as is said, by a violent storm, quite out of the course of our intended voyage, and a great way, namely, some hundreds of leagues, out of the ordinary course of the trade of mankind, I had great reason to consider it as a determination of Heaven, that, in this desolate place, and in this desolate manner, I should end my life. The tears would run plentifully down my face when I made these reflections; and sometimes I would expostulate with myself why Providence should thus completely ruin his creatures, and render them so absolutely miserable, so without help abandoned, so entirely depressed, that it could hardly be rational to be thankful for such a life.

But something always returned swift upon me to check these thoughts, and to reprove me; and, particularly, one day walking, with my gun in my hand, by the sea-side, I was very pensive upon the subject of my present condition, when reason, as it were, expostulated with me the other way, thus: "Well, you are in a desolate condition, it is true; but pray, remember, where are the rest of you? Did not you come eleven of you into the boat? Where are the ten? Why were they not saved and you lost? Why were you singled out? Is it better to be here or there?" And then I pointed to the sea. All evils are to be considered with the good that is in them, and with what worse attended them.

Then it occurred to me again, how well I was furnished for my subsistence, and what would have been my case if it had not happened, which was an hundred thousand to one, that the ship floated from the place where she first struck, and was driven so near the shore that I had time to get all things out of her. What would have been my case, if I had been to have lived in the condition in which I at first came on shore, without necessaries of life, or necessaries to supply or procure them? "Particularly," said I, aloud, though to myself, "what should I have done without a gun, without ammunition, without any tools to make anything, or to work with – without clothes, bedding, a tent or any manner of covering?" and that now I had all these to a sufficient quantity, and was in a fair way to provide myself in such a manner as to live without my gun when my ammunition was spent; so that I had a tolerable view of subsisting without any want, as long as I lived: for I considered, from the beginning, how I should provide for the accidents that might happen, and for the time that was to come, even not only after my ammunition should be spent, but even after my health and strength should decay.

I confess I had not entertained any notion of my ammunition being destroyed at one blast, I mean, my powder being blown up by lightning; and this made the thoughts of it so surprising to me when it lightened and thundered, as I observed just now.

And now, being about to enter into a melancholy relation of a scene of silent life, such, perhaps, as was never heard of in the world before, I shall take it from its beginning, and continue it in its order. It was, by my account, the 30th of September, when, in the manner as above said, I first set foot upon this horrid island, when the sun being, to us, in its autumnal equinox, was almost just over my head; for I reckoned myself, by observation, to be in the latitude of nine degrees twenty-two minutes north of the Line.

After I had been there about ten or twelve days, it came into my thoughts, that I should lose my reckoning of time for want of books, and pen and ink, and should even forget the Sabbath days from the working days; but, to prevent this, I cut it with my knife upon a large post in capital letters, and making it into a great cross, I set it up on the shore where I first landed, namely, I came on shore here on the 30th of September, 1659. Upon the sides of this square post, I cut every day a notch with my knife, and every seventh notch was as long again as the rest, and every first day of the month as long again as that long one; and thus I kept my calendar, or weekly, monthly, and yearly reckoning of time.

In the next place, we are to observe that, among the many things which I brought out of the ship in the several voyages, which, as above mentioned, I made to it, I got several things of less value, but not at all less useful to me, which I omitted setting down before; as, in particular, pens, ink, and paper, several parcels in the captain's, mate's, gunner's, and carpenter's keeping, three or four compasses, some mathematical instruments, dials, perspectives, charts, and books of navigation, all which I huddled together, whether I might want them or no. Also, I found three very good Bibles, which came to me in my cargo from England, and which I had packed up among my things; some Portuguese books also, and among them two or three Popish prayer-books, and several other books: all which I carefully secured. And I must not forget that we had in the ship a dog and two cats of whose eminent history I may have occasion to say something in its place; for I carried both the cats with me: and as for the dog, he jumped out of the ship of himself, and swam on shore to me the day after I went on shore with my first cargo, and was a trusty servant to me many years: I wanted nothing that he could fetch me, nor any company that he could make up to me – I only wanted to have him talk to me; but that he could not so. As I observed before, I found pen, ink, and paper, and I husbanded them to the utmost; and I shall show, that while my ink lasted, I kept things very exact; but after that was gone I could not, for I could not make any ink by any means that I could devise.

And this put me in mind that I wanted many things, notwithstanding all that I had amassed together; and of these, this of ink was one, as also spade, pickaxe, and shovel, to dig or remove the earth; needles pins, and thread. As for linen, I soon learnt to want that without much difficulty.

This want of tools made every work I did go on heavily, and it was near a whole year before I had entirely finished my little pale, or surrounded habitation; the piles, or stakes, which were as heavy as I could well lift, were a long time in cutting and preparing in the woods, and more by far in bringing home; so that I spent sometimes two days in cutting and bringing home one of those posts, and a third day in driving it into the ground; for which purpose I got a heavy piece of wood at first, but at last bethought myself of one of the iron crows, which, however, though I found it, yet it made driving those posts, or piles, very laborious and tedious work.

But what need I have been concerned at the tediousness of anything I had to do, seeing I had time enough to do it in? Nor had I any other employment, if that had been over, at least that I could foresee, except the ranging the island to seek for food, which I did more or less every day.

I now began to consider seriously my condition, and the circumstances I was reduced to, and I drew up the state of my affairs in writing, not so much to leave them to any that were to come after me (for I was like to have but few heirs), as to deliver my thoughts from daily poring upon them, and afflicting my mind; and as my reason began now to master my despondency, I began to comfort myself as well as I could, and to set the good against the evil, that I might have something to distinguish my case from worse; and stated it very impartially, like debtor and creditor, the comforts I enjoyed against the miseries I suffered, thus: –

EVIL

I am cast upon a horrible, desolate island, void of all hope of recovery.

I am singled out and separated, as it were, from all the world to be miserable.

I am divided from mankind, a solitaire, one banished from human society.

I have no clothes to cover me.

I am without any defence, or means to resist any violence of man or beast.

I have no soul to speak to, or relieve me.

GOOD

But I am alive, and not drowned, as all my ship's company was.

But I am singled out, too, from all the ship's crew, to be spared from death; and He that miraculously saved me from death, can deliver me from this condition.

But I am not starved and perishing on a barren place, affording no sustenance.

But I am in a hot climate, where, if I had clothes, I could hardly wear them.

But I am cast on an island where I see no wild beasts to hurt me, as I saw on the coast of Africa; and what if I had been ship-wrecked there?

But God wonderfully sent the ship in near enough to the shore, that I have gotten out so many necessary things as will either supply my wants, or enable me to supply myself, even as long as I live.

Upon the whole, here was an undoubted testimony, that there was scarce any condition in the world so miserable, but there was something *negative* or something *positive* to be thankful for in it; and let this stand as a direction from the experience of the most miserable of all conditions in this world, that we may always find in it something to comfort ourselves from, and to set in the description of good and evil on the credit side of the account.

Having now brought my mind a little to relish my condition, and given over looking out to sea, to see if I could spy a ship – I say, giving over these things, I began to apply myself to accommodate my way of living, and to make things as easy to me as I could.

I have already described my habitation, which was a tent, under the side of a rock, surrounded with a strong pale of posts and cables; but I might now rather call it a wall, for I raised a kind of wall up against it of turfs, about two feet thick on the outside; and after some time – I think it was a year and a half – I raised rafters from it, leaning to the rock, and thatched or covered it with boughs of trees, and such things as I could get to keep out the rain, which I found at some times of the year very violent.

I have already observed how I brought all my goods into this pale, and into the cave which I had made behind me: but I must observe, too, that at first this was a confused heap of goods, which, as they lay in no order, so they took up all my place: I had no room to turn myself, so I set myself to enlarge my cave and works farther into the earth; for it was a loose, sandy rock, which yielded easily to the labour I bestowed on it – and so, when I found I was pretty safe as to beasts of prey, I worked sideways to the right hand into the rock: and then, turning to the right again, worked quite out, and made me a door to come out, on the outside of my pale, or fortification.

This gave me not only egress and regress, as it were a back way to my tent and to my storehouse, but gave me room to stow my goods.

And now I began to apply myself to make such necessary things as I found I most wanted, particularly a chair and a table; for without these I was not able to enjoy the few comforts I had in the world – I could not write, or eat, or do several things with so much pleasure without a table.,

So I went to work; and here I must needs observe, that as reason is the substance and original of the mathematics, so, by stating and squaring everything by reason, and by making the most rational judgment of things, every man may be in time master of every mechanic art. I had never handled a tool in my life, and yet in time, by labour, application, and contrivance, I found at last that I wanted nothing but I could have made it, especially if I had had tools; however, I made abundance of things even without tools, and some with no more tools than an adze and a hatchet, which perhaps, were never made that way before, and that with infinite labour – for example, if I wanted a board, I had no other way but to cut down a tree, set it on edge before me, and hew it flat on either side with my axe, till I had brought it to be as thin as a plank, and then dub it smooth with my adze. It is true, by this method I could make but one board out of a whole tree; but this I had no remedy for but patience, any more than I had for the prodigious deal of time and labour which it took me up to make a plank or board; but my time and labour were little worth, and so they were as well employed one way as another.

However, I made me a table and a chair, as I observed above, in the first place – and this I did out of the short pieces of boards that I brought on my raft from the ship: but, when I had wrought out some boards, as above, I made large shelves of the breadth of a foot and a half, one over another, all along one side of my cave, to lay all my tools, nails, and iron-work, and in a word, to separate everything at large in their places, that I might come easily at them. I knocked pieces into the wall of the rock to hang my guns, and all things that would hang up.

So that, had my cave been to be seen, it looked like a general magazine of all necessary things; and I had everything so ready at my hand, that it was a great pleasure to me to see all my goods in such order, and especially to find my stock of all necessaries so great.

And now it was that I began to keep a journal of every day's employment; for indeed at first I was in too much a hurry; and not only hurry as to labour, but in too much discomposure of mind, and my journal would have been full of many dull things. For example, I must have said thus: – September the 30th, after I got to shore, and had escaped drowning, instead of being thankful to God for my deliverance, having first vomited with the great quantity of salt water which was gotten into my stomach, and recovering myself a little, I ran about the shore, wringing my hands, and beating my head and face, exclaiming at my misery, and crying out, I was undone, undone! till, tired and faint, I was forced to lie down on the ground to repose, but durst not sleep for fear of being devoured.

Some days after this, and after I had been on board the ship, and got all that I could out of her, yet I could not forbear getting up to the top of a little mountain, and looking out to sea, in hopes of seeing a ship; then fancy at a vast distance I spied a sail – please myself with the hopes of it – and then, after looking steadily till I was almost blind, lose it quite, and sit down and weep like a child, and thus increase my misery by my folly.

But having gotten over these things in some measure and having settled my household stuff and habitation, made me a table and a chair, and all as handsome about me as I could, I began to keep my journal, of which I shall here give you the copy (though in it will be told all these particulars over again), as long as it lasted; for having no more ink, I was forced to leave it off.

CHAPTER 5
THE JOURNAL

I begin a Journal – Various Schemes to
make Tools, etc. – Begin to build a house –
Discover Corn – Earthquake and Storm
– September 30, 1659.

I, poor miserable Robinson Crusoe, being shipwrecked during a
dreadful storm in the offing, came on shore on this dismal, unfortunate island, which I called the Island of Despair; all the rest of
the ship's company being drowned, and myself almost dead.

All the rest of that day I spent in afflicting myself at the dismal
circumstances I was brought to, namely, I had neither food, house,
clothes, weapon, nor place to fly to, and in despair of any relief, saw
nothing but death before me, either that I should be devoured by
wild beasts, murdered by savages, or starved to death for want of
food. At the approach of night I slept in a tree, for fear of wild creatures, but slept soundly, though it rained all night.

October I. – In the morning, I saw to my great surprise, the
ship had floated with the high tide, and was driven on shore again
much nearer the island; which, as it was some comfort on one
hand, for seeing her sit upright, and not broken to pieces, I hoped,
if the wind abated, I might get on board, and get some food and
necessaries out of her for my relief; so, on the other hand, it
renewed my grief at the loss of my comrades, who, I imagined, if
we had all stayed on board, might have saved the ship, or at least
that they would not have been all drowned as they were; and
that had the men been saved we might perhaps have built us a
boat out of the ruins of the ship, to have carried us to some other
part of the world, I spent great part of this day in perplexing myself

on these things; but at length, seeing the ship almost dry, I went upon the sand as near as I could, and then swam on board. This day also it continued raining, though with no wind at all.

From the 1st of October to the 24th. – All these days entirely spent in many several voyages to get all I could out of the ship, which I brought on shore, every tide of flood, upon rafts. Much rain also in these days, though with some intervals of fair weather; but it seems this was the rainy season.

Oct. 20. – I overset my raft, and all the goods I had upon it; but being in shoal water, and the things being chiefly heavy, I recovered many of them when the tide was out.

Oct. 25. – It rained all night and all day, with some gusts of wind; during which time the ship broke in pieces, the wind blowing a little harder than before, and was no more to be seen except the wreck of her, and that only at low water. I spent this day in covering and securing the goods which I had saved, that rain might not spoil them.

Oct. 26. – I walked about the shore almost all day, to find out a place to fix my habitation, greatly concerned to secure myself from any attack in the night, either from wild beasts or men. Towards night I fixed upon a proper place under a rock, and marked out a semicircle for my encampment, which I resolved to strengthen with a work, wall, or fortification, made of double piles, lined within with cable, and without with turf.

From the 26th to the 30th I worked very hard in carrying all my goods to my new habitation, though some part of the time it rained exceedingly hard.

The 31st, in the morning, I went out into the island with my gun, to seek for some food, and discover the country; when I killed a she-goat, and her kid followed me home, which I afterwards killed also, because it would not feed.

November 1. – I set up my tent under a rock, and lay there for the first night, making it as large as I could, with stakes driven in to swing my hammock upon.

Nov. 2. – I set up all my chests and boards, and the pieces of timber, which made my rafts, and with them formed a fence round me, a little within the place I had marked out for my fortification.

Nov. 3. – I went out with my gun, and killed two fowls like ducks, which were very good food. In the afternoon, went to work to make me a table.

Nov. 4. – This morning I began to order my times of work

– of going out with my gun, time of sleep, and time of diversion: namely, every morning, I walked out with my gun for two or three hours, if it did not rain, then employed myself to work till about eleven o'clock, then ate what I had to live on, and from twelve till two I lay down to sleep, the weather being excessively hot, and then in the evening to work again. The working part of this day and of the next were wholly employed in making my table, for I was yet but a very sorry workman, though time and necessity made me a complete natural mechanic soon after, as I believe it would do any one else.

Nov. 5. – This day went abroad with my gun and my dog, and killed a wild cat; her skin pretty soft, but her flesh good for nothing; every creature I killed I took off the skins and, preserved them. Coming back by the sea-shore, I saw many sorts of sea-fowls, which I did not understand; but was surprised, and almost frighted, with two or three seals, which, while I was gazing at, not well knowing what they were, got into the sea, and escaped me for that time.

Nov. 6. – After my morning walk, I went to work with my table again, and finished it, though not to my liking; nor was it long before I learned to mend it.

Nov. 7. – Now it began to be settled fair weather. The 7th, 8th, 9th, 10th, and part of the 12th (for the 11th was Sunday), I took wholly up to make me a chair, and with much ado brought it to a tolerable shape, but never to please me; and even in the making I pulled it in pieces several times. *Note.* – I soon neglected my keeping Sundays; for omitting my mark for them on my post, I forgot which was which.

Nov. 13. – This day it rained, which refreshed me exceedingly, and cooled the earth; but was accompanied with terrible thunder and lightning, which frighted me dreadfully for fear of my powder. As soon as it was over, I resolved to separate my stock of powder into as many little parcels as possible, that it might not be in danger.

Nov. 14, 15, 16. – These three days I spent in making little square chests or boxes, which might hold about a pound, or two pound at most, of powder; and so putting the powder in, I stowed it in places as secure and remote from one another as possible. On one of these three days I killed a large bird that was good to eat, but I knew not what to call it.

Nov. 17. – This day I began to dig behind my tent into the rock, to make room for my farther convenience. *Note.* – Three things I wanted exceedingly for this work, namely, a pick-axe, a shovel, and a wheelbarrow or basket; so I desisted from my work, and began to consider how to supply that want, and make me some tools: as for a pick-axe, I made use of the iron crows, which were proper enough, though heavy; but the next thing was a shovel or spade; this was so absolutely necessary, that indeed I could do nothing effectually without it, but what kind of one to make I knew not.

Nov. 18. – The next day, in searching the woods, I found a tree of that wood, or like it, which in the Brazils they call the iron tree, for its exceeding hardness: of this, with great labour, and almost spoiling my axe, I cut a piece, and brought it home too with difficulty enough, for it was exceeding heavy.

The excessive hardness of the wood, and having no other way, made me a long while upon this machine; for I worked it effectually by little and little into the form of a shovel or spade, the handle exactly shaped like ours in England, only that the broad part having no iron shod upon it at bottom, it would not last me so long; however, it served well enough for the uses which I had occasion to put it to; but never was a shovel, I believe, made after that fashion, or so long a-making.

I was still deficient, for I wanted a basket or a wheelbarrow: a basket I could not make by any means, having no such things as twigs, that would bend to make wicker-ware, at least not yet found out; and as to a wheelbarrow, I fancied I could make all but the wheel, but that I had no notion of, neither did I know how to go about it; besides, I had no possible way to make the iron gudgeons for the spindle, or axis, of the wheel, to run in, so I gave it over; and so, for carrying away the earth which I dug out of the cave, I made me a thing like a hod, which the labourers carry mortar in when they serve the bricklayers.

This was not so difficult to me as the making the shovel; and yet this, and the shovel, and the attempt which I made in vain to make a wheelbarrow, took me up no less than four days – I mean always excepting my morning walk with my gun, which I seldom failed; and seldom failed also bringing home something to eat.

Nov. 23. – My other work having now stood still, because of my making these tools, when they were finished I went on, and working every day, as my strength and time allowed, I spent eighteen days entirely in widening and deepening my cave, that it might hold my goods commodiously.

Note. – During all this time I worked to make this room, or cave, spacious enough to accommodate me as a warehouse, or magazine, a kitchen, a dining room, and a cellar: as for my lodging, I kept to the tent, except that sometimes, in the wet season of the year, it rained so hard that I could not keep myself dry, which caused me afterwards to cover all my place within my pale with long poles in the form of rafters, leaning against the rock, and load them with flags and large leaves of trees like a thatch.

December, 10. – I began now to think my cave, or vault, finished, when on a sudden (it seems I had made it too large) a great quantity of earth fell down from the top and one side, so much, that, in short, it frighted me, and not without reason too; for if I had been under it, I had never wanted a gravedigger. Upon this disaster I had a great deal of work to do over again; for I had the loose earth to carry out, and, which was of more importance, I had the ceiling to prop up, so that I might be sure no more would come down.

Dec. 11. – This day I went to work with it accordingly, and got two shores or posts pitched upright to the top, with two pieces of boards across over each post; this I finished the next day; and setting more posts up with boards, in about a week more I had the roof secured; and the posts standing in rows, served me for partitions to part off the house.

Dec. 17. – From this day to the 20th I placed shelves, and knocked up nails on the posts to hang everything up that could be hung up: and now I began to be in some order within doors.

Dec. 20. – Now I carried everything into the cave, and began to furnish my house, and set up some pieces of boards like a dresser, to order my victuals upon; but boards began to be very scarce with me; also, I made me another table.

Dec. 24. – Much rain all night and all day; no stirring out.

Dec. 25. – Rain all day.

Dec. 26. – No rain, and the earth much cooler than before, and pleasanter.

Dec. 27. – Killed a young goat, and lamed another, so that I caught it, and led it home in a string; when I had it home, I bound and splintered up its leg, which was broke. *N.B.* – I took such care of it that it lived, and the leg grew well and as strong as ever; but by nursing it so long it grew tame, and fed upon the little green at my door, and would not go away. This was the first time that I entertained a thought of breeding up some tame creatures, that I might have food when my powder and shot are all spent.

Dec. 28, 29, 30. – Great heats, and no breeze; so that there was no stirring abroad, except in the evening for food. This time I spent in putting all my things in order within doors.

January I. – Very hot still: but I went abroad early and late with my gun, and lay still in the middle of the day. This evening, going farther into the valleys which lay towards the centre of the island, I found there was plenty of goats, though exceedingly shy and hard to come at; however, I resolved to try if I could not bring my dog to hunt them down.

Jan. 2. – Accordingly, the next day I went out with my dog, and set him upon the goats; but I was mistaken, for they all faced about upon the dog; and he knew his danger too well, for he would not come near them.

Jan. 3. – I began my fence, or wall, which, being still jealous of my being attacked by somebody, I resolved to make very thick and strong.

N.B. – This wall being described before, I purposely omit what was said in the journal; it is sufficient to observe, that I was no less time than from the 3rd of January to the 14th of April, working, finishing, and perfecting this wall, though it was no more than about twenty-four yards in length, being a half circle from one place in the rock to another place about eight yards from it, the door of the cave being in the centre behind it.

All this time I worked very hard, the rains hindering me many days, nay sometimes weeks together; but I thought I should never be perfectly secure until this wall was finished: and it is scarce credible what inexpressible labour everything was done with, especially the bringing piles out of the woods, and driving them into the ground; for I made them much bigger than I need to have done.

When this wall was finished, and the outside double-fenced with a turf wall raised up close to it, I persuaded myself, that if any people were to come on shore there, they would not perceive anything like a habitation; and it was very well I did so, as may be observed hereafter, upon a very remarkable occasion.

During this time I made my rounds in the woods for game every day, when the rain permitted me, and made frequent discoveries in these walks, of something or other to my advantage; particularly, I found a kind of wild pigeons, who built, not as wood pigeons, in a tree, but rather as house pigeons, in the holes of the rocks; and taking some young ones, I endeavoured to breed them up tame, and did so; but when they grew older they flew away, which, perhaps, was at first for want of feeding them; for I had nothing to give them. However, I frequently found their nests and got their young ones, which was very good meat.

And now, in the managing my household affairs, I found myself wanting in many things, which I thought at first it was impossible for me to make, as indeed, as to some of them, it was – for instance, I could never make a cask to be hooped. I had a small runlet or two, as I observed before, but I could never arrive to the capacity of making one by them, though I spent many weeks about it; I could neither put in the heads, nor joint the staves so true to one another as to make them hold water, so I gave that also over.

In the next place, I was at great loss for candle, so that as soon as ever it was dark, which was generally by seven o'clock, I was obliged to go to bed. I remembered the lump of bees' wax with which I made candles in my African adventure, but I had none of that now. The only remedy I had was that, when I killed a goat I saved the tallow, and, with a little dish made of clay, which I baked in the sun, to which I added a wick of some oakum, I made me a lamp; and this gave me a light, though not a clear, steady light like a candle. In the middle of all my labours, it happened that, rummaging my things, I found a little bag, which, as I hinted before, had been filled with corn for the feeding of poultry, not for this voyage, but before, as I suppose, when the ship came from Lisbon. What little remainder of corn had been in the bag was all devoured with the rats, and I saw nothing in the bag but husks and dust; and being willing to have the bag for some other use – I think it was to put powder in, when I divided it for fear of the lightning, or some such use – I shook the husks of corn out of it, on one side of my fortification, under the rock.

It was a little before the great rains, just now mentioned, that I threw this stuff away, taking no notice of anything, and not so much as remembering that I had thrown anything there; when about a month after, or thereabout, I saw some few stalks of something green shooting out of the ground, which I fancied might be some plant I had not seen; but I was surprised and perfectly astonished, when, after a little longer time, I saw about ten or twelve ears come out, which were perfectly green barley, of the same kind as our European – nay, as our English barley.

It is impossible to express the astonishment and confusion of my thoughts on this occasion. I had hitherto acted upon no religious foundation at all. Indeed, I had very few notions of religion in my head, or had entertained any sense of anything that had befallen me, otherwise than as a chance, or, as we lightly say, what pleases God; without so much as inquiring into the end of Providence in these things, or his order in governing events in the world. But after I saw barley grow there, in a climate which I knew was not proper for corn, and especially, that I knew not how it came there, it startled me strangely, and I began to suggest, that God had miraculously caused this grain to grow, without any help of seed sown; and that it so was directed, purely for my sustenance on that wild miserable place.

This touched my heart a little, and brought tears out of my eyes, and I began to bless myself that such a prodigy of nature should happen upon my account; and this was the more strange to me, because I saw near it still, all along by the side of the rock, some other straggling stalks of rice, and which I knew, because I had seen it grow in Africa, when I was ashore there.

I not only thought these the pure productions of Providence for my support, but, not doubting but that there was more in the place, I went all over that part of the island where I had been before, peeping in every corner, and under every rock, to see for more of it, but I could not find any. At last, it occurred to my thought, that I had shook a bag of chickens' meat out in that place, and then the wonder began to cease; and I must confess, my religious thankfulness to God's providence began to abate too, upon discovering that all this was nothing but what was common, though I ought to have been as thankful for so strange and unforeseen a providence, as if it had been miraculous; for it was really the work of Providence, as to me, that should order or appoint ten or twelve grains of corn to remain unspoiled, when the rats had destroyed all the rest, as if it had been dropped from heaven – as also, that I should throw it out on that particular place, where, it being in the shade of a high rock, it sprang up immediately; whereas, if I had thrown it anywhere else at that time, it had been burnt up and destroyed.

I carefully saved the ears of corn, you may be sure, in their season, which was about the end of June, and laying up every corn, I resolved to sow them all again, hoping in time to have some quantity sufficient to supply me with bread; but it was not till the fourth year that I could allow myself the least grain of this corn to eat, and even then but sparingly, as I shall say afterwards in its order – for I lost all that I sowed the first season, by not observing the proper time – for I sowed it just before the dry season, so that it never came up at all, at least not as it would have done – of which in its place.

Besides this barley, there were, as above, twenty or thirty stalks of rice, which I preserved with the same care, and whose use was of the same kind, or to the same purpose, namely, to make me bread, or rather food; for I found ways to cook it up without baking, though I did that also after some time. But to return to my journal.

I worked excessively hard these three or four months to get my wall done; and the 14th of April I closed it up, contriving to go into it, not by a door, but over the wall by a ladder, that there might be no sign in the outside of my habitation.

April 16. – I finished the ladder; so I went up with the ladder to the top, and then pulled it up after me, and let it down in the inside. This was a complete enclosure to me; for within I had room enough, and nothing could come at me from without, unless it could first mount my wall.

The very next day after this wall was finished, I had almost had all my labour overthrown at once, and myself killed. The case was thus: As I was busy in the inside of it, behind my tent, just in the entrance into my cave, I was terribly frighted with a most dreadful surprising thing indeed; for on a sudden I found the earth come crumbling down from the roof of my cave, and from the edge of the hill, over my head, and two of the posts I had set up in the cave cracked in a frightful manner. I was heartily scared, but thought nothing of what was really the cause, only thinking that the top of my cave was falling in, as some of it had done before; and for fear I should be buried in it, I ran forward to my ladder, and not thinking myself safe there neither, I got over my wall for fear of the pieces of the hill, which I expected might roll down upon me. I was no sooner stept down upon the firm ground, but I plainly saw it was a terrible earthquake, for the ground I stood on shook three times at about eight minutes' distance, with three such shocks as would have overturned the strongest building that could be supposed to have stood on the earth; and a great piece of the top of a rock, which stood about half a mile from me, next the sea, fell down with such a terrible noise as I never heard in all my life: I perceived also the very sea was put into violent motion by it; and I believe the shocks were stronger under the water than on the island.

I was so amazed with the thing itself, having never felt the like, or discoursed with any one that had, that I was like one dead or stupefied; and the motion of the earth made my stomach sick, like one that was tossed at sea; but the noise of the falling of the rock awaked me, as it were, and, rousing me from the stupefied condition I was in, filled me with horror, and I thought of nothing then but the hill falling upon my tent and all my household goods, and burying all at once; and thus sunk my very soul within me a second time.

After the third shock was over, and I felt no more for some time, I began to take courage; and yet I had not heart enough to get over my wall again, for fear of being buried alive, but sat still upon the ground, greatly cast down and disconsolate, not knowing what to do. All this while I had not the least serious religious thought, nothing but the common: "Lord, have mercy upon me!" and when it was over that went away too.

While I sat thus, I found the air overcast, and grow cloudy, as if it would rain; soon after that, the wind rose by little and little, so that in less than half an hour it blew a most dreadful hurricane: the sea was all on a sudden covered over with foam and froth, the shore was covered with the breach of the water, the trees were torn up by the roots, and a terrible storm it was: and this held about three hours, and then began to abate, and in two hours more it was stark calm, and began to rain very hard.

All this while I sat upon the ground, very much terrified and dejected, when on a sudden it came into my thoughts, that these winds and rain being the consequence of the earthquake, the earth-quake itself was spent and over and I might venture into my cave again: with this thought my spirits began to revive, and the rain also helping to persuade me, I went in and sat down in my tent; but the rain was so violent, that my tent was ready to be beaten down with it; and I was forced to go into my cave, though very much afraid and uneasy, for fear it should fall on my head.

This violent rain forced me to a new work, namely, to cut a hole through my new fortification, like a sink, to let water go out, which would else have drowned my cave. After I had been in my cave some time, and found still no more shocks of the earthquake follow, I began to be more composed; and now, to support my spirits, which indeed wanted it very much, I went to my little store, and took a small cup of rum, which, however, I did then, and always, very sparingly, knowing I could have no more when that was gone.

It continued raining all that night and great part of the next day, so that I could not stir abroad; but, my mind being more composed, I began to think of what I had best do, concluding, that if the island was subject to these earthquakes, there would be no living for me in a cave, but I must consider of building me some little hut in an open place, which I might surround with a wall as I had done here, and so make myself secure from wild beasts or men: but concluded if I stayed where I was, I should certainly, one time or other, be buried alive.

With these thoughts, I resolved to remove my tent from the place where it stood, which was just under the hanging precipice of the hill, and which, if it should be shaken again, would certainly fall upon my tent. And I spent the two next days, being the 19th and 20th of April, in contriving where and how to remove my habitation.

The fear of being swallowed up alive made me that I never slept in quiet, and yet the apprehension of lying abroad without any fence was almost equal to it; but still, when I looked about, and saw how everything was put in order, how pleasantly concealed I was, and how safe from danger, it made me very loath to remove.

In the meantime, it occurred to me that it would require a vast deal of time for me to do this, and that I must be contented to run the venture where I was, till I had formed a camp for myself, and had secured it so as to remove to it. So, with this resolution, I composed myself for a time, and resolved that I would go to work with all speed, to build me a wall with piles and cables, etc., in a circle, as before, and set my tent up in it when it was finished; but that I would venture to stay where I was till it was finished, and fit to remove to. This was the 21st.

April 22. – The next morning I began to consider of means to put this resolve in execution, but I was at a great loss about my tools. I had three large axes, and abundance of hatchets (for we carried the hatchets for traffic with the Indians); but, with much chopping, and cutting knotty hard wood, they were all full of notches and dull; and, though I had a grindstone, I could not turn it, and grind my tools too; this cost me as much thought as a statesman would have bestowed upon a grand point of politics, or a judge upon the life and death of a man. At length I contrived a wheel with a string, to turn it with my foot, that I might have both my hands at liberty. *Note.* – I had never seen any such thing in England, or at least not to take notice how it was done, though since I have observed it is very common there; besides that my grindstone was very large and heavy. This machine cost me a full week's work to bring it to perfection.

April 28, 29. – These two whole days I took up in grinding my tools, my machine for turning my grindstone performing very well.

April 30. – Having perceived my bread had been low a great while, now I took a survey of it, and reduced myself to one biscuit-cake a-day, which made my heart very heavy.

CHAPTER 6

Ship driven farther aground – Procure
quantities of Stores from Wreck – Catch a
Turtle – Ill of a Fever and Ague – Terrible
Dream and serious Reflections – Find a Bible
in a Seaman's Chest

May 1. – In the morning, looking towards the seaside, the tide being
low, I saw something lie on the shore bigger than ordinary, and it
looked like a cask. When I came to it, I found a small barrel, and
two or three pieces of the wreck of the ship, which were driven on
shore by the late hurricane; and looking towards the wreck itself, I
thought it seemed to lie higher out of the water than it used to do.
I examined the barrel which was driven on shore, and soon found
it was a barrel of gunpowder, but it had taken water, and the powder
was caked as hard as a stone; however, I rolled it farther on shore
for the present, and went on upon the sands as near as I could to
the wreck of the ship to look for more.

When I came down to the ship, I found it strangely removed:
the forecastle, which lay before buried in sand, was heaved up at
least six feet; and the stern (which was broke to pieces, and parted
from the rest by the force of the sea, soon after I had left rummaging
her) was tossed, as it were, up, and cast on one side; and the sand
was thrown so high on that side next her stern, that whereas there
was a great piece of water before, so that I could not come within
a quarter of a mile of the wreck without swimming, I could now
walk quite up to her when the tide was out. I was surprised with
this at first, but soon concluded it must be done with the earthquake; and, as by this violence the ship was more broken open than
formerly, so many things came daily on shore, which the sea had

loosened, and which the winds and waters rolled by degrees to the land.

This wholly diverted my thoughts from the design of removing my habitation; and I busied myself mightily, that day especially, in searching whether I could make any way into the ship; but I found nothing was to be expected of that kind, for that all the inside of the ship was choked up with sand; however, as I had learned not to despair of anything, I resolved to pull everything to pieces that I could of the ship, concluding, that everything I could get from her would be of some use or other to me.

May 3. – I began with my saw, and cut a piece of a beam through, which I thought held some of the upper part or quarter-deck together, and when I had cut it through, I cleared away the sand as well as I could from the side which lay highest; but the tide coming in, I was obliged to give over for that time.

May 4. – I went a-fishing, but caught not one fish that I durst eat of, till I was weary of my sport, when, just going to leave off, I caught a young dolphin. I had made me a long line of some rope yarn, but I had no hooks, yet I frequently caught fish, as much as I cared to eat; all which I dried in the sun, and ate them dry.

May 5. – Worked on the wreck – cut another beam asunder, and brought three great fir planks off from the decks, which I tied together, and made swim on shore when the tide of flood came in.

May 6. – Worked on the wreck – got several iron bolts out of her, and other pieces of iron work; worked very hard, and came home very much tired, and had thoughts of giving it over.

May 7. – Went to the wreck again, but with an intent not to work, but found the weight of the wreck had brought itself down, the beams being cut; that several pieces of the ship seemed to lie loose, and the inside of the hold lay so open that I could see into it, but almost full of water and sand.

May 8. – Went to the wreck, and carried an iron crow to wrench up the deck, which lay now quite clear of the water or sand; I wrenched open two planks, and brought them on shore also with the tide: I left the iron crow in the wreck for next day.

May 9. – Went to the wreck, and with the crow made way into the body of the wreck, and felt several casks, and loosened them with the crow, but could not break them up: I felt also the roll of English lead, and could stir it, but it was too heavy to remove.

May 10, 11, 12, 13, 14. – Went every day to the wreck, and got a great many pieces of timber, and boards, or planks, and two or three hundredweight of iron.

May 15. – I carried two hatchets, to try if I could not cut a piece of the roll of lead, by placing the edge of one hatchet, and driving it with the other, but as it lay about a foot and a half in the water, I could not make any blow to drive the hatchet.

May 16. – It had blown hard in the night, and the wreck appeared more broken by the force of the water; but I stayed so long in the woods to get pigeons for food, that the tide prevented me going to the wreck that day.

May 17. – I saw some pieces of the wreck blown on shore, at a great distance, near two miles off me, but resolved to see what they were, and found it was a piece of the head, but too heavy for me to bring away.

May 24. – Every day to this day I worked on the wreck, and with hard labour I loosened some things so much with the crow that the first flowing tide, several casks floated out, and two of the seamen's chests; but the wind blowing from the shore, nothing came to land that day but pieces of timber, and a hogshead, which had some Brazil pork in it; but the salt water and the sand had spoiled it.

I continued this work every day to the 15th of June, except the time necessary to get food, which I always appointed during this part of my employment to be when the tide was up, that I might be ready when it was ebbed out; and by this time I had gotten timber, and plank, and iron-work enough to have built a good boat, if I had known how; and also I got at several times, and in several pieces, near one hundredweight of the sheet lead.

June 16. – Going down to the sea-side, I found a large tortoise or turtle; this was the first that I had seen, which it seems was only my misfortune, not any defect of the place, or scarcity; for had I happened to be on the other side of the island, I might have had hundreds of them every day, as I found afterwards, but perhaps had paid dear for them.

June 17*th* I spent in cooking the turtle; I found in her three score eggs; and her flesh was to me, at that time, the most savoury and pleasant that ever I tasted in my life, having had no flesh but of goats and fowls since I landed in this horrid place.

June 18. – Rained all day, and I stayed within. I thought at this time the rain felt cold, and I was something chilly, which I knew was not usual in that latitude.

June 19. – Very ill, and shivering, as if the weather had been cold.

June 20. – No rest all night, violent pains in my head, and feverish.

June 21. – Very ill, frighted almost to death with the apprehensions of my sad condition, to be sick, and no help. Prayed to God, for the first time since the storm off Hull; but scarce knew what I said, or why, my thoughts being all confused.

June 22. – A little better, but under dreadful apprehensions of sickness.

June 23. – Very bad again, cold and shivering, and then a violent headache.

June 24. – Much better.

June 25. – An ague – very violent; the fit held me seven hours, cold fit and hot, with faint sweats after it.

June 26. – Better; and, having no victuals to eat, took my gun, but found myself very weak; however, I killed a she-goat, and with much difficulty got it home, and broiled some of it, and ate; I would fain have stewed it, and made some broth, but had no pot.

June 27. – The ague again so violent that I lay a-bed all day, and neither ate nor drank. I was ready to perish for thirst, but so weak I had not strength to stand up, or to get myself any water to drink. Prayed to God again, but was light-headed; and when I was not, I was so ignorant that I knew not what to say, only I lay, and cried: "Lord, look upon me! Lord, pity me! Lord, have mercy upon me!" I suppose I did nothing else for two or three hours, till, the fit wearing off, I fell asleep, and did not wake till far in the night; when I waked, I found myself much refreshed, but weak, and exceedingly thirsty; however, as I had no water in my whole habitation, I was forced to lie till morning, and went to sleep again. In this second sleep I had this terrible dream, –

I thought that I was sitting on the ground, on the outside of my wall, where I sat when the storm blew after the earthquake, and that I saw a man descend from a great black cloud, in a bright flame of fire, and light upon the ground. He was all over as bright as a flame, so that I could but bear just to look towards him; his countenance was most inexpressibly dreadful, impossible for words to describe; when he stepped upon the ground with his feet, I thought the earth trembled, just as it had done before in the earthquake, and all the air looked to my apprehension as if it had been filled with flashes of fire.

He was no sooner landed upon the earth but he moved forward towards me, with a long spear, or weapon, in his hand, to kill me; and when he came to a rising ground, at some distance, he spoke to me, for I heard a voice so terrible that it is impossible to express the terror of it; all that I can say I understood was this: "Seeing all these things have not brought thee to repentance, now thou shalt die!" at which words I thought he lifted up the spear that was in his hand to kill me.

No one that shall ever read this account will expect that I should be able to describe the horrors of my soul at this terrible vision – I mean, that even while it was a dream, I even dreamed of those horrors; nor is it any more possible to describe the impression that remained upon my mind when I awaked and found it was but a dream!

I had, alas! no divine knowledge. What I had received by the good instruction of my father was then worn out by an uninterrupted series, for eight years, of seafaring wickedness, and a constant conversation with nothing but such as were, like myself, wicked and profane to the last degree. I do not remember that I had, in all that time, one thought that so much as tended either to looking upwards towards God, or inwards towards a reflection upon my own ways. But a certain stupidity of soul, without desire of good, or conscience of evil, had entirely overwhelmed me, and I was all that the most hardened, unthinking, wicked creature, among our common sailors, can be supposed to be, not having the least sense, either of the fear of God in danger, or of thankfulness to God in deliverances.

In the relating what is already past of my story this will be the more easily believed, when I shall add, that, through all the variety of miseries that had to this day befallen me, I never had so much as one thought of it being the hand of God, or that it was a just punishment for my sin, my rebellious behaviour against my father, or my present sins, which were great – or so much as a punishment for the general course of my wicked life. When I was on the desperate expedition on the desert shores of Africa, I never had so much as one thought of what would become of me, or one wish to God to direct me whither I should go, or keep me from the danger which apparently surrounded me, as well from voracious creatures as cruel savages: but I was merely thoughtless of a God, or a Providence, acted like a mere brute from the principles of nature, and by the dictates of common sense only, and indeed hardly that.

When I was delivered and taken up at sea by the Portugal captain, well used, and dealt justly and honourably with, as well as charitably, I had not the least thankfulness in my thoughts. When again I was shipwrecked, ruined, and in danger of drowning on this island, I was as far from remorse, or looking on it as a judgment – I only said to myself often, that I was *an unfortunate dog*, and born to be always miserable.

It is true, when I got on shore first here, and found all my ship's crew drowned, and myself spared, I was surprised with a kind of ecstasy, and some transports of soul, which, had the grace of God assisted, might have come up to true thankfulness; but it ended where it began, in a mere common flight of joy, or, as I may say, *being glad I was alive*, without the least reflection upon the distinguishing goodness of the Hand which had preserved me, and had singled me out to be preserved when all the rest were destroyed; or an inquiry why Providence had been thus merciful to me; even just the same common sort of joy which seamen generally have after they have got safe on shore from a shipwreck, which they drown all in the next bowl of punch, and forget almost as soon as it is over; and all the rest of my life was like it.

Even when I was afterwards, on due consideration, made sensible of my condition, how I was cast on this dreadful place, out of the reach of human kind, out of all hope of relief, or prospect of redemption, as soon as I saw but a prospect of living, and that I should not starve or perish for hunger, all the sense of my affliction wore off, and I began to be very easy, applied myself to the works proper for my preservation and supply, and was far enough from being afflicted at my condition, as a judgment from Heaven, or as the hand of God against me; these were thoughts which very seldom entered my head.

The growing up of the corn, as is hinted in my journal, had at first some little influence upon me, and began to affect me with seriousness, as long as I thought it had something miraculous in it; but as soon as ever that part of thought was removed, all the impression which was raised from it wore off also, as I have noted already.

Even the earthquake, though nothing could be more terrible in its nature, or more immediately directing to the invisible Power, which alone directs such things; yet no sooner was the first fright over, but the impression it had made went off also. I had no more sense of God or his judgments, much less of the present affliction of my circumstances being from His hand, than if I had been in the most prosperous condition of life.

But now, when I began to be sick, and a leisurely view of the miseries of death came to place itself before me; when my spirits began to sink under the burden of a strong distemper, and nature was exhausted with the violence of the fever, conscience, that had slept so long, began to awake, and I began to reproach myself with my past life, in which I had so evidently, by uncommon wickedness, provoked the justice of God to lay me under uncommon strokes, and to deal with me in so vindictive a manner.

These reflections oppressed me from the second or third day of my distemper; and in the violence, as well of the fever as of the dreadful reproaches of my conscience, extorted some words from me like praying to God, though I cannot say they were either a prayer, attended with desires or with hopes: it was rather the voice of mere fright and distress: my thoughts were confused, the convictions great upon my mind, and the horror of dying in such a miserable condition raised vapours into my head with the mere apprehensions; and, in these hurries of my soul, I knew not what my tongue might express: but it was rather exclamation, such as, "Lord! what a miserable creature am I! If I should be sick, I shall certainly die for want of help, and what will become of me!' Then the tears burst out of my eyes, and I could say no more for a good while.

In this interval, the good advice of my father came to my mind, and presently his prediction, which I mentioned in the beginning of this story, namely, that, if I did take this foolish step, God would not bless me, and I would have leisure hereafter to reflect upon having neglected his counsel, when there might be none to assist in my recovery. "Now," said I, aloud, "my dear father's words are come to pass: God's justice has overtaken me, and I have none to help or hear me. I rejected the voice of Providence, which had mercifully put me in a posture or station of life wherein I might have been happy and easy; but I would neither see it myself, nor learn to know the blessing of it from my parents. I left them to mourn over my folly, and now I am left to mourn over the consequences of it. I refused their help and assistance, who would have lifted me into the world, and would have made everything easy to me, and now I have difficulties to struggle with, too great for even nature itself to support, and no assistance, no help, no comfort, no advice." Then I cried out, "Lord, be my help; for I am in great distress!"

This was the first prayer, if I might call it so, that I had made for many years. But I return to my journal.

June 28. – Having been somewhat refreshed with the sleep I had had, and the fit being entirely off, I got up; and though the fright and terror of my dream was very great, yet I considered that the fit of the ague would return again the next day, and now was my time to get something to refresh and support myself, when I should be ill: and the first thing I did, I filled a large square case-bottle with water, and set it upon my table in reach of my bed; and to take off the chill or aguish disposition of the water, I put about a quarter of a pint of rum into it, and mixed them together; then I got me a piece of the goat's flesh, and broiled it on the coals, but could eat very little. I walked about, but was very weak, and withal very sad and heavy-hearted, under a sense of my miserable condition, dreading the return of my distemper the next day. At night, I made my supper of three of the turtle's eggs, which I roasted in the ashes, and ate, as we call it, in the shell; and this was the first bit of meat I had ever asked God's blessing to, even, as I could remember, in my whole life.

After I had eaten, I tried to walk, but found myself so weak that I could hardly carry the gun (for I never went out without that); so I went but a little way, and sat down upon the ground, looking out upon the sea, which was just before me, and very calm and smooth. As I sat here, some such thoughts occurred to me: –

What is the earth and sea, of which I have seen so much? Whence is it produced? And what am I, and all the other creatures – wild and tame, human and brutal – whence are we?

Sure we are all made by some secret Power, who formed the earth and sea, the air and sky – and who is that?

Then it followed most naturally: – It is God that has made it all. Well, but then – it came on strangely – if God has made all these things, He guides and governs them all, and all things that concern them; for the Being that could make all things must certainly have power to guide and direct them.

If so, nothing can happen in the great circuit of His works, either without His knowledge or appointment.

And if nothing happens without His knowledge, He knows that I am here, and in a dreadful condition; and if nothing happens without His appointment, He has appointed all this to befall me.

Nothing occurred to my thoughts to contradict any of these

conclusions; and, therefore, it rested upon me with the greater force, that it must needs be that God had appointed all this to befall, me – that I was brought to this miserable circumstance by His direction, He having the sole power, not of me only, but of everything that happened in the world. Immediately it followed: –

Why has God done this to me? What have I done to be thus used?

My conscience presently checked me in that inquiry, as if I had blasphemed; and methought it spoke to me like a voice: "Wretch! dost thou ask what thou hast done? Look back upon a dreadful misspent life, and ask thyself what thou hast not done? Ask why it is that thou wert not long ago destroyed? Why wert thou not drowned in Yarmouth Roads? killed in the fight, when the ship was taken by the Sallee man-of-war? devoured by the wild beasts on the coast of Africa; or drowned here, when all the crew perished but thyself? Dost thou ask. What have I done?"

I was struck with these reflections, as one astonished, and had not a word to say – no, not to answer to myself; but rose up, pensive and sad, walked back to my retreat, and went up over my wall, as if I had been going to bed; but my thoughts were sadly disturbed, and I had no inclination to sleep, so I sat down in my chair, and lighted my lamp, for it began to be dark. Now, as the apprehensions of the return of my distemper terrified me very much, it occurred to my thought that the Brazilians take no physic but their tobacco for almost all distempers; and I had a piece of a roll of tobacco in one of the chests, which was quite cured, and some also that was green, and not quite cured.

I went, directed by Heaven, no doubt; for in this chest I found a cure both for soul and body. I opened the chest, and found what I had looked for, namely, the tobacco; and as the few books I had saved lay there too, I took out one of the Bibles, which I mentioned before, and which, to this time, I had not found leisure, or so much as inclination, to look into – I say, I took it out and brought both that and the tobacco with me to the table.

What use to make of the tobacco, I knew not, as to my distemper, or whether it was good for it or no; but I tried several experiments with it, as if I was resolved it should hit one way or other. I first took a piece of a leaf, and chewed it in my mouth, which indeed, at first, almost stupefied my brain, the tobacco being green and strong, and I had not been much used to it; then I took some, and steeped it an hour or two in some rum, and resolved to take a dose of it when I lay down; and lastly, I burnt some upon a pan of coals, and held my nose close over the smoke of it, as long as I could bear it, as well for the heat as the virtue of it, and I held almost to suffocation.

In the interval of this occupation, I took up the Bible, and began to read; but my head was too much disturbed with the tobacco to bear reading, at least at that time; only, having opened the book casually, the first words that occurred to me were these: "Call on me in the day of trouble, and I will deliver; and thou shalt glorify me."

The words were very apt to my case, and made some impression upon my thoughts at the time of reading them, though not so much as they did afterwards; for, as for being delivered, the word had no sound, as I may say, to me. The thing was so remote, so impossible, in my apprehension of things, that I began to say, as the children of Israel did when they were promised flesh to eat, "Can God spread a table in the wilderness?" So I began to say, "Can God himself deliver me from this place?" And as it was not for many years that any hope appeared, this prevailed very often upon my thoughts. But, however, the words made a very great impression upon me, and I mused upon them very often. It grew now late and the tobacco had, as I said, dosed my head so much, that I inclined to sleep, so that I left my lamp burning in the cave, lest I should want anything in the night, and went to bed. But before I lay down I did what I never had done in all my life – I kneeled down and, prayed to God to fulfil the promise to me, that, if I called upon him in the day of trouble, he would deliver me. After my broken and imperfect prayer was over, I drank the rum, in which I had steeped the tobacco, which was so strong and rank of the tobacco, that indeed I could scarce get it down. Immediately upon this, I went to bed, and found presently it flew up into my head violently; but I fell into a sound sleep, and waked no more, till, by the sun, it must necessarily be near three o'clock in the afternoon the next day; nay, to this day, I am partly of the opinion, that I slept all the next day and night, and till almost three the day after; for otherwise, I know not how I should lose a day out of my reckoning, in the days of the week, as it appeared, some years after, I had done: for if I had lost it by crossing and recrossing the Line, I should have lost more than a day; but in my account it was lost, and I never knew which way.

Be that, however, one way or other; when I awaked, I found myself exceedingly refreshed, and my spirits lively and cheerful.

When I got up I was stronger than I was the day before, and my stomach better, for I was hungry; and in short, I had no fit the next day, but continued much altered for the better: this was the 29th.

The 30th was my well day, of course, and I went abroad with my gun, but did not care to travel too far: I killed a sea-fowl or two, something like a brand goose, and brought them home, but was not very forward to eat them; so I ate some more of the turtle's eggs, which were very good. This evening I renewed the medicine, which I had supposed did me good the day before, namely, the tobacco steeped in rum; only, I did not take so much as before, nor did I chew any of the leaf, or hold my head over the smoke; however, I was not so well the next day, which was the 1st of July, as I hoped I should have been; for I had a little spice of the cold fit, but it was not much.

July 2. – I renewed the medicine all the three ways, and dosed myself with it as at first, and doubled the quantity which I drank.

July 3. – I missed the fit for good and all, though I did not recover my full strength for some weeks after. While I was thus gathering strength, my thoughts ran exceedingly upon this Scripture, "I will deliver thee;" and the impossibility of my deliverance lay much upon my mind, in bar of my ever expecting it: but as I was discouraging myself with such thoughts, it occurred to my mind, that I pored so much upon my deliverance from the main affliction, that I disregarded the deliverance I had received, and I was, as it were, made to ask myself such questions as these: namely, Have I not been delivered, and wonderfully too, from sickness – from the most distressing condition that could be, and that was so frightful to me? and what notice had I taken of it? had I done my part? God had delivered me, but I had not glorified Him – that is to say, I had not owned and been thankful for that as a deliverance; and how could I expect greater deliverance?

This touched my heart very much, and immediately I kneeled down and gave God thanks aloud, for my recovery from my sickness.

July 4. – In the morning I took the Bible; and, beginning at the New Testament, I began seriously to read it, and imposed upon myself to read a while every morning and every night, not tying myself to the number of chapters, but as long as my thoughts should engage me. It was not long after I set seriously to this work, but I found my heart more deeply and sincerely affected with the wickedness of my past life. The impression of my dream revived; and the words,

"All these things have not brought thee to repentance," ran seriously in my thoughts. I was earnestly begging of God to give me repentance, when it happened providentially that very day, that, reading the Scripture, I came to these words: "He is exalted a Prince and a Saviour to give repentance, and to give remission." I threw down the book, and with my heart as well as my hand lifted up to heaven, in a kind of ecstasy of joy, I cried out aloud, "Jesus, thou Son of David! Jesus, thou exalted Prince and Saviour, give me repentance!"

This was the first time that I could say, in the true sense of the words, that I prayed in all my life; for now I prayed with a sense of my condition, and with a true Scripture view of hope, founded on the encouragement of the word of God; and from this time, I may say, I began to have hope that God would hear me.

Now I began to construe the words mentioned above, "Call on me, and I will deliver thee," in a different sense from what I had ever done before; for then I had no notion of anything being called deliverance, but my being delivered from the captivity I was in: for, though I was indeed at large in the place, yet the island was certainly a prison to me, and that in the worst sense of the word; but now I learnt to take it in another sense. Now I looked back on my past life with such horror, and my sins appeared so dreadful, that my soul sought nothing of God but deliverance from the load of guilt that bore down all my comfort. As for my solitary life, it was nothing; I did not so much as pray to be delivered from it, or think of it; it was all of no consideration in comparison of this; and I add this part here, to hint to whoever shall read it, that whenever they come to a true sense of things, they will find deliverance from sin a much greater blessing than deliverance from affliction.

But, leaving this part, I return to my journal.

My condition began now to be, though not less miserable as to my way of living, yet much easier to my mind; and my thoughts being directed, by a constant reading the Scripture and praying to God, to things of a higher nature, I had a great deal of comfort within, which till now I knew nothing of: also, as my health and strength returned, I bestirred myself to furnish myself with everything that I wanted, and make my way of living as regular as I could.

From the 4th of July to the 14th, I was chiefly employed in walking about with my gun in my hand, a little and a little at a time, as a man that was gathering up his strength after a fit of sickness; for it is hardly to be imagined how low I was, and to what weakness I was reduced. The application which I made use of was perfectly new, and, perhaps, what had never cured an ague before; neither can I recommend it to any one to practise by this experiment; and though it did carry off the fit, yet it rather contributed to weaken me, for I had frequent convulsions in my nerves and limbs for some time.

I learnt from it also this, in particular, that being abroad in the rainy season was the most pernicious thing to my health that could be, especially in those rains which came attended with storms and hurricanes of wind; for, as the rain which came in a dry season was always most accompanied with such storms, so I found this rain was much more dangerous than the rain which fell in September and October.

I had been now in this unhappy island above ten months; all possibility of deliverance from this condition seemed to be entirely taken from me; and I firmly believed, that no human shape had ever set foot upon that place. Having now secured my habitation, as I thought, fully to my mind, I had a great desire to make a more perfect discovery of the island, and to see what other productions I might find, which yet I knew nothing of.

CHAPTER 7

I begin survey of Island – Discover
Tobacco, Grapes, Lemons, and Sugar-canes,
wild, but no human inhabitants – My Cat
returns with Kittens – Shut myself up for
the Wet Season

It was the 15th of July that I began to take a more particular survey
of the island itself. I went up the creek first, where, as I hinted, I
brought my rafts on shore, I found, after I came about two miles
up that the tide did not flow any higher, and that it was no more
than a little brook of running water, very fresh and good; but this
being the dry season, there was hardly any water in some parts of
it, at least not enough to run into any stream, so as it could be
perceived.

On the banks of this brook I found many pleasant savannas
or meadows, plain, smooth, and covered with grass; and, on the
rising parts of them, next to the higher grounds (where the water,
as it might be supposed, never overflowed), I found a great deal of
tobacco, green, and growing to a great and very strong stalk; there
were diverse other plants, which I had no notion of, or understanding
about, and might perhaps have virtues of their own, which I could
not find out.

I searched for the cassava root, which the Indians in all that
climate make their bread of, but I could find none. I saw large plants
of aloes, but did not then understand them; I saw several sugar-
canes, but wild, and, for want of cultivation, imperfect. I contented
myself with these discoveries for this time, and came back musing
with myself what course I might take to know the virtue and goodness of any of the fruits or plants which I should discover, but could

bring it to no conclusion; for, in short, I had made so little observation while I was in the Brazils. that I knew little of the plants of the field: at least, very little that might serve me to any purpose now in my distress.

The next day, the 16th, I went up the same way again; and, after going something farther than I had done the day before, I found the brook and the savannas began to cease, and the country became more woody than before. In this part I found different fruits, and particularly I found melons upon the ground in great abundance, and grapes upon the trees; the vines had spread indeed over the trees, and the clusters of grapes were now just in their prime, very ripe and rich. This was a surprising discovery, and I was exceedingly glad of them; but I was warned by my experience to eat sparingly of them, remembering that when I was ashore in Barbary, the eating of grapes killed several of our Englishmen who were slaves there, by throwing them into fluxes and fevers; but I found an excellent use for these grapes, and that was to cure or dry them in the sun, and keep them as dried grapes or raisins are kept, which I thought would be, as indeed they were, as wholesome and as agreeable to eat, when no grapes might be had.

I spent all that evening there, and went not back to my habitation; which, by the way, was the first night, as I might say, I had lain from home. In the night I took my first contrivance, and got up into a tree, where I slept well, and the next morning proceeded upon my journey, travelling near four miles, as I might judge by the length of the valley, keeping still due north, with a ridge of hills on the south and north side of me.

At the end of this march I came to an opening, where the country seemed to descend to the west; and a little spring of fresh water, which issued out of the side of the hill by me, ran the other way, that is, due east; and the country appeared so fresh, so green, so flourishing, everything being in a constant verdure, or flourish of spring, that it looked like a planted garden.

I descended a little on the side of that delicious valley, surveying it with a secret kind of pleasure (though mixed with other afflicting thoughts), to think that this was all my own, that I was king and lord of all this country indefeasibly, and had a right of possession; and, if I could convey it, I might have it in inheritance, as completely as any lord of a manor in England. I saw here abundance of cocoa trees, orange, and lemon, and citron trees, but all wild, and few bearing any fruit; at least, not then: however, the green limes that I gathered were not only pleasant to eat, but very wholesome; and I mixed their juice afterwards with water, which made it very wholesome; and very cool and refreshing.

I found now I had business enough to gather and carry home; and resolved to lay up a store, as well of grapes as limes and lemons, to furnish myself for the wet season, which I knew was approaching.

In order to do this, I gathered a great heap of grapes in one place, and a lesser heap in another place; and a great parcel of limes and lemons in another place; and taking a few of each with me, I travelled homeward, and resolved to come again and bring a bag or sack, or what I could make, to carry the rest home.

Accordingly, having spent three days in this journey, I came home (so I must now call my tent and my cave); but before I got thither, the grapes were spoiled; the richness of the fruit and the weight of the juice having broken them and bruised them, they were good for little or nothing: as to the limes, they were good, but I could bring but a few.

The next day, being the 19th, I went back, having made me two small bags to bring home my harvest. But I was surprised, when coming to my heap of grapes which were so rich and fine when I gathered them, I found them all spread abroad, trod to pieces, and dragged about, some here, some there, and abundance eaten and devoured. By this I concluded there were some wild creatures thereabouts, which had done this; but what they were I knew not.

However, as I found there were no laying them up on heaps, and no carrying them away in a sack, but that one way they would be destroyed, and the other way they would be crushed with their own weight, I took another course; for I gathered a large quantity of the grapes, and hung them upon the out branches of the trees, that they might cure and dry in the sun; and as for the limes and lemons, I carried as many back as I could well stand under.

When I came home from this journey, I contemplated with great pleasure on the fruitfulness of that valley, and the pleasantness of the situation, the security from storms on that side of the water and wood; and concluded, that I had pitched upon a place to fix my abode, which was by far the worst part of the country. Upon the whole, I began to consider of removing my habitation, and to look out for a place, equally safe as where I now was situated, if possible, in that pleasant, fruitful part of the island.

DANIEL DEFOE

This thought ran along in my head, and I was exceedingly fond of it for some time, the pleasantness of the place tempting me; but when I came to a nearer view of it, and to consider that I was now by the seaside, where it was at least possible that something might happen to my advantage, and that the same ill fate that brought me hither, might bring some other unhappy wretches to the same place; and though it was scarce probable that any such thing should ever happen, yet, to enclose myself among the hills and woods in the centre of the island, was to anticipate my bondage, and to render such an affair not only improbable, but impossible; and that, therefore, I ought not by any means to remove.

However, I was so enamoured with this place that I spent much of my time there for the whole remaining part of the month of July; and though, upon second thoughts, I resolved, as above, not to remove, yet I built me a little kind of a bower, and surrounded it at a distance with a strong fence, being a double hedge, as high as I could reach, well staked, and filled between with brushwood; and here I lay very secure, sometimes two or three nights together, always going over it with a ladder, as before; so that I fancied now I had my country-house, and my sea-coast house, and this work took me up to the beginning of August.

I had but newly finished my fence, and began to enjoy my labour, when the rains came on, and made me stick close to my first habitation, for though I had made me a tent like the other, with a piece of sail, and spread it very well, yet I had not the shelter of a hill to keep me from storms, nor a cave behind me to retreat into when the rains were extraordinary. About the beginning of August, as I said, I had finished my bower, and begun to enjoy myself. The 3rd of August I found the grapes I had hung up were perfectly dried, and, indeed, were excellent good raisins of the sun; so I began to take them down from the trees, and it was very happy that I did so, for the rains which followed would have spoiled them, and I had lost the best part of my winter food; for I had above two hundred large bunches of them. No sooner had I taken them all down, and carried most of them home to my cave, but it began to rain; and from thence, which was the 14th of August, it rained more or less every day till the middle of October, and sometimes so violently that I could not stir out of my cave for several days.

In this season I was much surprised with the increase of my family: I had been concerned for the loss of one of my cats, who ran away from me, or, as I thought, had been dead; and I heard no more tale or tidings of her, till, to my astonishment, she came home, about the end of August, with three kittens. This was the more strange to me, because, though I had killed a wild cat, as I called it, with my gun, yet I thought it was a quite different kind from our European cats; yet the young cats were the same kind of house breed like the old ones; and both my cats being females, I thought it very strange: but from these three cats, I afterwards came to be so pestered with cats, that I was forced to kill them like vermin, or wild beasts, and to drive them from my house as much as possible.

From the 14th of August to the 26th, incessant rain, so that I could not stir, and was now very careful not to be much wet, In this confinement I began to be straitened for food; but venturing out twice, I one day killed a goat, and the last day, which was the 26th, found a very large tortoise, which was a treat to me, and my food was regulated thus: I ate a bunch of raisins for my breakfast, a piece of the goat's flesh, or of the turtle, for my dinner broiled (for, to my great misfortune, I had no vessel to boil or stew anything), and two or three of the turtle's eggs for supper.

During this confinement in my cover by the rain, I worked daily two or three hours at enlarging my cave; and, by degrees, worked it on towards one side, till I came to the outside of the hill, and made a door or way out, which came beyond my fence, or wall; and so I came in and out this way. But I was not perfectly easy at lying so open; for, as I had managed myself before, I was in a perfect enclosure, whereas now I thought I lay exposed; and yet I could not perceive that there was any living thing to fear, the biggest creature that I had ever seen upon the island being a goat.

September the 30th. – I was now come to the unhappy anniversary of my landing – I cast up the notches on my post, and found I had been on shore three hundred and sixty-five days. I kept this day as a solemn fast, setting it apart to a religious exercise, prostrating myself to the ground with the most serious humiliation, confessing myself to God, acknowledging His righteous judgment upon me, and praying to Him to have mercy on me, through Jesus Christ; and having not tasted the least refreshment for twelve hours, even till the going down of the sun, I then ate a biscuit-cake and a bunch of grapes, and went to bed, finishing the day as I began it.

I had all this time observed no Sabbath day, for as at first I had no sense of religion upon my mind, I had, after some time, omitted to distinguish the weeks, by making a longer notch than ordinary for the Sabbath day, and so did not really know what any of the days were; but now, having cast up the days as above, I found I had been there a year; so I divided it into weeks, and set apart every seventh day for a Sabbath; though I found, at the end of my account, I had lost a day or two of my reckoning.

A little after this my ink began to fail me, and so I contented myself to use it more sparingly, and to write down only the most remarkable events of my life, without continuing a daily memorandum of other things.

The rainy season and the dry season began now to appear regular to me, and I learned to divide them so as to provide for them accordingly. But I bought all my experience before I had it; and this, I am going to relate, was one of the most discouraging experiments that I made at all. I have mentioned that I had saved the few ears of barley and rice which I had so surprisingly found spring up, as I thought, of themselves, and believe there were about thirty stalks of rice, and about twenty of barley; and now I thought it a proper time to sow it after the rains, the sun being in its southern position going from me.

Accordingly, I dug up a piece of ground, as well as I could, with my wooden spade, and dividing it into two parts, I sowed my grain; but as it was sowing, it casually occurred to my thought, that I would not sow it all at first, because I did not know when was the proper time for it; so I sowed about two-thirds of the seeds, leaving about a handful of each.

It was a great comfort to me afterwards that I did so, for not one grain of that I sowed this time came to anything; for the dry months following, the earth having had no rain after the seed was sown, it had no moisture to assist its growth, and never came up at all, till the wet season had come again, and then it grew as if it had been newly sown.

Finding my first seed did not grow, which I easily imagined was the drought, I sought for a moister piece of ground to make another trial in; and I dug up a piece of ground near my new bower, and sowed the rest of my seed in February, a little before the vernal equinox; and this, having the rainy months of March and April to water it, sprung up very pleasantly, and yielded a very good crop; but having part of the seed left only, and not daring to sow all that I had yet, I had but a small quantity at last, my whole crop not amounting to above half a peck of each kind.

But by this experience I was made master of my business, and knew exactly when the proper season was to sow, and that I might expect two seed times and two harvests every year.

While this corn was growing, I made a little discovery which was of use to me afterwards. As soon as the rains were over, and the weather began to settle, which was about the month of November, I made a visit up the country to my bower, where, though I had not been for some months, yet I found all things just as I left them. The circle or double hedge that I had made was not only firm and entire, but the stakes which I had cut off of some trees that grew thereabouts, were all shot out, and grown with long branches as much as a willow tree usually shoots the first year after lopping its head. I could not tell what tree to call it that these stakes were cut from. I was surprised, and yet very well pleased, to see the young trees grow – and I pruned them, and led them up to grow as much alike as I could – and it is scarce credible how beautiful a figure they grew into in three years; so that, though the hedge made a circle of about twenty-five yards in diameter, yet the trees, for such I might now call them, soon covered it; and it was a complete shade, sufficient to lodge under all the dry season.

This made me resolve to cut some more stakes, and make me a hedge like this in a semicircle round my wall, I mean that of my first dwelling, which I did; and placing the trees, or stakes, in a double row, at above eight yards' distance from my first fence, they grew presently, and were at first a fine cover to my habitation, and afterwards served for a defence also, as I shall observe in its order.

I found now, that the seasons of the year might generally be divided, not into summer and winter, as in Europe, but into the rainy seasons and the dry seasons, which were generally thus: –

Half February, March, half April. – Rainy, the sun being then on or near the equinox.

Half April, May, June, July, half August. – Dry, the sun being then to the north of the Line.

Half August, September, half October. – Rain, the sun being then come back.

Half October, November, December, January, half February. – Dry, the sun being then to the south of the Line.

The rainy season sometimes held longer or shorter, as the winds happened to blow; but this was the general observation I made. After I had found, by experience, the ill-consequences of being abroad in the rain, I took care to furnish myself with provision beforehand, that I might not be obliged to go out; and I sat within doors as much as possible during the wet months.

In this time I found much employment (and very suitable also to the time), for I found great occasion of many things which I had no way to furnish myself with, but by hard labour and constant application; particularly, I tried many ways to make myself a basket; but all the twigs I could get for the purpose proved so brittle that they would do nothing. It proved of excellent advantage to me now, that when I was a boy I used to take great delight in standing at a basket-maker's in the town where my father lived, to see them make their wicker-ware; and being, as boys usually are, very officious to help, and a great observer of the manner how they worked those things, and sometimes lent a hand, I had by this means so full knowledge of the methods of it, that I wanted nothing but the materials; when it came into my mind, that the twigs of that tree from whence I cut my stakes that grew, might possibly be as tough as the sallows, and willows, and osiers, in England; and I resolved to try.

Accordingly, the next day I went to my country-house, as I called it, and, cutting some of the smaller twigs, I found them to my purpose as much as I could desire; whereupon I came the next time prepared with a hatchet to cut down a quantity, which I soon found, for there was a great plenty of them; these I set up to dry within my circle, or hedges, and when they were fit for use, I carried them to my cave; and here, during the next season, I employed myself in making (as well as I could) a great many baskets both to carry earth, or to carry or lay up anything, as I had occasion; and though I did not finish them very handsomely, yet I made them sufficiently serviceable for my purpose; and thus afterwards I took care never to be without them; and as my wicker-ware decayed, I made more; especially I made strong deep baskets to place my corn in, instead of sacks, when I should come to have any quantity of it.

Having mastered this difficulty, and employed a world of time about it, I bestirred myself to see, if possible, how to supply two wants; I had no vessels to hold anything that was liquid, except two runlets, which were almost full of rum, and some glass bottles, some of the common size, and others, which were case-bottles, square, for the holding of waters, spirits, etc. I had not so much as a pot to boil anything in, except a great kettle which I saved out of the ship, and which was too big for such cases as I desired it for, namely, to make broth, and stew a bit of meat by itself. The second thing I would fain have had was a tobacco-pipe, but it was impossible for me to make one; however, I found a contrivance for that too at last.

I employed myself in planting my second rows of stakes of piles, and in this wicker-work, all the summer, or dry season, when another business took me up more time than it could be imagined I could spare.

CHAPTER 8

Make second Survey of Island – Catch a
Parrot, which I teach to speak – Mode of
sleeping – Find other side of the Island
covered with Turtle and Sea-fowl – Catch
and tame a young Kid

I mentioned before, that I had a great mind to see the whole island,
and that I had travelled up the brook, and so on, to where I built
my bower, and where I had an opening quite to the sea, on the
other side of the island. I now resolved to travel quite across to the
sea-shore on that side. So, taking my gun and hatchet, and my dog,
and a larger quantity of powder and shot than usual, with two
biscuit-cakes, and a great bunch of raisins in my pouch, for my store,
I began my journey. When I had passed the vale where my bower
stood, as above, I came within view of the sea to the west; and it
being a very clear day, I fairly descried land, whether an island or
continent I could not tell; but it lay very high, extending from the
west to the west-south-west, at a very great distance; by my guess
it could not be less than fifteen or twenty leagues off.

I could not tell what part of the world this might be, otherwise than that I knew it must be part of America; and, as I concluded
by all my observations, must be near the Spanish dominions, and
perhaps was all inhabited by savages, where, if I should have landed,
I had been in a worse condition than I was now; and therefore I
acquiesced in the dispositions of Providence, which I began now to
own, and to believe ordered everything for the best – I say, I quieted
my mind with this, and left afflicting myself with fruitless wishes
of being there.

Besides, after some pause upon this affair, I considered, that if this land was the Spanish coast, I should certainly, one time or other, see some vessels pass or repass one way or other; but if not, then it was the savage coast between the Spanish country and Brazil, the inhabitants of which are indeed the worst of savages; for they are cannibals, or men-eaters, and fail not to murder and devour all the human bodies that fall into their hands.

With these considerations I walked very leisurely forward. I found that side of the island where I now was much pleasanter than mine – the open or savanna fields sweet, adorned with flowers and grass, and full of very fine woods. I saw abundance of parrots, and fain would I have caught one, if possible, to have kept it to be tame, and taught it to speak to me. I did, after some painstaking, catch a young parrot; for I knocked it down with a stick, and having recovered it, I brought it home, but it was some years before I could make him speak. However, at last I taught him to call me by my name very familiarly; but the accident that followed, though it be a trifle, will be very diverting in its place.

I was exceedingly diverted with this journey; I found in the low grounds, hares, as I thought them to be, and foxes, but they differed greatly from all the other kinds I had met with, nor could I satisfy myself to eat them, though I killed several; but I had no need to be venturous; for I had no want of food, and of that which was very good too; especially these three sorts; namely, goats, pigeons, and turtles, or tortoise, which added to my grapes, Leadenhall Market could not have furnished a better table than I, in proportion to the company; and though my case was deplorable enough, yet I had great cause for thankfulness, that I was not driven to any extremities for food; but rather plenty, even to dainties.

I never travelled in this journey above two miles outright in a day, or thereabouts; but I took so many turns and returns to see what discoveries I could make, that I came wearied enough to the place where I resolved to sit down for all night; and then either reposed myself in a tree, or surrounded myself with a row of stakes set upright in the ground, either from one tree to another, or so as no wild creature could come at me without waking me.

As soon as I came to the sea-shore, I was surprised to see that I had taken up my lot on the worst side of the island; for here, indeed, the shore was covered with innumerable turtles, whereas, on the other side, I had found but three in a year and a half. Here was also an infinite number of fowls of many kinds, some of which

I had not seen before, and many of them very good meat; but such as I knew not the names of, except those called penguins.

I could have shot as many as I pleased, but was very sparing of my powder and shot; and therefore had more mind to kill a she-goat, if I could, which I could better feed on; and though there were many goats here, more than on the other side of the island, yet it was with much more difficulty that I could come near them – the country being flat and even, and they saw me much sooner than when I was on the hills.

I confess this side of the country was much pleasanter than mine, but yet I had not the least inclination to remove; for, as I was fixed in my habitation, it became natural to me, and I seemed, all the while I was here, to be, as it were, upon a journey and from home; however, I travelled along the shore of the sea towards the east, I suppose, about twelve miles; and then, setting up a great pole upon the shore for a mark, I concluded I would go home again; and the next journey I took should be on the other side of the island, east from my dwelling, and so round, till I came to my post again – of which in its place.

I took another way to come back than that I went, thinking I could keep all the island so much in my view, that I could not miss finding my first dwelling by viewing the country – but I found myself mistaken; for, being come about two or three miles, I found myself descended into a very large valley, but so surrounded with hills, and those hills covered with woods, that I could not see which was my way by any direction but that of the sun, nor even then, unless I knew very well the position of the sun at that time of the day.

It happened, to my further misfortune, that the weather proved hazy for three or four days, while I was in this valley; and not being able to see the sun, I wandered about very uncomfortably, and at last was obliged to find out the sea-side, look for my post, and come back the same way I went; and then, by easy journeys, I turned homeward, the weather being exceedingly hot, and my gun, ammunition, hatchet, and other things, very heavy.

In this journey, my dog surprised a young kid, and seized upon it; and I running in to take hold of it, caught it, and saved it alive from the dog. I had a great mind to bring it home, if I could; for I had often been musing whether it might not be possible to get a kid or two, and so raise a breed of tame goats, which might supply me when my powder and shot should be spent.

I made a collar for this little creature, and, with a string which I made of some rope-yarn, which I always carried about me, I led him along, though with some difficulty, till I came to my bower, and there I enclosed him, and left him, for I was very impatient to be at home, from whence I had been absent above a month.

I cannot express what a satisfaction it was to me to come into my old hutch, and lie down in my hammock-bed: this little wandering journey, without a settled place of abode, had been so unpleasant to me, that my own house, as I called it to myself, was a perfect settlement to me compared to that; and it rendered everything about me so comfortable, that I resolved I would never go a great way from it again, while it should be my lot to stay on the island.

I reposed myself here a week, to rest and regale myself after my long journey; during which, most of the time was taken up in the weighty affair of making a cage for my poll, who began now to be a mere domestic, and to be mighty well acquainted with me. Then I began to think of the poor kid which I had pent in within my little circle, and resolved to go and fetch it home, and give it some food; accordingly I went, and found it where I left it; for, indeed, it could not get out, but was almost starved for want of food. I went and cut boughs of trees, and branches of such shrubs as I could find, and threw it over, and having fed it, I tied it as I did before, to lead it away; but it was so tame with being hungry, that I had no need to have tied it, for it followed me like a dog; and, as I continually fed it, the creature became so loving, so gentle, and so fond, that it became from that time one of my domestics also, and would never leave me afterwards.

The rainy season of the autumnal equinox was now come, and I kept the 30th of September in the same solemn manner as before, being the anniversary of my landing on the island, having now been there two years, and no more prospect of being delivered than the first day I came there. I spent the whole day in humble and thankful acknowledgments of the many wonderful mercies which my solitary condition was attended with, and without which it might have been infinitely more miserable. I gave humble and hearty thanks, that God had been pleased to discover to me even that it was possible I might be more happy in this solitary condition than I should have been in a liberty of society, and in all the pleasures of the world – that He could fully make up to me the deficiencies of my solitary state, and the want of human society, by His presence and the communication of His grace to my soul, supporting, comforting, and encouraging me to depend upon His providence here, and hope for His eternal presence hereafter.

It was now that I began sensibly to feel how much more happy the life I now led was, with all its miserable circumstances, than the wicked, cursed, abominable life I led all the past part of my days; and now, having changed both my sorrows and my joys, my very desires altered, my affections changed their gust, and my delights were perfectly new from what they were at my first coming, or, indeed, for the two years past.

Before, as I walked about, either on my hunting or for viewing the country, the anguish of my soul at my condition would break out upon me on a sudden, and my very heart would die within me to think of the woods, the mountains, the deserts I was in; and how I was a prisoner, locked up with the eternal bars and bolts of the ocean, in an uninhabited wilderness, without redemption. In the midst of the greatest composures of my mind, this would break out upon me like a storm, and made me wring my hands and weep like a child. Sometimes it would take me in the middle of my work, and I would immediately sit down and sigh, and look upon the ground for an hour or two together, and this was still worse to me; for if I could burst out into tears, or vent myself by words, it would go off; and the grief, having exhausted itself, would abate.

But now I began to exercise myself with new thoughts – I daily read the word of God, and applied all the comforts of it to my present state. One morning, being very sad, I opened the Bible upon these words, "I will never leave thee, nor forsake thee!" Immediately it occurred, that these words were to me; why else should they be directed in such a manner, just at the moment when I was mourning over my condition, as one forsaken of God and man? "Well then," said I, "if God does not forsake me, of what ill consequence can it be, or what matters it though the world should all forsake me, seeing, on the other hand, if I had all the world, and should lose the favour and blessing of God, there would be no comparison in the loss."

From this moment I began to conclude in my mind, that it was possible for me to be more happy in this forsaken, solitary condition, than it was probable I should have ever been in any particular state in the world; and with this thought I was going to give thanks to God for bringing me to this place.

I know not what it was, but something shocked my mind at that thought, and I durst not speak the words. "How canst thou be such a hypocrite," said I, even audibly, "to pretend to be thankful for a condition which, however thou mayst endeavour to be contented with, thou wouldst rather pray heartily to be delivered from?" So I stopped there: but though I could not say I thanked God for being there, yet I sincerely gave thanks to God for opening my eyes, by whatever afflicting providences, to see the former condition of my life, and to mourn for my wickedness, and repent, I never opened the Bible, or shut it, but my very soul within me blessed God for directing my friend in England, without any order of mine, to pack it up among my goods, and for assisting me afterwards to save it out of the wreck of the ship.

Thus, and in this disposition of mind, I began my third year; and though I have not given the reader the trouble of so particular an account of my works this year as at first, yet in general it may be observed, that I was very seldom idle, having regularly divided my time according to the several daily employments that were before me – such as, first, my duty to God, and reading the Scriptures, which I constantly set apart some time for, thrice every day; secondly, the going abroad with my gun for food, which generally took me up three hours every morning when it did not rain; thirdly, the ordering, curing, preserving, and cooking what I had killed or catched for my supply – these took up great part of the day; also it is to be considered, that in the middle of the day, when the sun was in the zenith, the violence of the heat was too great to stir out; so that about four hours in the evening was all the time I could be supposed to work in; with this exception, that sometimes I changed my hours of hunting and working, and went to work in the morning, and abroad with my gun in the afternoon.

To this short time allowed for labour, I desire may be added the exceeding laboriousness of my work; the many hours which, for want of tools, want of help and want of skill, everything that I did took up out of my time – for example, I was full two-and-forty days making me a board for a long shelf, which I wanted in my cave; whereas, two sawyers, with their tools and saw-pit, would have cut six of them out of the same tree in half a day.

My case was this: it was to be a large tree which was to be cut down, because my board was to be a broad one. The tree I was three days of cutting down, and two more cutting of the boughs, and reducing it to a log, or piece of timber. With inexpressible hacking and hewing, I reduced both the sides of it into chips, till it began to be light enough to move; then I turned it, and made one side of it smooth and flat, as a board, from end to end; then, turning that side downward, cut the other side till I brought the plank to be about three inches thick, and smooth on both sides. Any one may judge the labour of my hands in such a piece of work; but labour and patience carried me through that and many other things; I only observe this in particular, to show the reason why so much of my time went away with so little work, namely, that what might be a little to be done with help and tools, was a vast labour, and required a prodigious time to do alone, and by hand.

But notwithstanding this, with patience and labour I went through many things, and indeed everything that my circumstances made necessary for me to do, as will appear by what follows.

I was now, in the months of November and December, expecting my crop of barley and rice. The ground I had manured or dug up for them was not great; for as I observed, my seed of each was not above the quantity of half a peck, for I had lost one whole crop by sowing in the dry season; but now my crop promised very well, when on a sudden I found I was in danger of losing it all again by enemies of several sorts, which it was scarce possible to keep from it; as first, the goats and wild creatures which I called hares, which, tasting the sweetness of the blade, lay in it night and day, as soon as it came up, and ate it so close that it could get no time to shoot up into stalks.

This I saw no remedy for, but by making an enclosure about it with a hedge, which I did with a great deal of toil; and the more, because it required a great deal of speed, the creatures daily spoiling my corn. However, as my arable land was but small, suited to my crop, I got it totally well fenced in about three weeks' time, and shooting some of the creatures in the daytime, I set my dog to guard it in the night, tying him up to a stake at the gate, where he would stand and bark all night long; so in a little time the enemies forsook the place, and the corn grew very strong and well, and began to ripen apace.

But as the beasts ruined me before while my corn was in the blade, so the birds were as likely to ruin me now, when it was in the ear; for, going along by the place to see how it throve, I saw my little crop surrounded with fowls I know not how many sorts, which stood as it were watching till I should be gone. I immediately let fly among them (for I had always my gun with me). I had no sooner shot, but there rose up a little crowd of fowls, which I had not seen at all, from among the corn itself.

This touched me sensibly; for I foresaw that, in a few days, they would devour all my hopes; that I should be starved, and never be able to raise a crop at all – and what to do I could not tell; however, I resolved not to lose my corn, if possible, though I should watch it night and day. In the first place, I went among it to see what damage was already done, and found they had spoiled a good deal of it; but that, as it was yet too green for them, the loss was not so great, but the remainder was like to be a good crop, if it could be saved.

I stayed by it to load my gun and, then coming away, I could easily see all the thieves sitting upon all the trees about me, as if they only waited till I was gone away, and the event proved it to be so; for, as I walked off as if I was gone, I was no sooner out of their sight, but they dropped down one by one, into the corn again. I was so provoked that I could not have patience to stay till more came on, knowing that every grain they ate now was, as it might be said, a peck loaf to me in the consequence; but, coming up to the hedge, I fired again, and killed three of them. This was what I wished for; so I took them up, and served them as we serve notorious thieves in England, namely, hanged them in chains for a terror to others. It is impossible to imagine almost that this should have such an effect as it had; for the fowls would not only not come at the corn, but, in short, they forsook all that part of the island, and I could never see a bird near the place as long as my scarecrows hung there.

This I was very glad of, you may be sure; and about the latter end of December, which was our second harvest of the year, I reaped my corn.

I was sadly put to it for a scythe, or a sickle, to cut it down, and all I could do was to make one as well as I could, out of one of the broadswords, or cutlasses which I saved among the arms out of the ship. However, as my crop was but small, I had no difficulty to cut it down: in short, I reaped it my way, for I cut nothing off but the ears, and carried it away in a great basket which I had made, and so rubbed it out with my hands; and, at the end of all my harvesting, I found, that out of my half peck of seed I had near two bushels of rice, and above two bushels and a half of barley, that is to say, by my guess, for I had no measure at that time.

However, this was a great encouragement to me; and I foresaw that in time it would please God to supply me with bread; and yet here I was perplexed again, for I neither knew how to grind nor make meal of my corn, nor, indeed, how to clean it and part it; nor, if made into meal how to make bread of it; and if how to make it, yet I knew not how to bake it. These things being added to my desire of having a good quantity for store, and to secure a constant supply, I resolved not to taste any of this crop, but to preserve it all for seed against the next season, and, in the meantime, to employ all my study and hours of working to accomplish this great work of providing myself with corn and bread.

It might be truly said, that I now worked for my bread. It is a little wonderful, and what I believe few people have thought much upon, namely, the strange multitude of little things necessary in the providing, producing, curing, dressing, making, and finishing this one article of bread.

I, that was reduced to a mere state of nature, found this to be my daily discouragement, and was made more and more sensible of it every hour, even after I got the first handful of seed corn, which, as I have said, came up unexpectedly, and indeed to a surprise.

First, I had no plough to turn the earth, no spade or shovel to dig it. Well, this I conquered by making a wooden spade, as I observed before; but this did my work but in a wooden manner; and though it cost me a great many days to make it, yet, for want of iron, it not only wore out the sooner, but made my work the harder, and made it be performed much worse.

However, this I bore with too, and was content to work it out with patience, and bear with the badness of the performance. When the corn was sowed, I had no harrow, but was forced to go over it myself, and drag a great heavy bough of a tree over it to scratch the earth, as it may be called, rather than rake or harrow it.

When it was growing, or grown, I have observed already how many things I wanted, to fence it, secure it, mow or reap it, cure or carry it home, thresh, part it from the chaff, and save it. Then I wanted a mill to grind it, sieves to dress it, yeast and salt to make it into bread, and an oven to bake it in; and all these things I did without; as shall be observed, and yet the corn was an inestimable comfort and advantage to me too. But all this, as I said, made everything laborious and tedious to me, but that there was no help for; neither was my time so much loss to me, because, as I had divided it, a certain part of it was every day appointed to these works; and as I resolved to use none of the corn for bread till I had a greater quantity by me, I had the next six months to apply myself wholly, by labour and invention, to furnish myself with utensils proper for the performing all the operations necessary for making the corn, when I had it fit for my use.

But first I was to prepare more land, for I had now seed enough to sow above an acre of ground. Before I did this, I had a week's work at least to make me a spade, which, when it was done, was a very sorry one indeed, and very heavy, and required double labour to work with it; however, I went through that, and sowed my seeds in two large flat pieces of ground, as near my house as I could find them to my mind, and fenced them in with a good hedge, the stakes of which were all cut off that wood which I had set before, which I knew would grow; so that in one year's time I knew I should have a quick or living hedge, that would want but little repair. This work was not so little as to take me up less than three months; because great part of that time was in the wet season, when I could not go abroad.

Within doors, that is, when it rained and I could not go out, I found employment on the following occasions; always observing, that all the while I was at work, I diverted myself with talking to my parrot, and teaching him to speak; and I quickly learnt him to know his own name, and at last to speak it out pretty loud, Poll, which was the first word I ever heard spoken in the island by any mouth but my own. This, therefore, was not my work, but an assistant to my work; for now, as I said, I had a great employment upon my hands, as follows: namely, I had long studied, by some means or other, to make myself some earthen vessels, which indeed I wanted sorely, but knew not where to come at them; however, considering the heat of the climate, I did not doubt but, if I could find out any suitable clay, I might botch up some such pot as might, being dried by the sun, be hard enough and strong enough to bear handling, and to hold anything that was dry, and required to be kept so; and as this was necessary in preparing corn, meal, etc., which was the thing I was upon, I resolved to make some as large as I could, and fit only to stand like jars to hold what should be put into them.

CHAPTER 9

Make Earthenware – Mode of Baking – Build
a Boat – Unable to get it to the Water – Ink
and Biscuit exhausted, and Clothes worn out
– Contrive Dress of Skins

It would make the reader pity me, or rather laugh at me, to tell
how many awkward ways I took to raise this paste, what odd,
misshapen, ugly things I made; how many of them fell in, and
how many fell out, the clay not being stiff enough to bear its own
weight; how many cracked by the over-violent heat of the sun,
being set out too hastily; and how many fell to pieces with only
removing, as well before as after they were dried: and, in a word,
how, after having laboured hard to find the clay, to dig it, to temper
it, to bring it home, and work it, I could not make above two large
earthen ugly things – I cannot call them jars – in about two months'
labour.

However, as the sun baked these two very dry and hard, I
lifted them very gently up, and set them down again in two great
wicker baskets, which I had made on purpose for them, that they
might not break; and, as between the pot and the basket there
was a little room to spare, I stuffed it full of the rice and barley
straw; and these two pots being to stand always dry, I thought
would hold my dry corn, and perhaps the meal when the corn was
bruised.

Though I miscarried so much in my design for large pots,
yet I made several smaller things with better success: such as little
round pots, flat dishes, pitchers, and pipkins, anything my hand
turned to; and the heat of the sun baked them strangely hard.

But all this would not answer my end, which was to get an

earthen pot to hold what was liquid, and bear the fire, which none of these could do. It happened after some time, making a pretty large fire for cooking my meat, when I went to put it out, after I had done with it, I found a broken piece of one of my earthenware vessels in the fire, burnt as hard as a stone, and red as a tile. I was agreeably surprised to see it, and said to myself, that certainly they might be made to burn whole, if they would burn broken.

This set me to study how to order my fire, so as to make it burn me some pots. I had no notion of a kiln such as the potters burn in, or of glazing them with lead, though I had some lead to do it with; but I placed three large pipkins, and two or three pots, in a pile, one upon another, and placed my firewood all around it, with a great heap of embers under them. I piled the fire with fresh fuel round the outside, and upon the top, till I saw the pots in the inside red hot quite through, and observed that they did not crack at all: when I saw them clear red, I let them stand in that heat about five or six hours, till I found one of them, though it did not crack, did melt, or run; for the sand which was mixed with the clay melted by the violence of the heat, and would have run into glass if I had gone on; so I slacked my fire gradually, till the pots began to abate of the red colour, and watching them all night, that I might not let the fire abate too fast, in the morning I had three very good, I will not say handsome, pipkins, and two other earthen pots, as hard burnt as could be desired, and one of them perfectly glazed with the running of the sand.

After this experiment, I need not say that I wanted no sort of earthenware for my use; but I must needs say, as to the shapes of them, they were very indifferent, as any one may suppose, when I had no way of making them but as the children make dirt pies, or as a woman would make pies that never learnt to raise paste.

No joy at a thing of so mean a nature was ever equal to mine, when I found I had made an earthen pot that would bear the fire; and I had hardly patience to stay till they were cold, before I set one upon the fire again with some water in it, to boil me some meat, which it did admirably well; and with a piece of kid, I made some very good broth, though I wanted oatmeal, and several other ingredients requisite to make it so good as I would have had it.

My next concern was to get me a stone mortar to stamp or beat some corn in; for as to the mill, there was no thought of arriving to that perfection of art with one pair of hands. To supply this want, I was at a great loss; for, of all the trades in the world, I was as perfectly unqualified for a stone-cutter as for any whatever; neither had I any tools to go about it with. I spent many a day to find out a great stone big enough to cut hollow, and make fit for a mortar, and could find none at all, except what was in the solid rock, and which I had no way to dig, or cut out; nor indeed were the rocks in the island of hardness sufficient, but were all of a sandy crumbling stone, which would neither bear the weight of a heavy pestle, nor would break the corn without filling it with sand; so, after a great deal of time lost in searching for a stone, I gave it over, and resolved to look out for a great block of hard wood, which I found indeed much easier; and, getting one as big as I had strength to stir, I rounded it, and formed it on the outside with my axe and hatchet; and then, with the help of fire and infinite labour, made a hollow place in it, as the Indians in Brazil make their canoes. After this I made a great heavy pestle, or beater, of the wood called the iron-wood, and this I prepared and laid by against I had my next crop of corn, when I proposed to myself to grind, or rather pound, my corn, or meal, to make my bread.

My next difficulty was to make a sieve, or searce, to dress my meal, and part it from the bran and the husk, without which I did not see it possible I could have any bread. This was a most difficult thing, so much as but to think on; for, to be sure, I had nothing like the necessary things to make it with – I mean fine thin canvas, or stuff, to searce the meal through. And here I was at a full stop for many months; nor did I know really what to do; linen I had none left but what was mere rags; I had goat's hair, but neither knew I how to weave or spin it; and had I known how, here were no tools to work it with. All the remedy that I found for this was, that at last I did remember I had among the seamen's clothes which were saved out of the ship, some neckcloths of calico, or muslin; and with some pieces of these I made three small sieves, but proper enough for the work; and thus I made shift for some years. How I did afterwards, I shall show in its place.

The baking part was the next thing to be considered, and how I should make bread when I came to have corn; for, first, I had no yeast; as to that part, there was no supplying the want, so I did not concern myself much about it. But for an oven, I was, indeed, in great pain. At length I found out an expedient for that also, which was this: – I made some earthen vessels very broad, but not deep; that is to say, about two feet diameter, and not above nine inches deep; these I burnt in the fire, as I had done the others, and laid them by; and when I wanted to bake, I made a great fire upon the hearth, which I had paved with some square tiles of my own making and burning also – but I should not call them square.

When the firewood was burnt pretty much into embers, or live coals, I drew them forward upon this hearth, so as to cover it all over, and there I let them lie, till the hearth was very hot; then, sweeping away all the embers, I set down my loaf, or loaves, and, whelming down the earthen pot upon them, drew the embers all round the outside of the pot, to keep in, and add to the heat: and thus, as well as in the best oven in the world, I baked my barley-loaves, and became in a little time a good pastry-cook into the bargain; for I made myself several cakes of the rice, and puddings: indeed, I made no pies, neither had I anything to put into them, supposing I had, except the flesh either of fowls or goats.

It need not be wondered at, if all these things took me up most part of the third year of my abode here; for it is to be observed, that in the interval of these things I had my new harvest and husbandry to manage; for I reaped my corn in its season, and carried it home as well as I could, and laid it up in the ear, in my large baskets, till I had time to rub it out; for I had no floor to thrash it on, or instrument to thrash it with.

And now, indeed, my stock of corn increasing, I really wanted to build my barns bigger; I wanted a place to lay it up in; for the increase of the corn now yielded me so much, that I had of the barley about twenty bushels, and of the rice as much, or more; insomuch, that I now resolved to begin to use it freely, for my bread had been quite gone a great while; also I resolved to see what quantity would be sufficient for me a whole year, and to sow but once a year.

Upon the whole, I found that the forty bushels of barley and rice were much more than I could consume in a year; so I resolved to sow just the same quantity every year that I sowed the last, in hopes that such a quantity would fully provide me with bread, etc.

All the while these things were doing, you may be sure my thoughts ran many times upon the prospect of land which I had seen from the other side of the island; and I was not without secret wishes that I was on shore there, fancying that, seeing the main-land and an inhabited country, I might find some way or other to convey myself farther, and perhaps, at last find some means of escape.

But all this while I made no allowance for the dangers of such a condition, and how I might fall into the hands of savages, and, perhaps, such as I might have reason to think far worse than the lions and tigers of Africa – that, if I once came into their power, I should run a hazard more than a thousand to one of being killed, and, perhaps, of being eaten; for I had heard that the people of the Caribbean coasts were cannibals, or men-eaters; and I knew by the latitude that I could not be far off from that shore – that, suppose they were not cannibals, yet they might kill me, as many Europeans who had fallen into their hands had been served, even when they had been ten or twenty together; much more I that was but one, and could make little or no defence. All these things, I say, which I ought to have considered well off, and I did cast up in my thoughts afterwards, yet took none of my apprehensions at first: and my head ran mightily upon the thoughts of getting over to that shore.

Now I wished for my boy Xury, and the long-boat with the shoulder-of-mutton sail, with which I sailed above a thousand miles on the coast of Africa; but this was in vain. Then I thought I would go and look on our ship's boat, which, as I have said, was blown up upon the shore a great way in the storm, when we were first cast away. She lay almost where she did at first, but not quite, and was turned by the force of the waves and the winds almost bottom upwards, against the high ridge of a beachy rough sand, but no water about her as before.

If I had had hands to have refitted her, and have launched her into the water, the boat would have done very well, and I might have gone back into the Brazils with her easy enough; but I might have easily foreseen that I could not more turn her, and set her upright upon her bottom, than I could remove the island. However, I went to the wood, and cut levers and rollers, and brought them to the boat, resolving to try what I could do, suggesting to myself, that if I could but turn her down, I might easily repair the damage she had received, and she would be a very good boat, and I might go to sea in her very easily.

I spared no pains, indeed, in this piece of fruitless toil, and spent, I think, three or four weeks about it; at last, finding it impossible to heave it up with my little strength, I fell to the digging away the sand to undermine it, and so to make it fall down, setting pieces of wood to thrust and guide it right in the fall.

But when I had done this, I was unable to stir it up again,

or to get under it, much less to move it forward towards the water; so I was forced to give it over: and yet, though I gave over the hopes of the boat, my desire to venture over for the main increased, rather than decreased, as the means for it seemed impossible.

This at length set me upon thinking whether it was not possible to make myself a canoe, or periagua, such as the natives of those climates make, even without tools, or, as I might say, without hands, namely, of the trunk of a great tree. This I not only thought possible, but easy; and pleased myself extremely with the thoughts of making it, and with having much more convenience for it than any of the negroes or Indians; but not at all considering the particular inconveniences which I lay under more than the Indians did, namely, want of hands to move it into the water when it was made – a difficulty much harder for me to surmount than all the consequences of want of tools could be to them: for what was it to me that, when I had chosen a vast tree in the woods, I might with great trouble cut it down, if after I might be able with my tools to hew and dub the outside into the proper shape of a boat, and burn or cut out the inside to make it hollow, so as to make a boat of it – if, after all this, I must leave it just there where I found it, and was not able to launch it into the water?

One would have thought, I could not have had the least reflection upon my mind of my circumstances, while I was making this boat, but I should have immediately thought how I should get it into the sea; but my thoughts were so intent upon my voyage over the sea in it, that I never once considered how I should get it off the land; and it was really, in its own nature, more easy for me to guide it over forty-five miles of sea, than about forty-five fathoms of land, where it lay, to set it afloat in the water.

I went to work upon this boat the most like a fool that ever man did who had any of his senses awake. I pleased myself with the design, without determining whether I was ever able to undertake it; not but that the difficulty of launching my boat came often into my head; but I put a stop to my own inquiries into it by this foolish answer which I gave myself: Let me first make it, I'll warrant I'll find some way or other to get it along when it is done.

This was a most preposterous method; but the eagerness of my fancy prevailed, and to work I went, and felled a cedar tree – I question much whether Solomon ever had such a one for the building the temple at Jerusalem. It was five feet ten inches diameter at the lower part next the stump, and four feet eleven inches diameter at the end of twenty-two feet, after which it lessened for awhile, and then parted into branches. It was not without infinite labour that I felled this tree; I was twenty days hacking and hewing at it at the bottom; I was fourteen more getting the branches and limbs, and the vast spreading head of it, cut off, which I hacked and hewed through with my axe and hatchet with inexpressible labour; after this it cost me a month to shape it; and dub it to a proportion, and to something like the bottom of a boat, that it might swim upright as it ought to do. It cost me near three months more to clear the inside, and work it out so as to make an exact boat of it: this I did indeed without fire, by mere mallet and chisel and by the dint of hard labour, till I had brought it to be a very handsome periagua, and big enough to have carried six-and-twenty men, and consequently big enough to have carried me and all my cargo.

When I had gone through this work, I was extremely delighted with it; the boat was really much bigger than I ever saw a canoe or periagua, that was made of one tree, in my life; many a weary stroke it had cost, you may be sure, for there remained nothing but to get it into the water; and had I gotten it into the water I make no question but I should have begun the maddest voyage, and the most unlikely to be performed, that ever was undertaken.

But all my devices to get it into the water failed me, though they cost infinite labour too. I lay about one hundred yards from the water, and not more; but the first inconvenience was, it was uphill towards the creek. Well, to take away this discouragement, I resolved to dig into the surface of the earth, and so make a declivity: this I began, and it cost me a prodigious deal of pains; but who grudge pains that have their deliverance in view? but when this was worked through, and this difficulty managed, it was still much at one, for I could no more stir the canoe than I could the other boat.

Then I measured the distance of ground, and resolved to cut a dock, or canal, to bring the water up to the canoe, seeing I could not bring the canoe down to the water: well, I began this work, and when I began to enter into it, and calculated how deep it was to be dug, how broad, how the stuff was to be thrown out, I found that, by the number of hands I had, being none but my own, it must have been ten or twelve years before I should have gone through with it; for the shore lay high, so that at the upper end it must have been at least twenty feet deep; so at length, though with great reluctance, I gave this attempt over also.

This grieved me heartily; and now I saw, though too late, the folly of beginning a work before we count the cost, and before we judge rightly of our own strength to go through with it.

In the middle of this work I finished my fourth year in this place, and kept my anniversary with the same devotion, and with as much comfort, as ever before; for, by a constant study, and serious application of the word of God, and by the assistance of His grace, I gained a different knowledge from what I had before: I entertained different notions of things; I looked now upon the world as a thing remote, which I had nothing to do with, no expectation from, and indeed no desires about: in a word, I had nothing indeed to do with it, nor was ever like to have; so I thought it looked as we may perhaps look upon it hereafter, namely, as a place I had lived in, but was come out of it; and well I might say, as father Abraham to Dives, "Between me and thee there is a great gulf fixed."

In the first place, I was removed from all the wickedness of the world here. I had neither the lust of the flesh, the lust of the eye, nor the pride of life. I had nothing to covet, for I had all I was now capable of enjoying; I was lord of the whole manor; or, if I pleased, I might call myself king or emperor over the whole country which I had possession of: there were no rivals; I had no competitor, none to dispute sovereignty or command with me; I might have raised ship-loadings of corn, but I had no use for it, so I let as little grow as I thought enough for my occasion; I had tortoises or turtles enough, but now and then one was as much as I could put to any use; I had timber enough to have built a fleet of ships; I had grapes enough to have made wine, or to have cured into raisins, to have loaded that fleet when they had been built.

But all I could make use of was all that was valuable; I had enough to eat, and supply my wants, and what was all the rest to me? If I killed more flesh than I could eat, the dog must eat it, or the vermin; if I sowed more corn than I could eat, it must be spoiled. The trees that I cut down were lying to rot on the ground, I could make no more use of them than for fuel – and that I had no occasion for but to dress my food.

In a word, the nature and experience of things dictated to me, upon just reflection, that all the good things of this world are no further good to us than as they are for our use; and that, whatever we may heap up to give to others, we enjoy only as much as we can use, and no more. The most covetous griping miser in the world would have been cured of the vice of covetousness, if he had been in my case; for I possessed infinitely more than I knew what to do with. I had no room for desire, except it was of things which I had not, and they were but trifles, though indeed of great use to me. I had, as I hinted before, a parcel of money, as well gold as silver, about thirty-six pounds sterling: alas! there the nasty, sorry, useless stuff lay; I had no manner of business for it; and I often thought with myself, that I would have given a handful of it for a gross of tobacco-pipes, or for a handmill to grind my corn; nay, I would have given it all for sixpenny-worth of turnip and carrot-seed out of England, or for a handful of peas and beans, and a bottle of ink: as it was, I had not the least advantage by it, or benefit from it; but there it lay in a drawer, and grew mouldy with the damp of the cave, in the wet season; and if I had had the drawer full of diamonds, it had been the same case, and they had been of no manner of value to me, because of no use.

I had now brought my state of life to be much easier in itself than it was at first, and much easier to my mind as well as to my body. I frequently sat down to my meat with thankfulness, and admired the hand of God's providence, which had thus spread my table in the wilderness. I learnt to look more upon the bright side of my condition, and less upon the dark side, and to consider what I enjoyed rather than what I wanted – and this gave me sometimes such secret comforts, that I cannot express them – and which I take notice of here, to put those discontented people in mind of it, who cannot enjoy comfortably what God hath given them, because they see and covet something that He has not given them: all our discontents about what we want, appeared to me to spring from the want of thankfulness for what we have.

Another reflection was of great use to me, and doubtless, would be so to any one that should fall into such distress as mine was; and this was, to compare my present condition with what I at first expected it should be – nay, with what it would certainly have been – if the good providence of God had not wonderfully ordered the ship to be cast up near to the shore, where I not only could come at her, but could bring what I got out of her to the shore for my relief and comfort; without which I had wanted tools to work, weapons for defence, or gunpowder and shot for getting my food.

I spent whole hours, I may say whole days, in representing to myself, in the most lively colours, how I must have acted if I had got nothing out of the ship; how I could not have so much as got any food, except fish and turtles; and that, as it was long before I found any of them, I must have perished first – that I should have lived, if I had not perished, like a mere savage – that if I had killed a goat or a fowl by any contrivance, I had no way to flay or open them, or part the flesh from the skin and the bowels, or to cut it up; but must gnaw it with my teeth, and pull it with my claws, like a beast.

These reflections made me very sensible of the goodness of Providence to me, and very thankful for my present condition, with all its hardships and misfortunes; and this part also I cannot but recommend to the reflection of those who are apt, in their misery, to say, "Is any affliction like mine?" Let them consider how much worse the cases of some people are, and what their case might have been, if Providence had thought fit.

I had another reflection, which assisted me also to comfort my mind with hopes; and this was, comparing my present condition with what I had deserved, and had therefore reason to expect, from the hand of Providence. I had lived a dreadful life, perfectly destitute of the knowledge and fear of God. I had been well instructed by father and mother; neither had they been wanting to me in their early endeavours to infuse a religious awe of God into my mind, a sense of my duty, and of what the nature and end of my being required of me. But, alas I falling early into the seafaring life, which, of all lives, is the most destitute of the fear of God, though his terrors are always before them – I say, falling early into the seafaring life, and into seafaring company, all that little sense of religion which I had entertained was laughed out of me by my messmates – by a hardened despising of dangers, and the views of death, which grew habitual to me – by my long absence from all manner of opportunities to converse with anything but what was like myself, or to hear anything of what was good, or tended towards it.

So void was I of everything that was good, or of the least sense of what I was, or was to be, that in the greatest deliverance I enjoyed, such as my escape from Sallee, my being taken up by the Portuguese master of the ship, my being planted so well in Brazil, my receiving the cargo from England, and the like, I never once had the words, "Thank God!" so much as on my mind, or in my mouth; nor, in the greatest distress, had I so much thought as to pray to him, nor as much as to say, "Lord, have mercy upon me!" – no, not to mention the name of God, unless it was to swear by, and blaspheme it.

I had terrible reflections upon my mind for many months, as I have already observed, on the account of my wicked and hardened life past; and when I looked about me, and considered what particular providences had attended me, since my coming into this place, and how God had dealt bountifully with me – had not only punished me less than my iniquity deserved, but had so plentifully provided for me; this gave me great hopes that my repentance was accepted, and that God had yet mercies in store for me.

With these reflections I worked my mind up, not only to resignation to the will of God in the present disposition of my circumstances, but even to a sincere thankfulness of my condition; and that I, who was yet a living man, ought not to complain, seeing I had not the due punishment of my sins – that I enjoyed so many mercies, which I had no reason to have expected in that place – that I ought never more to repine at my condition, but to rejoice, and to give daily thanks for that daily bread, which nothing but a cloud of wonders could have brought – that I ought to consider I had been fed even by a miracle, even as great as that of feeding Elijah by ravens – nay, by a long series of miracles; and that I could hardly have named a place in the uninhabited part of the world where I could have been cast more to my advantage – a place where, as I had no society, which was my affliction on one hand, so I found no ravenous beasts, no furious wolves, or tigers, to threaten my life; no venomous creatures or poisonous, which I might have fed on to my hurt; no savages to murder and devour me.

In a word, as my life was a life of sorrow one way, so it was a life of mercy another; and I wanted nothing to make it a life of comfort, but to be able to make my sense of God's goodness to me, and care over me in this condition, be my daily desolation; and after I made a just improvement of these things, I went away, and was no more sad.

I had now been here so long, that many things which I brought on shore for my help were either quite gone or very much wasted, and near spent.

My ink, as I observed, had been gone for some time, all but a very little, which I eked out with water a little and a little, till it was so pale it scarce left any appearance of black upon the paper:

as long as it lasted, I made use of it to minute down the days of the month on which any remarkable thing happened to me; and first, by casting up times past, I remember that there was a strange occurrence of days in the various providences which befell me, and which, if I had been superstitiously inclined to observe days as fatal or fortunate, I might had had reason to have looked upon with a great deal of curiosity.

First, I had observed, that the same day that I broke away from my father and my friends, and ran away to Hull, in order to go to sea, the same day afterwards I was taken by the Sallee man-of-war, and made a slave.

The same day of the year that I escaped out of the wreck of the ship in Yarmouth Roads, that same day of the year afterwards I made my escape from Sallee in the boat.

The same day of the year I was born on, namely, the 20th of September, the same day I had my life so miraculously saved twenty-six years after, when I was cast on shore in this island; so that my wicked life, and solitary life, both began on a day.

The next thing to my ink's being wasted, was that of my bread, I mean the biscuit which I brought out of the ship. This I had husbanded to the last degree, allowing myself but one cake of bread a-day, for above a year: and yet I was quite without bread for a year before I got any corn of my own; and great reason I had to be thankful that I had any at all, the getting it being, as it has been already observed, next to miraculous.

My clothes, too, began to decay mightily: as to linen, I had none a good while, except some chequered shirts which I found in the chests of the other seamen, and which I carefully preserved, because many times I could bear no other clothes on but a shirt; and it was a very great help to me that I had, among all the men's clothes of the ship, almost three dozen shirts. There were also several thick watch-coats of the seamen, which were left behind, but they were too hot to wear; and though it is true that the weather was so violently hot that there was no need of clothes, yet I could not go quite naked – no, though I had been inclined to it, which I was not – nor could I abide the thoughts of it, though I was all alone.

One reason why I could not go quite naked was, I could not bear the heat of the sun so well when quite naked, as with some clothes on – nay, the very heat frequently blistered my skin; whereas, with a shirt on, the air itself made some motion, and

DANIEL DEFOE

whistling under the shirt, was twofold cooler than without it: no more could I bring myself ever to go out in the heat of the sun without a cap or a hat; the heat of the sun beating with such violence as it does in that place, would give me the headache presently, by darting so directly on my head, without a cap or hat on, so that I could not bear it; whereas if I put on my hat, it would presently go away.

Upon these views I began to consider about putting the few rags I had, which I called clothes, into some order; I had worn out all the waistcoats I had, and my business was now to try if I could not make jackets out of the great watch-coats which I had by me, and with such other materials as I had – so I set to work a-tailoring, or rather, indeed, a-botching – for I made most piteous work of it. However, I made shift to make two or three waistcoats, which I hoped would serve me a great while: as for breeches or drawers, I made but very sorry shift indeed till afterwards.

I have mentioned that I saved the skins of all the creatures that I killed – I mean four-footed ones – and I had hung them up stretched out with sticks in the sun; by which means some of them were so dry and hard that they were fit for little; but others, it seems, were very useful. The first thing I made of these was a great cap for my head, with the hair on the outside to shoot off the rain: and this I performed so well, that after this I made a suit of clothes wholly of those skins – that is to say, a waistcoat and breeches open at the knees, and both loose; for they were rather wanted to keep me cool, than to keep me warm. I must not omit to acknowledge that they were wretchedly made; for if I was a bad carpenter, I was a worse tailor: however, they were such as I made a very good shift with; and when I was abroad, if it happened to rain, the hair of the waistcoat and cap being outmost, I was kept very dry.

After this I spent a deal of time and pains to make me an umbrella: I was, indeed, in great want of one, and had a great mind to make one; I had seen them made in the Brazils, where they are very useful in the great heats which are there; and I felt the heats every jot as great here, and greater, too, being nearer the equinox; besides, as I was obliged to be much abroad, it was a most useful thing to me, as well for the rains as the heats. I took a world of pains at it, and was a great while before I could make anything likely to hold; nay, after I thought I had hit the way, I spoiled two or three before I made one to my mind; but at last

I made one that answered indifferently well. The main difficulty I found was to make it to let down; I could make it to spread; but if it did not let down too, and draw in, it would not be portable for me any way, but just over my head, which would not do. However, at last, as I said, I made one to answer: I covered it with skins, the hair upwards, so that it cast off the rain like a penthouse, and kept off the sun so effectually, that I could walk out in the hottest of the weather, with greater advantage than I could before in the coolest; and, when I had no need of it, I could close it, and carry it under my arm.

Thus I lived mighty comfortably, my mind being entirely composed by resigning to the will of God, and throwing myself wholly upon the disposal of His providence: this made my life better than sociable; for, when I began to regret the want of conversation, I would ask myself, whether thus conversing mutually with my own thoughts, and, as I hope I may say, with even my Maker, by ejaculations and petitions, was not better than the utmost enjoyment of human society in the world.

I cannot say that, after this, for five years, any extraordinary thing happened to me; but I lived on in the same course, in the same posture and place, just as before. The chief thing I was employed in, besides my yearly labour of planting my barley and rice, and curing my raisins, of both which I always kept up just enough to have a sufficient stock of the year's provisions beforehand – I say, besides this yearly labour, and my daily labour of going out with my gun, I had one labour to make me a canoe, which at last I finished: so that by digging a canal to it, six feet wide, and four feet deep, I brought it into the creek almost half a mile. As for the first, that was so vastly big, as I made it without considering beforehand, as I ought to do, how I should be able to launch it; so, never being able to bring it to the water or bring the water to it, I was obliged to let it lie where it was, as a memorandum to teach me to be wiser next time. Indeed; the next time, though I could not get a tree proper for it, and was in a place where I could not get the water to it, at any less distance than, as I have said, of near a half mile; yet, as I saw it practicable at last, I never gave it over; and, though I was near two years about it, yet I never grudged my labour, in hopes of having a boat to go off to sea at last.

CHAPTER 10

I float Canoe, and am driven out to Sea –
Reach the shore with difficulty – Fall asleep,
am awakened by a mysterious Voice

However, though my little periagua was finished, *yet* the size of it
was not at all answerable to the design which I had in view when
I made the first – I mean of venturing over to the terra firma, where
it was above forty miles broad; accordingly, the smallness of the
boat assisted to put an end to that design, and now I thought no
more of it. But as I had a boat, my next design was to make a tour
round the island; for, as I had been on the other side, in one place,
crossing, as I have already described it, over the land, so the discoveries I made in that journey made me very eager to see the other
parts of the coast; and now I had a boat, I thought of nothing but
sailing round the island.

For this purpose, and that I might do everything with discretion and consideration, I fitted up a little mast to my boat, and
made a sail to it out of some of the pieces of the ship's sails, which
lay in store, and of which I had a great store by me.

Having fitted my mast and sail, and tried the boat, I found
she would sail very well. Then I made little lockers and boxes at
each end of my boat, to put provisions, necessaries, and ammunition, etc., into, to be kept dry, either from rain, or the spray of
the sea; and a little long hollow place I cut in the inside of the
boat, where I could lay my gun, making a flap to hang down over
it to keep it dry.

I fixed my umbrella also in a step at the stern, like a mast,
to stand over my head, and keep the heat of the sun off me, like
an awning; and thus I every now and then took a little voyage

upon the sea, but never went far out, nor far from the little creek; but at last, being eager to view the circumference of my little kingdom, I resolved upon my tour, and accordingly I victualled my ship for the voyage – putting in two dozen of my loaves (cakes I should rather call them) of barley bread, an earthen pot full of parched rice (a food I ate a great deal of), a little bottom of rum, half a goat, and powder and shot for killing more, and two large watch-coats, of those which, as I mentioned before, I had saved out of the seamen's chests; these I took, one to lie upon, and the other to cover me in the night.

It was the 6th of November, in the sixth year of my reign, or my captivity, which you please, that I set out on this voyage, and I found it much longer than I expected; for though the island itself was not very large, yet when I came to the east side of it, I found a great ledge of rocks lie out about two leagues into the sea, some above water, some under it; and beyond this a shoal of sand, lying dry half a league more: so that I was obliged to go a great way out to sea to double that point.

When I first discovered them, I was going to give over my enterprise, and come back again, not knowing how far it might oblige me to go out to sea, and, above all, doubting how I should get back again; so I came to an anchor, for I had made me a kind of an anchor with a piece of broken grappling which I got out of the ship.

Having secured my boat, I took my gun, and went on shore, climbing up a hill, which seemed to overlook that point, where I saw the full extent of it, and resolved to venture.

In my viewing the sea from that hill where I stood, I perceived a strong, and indeed a most furious current, which ran to the east, and even came close to the point; and I took the more notice of it, because I saw there might be some danger, that when I came into it, I might be carried out to sea by the strength of it, and not be able to make the island again. And indeed, had I not gotten first upon this hill, I believe it would have been so; for there was the same current on the other side of the island, only that it set off at a farther distance; and I saw there was a strong eddy under the shore – so I had nothing to do but to get out of the first current, and I should presently be in an eddy.

I lay here, however, two days; because the wind blowing pretty fresh (at east-south-east, and that being just contrary to the said current), made a great breach of the sea upon the point;

so that it was not safe for me to keep too close to the shore for the breach, nor to go too far off because of the stream.

The third day, in the morning, the wind having abated overnight, the sea was calm, and I ventured: but I am a warning-piece again to all rash and ignorant pilots; for no sooner was I come to the point, when I was not my boat's length from the shore, but I found myself in a great depth of water and a current like the sluice of a mill. It carried my boat along with it, with such a violence that all I could do could not keep her so much as on the edge of it; but I found it hurried me farther and farther out from the eddy, which was on the left hand. There was no wind stirring to help me, and all that I could do with my paddles signified nothing; and now I began to give myself over for lost; for, as the current was on both sides of the island, I knew in a few leagues' distance they must join again, and then I was irrecoverably gone – nor did I see any possibility of avoiding it; so that I had no prospect before me but of perishing – not by the sea, for that was calm enough, but of starving for hunger. I had, indeed, found a tortoise on the shore, as big almost as I could lift, and had tossed it into the boat; and I had a great jar of fresh water, that is to say, one of my earthen pots; but what was all this to being driven into the vast ocean, where, to be sure, there was no shore, no mainland or island, for a thousand leagues at least?

And now I saw how easy it was for the providence of God to make the most miserable condition that mankind could be in worse. Now, I looked back upon my desolate solitary island as the most pleasant place in the world, and all the happiness my heart could wish for was to be there again; I stretched out my hands to it with eager wishes. "Oh, happy desert!" said I, "I shall never see thee more! Oh, miserable creature I" said I, "whither am I going?" Then I reproached myself with my unthankful temper, and how I had repined at my solitary condition; and now, what would I give to be on shore there again? Thus we never see the true state of our condition, till it is illustrated to us by its contraries; nor know how to value what we enjoy, but by the want of it. It is scarce possible to imagine the consternation I was in, being driven from my beloved island (for so it appeared to me now to be) into the wide ocean, almost two leagues, and in the utmost despair of ever recovering it again: however, I worked hard, till indeed my strength was almost exhausted, and kept my boat as much to the northward, that is, towards the side of the current which the eddy lay on, as possibly I could; when about noon, as the sun passed the meridian, I thought I felt a little breeze of wind in my face, springing up from the south-south-east. This cheered my heart a little, and especially when, in about half an hour more, it blew a pretty small gentle gale. By this time I was gotten at a frightful distance from the island; and, had the least cloud or hazy weather intervened, I had been undone another way too; for I had no compass on board, and should never have known how to have steered towards the island, if I had but once lost sight of it; but the weather continuing clear, I applied myself to get up my mast again, and spread my sail, standing away to the north as much as possible, to get out of the current.

Just as I had set my mast and sail, and the boat began to stretch away, I saw, even by the clearness of the water, some alteration of the current was near; for where the current was so strong, the water was foul; but perceiving the water clear, I found the current abate, and presently I found, to the east, at about half a mile, a breach of the sea upon some rocks: these rocks I found caused the current to part again, and as the main stress of it ran away more southerly, leaving the rocks to the north-east, so the other returned by the repulse of the rock, and made a strong eddy, which ran back again to the north-west with a very sharp stream.

They who know what it is to have a reprieve brought to them upon the ladder, or to be rescued from thieves just going to murder them, or who have been in such like extremities, may guess what my present surprise of joy was, and how gladly I put my boat into the stream of this eddy; and the wind also freshening, how gladly I spread my sail to it, running cheerfully before the wind, and with a strong tide or eddy under foot.

This eddy carried me about a league on my way back again directly towards the island, but about two leagues more towards the northward than the current lay, which carried me away at first; so that when I came near the island, I found myself open to the northern shore of it, that is to say, the other end of the island, opposite to that which I went out from.

When I had made something more than a league of way, by the help of this heavy current or eddy, I found it was spent, and served me no farther. However, I found that being between the two great currents, namely, that on the south side which had carried me away, and that on the north, which lay about two leagues on the other side – I say, between these two, in the west of the island, I found the water at least still, and running no way; and having still a breeze of wind fair for me, I kept on steering directly for the island, though not making such fresh way as I did before.

After four o'clock in the evening, being then within about a league of the island, I found the point of the rocks which occasioned this distance stretching out, as is described before, to the southward, and, casting off the current more southwardly, had, of course, made another eddy to the north; and this I found very strong, but not directly setting the way my course lay, which was due west, but almost full north. However, having a fresh gale, I stretched across this eddy, slanting north-west, and, in about an hour, came within about a mile of the shore, where, it being smooth water, I soon got to land.

When I was on shore, I fell on my knees, and gave God thanks for my deliverance, resolving to lay aside all thoughts of my deliverance by my boat; and, refreshing myself with such things as I had, I brought my boat close to the shore, in a little cove that I had espied under some trees, and laid me down to sleep, being quite spent with the labour and fatigue of the voyage.

I was now at a great loss which way to *get* home with my boat; I had run so much hazard, and knew too much the cause, to think of attempting it by the way I went out; and what might be at the other side (I mean the west side), I knew not, nor had I any mind to run any more ventures; so I only resolved in the morning to make my way westward along the shore, and to see if there was no creek where I might lay up my frigate in safety, so as to have her again if I wanted her. In about three miles, or thereabouts, coasting the shore, I came to a very good inlet, or bay, about a mile over, which narrowed till it came to a very little rivulet, or brook, where I found a convenient harbour for my boat, and where she lay as if she had been in a little dock made on purpose for her; here I put in, and having stowed my boat very safe, I went on shore to look about me, and see where I was.

I soon found I had but a little passed by the place where I had been before when I travelled on foot to that shore; so, taking nothing out of my boat but my gun and my umbrella, for it was exceedingly hot, I began my march. The way was comfortable enough, after such a voyage as I had been upon, and I reached my old bower in the evening, where I found everything standing as I left it; for I always kept it in good order, being, as I said before, my country-house.

I got over the fence, and laid me down in the shade to rest my limbs, for I was very weary, and fell asleep; but judge if you can, you that read my story, what a surprise I must be in, when I was awaked out of my sleep by a voice calling me by my name several times, "Robin, Robin, Robin Crusoe, poor Robin Crusoe! Where are you, Robin Crusoe? Where are you? Where have you been?"

I was dead asleep at first, being fatigued with rowing, or paddling, as it is called, the first part of the day, and walking the latter part, that I did not awake thoroughly, and dozing between sleeping and waking, thought I dreamed that somebody spoke to me; but as the voice continued to repeat "Robin Crusoe, Robin Crusoe!" at last I began to awake more perfectly, and was at first dreadfully frightened, and started up in the utmost consternation: but no sooner were my eyes open, but I saw my Poll sitting on the top of the hedge, and immediately knew that this was he that spoke to me; for just in such bemoaning language I had used to talk to him, and teach him; and he had learned it so perfectly, that he would sit upon my finger and lay his bill close to my face, and cry, "Poor Robin Crusoe, where are you? Where have you been? How came you here?" and such things as I taught him.

However, even though I knew it was the parrot, and that indeed it could be nobody else, it was a good while before I could compose myself. First, I was amazed how the creature got thither, and then how he should just keep about the place, and nowhere else; but as I was well satisfied it could be nobody but honest Poll, I got it over; and, holding out my hand, and calling him by his name, "Poll!" the sociable creature came to me, and sat upon my thumb, as he used to do, and continued talking to me – "Poor Robin Crusoe!" and "How did I come here?" and "Where had I been?" just as if he had been overjoyed to see me again; and so I carried him home along with me.

I had now had enough of rambling to sea for some time, and had enough to do for many days to sit still and reflect upon the danger I had been in. I would have been very glad to have had my boat again on my side of the island, but I knew not how it was practicable to get it about: as to the east side of the island, which I had gone round, I knew well enough there was no venturing that way; my very heart would shrink, and my very blood run chill, but to think of it: and as to the other side of the island, I did not know how it might be there; but supposing the current ran with the same force against the shore at the east, as it passed by it on the other, I might run the same risk of being driven down the stream, and carried by the island, as I had been before of being carried away from it. So with these thoughts I contented myself to be without any boat, though it had been the product of so many months' labour to make it, and of so many more to get it into the sea.

In this government of my temper, I remained near a year – lived a very sedate, retired life, as you may well suppose; and my thoughts being very much composed as to my condition, and fully comforted in resigning myself to the dispositions of Providence, I thought I lived really very happily in all things, except that of society.

I improved myself in this time in all the mechanic exercises which my necessities put me upon applying myself to; and I believe could, upon occasion, have made a very good carpenter, especially considering how few tools I had.

Besides this, I arrived at an unexpected perfection in my earthenware, and contrived well enough to make them with a wheel, which I found infinitely easier and better; because I made things round and shapeable, which before were filthy things indeed to look on. But I think I never was more vain of my own performance, or more joyful for anything I found out, than for my being able to make a tobacco-pipe; and though it was a very ugly clumsy thing when it was done, and only burnt red like other earthenware, yet as it was hard and firm, and would draw the smoke, I was exceedingly comforted with it – for I had been always used to smoke, and there were pipes in the ship, but I forgot them at first, not knowing there was tobacco in the island; and afterwards, when I searched the ship again, I could not come at any pipes at all.

In my wicker-ware I also improved much, and made abundance of necessary baskets, as well as my invention showed me, though not very handsome, yet convenient for my laying things up in, or fetching things home in. For example, if I killed a goat abroad, I could hang it up in a tree, flay it, and dress it, and cut it in pieces, and bring it home in a basket: and the like by a turtle, I could cut it up, take out the eggs, and a piece or two of the flesh, which was enough for me, and bring them home in a basket, and leave the rest behind me. Also large deep baskets were my receivers for my corn, which I always rubbed out as soon as it was dry, and cured, and kept it in great baskets instead of a granary.

I began now to perceive my powder abated considerably; and this was a want which it was impossible for me to supply, and I began seriously to consider what I must do when I should have no more powder – that is to say, how I should do to kill any goats. I had, as I observed, in the third year of my being here, kept a young kid, and bred her tame; I was in hopes of getting a he-kid, but I could not by any means bring it to pass, till my kid grew an old goat; and I could never find in my heart to kill her, till she died at last of mere age.

But being now in the eleventh year of my residence, and, as I have said, my ammunition growing low, I set myself to study some art to trap and snare the goats, to see whether I could not catch some of them alive; and, particularly, I wished to possess a she-goat great with young.

To this purpose I made snares to hamper them, and believe they were more than once taken in them; but my tackle was not good, for I had no wire, and always found them broken, and my bait devoured.

At length, I resolved to try a pitfall; so I dug several large pits in the earth, in places where I had observed the goats used to feed, and over these pits I placed hurdles, of my own making too, with a great weight upon them, and several times I put ears of barley, and dry rice, without setting the trap; and I could easily perceive that the goats had gone in, and eaten up the corn, for I could see the marks of their feet; at length, I set three traps in one night, and going the next morning, I found them all standing, and yet the bait eaten and gone. This was very discouraging; however, I altered my trap; and, not to trouble you with particulars, going one morning to see my traps, I found in one of them a large old he-goat, and in one of the other, three kids, a male, and two females.

As to the old one, I knew not what to do with him; he was so fierce, I durst not go into the pit to him – that is to say, to go about to bring him away alive, which was what I wanted. I could have killed him, but that was not my business, nor would it answer my end; so I even let him out, and he ran away as if he had been frightened out of his wits; but I did not then know what I afterwards learned, that hunger would tame a lion: if I had let him stay there three or four days without food, and then have carried him some water to drink, and then a little corn, he would have been as tame as one of the kids; for they are mighty sagacious and tractable creatures, where they are well used.

However, for the present I let him go, knowing no better at that time: then I went to the three kids; and, taking them one by one, I tied them with strings together, and with considerable difficulty brought them all home.

It was a good while before they would feed; but throwing them some sweet corn, it tempted them, and they began to be tame: and now I found that if I expected to supply myself with goat's flesh, when I had no powder or shot left, breeding up some tame was my only way, when, perhaps, I might have them about my house like a flock of sheep.

But then it presently occurred to me that I must keep the tame from the wild, or else they would always run wild when they grew up; and the only way for this was to have some enclosed piece of ground, well fenced, either with hedge or pale, to keep them in so effectually that those within might not break out, or those without break in.

This was a great undertaking for one pair of hands; yet as I saw there was an absolute necessity for doing it, my first piece of work was to find out a proper piece of ground, namely, where there was likely to be herbage for them to eat, water for them to drink, and cover to keep them from the sun.

Those who understand such enclosures will think I had very little contrivance when I pitched upon a place very proper for all these (being a plain open piece of meadowland, or savanna, as our people call it in the western colonies), which had two or three little drills of fresh water in it; and at one end was very woody – I say, they will smile at my forecast, when I shall tell them I began by enclosing of this piece of ground in such a manner that my hedge or pale must have been at least two miles about: nor was the madness of it so great as to the compass; for if it was ten miles about, I was like to have time enough to do it in; but I did not consider, that my goats would be as wild in so much compass as if they had had the whole island; and I should have so much room to chase them in that I should never catch them.

My hedge was begun and carried on, I believe, about fifty yards when this thought occurred to me; so I presently stopped short, and for the first beginning I resolved to enclose a piece of about one hundred and fifty yards in length, and a hundred yards in breadth, which, as it would maintain as many as I should have in any reasonable time, so, as my flock increased, I could add more ground to my enclosure.

This was acting with some prudence, and I went to work with courage. I was about three months hedging in the first piece; and till I had done it, I tethered the three kids in the best part of it, and used them to feed as near me as possible, to make them familiar; and very often I would go and carry them some ears of barley, or a handful of rice, and feed them out of my hand; so that after my enclosure was finished, and I let them loose, they would follow me up and down, bleating after me for a handful of corn.

This answered my end, and in about a year and a half I had a flock of about twelve goats, kids and all; and in two years more I had three-and-forty, besides several that I took and killed for my food; and after that I enclosed five several pieces of ground to feed them in, with little pens to drive them into, to take them as I wanted them, and gates out of one piece of ground into another.

But this was not all, for now I not only had got goat's flesh to feed on when I pleased, but milk too, a thing which indeed in my beginning I did not so much as think of, and which, when it came into my thoughts, was really an agreeable surprise; for now I set up my dairy, and had sometimes a gallon or two of milk in a day. And as nature, who gives supplies of food to every creature, dictates even naturally how to make use of it, so I, that never milked a cow, much less a goat, or saw butter or cheese made, very readily and handily, though after a great many essays and miscarriages, made me both butter and cheese, at last, and never wanted it afterwards.

How mercifully can our great Creator treat His creatures, even in those conditions in which they seem to be overwhelmed in destruction! How can He sweeten the bitterest providences, and give us cause to praise Him for dungeons and prisons! What a table was here spread for me, in a wilderness where I saw nothing at first but to perish for hunger!

It would have made a stoic smile, to have seen me and my little family sit down to dinner: there was my majesty, the prince and lord of the whole island; I had the lives of all my subjects at absolute command; I could hang, draw, give life and liberty, and take it away, and no rebels among all my subjects.

Then to see how like a king I dined too, all alone, attended by my servants. Poll, as if he had been my favourite, was the only person permitted to talk to me; my dog, which was now grown very old and crazy, and found no species to multiply his kind upon, sat always at my right hand; and two cats, one on one side of the table, and one on the other, expecting now and then a bit from my hand, as a mark of special favour.

But these were not the two cats which I brought on shore at first; for they were both of them dead, and had been interred near my habitation with my own hands; but one of them having multiplied by I know not what kind of creature, these were two which I preserved tame, whereas the rest ran wild into the woods, and became, indeed, troublesome to me at last; for they would often come into my house, and plunder me too, till at last I was obliged to shoot them, and did kill a great many: at length they left me. With this attendance, and in this plentiful manner I lived; neither could I be said to want anything but society, and of that, in some time after this, I was like to have too much.

CHAPTER 11

Description of my Dwelling and Enclosures
– Dreadful alarm on seeing Footprints on
the Shore – Take every precaution

I was somewhat impatient, as I had observed, to have the use of
my boat, though very loath to run any more hazard; and therefore sometimes I sat contriving ways to get her about the island,
and at other times I sat myself down contented enough without
her. But I had a strange uneasiness in my mind to go down to
the point of the island, where, as I have said in my last ramble,
I went up the hill to see how the shore lay, and how the current
set, that I might see what I had to do. This inclination increased
upon me every day, and at length I resolved to travel thither by
land, and following the edge of the shore, I did so; but had any
one in England been to meet such a man as I was, it must either
have frightened him, or raised a great deal of laughter; and as I
frequently stood still to look at myself, I could not but smile at
the notion of my travelling through Yorkshire with such an
equipage, and in such a dress. Be pleased to take a sketch of my
figure, as follows: –

I had a great high shapeless cap, made of goat's skin, with
a flap hanging down behind, as well to keep the sun from me as
to shoot the rain off from running into my neck; nothing being
so hurtful in these climates as the rain upon the flesh under the
clothes.

I had a short jacket of goat's skin, the skirts coming down
to about the middle of my thighs; and a pair of open-kneed
breeches of the same; the breeches were made of the skin of an
old he-goat, whose hair hung down such a length on either side,

that, like pantaloons, it reached to the middle of my legs. Stockings and shoes I had none; but I had made me a pair of something, I scarce knew what to call them, like buskins, to flap over my legs, and lace on either side like spatterdashes, but of a most barbarous shape, as indeed were all the rest of my clothes.

I had on a broad belt of goat's skin dried, which I drew together with two thongs of the same, instead of buckles; and in a kind of a frog on either side of this, instead of a sword and dagger, hung a little saw and a hatchet – one on one side, one on the other; I had another belt not so broad, and fastened in the same manner, which hung over my shoulder; and at the end of it, under my left arm hung two pouches, both made of goat's skin too, in one of which hung my powder, in the other my shot; at my back I carried my basket, on my shoulder my gun; and over my head a great clumsy ugly goat's skin umbrella, but which, after all, was the most necessary thing I had about me, next to my gun. As for my face, the colour of it was really not so mulatto-like as one might expect from a man not at all careful of it, and living within nine or ten degrees of the equinox. My beard I had once suffered to grow till it was about a quarter of a yard long; but as I had both scissors and razors sufficient, I had cut it pretty short, except what grew on my upper lip, which I had trimmed into a large pair of Mahometan whiskers, such as I had seen worn by some Turks whom I saw at Sallee; for the Moors did not wear such, though the Turks did: of these mustachios, or whiskers, I will not say they were long enough to hang my hat upon them; but they were of length and shape monstrous enough, and such as in England would have passed for frightful.

But all this is by the bye; for as to my figure, I had so few to observe, that it was of no manner of consequence – so I say no more to that part. In this kind of figure I went my new journey, and was out five or six days. I travelled first along the sea-shore directly to the place where I first brought my boat to an anchor, to *get* upon the rocks; and, having no boat now to take care of, I went over the land a nearer way, to the same height that I was upon before; when looking forward to the point of the rock which lay out, and which I was to double with my boat, as I said above, I was surprised to see the sea all smooth and quiet; no rippling, no motion, no current, any more than in any other places.

I was at a strange loss to understand this, and resolved to spend some time in the observing of it, to see if nothing from the sets of the tide had occasioned it: but I was presently convinced how it was; namely, that the tide of ebb setting from the west, and joining with the current of waters from some great river on the shore, must be the occasion of this current, and accordingly as the wind blew more forcibly from the west, or from the north, this current came near, or went farther from the shore; for, waiting thereabouts till evening, I went up to the rock again, and then, the tide of ebb being made, I plainly saw the current again as before, only that it ran farther off, being near half a league from the shore; whereas, in my case, it set close upon the shore, and hurried me in my canoe along with it, which at another time it would not have done.

This observation convinced me, that I had nothing to do but to observe the ebbing and the flowing of the tide, and I might very easily bring my boat about the island again: but when I began to think of putting it into practice I had such a terror upon my spirits at the remembrance of the danger I had been in, that I could not think of it again with any patience; but, on the contrary, I took up another resolution, which was more safe, though more laborious, and this was, that I would build, or rather make, me another periagua, or canoe; and so have one for one side of the island, and one for the other.

You are to understand, that now I had, as I may call it, two plantations in the island, one my little fortification, or tent, with the wall about it under the rock, with the cave behind me, which by this time I had enlarged into several apartments or caves, one within another. One of these, which was the driest and largest, and had a door out beyond my wall or fortification – that is to say, beyond where my wall joined to the rock – was all filled up with large earthen pots, of which I have given an account, and with fourteen or fifteen great baskets, which would hold five or six bushels each, where I laid up my stores of provision, especially my corn, some in the ear, cut off short from the straw, and the other rubbed out with my hands.

As for my wall, made as before with long stakes or piles, those piles grew all like trees, and were by this time grown so big, and spread so very much, that there was not the least appearance, to any one's view, of any habitation behind them.

Near this dwelling of mine, but a little farther within the land, and upon lower ground, lay my two pieces of corn ground, which I kept duly cultivated and sowed, and which duly yielded me their harvest in its season; and whenever I had occasion for more corn, I had more land adjoining, as fit as that.

Besides this, I had my country seat, and I had now a tolerable plantation there also; for first, I had my little bower, as I called it, which I kept in repair – that is to say, I kept the hedge which circled it in constantly fitted up to its usual height; the ladder standing always in the inside; I kept the trees, which at first were no more than stakes, but were now grown very firm and tall – I kept them always so cut that they might spread, and grow thick and wild, and make the more agreeable shade, which they did effectually to my mind. In the middle of this I had my tent always standing, being a piece of sail spread over poles set up for that purpose, and which never wanted any repair or renewing; and under this I had made me a squab, or couch, with the skins of the creatures I had killed, and with other soft things, and a blanket laid on them, such as belonged to our sea bedding, which I had saved, and a great watch-coat to cover me; and here, whenever I had occasion to be absent from my chief seat, I took up my country habitation.

Adjoining to this, I had my enclosures for my cattle, that is to say, my goats: and as I had taken an inconceivable deal of pains to fence and enclose this ground, I was so uneasy to see it kept entire, lest the goats should break through, that I never left off, till, with infinite labour, I had stuck the outside of the hedge so full of small stakes, and so near to one another that it was rather a pale than a hedge, and there was scarce room to put a hand through between them, which afterwards, when those stakes grew, as they all did in the next rainy season, made the enclosure strong like a wall – indeed, stronger than any wall.

This will testify for me that I was not idle, and that I spared no pains to bring to pass whatever appeared necessary for my comfortable support; for I considered the keeping up a breed of tame creatures thus at my hand, would be a living magazine of flesh, milk, butter, and cheese for me, as long as I lived in the place, if it were to be forty years; and that keeping them in my reach depended entirely upon my perfecting my enclosures to such a degree that I might be sure of keeping them together; which by this method, indeed, I so effectually secured, that, when these little stakes began to grow, I had planted them so very thick I was forced to pull some of them up again, In this place also I had my grapes growing, which I principally depended on for my winter store of raisins, and which I never failed to preserve very carefully, as the best and most agreeable dainty of my whole diet; and, indeed, they were not agreeable only, but physical, wholesome, nourishing, and refreshing to the last degree.

As this was also about half-way between my other habitation and the place where I had laid up the boat, I generally stayed and lay here on my way thither; for I used frequently to visit my boat, and I kept all things about or belonging to her in very good order. Sometimes I went out in her to divert myself; but no more hazardous voyages would I go, nor scarce ever above a stone's cast or two from the shore, I was so apprehensive of being hurried out of my knowledge again by the currents, or winds, or any other accident. But now I come to a new scene of my life.

It happened one day about noon, going towards my boat, I was exceedingly surprised with the print of a man's naked foot on the shore, which was very plain to be seen in the sand: I stood like one thunderstruck, or as if I had seen an apparition; I listened, I looked round me – I could hear nothing, nor see anything: I went up to a rising ground to look farther; I went up the shore and down the shore, but it was all one, I could see no other impression but that one; I went to it again to see if there were any more, and to observe if it might not be my fancy; but there was no room for that, for there was exactly the very print of a foot, toes, heel, and every part of a foot; how it came thither I knew not, nor could in the least imagine. But after innumerable fluttering thoughts, like a man perfectly confused, and out of myself, I came home to my fortification, not feeling, as we say, the ground I went on, but terrified to the last degree, looking behind me at every two or three steps, mistaking every bush and tree, and fancying every stump at a distance to be a man; nor is it possible to describe how many various shapes an affrighted imagination represented things to me in – how many wild ideas were formed every moment in my fancy – and what strange unaccountable whimsies came into my thoughts by the way.

When I came to my castle, for so I think I called it ever after this, I fled into it like one pursued; whether I went over by the ladder, at first contrived, or in at the hole in the rock, which I called a door, I cannot remember; for never frighted hare fled to cover, or fox to earth, with more terror of mind than I to this retreat.

I had no sleep that night: the farther I was from the

occasion of my fright, the greater my apprehensions were; which is something contrary to the nature of such things, and especially to the usual practice of all creatures in fear. But I was so embarrassed with my own frightful ideas of the thing, that I formed nothing but dismal imaginations to myself, even though I was now a great way off it. Sometimes I fancied it must be the devil; and reason joined in with me upon this supposition. For how should any other thing in human shape come into the place? Where was the vessel that brought them? What marks were there of any other footsteps? And how was it possible that a man should come there? But then to think that Satan should take human shape upon him in such a place, where there could be no manner of occasion for it but to leave the print of his foot behind him, and that even for no purpose too (for he could not be sure I should see it), this was an amazement the other way: I considered that the devil might have found out abundance of other ways to have terrified me, than this of the single print of a foot; that, as I lived quite on the other side of the island, he should never have been so simple as to leave a mark in a place where it was ten thousand to one whether I should ever see it or not, and in the sand too, which the first surge of the sea upon a high wind would have defaced entirely. All this seemed inconsistent with the thing itself, and with all notions we usually entertain of the subtlety of the devil.

Abundance of such things as these assisted to argue me out of all apprehensions of its being the devil; and I presently concluded that it must be some more dangerous creature – namely, that it must be some of the savages of the mainland over against me, who had wandered out to sea in their canoes, and, either driven by the currents, or by contrary winds, had made the island, and had been on shore, but were gone away again to sea, being as loath, perhaps, to have stayed in this desolate island, as I would have been to have had them.

While these reflections were rolling upon my mind, I was very thankful in my thought, that I was so happy as not to be thereabouts, at that time, or that they did not see my boat, by which they would have concluded that some inhabitants had been in the place, and perhaps have searched farther for me. Then terrible thoughts racked my imagination, about their having found my boat, and that there were people here; and that if so, I should certainly have them come again in greater numbers, and devour me: that if it should happen so that they should not find me, yet they would find my enclosure, destroy all my corn, carry away all my flock of tame goats, and I should perish at last for mere want.

Thus my fear banished all my religious hope; all that former confidence in God, which was founded upon such wonderful experience as I had had of His goodness, now vanished; as if He that had fed me by a miracle hitherto, could not preserve by His power the provision which He had made for me by His goodness. I reproached myself with my laziness, that I would not sow any more corn one year than would just serve me till the next season, as if no accident could intervene to prevent my enjoying the crop that was upon the ground. And this I thought so just a reproof, that I resolved for the future to have two or three years' corn beforehand, so that, whatever might come, I might not perish for want of bread.

How strange a chequer-work of Providence is the life of man! And by what secret differing springs are the affections hurried about, as differing circumstances present! To-day we love what to-morrow we hate – to-day we seek what to-morrow we shun – to-day we desire what to-morrow we fear, nay, even tremble at the apprehensions of. This was exemplified in me at this time in the most lively manner imaginable; for I, whose only affliction was, that I seemed banished from human society, that I was alone, circumscribed by the boundless ocean, cut off from mankind, and condemned to what I called a silent life; that I was as one whom Heaven thought not worthy to be numbered among the living, or to appear among the rest of his creatures; that to have seen one of my own species would have seemed to me a raising me from death to life, and the greatest blessing that Heaven itself, next to the supreme blessing of salvation, could bestow – I say, that I should now tremble at the very apprehensions of seeing a man, and was ready to sink into the ground at but the shadow, or silent appearance, of a man's having set his foot on the island.

Such is the uneven state of human life, and it afforded me a great many curious speculations afterwards, when I had little recovered my first surprise: I considered that this was the station of life the infinitely wise and good providence of God had determined for me; that as I could not foresee what the ends of divine wisdom might be in all this, so I was not to dispute His sovereignty, who, as I was His creature, had an undoubted right by creation to govern and dispose of me absolutely as He thought fit; and who, as I was a creature who had offended Him, had likewise a judicial right to condemn me to what punishment He thought fit; and that it was my part to submit to bear His indignation, because I had sinned against Him.

I then reflected, that God, who was not only righteous but omnipotent, as He had thought fit thus to punish and afflict me, so He was able to deliver me; that if He did not think fit to do it it was my unquestioned duty to resign myself absolutely and entirely to His will; and, on the other hand, it was my duty also to hope in Him, pray to Him, and quietly to attend the dictates and directions of His daily providence.

These thoughts took me up many hours, days-nay, I may say, weeks and months; and one particular effect of my cogitations on this occasion I cannot omit; namely, one morning early, lying in my bed, and filled with thoughts about my danger from the appearance of savages, I found it discomposed me very much; upon which these words of the Scripture came into my thoughts, "Call upon me in the day of trouble, and I will deliver thee, and thou shalt glorify me."

Upon this, rising cheerfully out of my bed, my heart was not only comforted, but I was guided and encouraged to pray earnestly to God for deliverance. When I had done praying, I took up my Bible, and opening it to read, the first words that presented to me were, "Wait on the Lord, and be of good cheer, and he shall strengthen thy heart: wait, I say, on the Lord." It is impossible to express the comfort this gave me; and in return, I thankfully laid down the book, and was no more sad, at least on that occasion.

In the midst of these cogitations, apprehensions, and reflections, it came into my thoughts one day that all this might be a mere chimera of my own, that this foot might be the print of my own foot, when I came on shore from my boat. This cheered me up a little too, and I began to persuade myself it was all a delusion – that it was nothing else but my own foot; and why might I not come that way from my boat, as well as I was going that way to the boat. Again, I considered also, that I could by no means tell for certain where I had trod, and where I had not; and that if at last this was only the print of my own foot, I had played the part of those fools who strive to make stories of spectres and apparitions, and then are themselves frighted at them more than anybody else.

Now I began to take courage, and to peep abroad again – for I had not stirred out of my castle for three days and nights, so that I began to starve for provision; for I had little or nothing within doors, but some barley-cakes and water. Then I knew that my goats wanted to be milked too, which usually was my evening diversion – and the poor creatures were in great pain and inconvenience for want of it; and, indeed, it almost spoiled some of them, and almost dried up their milk.

Heartening myself, therefore, with the belief that this was nothing but the print of one of my own feet (and so I might be truly said to start at my own shadow), I began to go abroad again, and went to my country-house to milk my flock; but to see with what fear I went forward, how often I looked behind me, how I was ready, every now and then, to lay down my basket, and run for my life, it would have made any one have thought I was haunted with an evil conscience, or that I had been lately most terribly frighted; and so indeed I had.

However, as I went down thus two or three days, and having seen nothing, I began to be a little bolder, and to think there was really nothing in it but my own imagination; but I could not persuade myself fully of this, till I should go down to the shore again and see this print of a foot, and measure it by my own, and see if there was any similitude or fitness, that I might be assured it was my own foot. But when I came to the place first, it appeared evidently to me, that when I laid up my boat, I could not possibly be ashore anywhere thereabouts. Secondly, when I came to measure the mark with my own foot, I found my foot not so large by a great deal. Both these things filled my head with new imaginations, and gave me the vapours again to the highest degree; so that I shook with cold like one in an ague, and I went home again, filled with the belief that some man or men had been on shore there; or, in short, that the island was inhabited, and I might be surprised before I was aware; and what course to take for my security I knew not.

Oh, what ridiculous resolutions men take when possessed with fear! It deprives them of the use of those means which reason offers for their relief. The first thing I proposed to myself was, to throw down my enclosures, and turn all my tame cattle wild into the woods, that the enemy might not find them, and then frequent the island in prospect of the same, or the like booty; then to the simple thing of digging up my two corn fields, that they might not find such a grain there, and still be prompted to frequent the island; then to demolish my bower and tent, that they might not see any vestiges of my habitation, and be prompted to look farther, in order to find out the persons inhabiting.

These were the subjects of the first night's cogitation after I was come home again, while the apprehensions which had so overrun my mind were fresh upon me, and my head was full of vapours, as above. Thus, fear of danger is ten thousand times more terrifying than danger itself, when apparent to the eyes; and we find the burden of anxiety greater by much than the evil which we are anxious about: but, which was worse than all this, I had not that relief in this trouble, from the resignation I used to practise, that I hoped to have. I looked, I thought, like Saul, who complained, not only that the Philistines were upon him, but that God had forsaken him; for I did not now take due ways to compose my mind, by crying to God in my distress, and resting upon His providence, as I had done before, for my defence and deliverance; which, if I had done, I had at least been more cheer-fully supported under this new surprise, and perhaps carried through it with more resolution.

This confusion of my thoughts kept me waking all night; but in the morning I fell asleep, and having, by the amusement of my mind, been, as it were, tired and my spirits exhausted, I slept very soundly, and awaked much better composed than I had ever been before. And now I began to think sedately; and, upon the utmost debate with myself, I concluded, that this island which was so exceeding pleasant, fruitful, and no farther from the main-land than as I had seen was not so entirely abandoned as I might imagine; that although there were no stated inhabitants who lived on me spot, yet that there might sometimes come boats off from the shore, who, either with design, or perhaps never but when they were driven by cross winds, might come to this place: that I had lived here fifteen years now, and had not met with the least shadow or figure of any people before; and that, if at any time they should be driven here, it was probable they went away again as soon as ever they could, seeing they had never thought fit to fix there upon any occasion, to this time: that the most I could suggest any danger from, was from any such casual accidental landing of straggling people from the main, who, as it was likely, if they were driven hither, were here against their wills: so they made no stay here, but went off again with all possible speed, seldom staying one night on shore, lest they should not have the help of the tides and daylight back again; and that therefore I had nothing to do but to consider of some safe retreat, in case I should see any savages land upon the spot.

Now I began sorely to repent that I had dug my cave so large as to bring a door through again, which door, as I said, came out beyond where my fortification joined to the rock. Upon maturely considering this, therefore, I resolved to draw me a second fortification in the manner of a semicircle, at a distance from my wall, just where I had planted a double row of trees about twelve years before, of which I made mention; these trees having been planted so thick before, there wanted but a few piles to be driven between them, that they should be thicker and stronger, and my wall would soon be finished.

So that I now had a double wall, and my outer wall was thickened with pieces of timber, old cables, and everything I could think of, to make it strong: having in it seven little holes, about as big as I might put my arm out at. In the inside of this I thickened my wall to about ten feet thick, continually bringing earth out of my cave, and laying it at the foot of the wall, and walking upon it; and through the seven holes I contrived to plant the muskets, of which I took notice that I got seven on shore out of the ship: these, I say, I planted like my cannon, and fitted them into frames that held them like a carriage, that so I could fire all the seven guns in two minutes' time. This wall I was many a weary month in finishing, and yet never thought myself safe till it was done.

When this was done, I stuck all the ground without my wall, for a great way every way, as full with stakes or sticks of the osier-like wood, which I found so apt to grow, as they could well stand; insomuch, that I believe I might set in near twenty thousand of them, leaving a pretty large space between them and my wall, that I might have room to see an enemy, and they might have no shelter from the young trees, if they attempted to approach my outer wall.

Thus in two years' time I had a thick grove; and in five or six years' time I had a wood before my dwelling, grown so monstrous thick and strong, that it was, indeed, perfectly impassable; and no man, of what kind soever, would ever imagine that there was anything beyond it, much less a habitation. As for the way I proposed myself to go in and out (for I left no avenue), it was by setting two ladders; one to a part of the rock which was low, and then broke in, and left room to place another ladder upon that; so when the two ladders were taken down, no man living could come down to me without mischiefing himself; and if they had come down they were still on the outside of my outer wall.

Thus I took all the measures human prudence could suggest for my own preservation; and it will be seen at length, that they were not altogether without just reason – though I foresaw nothing at that time more than my mere fear suggested.

While this was doing, I was not altogether careless of my other affairs, for I had a great concern upon me for my little herd of goats; they were not only a present supply to me upon every other occasion, and to be sufficient for me without the expense of powder and shot, but also abated the fatigue of my hunting after the wild ones; and I was loath to lose the advantage of them, and to have them all to nurse up over again.

To this purpose, after long consideration, I could think but of two ways to preserve them: one was to find another convenient place to dig a cave under ground, and to drive them into it every night; and the other was to enclose two or three little bits of land, remote from one another, and as much concealed as I could, where I might keep about half a dozen young goats in each place, so that if any disaster happened to the flock in general, I might be able to raise them again with little trouble and time; and this, though it would require a great deal of time and labour, I thought was the most rational design.

Accordingly, I spent some time to find out the most retired parts of the island; and I pitched upon one which was as private, indeed, as my heart could wish, for it was a little damp piece of ground in the middle of the hollow and thick woods, where, as is observed, I almost lost myself once before, endeavouring to come back that way from the eastern part of the island. Here I found a clear piece of land, near three acres, so surrounded with woods that it was almost an enclosure by nature; at least, it did not want near so much labour to make it so, as the other pieces of ground I had worked so hard at.

I immediately went to work with this piece of ground, and in less than a month's time I had so fenced it round that my flock, or herd, call it which you please, which were not so wild now as at first they might be supposed to be, were well enough secured in it. So, without any further delay, I removed ten she-goats and two he-goats to this piece; and when there, I continued to perfect the fence, till I had made it as secure as the other, which, however, I did at more leisure, and it took me up the more time by a great deal.

CHAPTER 12

I observe a Canoe out at Sea – Find the
remnant of a Cannibal feast – Horror
thereon – Double arm myself – Discover a
Cave in which I form my Magazine – Fears
of the Savages begin to subside

All this labour I was at the expense of, purely from my apprehensions on the account of the print of a man's foot, which I had seen; for as yet I never saw any human creature come near the island, and I had now lived two years under these uneasinesses, which, indeed, made my life much less comfortable than it was before, as may well be imagined by any who know what it is to live in the constant snare of the fear of man: and this I must observe with grief, too, that the discomposure of my mind had too great impressions also upon the religious part of my thoughts; for the dread and terror of falling into the hands of savages and cannibals lay so upon my spirits, that I seldom found myself in a due temper for application to my Maker; at least, not with the sedate calmness and resignation of soul which I was wont to do. I rather prayed to God as under great affliction and pressure of mind, surrounded with danger, and in expectation every night of being murdered and devoured before the morning; and I must testify from my experience, that a temper of peace, thankfulness, love, and affection, is much more the proper frame for prayer than that of terror and discomposure; and that, under the dread of mischief impending, a man is no more fit for a comforting performance of the duty of praying to God, than he is for repentance on a sick bed – for these discomposures affect the mind as others do the body – and the discomposure of the mind must necessarily be as great a disability as that of the body, and much greater; praying to God being properly an act of the mind, not of the body.

But to go on, After I had thus secured one part of my little living stock, I went about the whole island searching for another private place to make such another deposit; when wandering more to the west point of the island than I had ever done yet, and looking out to sea, I thought I saw a boat upon the sea at a great distance. I had found a perspective glass or two in one of the seamen's chests which I saved out of our ship; but I had it not about me, and this was so remote, that I could not tell what to make of it, though I looked at it till my eyes were not able to look any longer – whether it was a boat or not, I did not know; but as I descended from the hill, I could see no more of it, so I gave it over; only I resolved to go no more without a perspective glass in my pocket.

When I was come down the hill to the end of the island, where indeed I had never been before, I was presently convinced that the seeing the print of a man's foot was not such a strange thing in the island as I imagined; and, but that it was a special providence that I was cast upon the side of the island where the savages never came, I should easily have known, that nothing was more frequent than for the canoes from the main, when they happened to be a little too far out to sea, to shoot over to that side of the island for harbour; likewise, as they often meet and fought in their canoes, the victors, having taken any prisoners would bring them over to this shore, where, according to their dreadful customs, being all cannibals, they would kill and eat them – of which hereafter.

When I was come down the hill to the shore, as I said above, being the south-west point of the island, I was perfectly confounded and amazed; nor is it possible for me to express the horror of my mind, at seeing the shore spread with skulls, hands, feet, and other bones of human bodies; and, particularly, I observed a place where there had been a fire made, and a circle dug in the earth, like a cock-pit, where I supposed the savage wretches had sat down to their inhuman feastings upon the bodies of their fellow-creatures.

I was so astonished at the sight of these things that I entertained no notions of any danger to myself from it for a long while; all my apprehensions were buried in the thoughts of such a pitch of inhuman, hellish brutality, and the horror of the degeneracy of human nature; which, though I had heard of often, yet I never had so near a view of before – in short, I turned away my face from the horrid spectacle; my stomach grew sick, and I was just at the point of fainting, when nature discharged the disorder from my stomach, and having vomited with an uncommon violence, I was a little relieved, but could not bear to stay in the place a moment; so I got me up the hill again with all the speed I could, and walked on towards my own habitation.

When I came a little out of that part of the island, I stood still a while as amazed; and then recovering myself, I looked up with the utmost affection of my soul, and with a flood of tears in my eyes, gave God thanks, that had cast my first lot in a part of the world where I was distinguished from such dreadful creatures as these; and that, though I had esteemed my present condition very miserable, had yet given me so many comforts in it, that I had still more to give thanks for than to complain of; and this above all, that I had, even in this miserable condition, been comforted with the knowledge of Himself, and the hope of His blessing, which was a felicity more than sufficiently equivalent to all the misery which I had suffered, or could suffer.

In this frame of thankfulness I went home to my castle, and began to be much easier now, as to the safety of my circumstances, than ever I was before – for I observed, that these wretches never came to this island in search of what they could get – perhaps not seeking, not wanting, or not expecting anything here, and having often, no doubt, been up in the covered woody part of it, without finding anything to their purpose. I knew I had been here now almost eighteen years, and never saw the least footsteps of a human creature there before; and might be here eighteen more as entirely concealed as I was now, if I did not discover myself to them, which I had no manner of occasion to do, it being my only business to keep myself entirely concealed where I was, unless I found a better sort of creatures than cannibals to make myself known to.

Yet I entertained such an abhorrence of the savage wretches that I have been speaking of, and of the wretched inhuman custom of their devouring and eating one another up, that I continued pensive and sad, and kept close within my own circle for almost two years after this; when I say my own circle, I mean by it my three plantations, namely, my castle, my country seat, which I called my bower, and my enclosure in the wood; nor did I look after this for any other use than as an enclosure for my goats; for the aversion which nature gave me to these hellish wretches was such, that I was as fearful of seeing them as of seeing the devil himself; nor did I so much as go to look after my boat in all this time, but began rather to think of making me another; for I could not think of ever making any more attempts to bring the other boat round the island to me, lest I should meet with some of those creatures at sea, in which, if I had happened to have fallen into their hands, I knew what would have been my lot.

Time, however, and the satisfaction I had that I was in no danger of being discovered by these people, began to wear off my uneasiness about them, and I began to live just in the same composed manner as before; only with this difference, that I used more caution, and kept my eyes more about me than I did before, lest I should happen to be seen by any of them; and particularly, I was more cautious of firing my gun, lest any of them on the island should happen to hear it; and it was therefore a very good providence to me that I had furnished myself with a tame breed of goats, that I had no need to hunt any more about the woods, or shoot at them; and if I did catch any more of them after this, it was by traps and snares, as I had done before – so that for two years after this, I believe I never fired my gun once off, though I never went out without it: and, which was more, as I had saved three pistols out of the ship, I always carried them out with me, or at least two of them, sticking them in my goat-skin belt; I likewise furbished up one of the great cutlasses that I had out of the ship, and made me a belt to put it in also: so that I was now a most formidable fellow to look at when I went abroad, if you add to the former description of myself, the particular of two pistols, and a great broadsword hanging at my side in a belt, but without a scabbard.

Things going on thus, as I have said, for some time, I seemed, excepting these cautions, to be reduced to my former calm sedate way of living. All these things tended to show me more and more how far my condition was from being miserable, compared to some others – nay, to many other particulars of life, which it might have pleased God to have made it my lot. It put me upon reflecting, how little repining there would be among mankind, at any condition of life, if people would rather compare their condition with those that are worse, in order to be thankful, than to be always comparing them with those which are better, to assist their murmurings and complainings.

As in my present condition there was not really many things which I wanted, so indeed I thought that the frights I had been in about these savage wretches, and the concern I had been in for my own preservation, had taken off the edge of my invention for my own conveniences, and I had dropped a good design, which I had once bent my thoughts upon, and that was, to try if I could not make some of my barley into malt, and then to try to brew myself some beer. This was really a whimsical thought, and I reproved myself often for the simplicity of it; for I presently saw there would be the want of several things necessary to the making my beer, that would be impossible for me to supply; as, first, casks to preserve it in, which was a thing that, as I have observed already, I could never compass – no, though I spent not many days, but weeks, nay, months in attempting it, but to no purpose. In the next place, I had no hops to make it keep, no yeast to make it work, no copper or kettle to make it boil; and yet, had not all these things intervened – I mean the frights and terrors I was in about the savages – I had under-taken it, and perhaps brought it to pass too; for I seldom gave anything over without accomplishing it, when I once had it in my head enough to begin it.

But my invention now ran quite another way; for night and day I could think of nothing but how I might destroy some of these monsters in their cruel, bloody entertainment, and, if possible, save the victim they should bring hither to destroy, It would take up a larger volume than this whole work is intended to be, to set down all the contrivances I hatched, or rather brooded upon in my thoughts, for the destroying these creatures, or at least frightening them, so as to prevent their coming hither any more; but all was abortive – nothing could be possible to take effect, unless I was to be there to do it myself; and what could one man do among them, when perhaps there might be twenty or thirty of them together, with their darts, or their bows and arrows, with which they could shoot as true to a mark as I could with my gun?

Sometimes I contrived to dig a hole under the place where they made their fire, and put in five or six pounds of gunpowder, which, when they kindled their fire, would consequently take fire, and blow up all that was near it; but as, in the first place, I should be very loath to waste so much powder upon them, my store now being within the quantity of a barrel, so neither could I be sure of it going off at any certain time, when it might surprise them, and at best, that it would little more than just blow the fire about their ears, and fright them, but not sufficient to make them forsake the place, so I laid it aside, and then proposed that I would place myself in ambush, in some convenient place, with my three guns all double loaded, and in the middle of their bloody ceremony, let fly at them, when I should be sure to kill or wound perhaps two or three at every shot; and then, falling in upon them with my three pistols, and my sword, I made no doubt but that, if there were twenty, I should kill them all. This fancy pleased my thoughts for some weeks, and I was so full of it that I often dreamed of it, and sometimes, that I was just going to let fly at them in my sleep.

I went so far with it in my imagination that I employed myself several days to find out proper places to put myself in ambuscade, as I said, to watch for them, and I went frequently to the place itself, which was now grown more familiar to me; and especially while my mind was thus filled with thoughts of revenge, and of a bloody putting twenty or thirty of them to the sword, as I may call it, but the horror I had at the place, and at the signals of the barbarous wretches devouring one another, abated my malice.

Well, at length I found a place in the side of the hill, where I was satisfied I might securely wait till I saw any of the boats coming, and might then, even before they would be ready to come on shore, convey myself unseen into the thickets of trees, in one of which there was a hollow large enough to conceal me entirely, and where I might sit, and observe all their bloody doings, and take my full aim at their heads, when they were so close together as that it would be next to impossible that I should miss my shot, or that I could fail wounding three or four of them at the first shot.

In this place, then, I resolved to fix my design; and accordingly, I prepared two muskets and my ordinary fowling-piece. Two muskets I loaded with a brace of slugs each, and four or five smaller bullets, about the size of pistol bullets, and the fowling-piece I loaded with near a handful of swan-shot, of the largest size; I also loaded my pistols with about four bullets each: and in this posture, well provided with ammunition for a second and third charge, I prepared myself for my expedition.

After I had thus laid the scheme of my design, and in my imagination put in practice, I continually made my tour every morning up to the top of the hill, which was from my castle, as I called it, about three miles or more, to see if I could observe any boats upon the sea, coming near the island, or standing towards it; but I began to tire of this hard duty, after I had for two or three months constantly kept my watch, but came always back without any discovery, there having not in all that time been the least appearance, not only on or near the shore, but not on the whole ocean, so far as my eyes or glasses could reach every way.

As long as I kept up my daily tour to the hill to look out, so long also I kept up the vigour of my design, and my spirits seemed to be all the while in a suitable frame for so outrageous an execution as the killing twenty or thirty naked savages for an offence, which I had not at all entered into a discussion of in my thoughts, any further than my passions were at first fired by the horror I conceived at the unnatural custom of the people of that country, who, it seems, had been suffered by Providence, in His wise disposition of the world, to have no other guide than that of their own abominable and vitiated passions; and consequently were left, and perhaps had been for some ages, to act such horrid things, and receive such dreadful customs, as nothing but nature, entirely abandoned of Heaven, and actuated by some hellish degeneracy, could have run them into; but now, when, as I have said, I began to be weary of the fruitless excursion which I had made so long and so far every morning, in vain, so my opinion of the action itself began to alter, and I began, with cooler and calmer thoughts, to consider what it was I was going to engage in – what authority or call I had to pretend to be judge and executioner upon these men as criminals, whom Heaven had thought fit for so many ages to suffer unpunished to go on, and to be, as it were, the executioners of His judgments upon one another; also, how far these people were offenders against me, and what right I had to engage in the quarrel of that blood which they shed promiscuously one upon another. I debated this very often with myself thus; – How do I know what God Himself judges in this particular case? It is certain these people do not commit this as a crime; it is not against their own consciences reproving, or their light reproaching them. They do not know it to be an offence, and then commit it in defiance of divine justice, as we do in almost all the sins we commit. They think it no more a crime to kill a captive taken in war than we do to kill an ox, nor to eat human flesh than we do to eat mutton.

When I had considered this a little, it followed necessarily that I was certainly in the wrong in it – that these people were not murderers in the sense that I had before condemned them in my thoughts, any more than those Christians were murderers, who often put to death the prisoners taken in battle; or more frequently, upon many occasions, put whole troops of men to the sword, without giving quarter, though they threw down their arms and submitted.

In the next place, it occurred to me, that albeit the usage they gave one another was thus brutish and inhuman, yet it was really nothing to me: these people had done me no injury – that if they attempted me, or I saw it necessary, for my immediate preservation, to fall upon them, something might be said for it; but that I was yet out of their power, and they had really no knowledge of me, and consequently no design upon me, and, therefore, it could not be just for me to fall upon them – that this would justify the conduct of the Spaniards in all their barbarities practised in America, where they destroyed millions of these people, who, however they were idolaters and barbarians, and had several bloody and barbarous rites in their customs – such as sacrificing human bodies to their idols – were yet, as to the Spaniards, very innocent people; and that the rooting them out of the country is spoken of with the utmost abhorrence and detestation, even by the Spaniards themselves, at this time, and by all other Christian nations of Europe, as a mere butchery, a bloody and unnatural piece of cruelty, unjustifiable either to God or man, and such, as for which the very name of a Spaniard is reckoned to be frightful and terrible to all people of humanity, or of Christian compassion: as if the kingdom of Spain were particularly eminent for the product of a race of men who were without principles of tenderness, or the common bowels of pity to the miserable, which is reckoned to be a mark of a generous temper in the mind.

These considerations really put me to a pause, and to a kind of a full stop; and I began by little and little to be off my design, and to conclude I had taken a wrong measure in my resolutions to attack the savages – that it was not my business to meddle with them, unless they first attacked me, and this it was my business, if possible, to prevent; but that, if I were discovered and attacked, then I knew my duty.

On the other hand, I argued with myself, that this really was not the way to deliver myself, but entirely to ruin and destroy myself; for unless I was sure to kill every one that not only should be on shore at that time, but that should ever come on shore afterwards – if but one of them escaped to tell their country people what had happened, they would come over again by thousands to revenge the death of their fellows: and I should only bring upon myself a certain destruction, which at present I had no manner of occasion for.

Upon the whole, I concluded, that neither in principles, nor in policy, I ought one way or other to concern myself in this affair – that my business was, by all possible means, to conceal myself from them, and not to leave the least signal to them to guess by that there were any living creatures upon the island, I mean of human shape.

Religion joined in with this prudential resolution, and I was convinced now many ways that I was perfectly out of my duty, when I was laying all my bloody schemes for the destruction of innocent creatures – I mean, innocent as to me: as to the crimes they were guilty of towards one another, I had nothing to do with them; they were national punishments to make a just retribution for national offences, and to bring public judgments upon those who offended in a public manner, by such ways as best please God.

This appeared so clear to me now, that nothing was a greater satisfaction to me, than that I had not been suffered to do a thing which I now saw so much reason to believe would have been no less a sin than that of wilful murder, if I had committed it; and I gave most humble thanks on my knees to God, that had thus delivered me from blood-guiltiness, beseeching Him to grant me the protection of His providence, that I might not fall into the hands of barbarians, or that I might not lay my hands upon them, unless I had a more clear call from Heaven to do it, in defence of my own life.

In this disposition I continued for near a year after this: and so far was I from desiring an occasion for falling upon these wretches, that in all that time I never once went up the hill to see whether there were any of them in sight, or to know whether any of them had been on shore there or not, that I might not be tempted to renew any of my contrivances against them, or be provoked, by any advantage which might present itself, to fall upon them; only this I did – I went and removed my boat, which I had on the other side of the island, and carried it down to the east end of the whole island, where I ran it into a little cove which I found under some high rocks, and where I knew, by reason of the currents, the savages durst not, at least would not, come with their boats, upon any account whatsoever.

With my boat I carried away everything that I had left there belonging to her, though not necessary for the bare going thither – namely, a mast and sail, which I had made for her, and a thing like an anchor, but, indeed, which could not be called either anchor or grappling – however, it was the best I could make of its kind. All these I removed, that there might not be the least shadow of any discovery, or any appearance of any boat, or of any habitation upon the island.

Besides this, I kept myself, as I said, more retired than ever, and seldom went from my cell, other than upon my constant employment – namely, to milk my she-goats, and manage my little flock in the wood, which, as it was quite on the other part of the island, was quite out of danger; for certain it is, that these savage people, who sometimes haunted this island, never came with any thoughts of finding anything here, and consequently never wandered from the coast; and I doubt not but they might have been several times on shore, after my apprehensions of them had made me cautious, as well as before; and, indeed, I looked back with some horror upon the thoughts of what my condition would have been, if I had chopped upon them, and been discovered before that, when naked and unarmed, except with one gun, and that loaded often only with small shot. I walked everywhere, peeping and peering about the island, to see what I could get – what a surprise I should have been in, if, when I discovered the print of a man's foot, I had instead of that seen fifteen or twenty savages, and found them pursuing me, and, by the swiftness of their running, no possibility of my escaping them.

The thoughts of this sometimes sunk my very soul within me, and distressed my mind so much that I could not soon recover it; to think what I should have done, and how I not only should not have been able to resist them, but even should not have had presence of mind enough to do what I might have done, much less what now, after so much consideration and preparation, I might be able to do. Indeed, after serious thinking of these things, I would be very melancholy, and sometimes it would last a great while; but I resolved it at last all into thankfulness to that Providence which had delivered me from so many unseen dangers, and had kept me from those mischiefs which I could no way have been the agent in delivering myself from; because I had not the least notion of any such thing depending, or the least supposition of its being possible.

This renewed a contemplation, which often had come to my thoughts in former time, when first I began to see the merciful dispositions of Heaven, in the dangers we run through in this life, how wonderfully we are delivered when we know nothing of it – how, when we were in a quandary (as we call it), a doubt or hesitation whether to go this way or that way, a secret hint shall direct us this way, when we intend to go another way – nay, when sense, our own inclination, and perhaps business, has called to go the other way, yet a strange impression upon the mind, from we know not what springs, and by we know not what power, shall overrule us to go this way: and it shall afterwards appear, that had we gone that way which we would have gone, and even to our imagination ought to have gone, we should have been ruined and lost. Upon these, and many like reflections, I afterwards made it a certain rule with me, that whenever I found those secret hints, or pressings of my mind, to doing or not doing anything that presented, or to going this way or that way, I never failed to obey the secret dictate; though I knew no other reason for it, than that such a pressure or such a hint hung upon my mind. I could give many examples of the success of this conduct in the course of my life, but more especially in the latter part of my inhabiting this unhappy island; besides many occasions which it is very likely I might have taken notice of, if I had seen with the same eyes then that I saw with now. But it is never too late to be wise; and I cannot but advise all considering men, whose lives are attended with such extraordinary incidents as mine, or even though not so extraordinary, not to slight such secret intimations of Providence, let them come from what invisible intelligence they will – that I shall not discuss, and perhaps cannot account for; but certainly they are a proof of the converse of spirits, and the secret communication between those embodied and those unembodied – and such a proof as can never be withstood – of which I shall have occasion to give some very remarkable instances, in the remainder of my solitary residence in this dismal place.

I believe the reader of this will not think it strange, if I confess that these anxieties, these constant dangers I lived in, and the concern that was now upon me, put an end to all invention, and to all the contrivances that I had laid for my future accommodations and conveniences. I had the care of my safety more now upon my hands than that of my food. I cared not to drive a nail, or chop a stick of wood now, for fear the noise I should make should be heard – much less would I fire a gun, for the same reason – and, above all, I was very uneasy at making any fire, lest the smoke, which is visible at a great distance in the day, should betray me; and, for this reason, I removed that part of my business which required fire, such as burning of pots and pipes, etc., into my new apartment in the wood; where, after I had been some time, I found, to my unspeakable consolation, a mere natural cave in the earth which went in a vast way, and where, I dare say, no savage, had he been at the mouth of it, would be so hardy as to venture in, nor indeed would any man else, but one who, like me, wanted nothing so much as a safe retreat.

The mouth of this hollow was at the bottom of a great rock, where, by mere accident (I would say, if I did not see an abundant reason to ascribe all such things now to Providence), I was cutting down some thick branches of trees to make charcoal; and before I go on, I must observe the reason of my making this charcoal, which was thus: –

I was afraid of making a smoke about my habitation, as I said before; and yet I could not live there without baking my bread, cooking my meat, etc.; so I contrived to burn some wood here, as I had seen done in England, under turf, till it became chark, or dry coal; and then putting the fire out, I preserved the coal to carry home, and perform the other services which fire was wanting for at home, without danger or smoke.

But this by the by. While I was cutting down some wood here, I perceived that behind a very thick branch of low brushwood or underwood, there was a kind of hollow place; I was curious to look into it, and getting with difficulty into the mouth of it, I found it was pretty large, that is to say, sufficient for me to stand upright in it, and perhaps another with me; but I must confess to you I made more haste out than I did in, when, looking farther into the place, which was perfectly dark, I saw two broad shining eyes of some creature, whether devil or man I knew not, which twinkled like two stars, the dim light from the cave's mouth shining directly in and making the reflection.

However, after some pause, I recovered myself, and began to call myself a thousand fools, and tell myself, that he that was afraid to see the devil was not fit to live twenty years in an island all alone, and that I durst to believe there was nothing in this cave that was more frightful than myself. Upon this, plucking up my courage, I took up a large firebrand, and in I rushed again, with the stick flaming in my hand; I had not gone three steps in, but I was almost as much frightened as I was before, for I heard a very loud sigh, like that of a man in some pain, and it was followed by a broken noise, as if of words half expressed and then a deep sigh again. I stepped back, and was indeed struck with such a surprise that it put me into a cold sweat; and if I had had a hat on my head, I will not answer for it that my hair might not have lifted it off. But still plucking up my spirits as well as I could, and encouraging myself a little with considering that the power and presence of God was everywhere, and was able to protect me; upon this I stepped forward again, and by the light of the firebrand, holding it up a little over my head, I saw lying on the ground a most monstrous frightful old he-goat, just making his will, as we say, gasping for life, and dying, indeed, of mere old age.

I stirred him a little, to see if I could *get* him out, and he essayed to get up, but was not able to raise himself; and I thought with myself, he might even lie there, for if he had frightened me so, he would certainly fright any of the savages if any of them should be so hardy as to come in there, while he had any life in him.

I was now recovered from my surprise, and began to look round me, when I found the cave was but very small; that is to say, it might be about twelve feet over, but in no manner of shape, either round or square, no hands having ever been employed in making it but those of mere nature; I observed also, that there was a place at the farther side of it that went in farther, but so low that it required me to creep upon my hands and knees to get into it, and whither it went I knew not: so, having no candle, I gave it over for some time, but resolved to come again the next day, provided with candles and a tinder-box, which I had made of the lock of one of the muskets, with some wild-fire in the pan.

Accordingly, the next day I came provided with six large candles of my own making, for I made very good candles now of goats' tallow; and, going into this low place, I was obliged to creep upon all fours, as I have said, almost ten yards, which, by the way, I thought was a venture bold enough, considering that I knew not how far it might go, or what was beyond it. When I was got through the strait, I found the roof rose higher up, I believe near twenty feet; but never was such a glorious sight seen in the island, I dare say, as it was, to look round the sides and roof of this vault or cave. The walls reflected an hundred thousand lights to me from my two candles; what it was in the rock, whether diamonds or any other precious stones, or gold, which I rather supposed it to be, I knew not.

The place I was in was a most delightful cavity, or grotto, of its kind, as could be expected, though perfectly dark; the floor was dry and level, and had a sort of small loose gravel upon it, so that there was no nauseous creature to be seen; neither was there any damp or wet on the sides of the roof: the only difficulty in it was the entrance, which, however, as it was a place of security, and such a retreat as I wanted, I thought that was a convenience, so that I was really rejoiced at the discovery, and resolved, without any delay, to bring some of those things which I was most anxious about to this place; particularly, I resolved to bring hither my magazine of powder, and all my spare arms, namely, two fowling-pieces (for I had three in all), and three muskets (for of them I had eight in all); so I kept at my castle only five which stood ready mounted, like pieces of cannon, on my outmost fence, and were ready also to take out upon any expedition.

Upon this occasion of removing my ammunition, I was obliged to open the barrel of powder which I took up out of the sea, and which had been wet, and I found that the water had penetrated about three or four inches into the powder on every side, which, caking and growing hard, had preserved the inside like a kernel in a shell, so that I had nearly sixty pounds of very good powder in the centre of the cask; and this was an agreeable discovery to me at that time; so I carried all away thither, never keeping above two or three pounds of powder with me in my castle, for fear of a surprise of any kind; I also carried thither all the lead I had left for bullets.

I fancied myself now like one of the ancient giants, which were said to live in caves and holes in the rocks, where none could come at them; for I persuaded myself while I was here, if five hundred savages were to hunt me, they could never find me out; or if they did they would not venture to attack me here.

The old goat which I found expiring died in the mouth of the cave the next day after I made this discovery; and I found it much easier to dig a great hole there, and throw him in and cover him with earth, than to drag him out; so I interred him there, to prevent offence to my nose.

CHAPTER 13

My Twenty-third Year of Residence –
Discover Savages round a Fire holding a
Cannibal feast – Determine to destroy the
next Party – A Ship lost off the Island –
Board the Wreck and secure Stores

I was now in my twenty-third year of residence in this island,
and was so naturalised to the place and to the manner of living
that could I have but enjoyed the certainty that no savages would
come to the place to disturb me, I could have been content to
have capitulated for spending the rest of my time there, even to
the last moment, till I had laid me down and died, like the old
goat in the cave: I had also arrived to some little diversions and
amusements, which made the time pass more pleasantly with me
a great deal than it did before; as, first, I had taught my Poll, as
I noted before, to speak; and he did it so familiarly, and talked
so articulately and plain, that it was very pleasant to me, and he
lived with me no less than six-and-twenty years: how long he
might live afterwards I knew not, though I know they have a
notion in the Brazils that they live a hundred years; perhaps some
of my Polls may be alive there still, calling after Poor Robin Crusoe
to this day: I wish no Englishman the ill luck to come there and
hear them; but if he did, he would certainly believe it was the
devil. My dog was a very pleasant and loving companion to me
for no less than sixteen years of my time, and then died of mere
old age. As for my cats, they multiplied, as I have observed, to
that degree that I was obliged to shoot several of them at first,
to keep them from devouring me and all I had; but at length,
when the two old ones I brought with me were gone, and after

some time continually driving them from me, and letting them have no provision with me, they all ran wild into the woods, except two or three favourites, which I kept tame, and whose young, when they had any, I always drowned, and these were part of my family: besides these, I always kept two or three household kids about me, which I taught to feed out of my hand; and I had also more parrots, which talked pretty well, and would all call Robin Crusoe, but none like my first; nor, indeed, did I take the pains with any of them that I had done with him. I had also several tame sea-fowls, whose names I know not, which I caught upon the shore, and cut their wings; and the little stakes which I had planted before my castle wall being now grown up to a good thick grove, these fowls all lived among these low trees, and bred there, which was very agreeable to me; so that, as I said above, I began to be very well contented with the life I led, if it might but have been secured from the dread of savages.

But it was otherwise directed; and it might not be amiss for all people, who shall meet with my story, to make this just observation from it, namely, how frequently, in the course of our lives, the evil which in itself we seek most to shun, and which, when we are fallen into, is the most dreadful to us, is oftentimes the very means or door of our deliverance, by which alone we can be raised again from the affliction we are fallen into. I could give many examples of this in the course of my unaccountable life; but in nothing was it more particularly remarkable, than in that circumstances of my last years of solitary residence in this island.

It was now the month of December, as I said above, in my twenty-third year; and this being the southern solstice – for winter I cannot call it – was the particular time of my harvest, and required my being pretty much abroad in the fields; when, going out pretty early in the morning, even before it was thorough daylight, I was surprised with seeing a light of some fire upon the shore, at a distance from me of about two miles, towards the end of the island where I had observed some savages had been, as before; but not on the other side, but, to my great affliction, it was on my side of the island.

I was, indeed, terribly surprised at the sight, and stopped short within my grove, not daring to go out, lest I might be surprised; and yet, I had no more peace within, from the apprehensions I had, that if these savages, in rambling over the island, should find my corn standing, or cut, or any of my works and improvements, they would immediately conclude that there were people in the place, and would then never give over till they found me out. In this extremity I went back directly to my castle, pulled up the ladder after me, having made all things without look as wild and natural as I could.

Then I prepared myself within, putting myself in a posture of defence: I loaded all my cannon, as I called them – that is to say, my muskets – which were mounted upon my fortification, and all my pistols, and resolved to defend myself to the last gasp; not forgetting seriously to recommend myself to the divine protection, and earnestly to pray to God to deliver me out of the hands of the barbarians; and in this posture I continued about two hours, but began to be mighty impatient for intelligence abroad, for I had no spies to send out.

After sitting a while longer, and musing what I should do in this case, I was not able to bear sitting in ignorance longer; so, setting up my ladder to the side of the hill where there was a flat place, as I observed before, and then pulling the ladder up after me, I set it up again, and mounted to the top of the hill; and pulling out my perspective glass, which I had taken on purpose, I laid me down flat on my belly on the ground, and began to look for the place. I presently found there were no less than nine naked savages sitting round a small fire they had made; not to warm them – for they had no need of that, the weather being extremely hot – but, as I suppose, to dress some of their barbarous diet of human flesh which they had brought with them, whether live or dead I could not know.

They had two canoes with them, which they had hauled up upon the shore; and as it was then tide of ebb, they seemed to me to wait the return of the flood to go away again. It is not easy to imagine what confusion this sight put me into, especially seeing them come on my side the island and so near me too; but when I observed their coming must be always with the current of the ebb, I began afterwards to be more sedate in my mind, being satisfied that I might go abroad with safety all the time of tide of flood, if they were not on shore before; and, having made this observation, I went abroad about my harvest work with the more composure.

As I expected, so it proved; for as soon as the tide made to the westward, I saw them all take boat, and row (or paddle, as we call it) all away: I should have observed, that for an hour and more before they went off, they went to dancing, and I could easily discern their postures and gestures by my glasses: I could only perceive, by my nicest observation, that they were stark naked, and had not the least covering upon them; but whether they were men or women, that I could not distinguish.

As soon as I saw them shipped and gone, I took two guns upon my shoulders, and two pistols at my girdle, and my great sword by my side, without a scabbard; and with all the speed I was able to make, I went away to the hill, where I had discovered the first appearance of all. As soon as I got thither, which was not less than two hours (for I could not go apace, being so loaded with arms as I was), I perceived there had been three canoes more of savages on that place; and looking out farther, I saw they were all at sea together, making over for the main.

This was a dreadful sight to me, especially when, going to the shore, I could see the marks of horror which the dismal work they had been about had left behind it, namely, the blood, the bones, and part of the flesh of human bodies, eaten and devoured by those wretches with merriment and sport. I was so filled with indignation at the sight, that I began now to premeditate the destruction of the next that I saw there, let them be who or how many soever.

It seemed evident to me, that the visits which they thus made to this island were not very frequent; for it was above fifteen months before any more of them came on shore there again – that is to say, I never saw them, or any footsteps or signals of them, in all that time; for as to the rainy seasons, then they are sure not to come abroad, at least not so far; yet all this while I lived uncomfortably, by reason of constant apprehensions I was in of their coming upon me by surprise – from whence I observe, that the expectation of evil is more bitter than the suffering, especially if there is no room to shake off that expectation, or those apprehensions.

During all this time, I was in the murdering humour, and took up most of my hours, which should have been better employed, in contriving how to circumvent and fall upon them the very next time I should see them, especially if they should be divided, as they were the last time, into two parties; nor did I consider at all, that if I killed one party, suppose ten or a dozen, I was still the next day, or week, or month, to kill another, and so another, even *ad infinitum*, till I should be at length no less a murderer than they were in being men-eaters, and perhaps much more so.

I spent my days now in great perplexity and anxiety of mind, expecting that I should one day or other fall into the hands of those merciless creatures; if I did at any time venture abroad, it was not without looking round me with the greatest care and caution imaginable; and now I found to my great comfort, how happy it was that I had provided a tame flock or herd of goats; for I durst not, upon any account, fire my gun, especially near that side of the island where they usually came, lest I should alarm the savages; and if they had fled from me now, I was sure to have them come back again, with perhaps two or three hundred canoes with them in a few days, and then I knew what to expect.

However, I wore out a year and three months more before I ever saw any more of the savages, and then I found them again, as I shall soon observe. It is true, they might have been there once or twice, but either they made no stay, or at least I did not hear them; but in the month of May, as near as I could calculate, and in my four-and-twentieth year. I had a very strange encounter with them, of which in its place.

The perturbation of my mind during this fifteen or sixteen months' interval was very great; I slept unquiet, dreamed always frightful dreams, and often started out of my sleep in the night: in the day great troubles overwhelmed my mind; in the night I dreamed often of killing the savages, and the reasons why I might justify the doing of it. But to waive all this for a while: it was in the middle of May, on the sixteenth day, I think, as well as my poor wooden calendar would reckon, for I marked all upon the post still – I say, it was on the sixteenth of May that it blew a great storm of wind all day, with a great deal of lightning and thunder, and a very foul night was after it: I know not what was the particular occasion of it; but as I was reading in the Bible, and taken up with serious thoughts about my present condition, I was surprised with the noise of a gun, as I thought, fired at sea.

This was, to be sure, a surprise of a quite different nature from any I had met with before; for the notions this put into my thoughts were quite of another kind. I started up in the greatest haste imaginable; and, in a trice, clapped up my ladder to the middle place of the rock, and pulled it after me, and, mounting it the second time, got to the top of the hill; that very moment a flash of fire bade me listen for a second gun, which, accordingly, in about half a moment, I heard, and, by the sound, knew that it was from that part of the sea where I was driven out with the current in my boat.

I immediately considered that this must be some ship in distress, and that they had some comrade, or some other ship in company, and fired these guns for signals of distress, and to obtain help. I had this presence of mind that minute, as to think that though I could not help them, it might be they might help me; so I brought together all the dry wood I could get at hand, and making a good handsome pile, I set it on fire upon the hill. The wood was dry, and blazed freely, and, though the wind blew very hard, yet it burnt fairly out, so that I was certain, if there was any such thing as a ship, they must needs see it; and no doubt they did, for as soon as ever my fire blazed up, I heard another gun, and after that several others, all from the same quarter. I plied my fire all night long till day broke; and when it was broad day, and the air cleared up, I saw something at a great distance at sea, full east of the island, whether a sail or a hull I could not distinguish, no, not with my glasses, the distance was so great, and the weather still something hazy also; at least it was so out at sea.

I looked frequently at it all that day, and soon perceived that it did not move, so I presently concluded that it was a ship at anchor; and being eager, you may be sure, to be satisfied, I took my gun in my hand, and ran towards the south-east side of the island, to the rocks, where I had been formerly carried away with the current; and getting up there, the weather by this time being perfectly clear, I could plainly see to my great sorrow, the wreck of a ship cast away in the night upon those concealed rocks which I found when I was out in my boat; and which rocks, as they checked the violence of the stream, and made a counter stream, or eddy, were the occasion of my recovering then from the most desperate, hopeless condition that ever I had been in all my life.

Thus, what is one man's safety is another man's destruction; for it seems these men, whoever they were, being out of their knowledge, and the rocks being wholly under water, had been driven upon them in the night, the wind blowing hard at east and east-north-east. Had they seen the island, as I must necessarily suppose they did not, they must, as I thought, have endeavoured to have saved themselves on shore by the help of their boat; but the firing of their guns for help, especially when they saw, as

I imagined, my fire, filled me with many thoughts; first, I imagined that, upon seeing my light, they might have put themselves into their boat, and have endeavoured to make the shore, but that the sea going very high, they might have been cast away; other times I imagined, that they might have lost their boat before, as might be the case many ways; as particularly, by the breaking of the sea upon their ship, which many times obliges men to stave or take in pieces their boat, and sometimes to throw it overboard with their own hand; other times I imagined they had some other ship or ships in company, who, upon the signals of distress they had made, had taken them up and carried them off: other whiles I fancied they were all gone off to sea in their boat, and being hurried away by the current that I had been formerly in, were carried out into the great ocean, where there was nothing but misery and perishing; and that perhaps they might, by this time, be starving, and in a condition to eat one another.

All these were but conjectures at best; so, in the condition I was in, I could do no more than look upon the misery of the poor men, and pity them; which had still this good effect upon my side, that it gave me more and more cause to give thanks to God, who had so happily and comfortably provided for me in my desolate condition, and that, of two ships' companies, who were now cast away upon this part of the world, not one life should be spared but mine. I learned here again to observe, that it is very rare that the providence of God casts us into any condition of life so low, or any misery so great, but we may see something or other to be thankful for, and may see others in worse circumstances than our own.

Such certainly was the case of these men, of whom I could not so much as see room to suppose any of them were saved; nothing could make it rational so much as to wish or expect that they did not all perish there, except the possibility only of their being taken up by another ship in company – and this was but mere possibility indeed; for I saw not the least signal or appearance of any such thing.

I cannot explain, by any possible energy of words, what a strange longing, or hankering of desire, I felt in my soul upon this sight – breaking out sometimes thus: "Oh! that there had been but one or two, nay, but one soul saved out of the ship, to have escaped to me, that I might have had but one companion, one fellow-creature, to have spoken to me, and to have conversed with!"

In all the time of my solitary life I never felt so earnest, so strong a desire after the society of my fellow-creatures, or so deep a regret at the want of it.

There are some secret moving springs in the affections, which, when they are set a-going by some object in view, or be it some object though not in view, yet rendered present to the mind by the power of imagination, that motion carries out the soul by its impetuosity to such violent eager embracings of the object, that the absence of it is insupportable.

Such were these earnest wishings that but one man had been saved! Oh, that it had been but one! I believe I repeated the words, "Oh, that it had been but one!" a thousand times; and my desires were so moved by it, that when I spoke the words, my hands would clench together, and my fingers press the palms of my hands, that if I had had any soft thing in my hand, it would have crushed it involuntarily; and my teeth in my head would strike together, and set against one another so strong, that for some time I could not part them again.

Let the naturalist explain these things, and the reason and manner of them; all I can say of them is, to describe the fact, which was ever surprising to me when I found it, though I knew not from what it should proceed: it was doubtless the effect of ardent wishes, and of strong ideas formed in my mind, realising the comfort which the conversation of one of my fellow Christians would have been to me.

But it was not to be; either their fate, or mine, or both, forbade it; for till the last year of my being on this island, I never knew whether any were saved out of that ship or no; and had only the affliction, some days after, to see the corpse of a drowned boy come on shore, at the end of the island which was next the shipwreck: he had on no clothes but a seaman's waistcoat, a pair of open-kneed linen drawers, and a blue linen shirt; but nothing to direct me so much as to guess what nation he was of. He had nothing in his pocket but two pieces of eight, and a tobacco pipe: the last was to me of ten times more value than the first.

It was now calm, and I had a great mind to venture out in my boat to this wreck, not doubting but I might find something on board that might be useful to me; but that did not altogether press me so much, as the possibility that there might yet be some living creature on board, whose life I might not only save, but might, by saving that life, comfort my own to the last degree: and this thought clung so to my heart, that I could not be quiet night nor day, but I must venture out in my boat on board this wreck; and committing the rest to God's providence, I thought the impression was so strong upon my mind that it could not be resisted, that it must come from some invisible direction, and that I should be wanting to myself if I did not go.

Under the power of this impression, I hastened back to my castle, prepared everything for my voyage, took a quantity of bread, a great pot of fresh water, a compass to steer by, a bottle of rum (for I had still a great deal of that left), a basket full of raisins; and thus loading myself with everything necessary, I went down to my boat, got the water out of her, and got her afloat, loaded all my cargo in her, and then went home again for more: my second cargo was a great bagful of rice, the umbrella to set up over my head for shade, another large pot full of fresh water, and about two dozen of my small loaves, or barley cakes, more than before, with a bottle of goat's milk, and a cheese; all which, with great labour and sweat, I brought to my boat; and, praying to God to direct my voyage, I put out, and, rowing or paddling the canoe along the shore, I came at last to the utmost point of the island, on that side, namely, north-east. And now I was to launch out into the ocean, and either to venture or not to venture: I looked on the rapid currents which ran constantly on both sides of the island, at a distance, and which were very terrible to me, from the remembrance of the hazard I had been in before, and my heart began to fail me; for I foresaw, that if I was driven into either of those currents, I should be carried a vast way out to sea, and perhaps out of reach or sight of the island again; and that then, as my boat was but small, if any little gale of wind should rise, I should be inevitably lost.

These thoughts so oppressed my mind, that I began to give over my enterprise; and having hauled my boat into a little creek on the shore, I stepped out, and sat me down upon a little spot of rising ground, very pensive and anxious, between fear and desire, about my voyage; when, as I was musing, I could perceive that the tide was turned, and the flood came on, upon which my going was for so many hours impracticable; upon this, it presently occurred to me, that I should go up to the highest piece of ground I could find, and observe, if I could, how the sets of the tide or currents lay, when the flood came in, that I might judge whether, if I was driven one way out, I might not expect to be driven another way home, with the same rapidness of the currents. This thought was no sooner in my head, but I cast my eye upon a little hill which sufficiently overlooked the sea both ways, and from whence I had a clear view of the currents, or sets of the tide, and which way I was to guide myself in my return; here I found, that as the current of the ebb set out close by the south point of the island, so the current of the flood set in close by the shore of the north side; and that I had nothing to do but to keep to the north side of the island in my return, and I should do well enough.

Encouraged with this observation, I resolved the next morning to set out with the first of the tide; and, reposing myself for that night in the canoe, under the great watch-coat I mentioned, I launched out. I made first a little out to sea full north, till I began to feel the benefit of the current, which set eastward, and which carried me at a great rate, and yet did not so hurry me as the southern side current had done before, and so as to take from me all government of the boat; but, having a strong steerage with my paddle, I went, I say, at a great rate, directly for the wreck, and in less than two hours I came up to it.

It was a dismal sight to look at: the ship, which by its building was Spanish, stuck fast, jammed in between two rocks; all the stern and quarter of her was beaten to pieces with the sea: and as her forecastle, which had stuck in the rocks, had run on with great violence, her mainmast and foremast were brought by the board, that is to say, broken short off; but her bowsprit was sound, and the head and bow appeared firm. When I came close to her, a dog appeared upon her, which, seeing me coming, yelped and cried, and as soon as I called him, jumped into the sea to come to me, and I took him into the boat, but found him almost dead for hunger and thirst: I gave him a cake of my bread, and he ate it like a ravenous wolf that had been starving a fortnight in the snow; I then gave the poor creature some fresh water, with which, if I would have let him, he would have burst himself.

After this I went on board. The first sight I met with was two men drowned in the cook-room, or forecastle of the ship, with their arms fast about one another. I concluded, as is indeed probable, that when the ship struck, it being in a storm, the sea broke so high, and so continually over her, that the men were not able to bear it, and were strangled with the constant rushing in of the water, as much as if they had been under water. Besides the dog, there was nothing left in the ship that had life, nor any goods that I could see, but what was spoiled by the water: there were some casks of liquor, whether wine or brandy I knew not, which lay lower in the hold, and which, the water, being ebbed out, I could see; but they were too big to meddle with: I saw several chests, which I believed belonged to some of the seamen, and I got two of them into the boat without examining what was in them.

Had the stern of the ship been fixed, and the fore part broken off, I am persuaded I might have made a good voyage; for, by what I found in these two chests, I had room to suppose the ship had a great deal of wealth on board: and if I may guess by the course she steered, she must have been bound from Buenos Ayres, or the Rio de la Plata, in the south part of America, beyond the Brazils, to the Havanna, in the Gulf of Mexico, and so, perhaps, to Spain; she had, no doubt, a great treasure in her, but of no use at that time to anybody; and what became of the rest of her people I then knew not.

I found, besides these chests, a little cask full of liquor, of about twenty gallons, which I got into my boat with much difficulty. There were several muskets in the cabin, and a great powder-horn, with about four pounds of powder in it; as for the muskets, I had no occasion for them, so I left them, but took the powder-horn. I took a fire-shovel and tongs, which I wanted extremely, as also two little brass kettles, a copper-pot to make chocolate, and a gridiron; and with this cargo, and the dog, I came away, the tide beginning to make home again; and the same evening, about an hour within night, I reached the island again, weary and fatigued to the last degree.

I reposed that night in the boat, and in the morning I resolved to harbour what I had gotten in my new cave, not to carry it home to my castle. After refreshing myself, I got all my cargo on shore; and began to examine the particulars; the cask of liquor I found to be a kind of rum, but not such as we had at the Brazils; and, in a word, not at all good: but, when I came to open the chests, I found several things which I wanted; for example, I found in one a fine case of bottles, of an extraordinary kind, and filled with cordial waters, fine, and very good; the bottles held about three pints each, and were tipped with silver. I found two pots of very good succades or sweetmeats, so fastened also on top, that the salt water had not hurt them, and two more of the same, which the water had spoiled; I found some very good shirts, which were very welcome to me, and about a dozen and a half of white linen handkerchiefs and coloured neckcloths; the former were also very welcome, being exceedingly refreshing to wipe my face in a hot day. Besides this, when I came to the till in the chests, I found there three great bags of pieces of eight, which held about eleven hundred pieces in all; and in one of them, wrapt up in a paper, six doubloons of gold, and some small bars or wedges of gold; I suppose they might all weigh near a pound.

The other chest I found had some clothes in it, but of little value; but, by the circumstances, it must have belonged to the gunner's mate, as there was no powder in it, but about two pounds of glazed powder in the three flasks, kept, I suppose, for charging their fowling-pieces on occasion. Upon the whole, I got very little by this voyage that was of much use to me; for, as to the money, I had no manner of occasion for it – it was to me as the dirt under my feet; and I would have given it all for three or four pair of English shoes and stockings, which were things I greatly wanted, but had not had on my feet now for many years: I had, indeed, got two pair of shoes now, which I took off the feet of the two drowned men whom I saw in the wreck; and I found two pair more in one of the chests, which were very welcome to me; but they were not like our English shoes, either for ease or service, being rather what we call pumps than shoes. I found in the seaman's chest about fifty pieces of eight in royals, but no gold: I suppose this belonged to a poorer man than the other, which seemed to belong to some officer.

Well, however, I lugged the money home to my cave, and laid it up, as I had done that before which I brought from our own ship; but it was great pity, as I said, that the other part of the ship had not come to my share, for I am satisfied I might have loaded my canoe several times over with money, which, if I had ever escaped to England, would have lain here safe enough till I might have come again and fetched it.

Having now brought all my things on shore, and secured them, I went back to my boat, and rowed and paddled her along the shore to her old harbour, where I laid her up, and made the best of my way to my old habitation, where I found everything safe and quiet; so I began to repose myself, live after my old fashion, and take care of my family affairs; and for a while I lived easy enough, only that I was more vigilant than I used to be, looked out oftener, and did not go abroad so much; and if at any time I did stir with any freedom, it was always to the east part of the island, where I was pretty well satisfied the savages never came, and where I could go without so many precautions, and such a load of arms and ammunition as I always carried with me, if I went the other way.

CHAPTER 14

An Extraordinary Dream – Discover five
Canoes of Savages on Shore – Observe two
taken to be eaten – I save the life of one –
Christen him Friday, and make him my
Servant

I lived in this condition near two years more, but my unlucky
head, that was always to let me know it was born to make my
body miserable, was all these two years filled with projects and
designs how, if it were possible, I might get away from this island
– for sometimes I was for making another voyage to the wreck,
though my reason told me, that there was nothing left there worth
the hazard of my voyage – sometimes for a ramble one way, sometimes another – and I believe verily, if I had had the boat that I
went from Sallee in, I should have ventured to sea, bound
anywhere, I knew not whither.

I have been, in all my circumstances, a memento to those
who are touched with that general plague of mankind, whence,
for aught I know, one half of their miseries flow – I mean, that of
not being satisfied with the station wherein God and nature hath
placed them – for, not to look back upon my primitive condition,
and the excellent advice of my father, the opposition to which was,
as I may call it, my original sin, my subsequent mistakes of the
same kind have been the means of my coming into this miserable
condition; for had that Providence, which so happily had seated
me at the Brazils as a planter, blessed me with confined desires,
and could I have been contented to have gone on gradually, I might
have been by this time – I mean in the time of my being on this
island – one of the most considerable planters in the Brazils; nay,

I am persuaded, that by the improvements I had made in that little time I lived there, and the increase I should probably have made if I had stayed, I might have been worth a hundred thousand moidores: and what business had I to leave a settled fortune, well stocked plantation, improving and increasing, to turn supercargo to Guinea, to fetch negroes, when patience and time would have so increased our stock at home, that we could have bought them at our own doors from those whose business it was to fetch them? And though it had cost us something more, yet the difference of that price was by no means worth saving at so great a hazard.

But as this is ordinarily the fate of young heads, so reflection upon the folly of it is as ordinarily the exercise of more years, or of the dear bought experience of time – and so it was with me now; and yet, so deep had the mistake taken root in my temper, that I could not satisfy myself in my station, but was continually poring upon the means and possibility of my escape from this place; and that I may, with the greater pleasure to the reader, bring on the remaining part of my story, it may not be improper to give some account of my first conceptions on the subject of this foolish scheme for my escape; and how, and upon what foundation, I acted.

I am now to be supposed to be retired into my castle after my late voyage to the wreck, my frigate laid up, and secured under water as usual, and my condition restored to what it was before. I had more wealth, indeed, than I had before, but was not all the richer; for I had no more use of it than the Indians of Peru had before the Spaniards came thither.

It was one of the nights in the rainy season in March, the four-and-twentieth year of my first setting foot on this island of solitariness; I was lying in my bed, or hammock, awake, and very well in health – had no pain, no distemper, no uneasiness of body, no, nor any uneasiness of mind more than ordinary, but could by no means close my eyes, that is, so as to sleep; no, not a wink all night long, otherwise than as follows: –

It is impossible as needless to set down the innumerable crowd of thoughts that whirled through that great thoroughfare of the brain, the memory, In this night's time. I ran over the whole history of my life in miniature, or by abridgement, as I may call it, to my coming to this island; and also of that part of my life since I came to this island. In my reflections upon the state of my case, since I came on shore on this island, I was comparing the happy posture of my affairs, in the first years of my habitation here, to that course of anxiety, fear, and care, which I had lived in ever since I had seen the print of a foot in the sand; not that I did not believe the savages had frequented the island even all the while, and might have been several hundreds of them at times on the shore there, but as I had never known it, and was incapable of any apprehensions about it, my satisfaction was perfect, though my danger was the same; and I was as happy in not knowing my danger, as if I had never really been exposed to it. This furnished my thoughts with many very profitable reflections, and particularly this one: How infinitely good that Providence, which has settled in its government of mankind such narrow bounds to his sight and knowledge of things; and though he walks in the midst of so many thousand dangers, the sight of which, if discovered to him, would distract his mind and sink his spirits, he is kept serene and calm, by having the events of things hid from his eyes, and knowing nothing of the dangers which surround him!

After these thoughts had for some time entertained me, I came to reflect seriously upon the real danger I had been in for so many years in this very island; and how I had walked about in the greatest security, and with all possible tranquillity, even, perhaps, when nothing but a brow of a hill, a great tree, or the casual approach of night, had been between me and the worst kind of destruction – namely, that of falling into the hands of the cannibals and savages, who would have seized on me with the same view as I did on a goat or a turtle, and have thought it no more a crime to kill and devour me than I did of a pigeon or curlew. I should unjustly slander myself, if I should say I was not sincerely thankful to my great Preserver, to whose singular protection I acknowledged with great humility, that all these unknown deliverances were due, and without which I should inevitably have fallen into their merciless hands.

When these thoughts were over, my head was for some time taken up in considering the nature of those wretched creatures, I mean the savages; and how it came to pass in the world, that the wise Governor of all things should give up any of his creatures to such inhumanity – nay, to something so much below even brutality itself – as to devour its own kind: but as this ended in some (at that time fruitless) speculations, it occurred to me to inquire what part of the world these wretches lived in: how far off the coast it was from whence they came; what they ventured so far from home for; what kind of boats they had; and why I might not order myself, and my business, so that I might be as able to go over thither as they were to come to me.

I never so much as troubled myself to consider what I should do with myself when I came thither; what should become of me if I fell into the hands of the savages; or how I should escape from them if they attempted to take me; no, nor so much as how it was possible for me to reach the coast, and not be attacked by some or other of them, without any possibility of delivering myself; and if I should not fall into their hands, what I should do for provision, or whither I should bend my course: none of these thoughts, I say, so much as came in my way; but my mind was wholly bent upon the notion of my passing over in my boat to the mainland. I looked back upon my present condition as the most miserable that could possibly be; that I was not able to throw myself into anything but death that could be called worse; that if I reached the shore of the main, I might perhaps meet with relief; or I might coast along, as I did on the shore of Africa, till I came to some inhabited country, and where I might find some relief; and after all, perhaps, I might fall in with some Christian ship that might take me in; and if the worst came to the worst, I could but die; which would put an end to all these miseries at once. Pray, note, all this was the fruit of a disturbed mind – an impatient temper, made, as it were, desperate by the long continuance of my troubles, and the disappointments I had met in the wreck I had been on board of, and where I had been so near the obtaining of what I so earnestly longed for, namely, somebody to speak to, and to learn some knowledge from, of the place where I was, and of the probable means of my deliverance – I say, I was agitated wholly by these thoughts. All my calm of mind in my resignation to Providence, and waiting the issue of the dispositions of Heaven, seemed to be suspended; and I had, as it were, no power to turn my thoughts to anything but the project of a voyage to the main, which came upon me with such force, and such an impetuosity of desire, that it was not to be resisted.

When this had agitated my thoughts for two hours or more, with such violence that it set my very blood into a ferment, and my pulse beat as high as if I had been in a fever, merely with the extraordinary fervour of my mind about it, nature, as if I had been fatigued and exhausted with the very thought of it, threw me into a sound sleep: one would have thought I should have dreamed of it; but I did not, nor of anything relating to it; but I dreamed, that as I was going out in the morning, as usual, from my castle, I saw upon the shore two canoes and eleven savages coming to land, and that they brought with them another savage, whom they were going to kill, in order to eat him, when, on a sudden, this savage that they were going to kill, jumped away, and ran for his life; then, I thought in my sleep, that he came running into my little thick grove, before my fortification, to hide himself; and that I, seeing him alone, and not perceiving that the others sought him that way, showed myself to him, and smiling upon him, encouraged him; that he kneeled down to me, seeming to pray me to assist him; upon which I showed my ladder, made him go up it, and carried him into my cave, and he became my servant; and that as soon as I got this man I said to myself, "Now, I may certainly venture to the mainland; for this fellow will serve me as a pilot, and will tell me what to do, and whither to go for provisions, and whither not to go for fear of being devoured; what places to venture into, and what to escape." I waked with this thought, and was under such inexpressible impressions of joy at the prospect of my escape in my dream, that the disappointment which I felt upon coming to myself, and finding that it was no more than a dream, were equally extravagant the other way, and threw me into a very great dejection of spirit.

Upon this, however, I made this conclusion, that my only way to go about an attempt for an escape was, if possible, to get a savage in my possession; and, if possible, it should be one of their prisoners whom they had condemned to be eaten, and should bring hither to kill: but these thoughts still were attended with this difficulty, that it was impossible to effect this, without attacking a whole caravan of them, and killing them all; and this was not only a very desperate attempt, and might miscarry, but, on the other hand, I had greatly scrupled the lawfulness of it to myself, and my heart trembled at the thought of shedding so much blood, though it was for my deliverance. I need not repeat the arguments which occurred to me against this, they being the same mentioned before: but though I had other reasons to offer now, namely, that those men were enemies to my life, and would devour me if they could; that it was self-preservation, in the highest degree, to deliver myself from this death of a life, and was acting in my own defence, as much as if they were actually assaulting me, and the like; I say, though these things argued for it, yet the thoughts of shedding human blood for my deliverance were very terrible to me, and such as I could by no means reconcile myself to a great while.

However, at last, after many secret disputes with myself, and after great perplexities about it (for all these arguments, one way and another, struggled in my head a long time), the eager prevailing desire of deliverance at length mastered all the rest, and I resolved, if possible, to get one of these savages into my hands, cost what it would. The next thing, then, was to contrive how to do it; and this indeed was very difficult to resolve on; but as I could pitch on no possible means for it, so I resolved to put myself upon the watch to see them when they came on shore, and leave the rest to the event, taking such measures as the opportunity should present, let it be what it would.

With these resolutions in my thoughts, I set myself upon the scout as often as possible, and indeed, so often, till I was heartily tired of it; for it was above a year and a half that I waited, and for a great part of that time went out to the west end and to the southwest corner of the island, almost every day, to see the canoes, but none appeared, This was very discouraging, and began to trouble me much; though I cannot say that it did in this case, as it had done some time before that, namely, wear off the edge of my desire to the thing; but the longer it seemed to be delayed, the more eager I was for it; in a word, I was not at first more careful to shun the sight of these savages, and avoid being seen by them, than I was now eager to be upon them.

Besides, I fancied myself able to manage one, nay, two or three savages, if I had them, so as to make them entirely slaves to me, to do whatever I should direct them, and to prevent their being able, at any time to do me any hurt. I was a great while that I pleased myself with this affair, but nothing still presented; all my fancies and schemes came to nothing, for no savages came near me for a great while.

About a year and a half after I had entertained these notions, and by long musing had, as it were, resolved them all into nothing, for want of an occasion to put them in execution, I was surprised one morning early with seeing no less than five canoes all on shore together, on my side the island, and the people who belonged to them all landed, and out of my sight; the number of them broke all my measures; for seeing so many, and knowing that they always come four, or six, or sometimes more, in a boat, I could not tell what to think of it, or how to take any measures to attack twenty or thirty men single-handed; so, I lay still in my castle, perplexed and discomforted; however, I put myself into all the same postures for an attack that I had formerly provided, and was just ready for action if anything had presented. Having waited a good while, listening to hear if they made any noise, at length, being very impatient, I set my guns at the foot of my ladder, and clambered up to the top of the hill by my two stages, as usual, standing so, however, that my head did not appear above the hill, so that they could not perceive me by any means. Here I observed, by the help of my perspective glass, that they were no less than thirty in number; that they had a fire kindled, and they had meat dressed: how they cooked it, that I knew not, or what it was; but they were all dancing in I know not how many barbarous gestures and figures, their own way, round the fire.

When I was thus looking on them, I perceived, by my perspective, two miserable wretches dragged from the boats, where, it seems, they were laid by, and were now brought out for the slaughter: I perceived one of them immediately fall, being knocked down, I suppose, with a club or wooden sword, for that was their way; and two or three others were at work immediately, cutting him open for their cookery, while the other victim was left standing by himself, till they should be ready for him. At that very moment, this poor wretch, seeing himself a little at liberty, nature inspired him with hopes of life, and he started away from them, and ran with incredible swiftness along the sands, directly towards me – I mean towards the part of the coast where my habitation was.

I was dreadfully frightened (that I must acknowledge) when I perceived him to run my way, and especially when, as I thought, I saw him pursued by the whole body; and now I expected that part of my dream was coming to pass, and that he would certainly take shelter in my grove; but I could not depend, by any means, upon my dream for the rest of it, namely, that the other savages would not pursue him thither, and find him there. However, I kept my station, and my spirits began to recover, when I found that there were not above three men that followed him; and still more was I encouraged when I found that he outstripped them exceedingly in running, and gained ground of them – so that if he could but hold it for half an hour, I saw easily he would fairly get away from them all.

There was between them and my castle the creek, which I mentioned often at the first part of my story, when I landed my cargoes out of the ship, and this I knew he must necessarily swim over, or the poor wretch would be taken there: but when the savage escaping came thither, he made nothing of it, though the tide was then up; but plunging in, swam in about thirty strokes or thereabouts, landed, and ran on with exceeding strength and swiftness. When the three pursuers came to the creek, I found that two of them could swim, but the third could not, and that he, standing on the other side, looked at the other, but went no farther; and soon after went softly back again, which, as it happened, was very well for him in the main.

I observed, that the two who swam were yet more than twice as long swimming over the creek as the fellow was that fled from them. It came now very warmly upon my thoughts, and indeed irresistibly, that now was my time to get a servant, and perhaps a companion, or assistant, and that I was called plainly by Providence to save this poor creature's life. I immediately got down the ladders with all possible expedition, fetched my two guns, for they were both at the foot of the ladder, as I observed above; and getting up again with the same haste to the top of the hill, I crossed towards the sea; and having a very short cut, and all down hill, clapped myself in the way between the pursuers and the pursued, halloing aloud to him that fled, who, looking back, was at first perhaps as much frightened at me as at them; but I beckoned with my hand to him to come back – and in the meantime I slowly advanced towards the two that followed – then rushing at once upon the foremost, I knocked him down with the stock of my piece – I was loath to fire, because I would not have the rest hear, though at that distance it would not have been easily heard – and being out of sight of the smoke, too, they would not have easily known what to make of it. Having knocked this fellow down, the other who pursued him stopped, as if he had been frightened, and I advanced apace towards him; but as I came nearer, I perceived presently he had a bow and arrow, and was fitting it to shoot at me; so I was then necessitated to shoot at him first, which I did, and killed him at the first shot. The poor savage who fled, but had stopped, though he saw both his enemies fallen, and killed (as he thought), yet was so frightened with the fire and noise of my piece, that he stood stock-still, and neither came forward nor went backward, though "he seemed rather inclined to fly still than to come on. I hallooed again to him, and made signs to come forward, which he easily understood, and came a little way, then stopped again, and then a little farther, and stopped again; and I could then perceive that he stood trembling, as if he had been taken prisoner, and had just been to be killed, as his two enemies were. I beckoned him again to come to me, and gave him all the signs of encouragement that I could think of; and he came nearer and nearer, kneeling down every ten or twelve steps, in token of acknowledgment for saving his life. I smiled at him, and looked pleasantly, and beckoned to him to come still nearer. At length he came close to me, and then he kneeled down again, kissed the ground, and laid his head upon the ground, and, taking me by the foot, set my foot upon his head. This, it seems, was in token of swearing to be my slave for ever. I took him up, and made much of him, and encouraged him all I could. But there was more work to do yet; for I perceived the savage whom I knocked down was not killed, but stunned with the blow, and began to come to himself: so I pointed to him, and showed him the savage, that he was not dead; upon this he spoke some words to me, and though I could not understand them, yet I thought they were pleasant to hear, for they were the first sound of a man's voice that I had heard, my own excepted, for above five-and-twenty years. But there was no time for such reflections now; the savage, who was knocked down, recovered himself so far as to sit up upon the ground; and I perceived that my savage began to be afraid; but when I saw that, I presented my other piece at the man, as if I would shoot him: upon this my savage, for so I called him now, made a motion to me to lend him my sword, which hung naked in a belt by my side – so I did: he no sooner had it, but he runs to his enemy, and at one blow cuts off his head so cleverly, no executioner in Germany could have done it sooner or better, which I thought very strange for one who, I had reason to believe, never saw a sword in his life before, except their own wooden swords: however, it seems, as I learned afterwards, they make their wooden swords so sharp, so heavy, and the wood is so hard that they will cut off heads even with them – ay, and arms, and that at one blow too. When he had done this, he comes laughing to me in sign of triumph, and brought me the sword again, and, with abundance of gestures, which I did not understand, laid it down, with the head of the savage that he had killed, just before me.

But that which astonished him most was, to know how I had

killed the other Indian so far off; so, pointing to him, he made signs to me to let him go to him; so I bade him go, as well as I could. When he came to him, he stood like one amazed, looking at him – turned him first on one side, then on the other – looked at the wound the bullet had made, which, it seems, was just in his breast, where it made a hole, and no great quantity of blood had followed; but he had bled inwardly, for he was quite dead. Then he took up his bow and arrows, and came back; so I turned to go away, and beckoned him to follow me, making signs to him that more might come after him.

Upon this he signed to me that he should bury them with sand, that they might not be seen by the rest, if they followed; and so I made signs again to him to do so. He fell to work, and in an instant he had scraped a hole in the sand with his hands, big enough to bury the first in, and then dragged him into it, and covered him, and did so also by the other; I believe he had buried them both in a quarter of an hour: then calling him away, I carried him not to my castle, but quite away to my cave, on the farther part of the island; so I did not let my dream come to pass in that part, namely, that he came into my grove for shelter.

Here I gave him bread and a bunch of raisins to eat, and a draught of water, which I found he was, indeed, in great distress for, by his running; and, having refreshed him, I made signs for him to go lie down and sleep, pointing to a place where I had laid a great parcel of rice-straw, and a blanket upon it, which I used to sleep upon myself sometimes; so the poor creature lay down, and went to sleep.

He was a comely, handsome fellow, perfectly well made, with straight, long limbs, not too large, tall, and well shaped, and, as I reckon, about twenty-six years of age. He had a very good countenance, not a fierce and surly aspect, but seemed to have something very manly in his face, and yet he had all the sweetness and softness of an European in his countenance, too, especially when he smiled: his hair was long and black, not curled like wool; his forehead very high and large, and a great vivacity and sparkling sharpness in his eyes. The colour of his skin was not quite black, but very tawny, and yet not of an ugly yellow nauseous tawny, as the Brazilians, and Virginians, and other natives of America are, but of a bright kind of a dun olive colour, that had in it something very agreeable, though not very easy to describe. His face was round and plump, his nose small, not flat like the negroes, a very good mouth, thin lips, and his teeth fine, well set, and white as ivory. After he had slumbered, rather than slept, above half an hour, he waked again, and comes out of the cave to me, for I had been milking my goats, which I had in the enclosure just by: when he espied me, he came running to me, laying himself down again upon the ground, with all the possible signs of an humble, thankful disposition, making many antic gestures to show it. At last he lays his head flat upon the ground, close to my foot, and sets my other foot upon his head, as he had done before; and, after this, he made all the signs to me of subjection, servitude, and submission imaginable, to let me know how much he would serve me as long as he lived. I understood him in many things, and let him know I was very well pleased with him. In a little time I began to speak to him, and teach him to speak to me; and, first, I made him know his name should be Friday, which was the day I saved his life, and I called him so for the memory of the time: I likewise taught him to say Master, and then let him know that was to be my name: I likewise taught him to say Yes and No, and to know the meaning of them. I gave him some milk in an earthen pot, and let him see me drink it before him, and sop my bread in it; and I gave him a cake of bread to do the like, which he quickly complied with, and made signs that it was very good for him.

I kept there with him all that night; but as soon as it was day I beckoned him to come with me, and let him know I would give him some clothes, at which he seemed very glad, for he was stark naked. As we went by the place where he had buried the two men, he pointed exactly to the spot, and showed me the marks that he had made to find them again, making signs to me that we should dig them up again and eat them: at this I appeared very angry, expressed my abhorrence of it, made as if I would vomit at the thoughts of it, and beckoned with my hand to him to come away, which he did immediately, with great submission. I then led him up to the top of the hill, to see if his enemies were gone, and pulling out my glass, I looked, and saw plainly the place where they had been, but no appearance of them or of their canoes, so that it was plain that they were gone, and had left their two comrades behind them, without any search after them.

But I was not content with this discovery: but, having now more courage, and, consequently, more curiosity, I took my man Friday with me, giving him the sword in his hand, with the bow and arrows at his back, which I found he could use very dexterously,

DANIEL DEFOE

making him carry one gun for me, and I two for myself, and away we marched to the place where these creatures had been; for I had a mind now to *get* some fuller intelligence of them. When I came to the place, my very blood ran chill in my veins, and my heart sank within me, at the horror of the spectacle: indeed, it was a dreadful sight, at least it was so to me, though Friday made nothing of it; the place was covered with human bones, the ground dyed with the blood, great pieces of flesh left here and there, half eaten, mangled, and scorched; and, in short, all the tokens of the triumphant feast they had been making there after a victory over their enemies. I saw three skulls, five hands, and the bones of three or four legs and feet, and abundance of other parts of the bodies; and Friday, by his signs, made me understand that they brought over four prisoners to feast upon; that three of them were eaten up and that he, pointing to himself, was the fourth; that there had been a great battle between them and their next king, whose subjects, it seems, he had been one of; and that they had taken a great number of prisoners, all which were carried to several places by those that had taken them in the fight, in order to feast upon them, as was done here by these wretches upon those they brought hither.

I caused Friday to gather all the skulls, bones, flesh, and whatever remained, and lay them together on a heap, and make a great fire upon it, and burn them all to ashes. I found Friday had still a hankering stomach after some of the flesh, and was still a cannibal in his nature; but I discovered so much abhorrence at the very thoughts of it, and at the least appearance of it, that he durst not discover it; for I had, by some means, let him know that I would kill him if he offered it.

When we had done this, we came back to our castle, and there I fell to work for my man Friday: and, first of all, I gave him a pair of linen drawers, which I had out of the poor gunner's chest I mentioned, and which I found in the wreck; and which, with a little alteration, fitted him very well; then I made him a jerkin of goat's skin, as well as my skill would allow, and I was now grown a tolerably good tailor; and I gave him a cap, which I had made of a hare's skin, very convenient, and fashionable enough: and thus he was dressed, for the present, tolerably well, and mighty well was he pleased to see himself almost as well clothed as his master. It is true, he went awkwardly in these things at first; wearing the drawers was very awkward to him, and the sleeves of

178

the waistcoat galled his shoulders and the inside of his arms; but a little easing them where he complained they hurt him, and using himself to them, at length he took to them very well.

The next day after I came home to my hutch with him, I began to consider where I should lodge him; and that I might do well for him, and yet be perfectly easy myself, I made a little tent for him in the vacant place between my two fortifications, in the inside of the last, and in the outside of the first; and as there was a door or entrance there into my cave, I made a formal framed door-case, and a door to it of boards, and set it up in the passage, a little within the entrance; and, causing the door to open on the inside, I barred it up in the night, taking in my ladders too: so that Friday could no way come at me in the inside of my innermost wall, without making so much noise in getting over, that it must needs awaken me; for my first wall had now a complete roof over it of long poles, covering all my tent, and leaning up to the side of the hill, which was again laid across with small sticks instead of laths, and then thatched over a great thickness with rice straw, which was strong like reeds; and at the hole or place which was left to go in or out by the ladder, I had placed a kind of trap-door, which if it had been attempted on the outside, would not have opened at all, but would have fallen down, and made a great noise; and as to weapons, I took them all into my side every night.

But I needed none of all this precaution; for never man had a more faithful, loving, sincere servant than Friday was to me; without passions, sullenness, or designs; perfectly obliging and engaging, his very affections were tied to me like those of a child to a father, and I dare say he would have sacrificed his life for the saving mine upon any occasion whatsoever: the many testimonies he gave me of this put it out of doubt, and soon convinced me, that I needed to use no precautions as to my safety on his account.

This frequently gave me occasion to observe, and that with wonder, that however it had pleased God in His providence, and in the government of the works of His hands, to take from so great a part of the world of His creatures the best uses to which their faculties and the powers of their souls are adapted; yet that He has bestowed upon them the same powers, the same reason, the same affections, the same sentiments of kindness and obligation, the same passions and resentments of wrongs, the same sense of gratitude, sincerity, fidelity and all the capacities of doing good, and receiving good, that He has given to us; and that, when He pleases to offer them occasions of exerting these, they are as ready, nay, more ready to apply, them to the right uses, for which they are bestowed, than we are. And this made me very melancholy sometimes, in reflecting, as the several occasions presented, how mean a use we make of all these, even though we have these powers enlightened by the great lamp of instruction, the Spirit of God, and by the knowledge of His word, added to our understanding; and why it has pleased God to hide the like saving knowledge from so many millions of souls, who, if I might judge by this poor savage, would make a much better use of it than we did.

From hence I sometimes was led too far to invade the sovereignty of Providence, and, as it were, arraign the justice of so arbitrary a disposition of things, that should hide that light from some, and reveal it to others, and yet expect a like duty from both; but I shut it up, and checked my thoughts with this conclusion – first, that we do not know by what light and law these should be condemned; but that as God is necessarily, and by the nature of His being, infinitely holy and just, so it could not be but that if these creatures were all sentenced to absence from Himself, it was on account of sinning against that light, which, as the Scripture says, was a law to themselves, and by such rules as their consciences would acknowledge to be just, though the foundation was not discovered to us: and, secondly, that still, as we are all clay in the hand of the potter, no vessel could say to Him, "Why hast thou formed me thus?"

But to return to my new companion. I was greatly delighted with him, and made it my business to teach him everything that was proper to make himself useful, handy and helpful, but especially to make him speak, and understand me when I spoke: and he was the aptest scholar that ever was; and particularly was so merry, so constantly diligent, and so pleased when he could but understand me, or make me understand him, that it was very pleasant to me to talk to him. And now my life began to be so easy, that I began to say to myself, that could I but have been safe from more savages, I cared not if I was never to remove from the place where I lived.

CHAPTER 15

I civilise Friday – He considers my gun an intelligent Being – Begins to talk English – A Dialogue – I instruct him in Religion – He describes some White Men who still lived in his Country

After I had been two or three days returned to my castle, I thought, that in order to bring Friday off from his horrid way of feeding, and from the relish of a cannibal's stomach. I ought to let him taste other flesh; so I took him out with me one morning to the woods. I went, indeed, intending to kill a kid out of my own flock, and bring it home and dress it; but as I was going, I saw a she-goat lying down in the shade, and two young kids sitting by her. I catched hold of Friday: "Hold," said I, "stand still;" and made signs to him not to stir. Immediately I presented my piece, shot, and killed one of the kids. The poor creature, who had at a distance indeed seen me kill the savage his enemy, but did not know, nor could imagine how it was done, was sensibly surprised, trembled and shook, and looked so amazed, that I thought he would have sunk down: he did not see the kid I had shot at, or perceived I had killed it, but ripped up his waistcoat to feel if he was not wounded; and, as I found presently, thought I was resolved to kill him, for he came and kneeled down to me, and embracing my knees, said a great many things I did not understand: but I could easily see that his meaning was to pray me not to kill him.

I soon found a way to convince him that I would do him no harm; and taking him up by the hand, laughed at him, and pointing to the kid which I had killed, beckoned him to run and fetch it, which he did; and while he was wondering and looking to see how the creature was killed, I loaded my gun again, and by-and-by I saw a great fowl, like a hawk, sit upon a tree within shot; so to let Friday understand a little what I would do, I called him to me again, pointing at the fowl, which was indeed a parrot, though I thought it had been a hawk – I say, pointing to the parrot, and to my gun, and to the ground under the parrot, to let him see I would make him fall, I made him understand that I would shoot and kill that bird; accordingly, I fired, and bid him look, and immediately he saw the parrot fall. He stood like one frighted again, notwithstanding all that I had said to him; and I found he was the more puzzled, because he did not see me put anything into the gun, but thought there must be some wonderful fund of death and destruction in that thing, able to kill man, beast, bird or anything, near and far off; for the astonishment this created in him was such as could not wear off for a long time; and I believe, if I would have let him, he would have worshipped me and my gun. As for the gun itself, he would not so much as touch it for several days after, but would speak to it, and talk to it, as if it had answered him, when he was by himself; which, as I afterwards learned of him, was to desire it not to kill him.

Well, after his astonishment was a little over at this, I pointed to him to run and fetch the bird I had shot, which he did, but stayed some time; for the parrot, not being quite dead, had fluttered a good way off from the place where she fell; however, he found her, took her up, and brought her to me; and as I had perceived his ignorance about the gun before, I took this advantage to charge the gun again, and not let him see me do it, that I might be ready for any other mark that might present; but nothing else offered at that time: so I brought home the kid; and the same evening I took the skin off, and cut it out as well as I could, and having a pot for that purpose, I boiled or stewed some of the flesh, and made some very good broth. After I had begun to eat some, I gave some to my man, who seemed very glad of it, and liked it very well; but that which was strangest to him was, to see me eat salt with it. He made a sign to me that the salt was not good to eat; and putting a little into his own mouth, he seemed to nauseate it, and would spit and sputter at it, washing his mouth with fresh water after it. On the other hand, I took some meat in my mouth without salt, and I pretended to spit and sputter for want of salt, as fast as he had done at the salt; but it would not do, he would never care for salt with meat, or in his broth; at least not a great while, and then but a very little.

Having thus fed him with boiled meat and broth, I was resolved to feast him the next day with roasting a piece of the kid: this I did by hanging it before the fire in a string, as I had seen many people do in England, setting two poles up, one on each side of a fire, and one cross on the top, and tying the string to the cross stick, letting the meat run continually: this Friday admired very much; but when he came to taste the flesh, he took so many ways to tell me how well he liked it, that I could not but understand him; and at last he told me he would never eat man's flesh any more, which I was very glad to hear.

The next day I set him to work to beating some corn out, and sifting it in the manner I used to do, as I observed before; and he soon understood how to do it as well as I, especially after he had seen what the meaning of it was, and that it was to make bread of; for after that I let him see me make my bread, and bake it too; and in a little time Friday was able to do all the work for me, as well as I could do it myself.

I began now to consider, that, having two mouths to feed instead of one, I must provide more ground for my harvest, and plant a larger quantity of corn than I used to do; so I marked out a larger piece of land, and began the fence in the same manner as before, in which Friday not only worked very willingly and very hard, but did it very cheerfully; and I told him what it was for, that it was for corn to make more bread, because he was now with me, and that I might have enough for him and myself too: he appeared very sensible of that part, and let me know that he thought I had much more labour upon me on his account than I had for myself, and that he would work the harder for me, if I would tell him what to do.

This was the pleasantest year of all the life I led in this place. Friday began to talk pretty well, and understood the names of almost everything I had occasion to call for, and of every place I had to send him to, and talk a great deal to me; so that, in short, I began now to have some use for my tongue again, which indeed I had very little occasion for before – that is to say, about speech. Besides the pleasure of talking to him, I had a singular satisfaction in the fellow himself: his simple unfeigned honesty appeared to

me more and more every day, and I began really to love the creature; and on his side, I believe, he loved me more than ever it
was possible for him ever to love anything before.

I had a mind once to try if he had any hankering inclination to his own country again; and having learned him English
so well, that he could answer me almost any questions, I asked
him, whether the nation that he belonged to never conquered in
battle? At which he smiled, and said, "Yes, yes, we always fight
the better" – that is, he meant, always get the better in fight –
and so we began the following discourse: "You always fight the
better!" said I: "how came you to be taken prisoner, then,
Friday?"

Friday – My nation beat much for all that.

Master – How beat? If your nation beat them, how came you
to be taken?

Friday – They more than my nation in the place where me
was; they take one, two, three, and me: my nation overheat them
in the yonder place, where me no was; there my nation take one,
two, great thousand.

Master – But why did not your side recover you from the hands
of your enemies, then?

Friday – They run, one, two, three, and me, and make go in
the canoe; my nation have no canoe that time.

Master – Well, Friday, and what does your nation do with the
men they take? Do they carry them away, and eat them as these
did?

Friday – Yes, my nation eat mans too, eat all up.

Master – Where do they carry them?

Friday – Go to other place where they think.

Master – Do they come hither?

Friday – Yes, yes, they come hither; come other else place.

Master – Have you been here with them?

Friday – Yes, I have been here [points to the northwest side
of the island, which, it seems, was their side].

By this I understood, that my man Friday had formerly been
among the savages who used to come on shore on the farther part
of the island, on the said man-eating occasions that he was now
brought for; and some time after, when I took the courage to carry
him to that side, being the same I formerly mentioned, he
presently knew the place, and told me, he was there once, when
they ate up twenty men, two women, and one child: he could not

tell twenty in English, but he numbered them by laying so many stones in a row, and pointing to me to tell them over.

I have told this passage because it introduces what follows; that after I had had this discourse with him, I asked him how far it was from our island to the shore, and whether the canoes were not often lost – he told me there was no danger, no canoes ever lost; but that after a little way out to sea, there was a current and a wind always one way in the morning, the other in the afternoon.

This I understood to be no more than the sets of the tide, as going out, or coming in; but I afterwards understood it was occasioned by the great draught and reflux of the mighty river Oroonoque, in the mouth of which river, as I thought afterwards, our island lay; and that this land which I perceived to the west and north-west, was the great island Trinidad, on the north point of the mouth of the river. I asked Friday a thousand questions about the country, the inhabitants, the sea, the coast, and what nations were near – he told me all he knew with the greatest openness imaginable. I asked him the names of the several nations of his sort of people, but could get no other name than Caribs; from whence I easily understood, that these were the Caribbees, which our maps place on that part of America which reaches from the mouth of the river Oroonoque to Guinea, and onwards to St. Martha. He told me, that up a great way beyond the moon – that was, beyond the setting of the moon, which must be west from their country – there dwelt white-bearded men, like me, and pointed to my great whiskers, which I mentioned before; and that they had killed much mans – that was his word – by which I understood he meant the Spaniards, whose cruelties in America had been spread over the whole countries, and were remembered by all the nations from father to son.

I inquired if he could tell me how I might come from this island, and get among those white men; he told me, "Yes, yes, I might go into two canoe." I could not understand what he meant by two canoe; till at last, with great difficulty, I found he meant, that it must be in a large great boat as big as two canoes.

This part of Friday's discourse began to relish with me very well; and from this time I entertained some hopes, that one time or other I might find an opportunity to make my escape from this place, and that this poor savage might be a means to help me to do it.

During the long time that Friday had now been with me, and that he began to speak to me, and understand me, I was not wanting to lay a foundation of religious knowledge in his mind; particularly I asked him one time, Who made him? The poor creature did not understand me at all, but thought I had asked who was his father; but I took it by another handle, and asked him, Who made the sea, the ground he walked on, and the hills and woods? He told me it was one old Benamuckee, that lived beyond all: he could describe nothing of this great person, but that he was very old – much older, he said, than the sea or the land, than the moon or the stars. I asked him then, if this old person had made all things, why did not all things worship him? He looked very grave, and, with a perfect look of innocence, said, All things said O! to him. I asked him if the people who die in his country went away anywhere? He said, Yes, they all went to Benamuckee. Then I asked him, whether those they eat up went thither too? He said Yes.

From these things I began to instruct him in the knowledge of the true God. I told him, that the great Maker of all things lived there, pointing up towards heaven; that He governs the world by the same power and providence by which He made it; that He was omnipotent, could do everything for us, give everything to us, take everything from us: and thus, by degrees, I opened his eyes. He listened with great attention, and received with pleasure the notion of Jesus Christ being sent to redeem us, and of the manner of making our prayers to God, and His being able to hear us, even in heaven: he told me one day, that if our God could hear us up beyond the sun, He must needs be a greater god than their Benamuckee, who lived but a little way off, and yet could not hear, till they went up to the great mountains, where he dwelt, to speak to him. I asked him if ever he went thither to speak to him? He said, No, they never went that were young men; none went thither but the old men, whom they called their Oowookakee; that is, as I made him explain it to me, their religious or clergy; and that they went to say O! (so he called saying prayers), and then came back, and told them what Benamuckee said. By this I observed, that there is priestcraft even among the most blinded ignorant Pagans in the world; and the policy of making a secret of religion, in order to preserve the veneration of the people to the clergy, is to be found among all religions in the world, even among the most brutish and barbarous savages.

I endeavoured to clear up this fraud to my man Friday, and told him, that the pretence of their old men going up to the mountains to say O! to their god Benamuckee, was a cheat; and their bringing word from thence what he said, was much more so; that if they met with any answer, or spoke with any one there, it must be with an evil spirit; and then I entered into a long discourse with him about the devil, the original of him, his rebellion against God, his enmity to man, the reason of it, his setting himself up in the dark parts of the world to be worshipped instead of God, and as God, and the many stratagems he made use of to delude mankind to their ruin; how he had a secret access to our passions and to our affections, to adapt his snares so to our inclinations as to cause us even to be our own tempters, and to run upon our own destruction by our own choice.

I found it was not so easy to imprint right notions in his mind about the devil, as it was about the being of a God: nature assisted all my arguments to evidence to him even the necessity of a great First Cause, and overruling governing Power, a secret directing Providence, and of the equity and justice of paying homage to Him that made us, and the like; but there appeared nothing of all this in the notion of an evil spirit, of his original, his being, his nature, and, above all, of his inclination to do evil, and to draw us in to do so too: and the poor creature puzzled me once in such a manner, by a question merely natural and innocent, that I scarce knew what to say to him.

I had been talking a great deal to him of the power of God, His omnipotence, His dreadful aversion to sin, His being a consuming fire to the workers of iniquity; how, as He had made us all, He could destroy us, and all the world, in a moment: and he listened with great seriousness to me all the while. After this, I had been telling him how the devil was God's enemy in the hearts of men, and used all his malice and skill to defeat the good designs of Providence, and to ruin the kingdom of Christ in the world, and the like. "Well," says Friday, "but you say God is so strong, so great, is He not much strong, much might, as the devil?" "Yes, yes," said I, "Friday, God is stronger than the devil; God is above the devil; and therefore we pray to God to tread him under our feet, and enable us to resist his temptations, and quench his fiery darts." "But," says he, again, "if God much strong, much might, as the devil, why God not kill the devil, so make him no more wicked?"

I was strangely surprised at his question; and, after all, though I was now an old man, yet I was but a young doctor, and ill enough qualified for a casuist, or a solver of difficulties: and, at first, I could not tell what to say: so I pretended not to hear him, and asked him what he said? But he was too earnest for an answer to forget his question, so that he repeated it in the very same broken words as above. By this time I had recovered myself a little, and I said, "God will at last punish him severely, he is reserved for the judgment, and is to be cast into the bottomless pit to dwell with everlasting fire." This did not satisfy Friday; but he returns upon me, repeating my words, "Reserve at last! me no understand: but why not kill the devil, not kill great ago?" "You may as well ask me," said I, "why God does not kill you and me, when we do wicked things here that offend Him: we are preserved to repent and be pardoned." He muses a while at this. "Well, well," says he, mighty affectionately, "that well: so you, I, devil, all wicked, all preserve, repent, God pardon all." Here I was run down again by him to the last degree, and it was a testimony to me, how the mere notions of nature, though they will guide reasonable creatures to the knowledge of a God, and of a worship or homage due to the supreme being of God, as the consequence of our nature, yet nothing but divine revelation can form the knowledge of Jesus Christ, and of a redemption purchased for us; of a Mediator; of a new covenant; and of an Intercessor at the footstool of God's throne – I say, nothing but a revelation from Heaven can form these in the soul; and that therefore the Gospel of our Lord and Saviour Jesus Christ, I mean the Word of God, and the Spirit of God, promised for the guide and sanctifier of His people, are the absolutely necessary instructors of the souls of men in the saving knowledge of God, and the means of salvation.

I therefore diverted the present discourse between me and my man, rising up hastily, as upon some sudden occasion of going out; then sending him for something a great way off, I seriously prayed to God, that he would enable me to instruct savingly this poor savage, assisting, by His Spirit, the heart of the poor ignorant creature to receive the light of the knowledge of God in Christ, reconciling him to Himself, and would guide me to speak so to him from the Word of God, as his conscience might be convinced, his eyes opened, and his soul saved. When he came again to me, I entered into a long discourse with him upon the subject of the redemption of man by the Saviour of the world; and of the doctrine of the Gospel preached from heaven, namely, of repentance towards God, and faith in our blessed Lord Jesus: I then explained to him, as well as I could, why our blessed Redeemer took not on Him the nature of angels but the seed of Abraham, and how, for that reason, the fallen angels had no share in the redemption; that He came only to the lost sheep of the house of Israel, and the like.

I had, God knows, more sincerity than knowledge in all the methods I took for this poor creature's instruction; and must acknowledge, what I believe all that act upon the same principle will find, that in laying things open to him, I really informed and instructed myself in many things that either I did not know, or had not fully considered before, but which occurred naturally to my mind upon my searching into them for the information of this poor savage: and I had more affection in my inquiry after things upon this occasion than ever I felt before; so that, whether this poor wild wretch was the better for me or no, I had great reason to be thankful that ever he came to me. My grief sat lighter upon me, my habitation grew comfortable to me beyond measure; and when I reflected that in this solitary life, which I had been confined to, I had not only been moved myself, to look up to Heaven, and to seek to the hand that brought me thither, but was now to be made an instrument, under Providence, to save the life, and, for aught I knew, the soul, of a poor savage, and bring him to the true knowledge of religion and of the Christian Doctrine, that he might know Jesus Christ, to know whom is life eternal – I say, when I reflected upon all these things, a secret joy ran through every part of my soul, and I frequently rejoiced that ever I was brought to this place, which I had often thought the most dreadful of all afflictions that could possibly have befallen me.

In this thankful frame I continued all the remainder of my time; and the conversation which employed the hours between Friday and me was such as made the three years which we lived there together perfectly and completely happy, if any such thing as complete happiness can be found in a sublunary state, The savage was now a good Christian, a much better than I; though

I have reason to hope, and bless God for it, that we were equally penitent, and comforted, restored penitents. We had here the word of God to read, and no farther off from His Spirit to instruct than if we had been in England.

I always applied myself to reading the Scripture, and to let him know, as well as I could, the meaning of what I read; and he again, by his serious inquiries and questions, made me, as I said before, a much better scholar in the Scripture knowledge, than I should ever have been by my own private reading. Another thing I cannot refrain from observing here also from experience, in this retired part of my life, namely, how infinite and inexpressible a blessing it is, that the knowledge of God, and of the doctrine of salvation by Christ Jesus, is so plainly laid down in the word of God, so easy to be received and understood, that as the bare reading the Scripture made me capable of understanding enough of my duty to carry me directly on to the great work of sincere repentance for my sins, and laying hold of a Saviour for life and salvation, to a stated reformation of practice, and obedience to all God's commands, and this without any teacher or instructor (I mean human); so the plain instruction sufficiently served to the enlightening this savage creature, and bringing him to be such a Christian as I have known few equal to him in my life.

As to the disputes, wranglings, strife, and contention which have happened in the world about religion, whether niceties in doctrines, or schemes of church government, they were all perfectly useless to us, as, for aught I can yet see, they have been to all the rest in the world. We had the sure guide to heaven, namely, the Word of God; and we had, blessed be God! comfortable views of the Spirit of God, teaching and instructing us by His word, leading us into all truth, and making us both willing and obedient to the instruction of His word; and I cannot see the least use that the greatest knowledge of the disputed points in religion, which have made such confusions in the world, would have been to us, if we could have obtained it. But I must go on with the historical part of things, and take every part in its order.

After Friday and I became more intimately acquainted, and that he could understand almost all said to him, and speak fluently, though in broken English, to me, I acquainted him with my own story, or at least so much of it as related to my coming into the place, how I had lived there, and how long: I let him into the mystery (for such it was to him) of gunpowder and bullets, and taught him how to shoot: I gave him a knife, which he was wonderfully delighted with; and I made him a belt with a frog hanging to it, such as in England we wear hangers in; and in the frog, instead of a hanger, I gave him a hatchet, which was not only as good a weapon in some cases, but much more useful upon many occasions.

I described to him the countries of Europe, and particularly England, which I came from; how we lived, how we worshipped God, how we behaved to one another, and how we traded in ships to all the parts of the world. I gave him an account of the Wreck which I had been on board of, and showed him, as near as I could, the place where she lay; but she was all beaten in pieces long before, and quite gone. I showed him the ruins of our boat, which we lost when we escaped, and which I could not stir with my whole strength then, but was now fallen almost all to pieces. Upon seeing this boat, Friday stood musing a great while, and said nothing; I asked him what it was he studied upon? At last, says he, "Me see such boat like come to place at my nation."

I did not understand him a good while; but at last, when I had examined further into it, I understood by him that a boat, such as that had been, came on shore upon the country where he lived – that is, as he explained it, was driven thither by stress of weather. I presently imagined that some European ship must have been cast away upon their coast, and the boat might get loose, and drive ashore; but was so dull, that I never once thought of men making escape from a wreck thither, much less whence they might come – so I only inquired after a description of the boat.

Friday described the boat to me well enough; but brought me better to understand him, when he added, with some warmth, "We save the white mans from drown." Then I presently asked him, if there were any white mans, as he called them, in the boat? "Yes,' he said, "the boat full of white mans." I asked him, how many? He told upon his fingers seventeen. I asked him, what became of them? He told me, "They live, they dwell at my nation."

This put new thoughts into my head again; for I presently imagined, that these might be the men belonging to the ship that was cast away in sight of my island, as I now called it; and who, after the ship was struck on the rock, and they saw her inevitably lost, had saved themselves in their boat, and were landed upon that wild shore among the savages.

Upon this I inquired of him more critically, what was become of them? He assured me they lived still there, that they had been there about four years, that the savages let them alone, and gave them victuals to live, I asked him how it came to pass they did not kill them, and eat them? He said, "No, they make brother with them" – that his, as I understood him, a truce: and then he added, "They eat no mans but when make the war fight" – that is to say, they never eat any men but such as come to fight with them, and are taken in battle.

It was after this some considerable time, that being on the top of the hill, at the east side of the island, from whence, as I have said, I had in a clear day discovered the main or continent of America, Friday, the weather being very serene, looks very earnestly towards the mainland, and, in a kind of surprise, falls a-jumping and dancing, and calls out to me, for I was at some distance from him: I asked him what was the matter? "Oh, joy!" says he, "oh, glad! there see my country, there my nation!"

I observed an extraordinary sense of pleasure appeared in his face, and his eyes sparkled, and his countenance discovered a strange eagerness, as if he had a mind to be in his own country again; and this observation of mine put a great many thoughts into me, which made me at first not so easy about my new man Friday as I was before; and I made no doubt but that if Friday could get back to his own nation, he would not only forget all his religion, but all his obligations to me: and would be forward enough to give his countrymen an account of me, and come back, perhaps, with a hundred or two of them, and make a feast upon me, at which he might be as merry as he used to be with those of his enemies, when they were taken in war.

But I wronged the poor honest creature very much, for which I was very sorry afterwards; however, as my jealousy increased, and held me some weeks, I was a little more circumspect, and not so familiar and kind to him as before; in which I was certainly in the wrong too, the honest grateful creature having no thought about it, but what consisted of the best principles, both as a religious Christian and as a grateful friend, as appeared afterwards to my full satisfaction.

Whilst my jealousy of him lasted, you may be sure I was every day pumping him, to see if he would discover any of the new thoughts which I suspected were in him; but I found everything he said was so honest and so innocent, that I could find nothing to nourish my suspicion; and in spite of all my uneasiness he made me at last entirely his own again – nor did he in the least perceive that I was uneasy – and therefore I could not suspect him of deceit.

One day, walking up the same hill, but the weather being hazy at sea, so that we could not see the continent, I called to him, and said, "Friday, do not you wish yourself in your own country, your own nation?" "Yes," he said, "I be much O glad to be at my own nation." "What would you do there!" said I; "would you turn wild again, eat men's flesh again, and be a savage as you were before?" He looked full of concern, and, shaking his head, said, "No, no! Friday tell them to live good, tell them to pray God, tell them to eat corn bread, cattle flesh, milk, no eat man again," "Why, then," said I to him, "they will kill you!" He looked grave at that, and then said, "No, they no kill me; they willing love learn" – he meant by this, they would be willing to learn. He added, they learned much of the bearded mans that came in the boat. Then I asked him if he would go back to them? He smiled at that, and told me he could not swim so far. I told him I would make a canoe for him. He told me he would go if I would go with him. "I go!" said I, "why, they will eat me if I come there!" "No, no!" says he, "me make them no eat you, me make they much love you" – he meant he would tell them how I had killed his enemies and saved his life, and so he would make them love me. Then he told me how kind they were to seventeen white men, or bearded men, as he called them, who came on shore in distress.

From this time, I confess, I had a mind to venture over, and see if I could possibly join with these bearded men, who, I made no doubt, were Spaniards or Portuguese; not doubting but, if I could, we might find some method to escape from thence, being upon the continent, and a good company together, better than I could from an island forty miles off the shore, and alone without help. So, after some days, I took Friday to work again, by way of discourse, and told him I would give him a boat to go back to his own nation; and accordingly, I carried him to my frigate, which lay on the other side of the island; and having cleared it of water (for I always kept it sunk in the water), I brought it out, showed it him and we both went into it.

I found he was a most dexterous fellow at managing it, would make it go almost as swift and fast again as I could; so when he was in, I said to him, "Well, now, Friday, shall we go to your nation?" He looked very dull at my saying so, which it seems was because he thought the boat too small to go so far. I told him then I had a bigger; so the next day I went to the place where the first boat lay which I had made, but which I could not get into the water: he said that was big enough; but then, as I had taken no care of it, and it had lain two or three-and-twenty years there, the sun had so split and dried it, that it was in a manner rotten. Friday told me such a boat would do very well, and would carry "much enough vittle, drink, bread" – that was his way of talking.

CHAPTER 16

I determine to go to the Continent –
Friday and I construct a Boat – Friday
brings intelligence of Savages on Shore –
Friday and I save the life of a Spaniard –
Discover a poor Indian in a Canoe, who
turns out to be Friday's Father

Upon the whole, I was by this time so fixed upon my design of going over with him to the continent, that I told him we would go and make one as big as that, and he should go home in it. He answered not one word, but looked very grave and sad. I asked him what was the matter with him? He asked me again, thus, "Why you angry mad with Friday? what me done?" I asked him what he meant? I told him I was not angry with him at all. "No angry: no angry!" says he, repeating the words several times; "why send Friday home away to my nation?" "Why," said I, "Friday, did you not say you wished you were there?" "Yes, yes," says he, "wish be both there; no wish Friday there, no master there." In a word, he would not think of going there without me. "I go there, Friday!" said I; "what should I do there?" He turned very quick upon me at this. "You do great deal much good," says he; "you teach wild mans to be good, sober, tame mans; you tell them know God, pray God, and live new life." "Alas, Friday," said I, "thou knowest not what thou sayest; I am but an ignorant man myself." "Yes yes," says he, "you teachee me good, you teachee them good." "No, no, Friday," said I, "you shall go without me; leave me here to live by myself, as I did before." He looked confused again at that word, and running to one of the hatchets which he used to wear, he takes it up hastily, and gives it me. "What must I do with this?" said I to him. "You take kill Friday," says he. "What must I kill you for?" said I again. He returns very quick, "What you send Friday away for? Take kill Friday, no send Friday away." This he spoke so earnestly, that I saw tears stand in his eyes. In a word, I so plainly discovered the utmost affection in him to me, and a firm resolution in him, that I told him then, and often after, that I would not send him away from me, if he was willing to stay with me.

Upon the whole, as I found by all his discourse a settled affection to me, and that nothing should part him from me, so I found all the foundation of his desire to go to his own country, was laid in his ardent affection to the people and his hopes of my doing them good – a thing which, as I had no notion of myself, so I had not the least thought, or intention, or desire of undertaking it. But still I found a strong inclination to my attempting an escape, as above, founded on the supposition gathered from the former discourse – namely, that there were seventeen bearded men there; and therefore, without delay, I went to work with Friday, to find out a great tree proper to fell, and make a large periagua, or canoe, to undertake the voyage. There were trees enough in the island to have built a little fleet, not of periaguas and canoes only, but of good large vessels: but the main thing I looked at, was to get one so near the water that we might launch it when it was made, to avoid the mistake I committed at first.

At last Friday pitched upon a tree, for I found he knew much better than I what kind of wood was fittest for it; nor can I tell to this day what wood to call the tree we cut down, except that it was very like the tree we call fustic, or between that and the Nicaragua wood, for it was much of the same colour and smell. Friday was for burning the hollow or cavity of this tree out, to make it into a boat: but I showed him how rather to cut it out with tools, which, after I showed him how to use, he did very handily; and in about a month's hard labour we finished it, and made it very handsome, especially when, with our axes, which I showed him how to handle, we cut and hewed the outside into the true shape of a boat. After this, however, it cost us near a fortnight's time to get her along, as it were, inch by inch, upon great rollers, into the water; but when she was in, she would have carried twenty men with great ease.

When she was in the water, and though she was so big, it amazed me to see with what dexterity, and how swift, my man Friday could manage her, turn her, and paddle her along; so I asked him if he would, and if we might, venture over in her? "Yes," he

said, "he venture over in her very well, though great blow wind."
However, I had a further design which he knew nothing of, and
that was, to make a mast and sail, and to fit her with an anchor and
cable. As to a mast, that was easy enough to get; so I pitched upon
a straight young cedar tree, which I found near the place, and which
there was a great plenty of in the island; and I set Friday to work
to cut it down, and gave him directions how to shape and order it;
but, as to the sail, that was my particular care; I knew I had old
sails, or rather pieces of old sails, enough; but, as I had had them
now twenty-six years by me, and had not been very careful to
preserve them, not imagining that I should ever have this kind of
use for them, I did not doubt but that they were all rotten – and,
indeed, most of them were so; however, I found two pieces which
appeared pretty good, and with these I went to work, and with great
a deal of pains, and awkward tedious stitching (you may be sure)
for want of needles, I at length made a three-cornered ugly thing,
like what we call in England a shoulder-of-mutton sail, to go with
a boom at bottom, and a little short sprit at the top, such as usually
our ships' long-boats sail with, and such as I best knew how to
manage; because it was such a one as I used in the boat in which
I made my escape from Barbary, as related in the first part of my
story.

I was near two months performing this last work, namely,
rigging and fitting my mast and sails; for I finished them very
complete, making a small stay, and a sail or foresail to it, to assist
if we should turn to windward; and, which was more than all, I
fixed a rudder to the stern of her, to steer with; and though I was
but a bungling shipwright, yet as I knew the usefulness, and even
necessity, of such a thing, I applied myself with so much pains to
do it, that at last I brought it to pass, though, considering the many
dull contrivances I had for it that failed, I think it cost me almost
as much labour as making the boat.

After all this was done, I had my man Friday to teach as to
what belonged to the navigation of my boat; for though he knew
very well how to paddle the canoe, he knew nothing what belonged
to a sail and a rudder, and was the more amazed when he saw me
work the boat to and again in the sea by the rudder, and how the
sail jibed and filled this way or that way, as the course we sailed
changed – I say, when he saw this, he stood like one astonished and
amazed: however, with a little use, I made all these things familiar
to him, and he became an expert sailor, except that as to the compass

DANIEL DEFOE

I could make him understand very little of that: on the other hand, as there was very little cloudy weather, and seldom or never any fogs, in those parts, there was the less occasion for a compass, seeing the stars were always to be seen by night, and the shore by day, except in the rainy seasons; and then nobody cared to stir abroad, either by land or sea.

I was now entered on the seven-and-twentieth year of my captivity in this place; though the three last years that I had this creature with me, ought rather to be left out of the account, my habitation being quite of another kind than in all the rest of my time. I kept the anniversary of my landing here with the same thankfulness to God, for his mercies as at first; and if I had such cause of acknowledgment at first I had much more so now, having such additional testimonies of the care of Providence over me, and the great hopes I had of being effectually and speedily delivered; for I had an invincible impression upon my thoughts that my deliverance was at hand and that I should not be another year in this place. However I went on with my husbandry, digging, planting, and fencing, as usual; I gathered and cured my grapes, and did every necessary thing, as before.

The rainy season was in the meantime upon me, when I kept more within doors than at other times; so I stowed our new vessel as secure as we could, bringing her up into the creek, where, as I said in the beginning, I landed my rafts from the ship; and hauling her up to the shore, at high-water mark, I made my man Friday dig a little dock, just big enough for her to float in; and then, when the tide was out, we made a strong dam across the end of it, to keep the water out; and so she lay dry, as to the tide, from the sea; and, to keep the ram off, we laid a great many boughs of trees, so thick that she was as well thatched as a house; and thus we waited for the months of November and December, in which I designed to make my adventure.

When the settled season began to come in, as the thought of my design returned with the fair weather, I was preparing daily for the voyage; and the first thing I did was to lay up a certain quantity of provision, being the store for the voyage, and intended in a week or a fortnight's time, to open the dock and launch out our boat. I was busy one morning upon something of this kind, when I called to Friday, and bade him go to the sea-shore and see if he could find a turtle, or tortoise, a thing which we generally got once a-week, for the sake of the eggs as well as the flesh. Friday had not been long gone when he came running back, and flew over my outward wall, or fence, like one that felt not the ground or the steps he set his feet on; and before I had time to speak to him, he cried out to me: "Oh, master! Oh, master! Oh, sorrow! Oh, bad!" "What's the matter, Friday? said I. "Oh, yonder there," says he, "one, two, three canoe! one, two three!" By this way of speaking, I concluded there were six; but, on inquiry, I found there were but three. "Well, Friday," said I, "do not be frighted;" so I heartened him up as well as I could. However, I saw the poor fellow was most terribly scared; for nothing ran in his head but that they were come to look for him, and would cut him in pieces and eat him. The poor fellow trembled so, that I scarce knew what to do with him. I comforted him as well as I could, and told him I was in as much danger as he, and that they would eat me as well as him. "But," said I, "Friday, we must resolve to fight them: can you fight, Friday?" "Me shoot," says he, "but there come many great number." "No matter for that," said I again; "our guns will fright them that we do not kill." So I asked him, whether, if I resolved to defend him, he would defend me, and stand by me, and do just as I bade him? He said, "Me die when you bid die, master." So I went and fetched a good dram of rum, and gave him; for I had been so good a husband of my rum that I had a great deal left, When he had drunk it, I made him take the two fowling-pieces which we always carried, and load them with large swan-shot as big as small pistol bullets; then I took four muskets, and loaded them with two slugs and five small bullets each; and my two pistols I loaded with a brace of bullets each – I hung my great sword, as usual, naked by my side, and gave Friday his hatchet.

When I had thus prepared myself, I took my perspective glass, and went up to the side of the hill to see what I could discover; and I found quickly, by my glass, that there were one-and-twenty savages, three prisoners, and three canoes; and that their whole business seemed to be the triumphant banquet upon these three human bodies – a barbarous feast, indeed, but nothing more than, as I had observed, was usual with them.

I observed also that they were landed, not where they had done when Friday made his escape, but nearer to my creek, where the shore was low, and where a thick wood came close almost down to the sea – this, with the abhorrence of the inhuman errand these wretches came about, so filled me with indignation, that I came down again to Friday, and told him I was resolved to go down to

DANIEL DEFOE

them and kill them all, and asked him if he would stand by me. He was now gotten over his fright, and his spirits being a little raised with the dram I had given him, he was very cheerful, and told me, as before, he would die when I bid die.

In this fit of fury, I took first and divided the arms, which I had charged, as before, between us; I gave Friday one pistol to stick in his girdle, and three guns upon his shoulder, and I took one pistol and the other three myself; and in this posture we marched out. I took a small bottle of rum in my pocket, and gave Friday a large bag with more powder and bullets; and as to orders, I charged him to keep close behind me, and not to stir, shoot, or do anything till I bade him; and, in the meantime, not to speak a word. In this posture I fetched a compass to my right hand of near a mile, as well to get over the creek as to get into the wood; so that I might come within shot of them before I could be discovered, which I had seen by my glass it was easy to do. While I was making this march, my former thoughts returning, I began to abate my resolution – I do not mean that I entertained any fear of their number; for as they were naked, unarmed wretches, it is certain I was superior to them, nay, though I had been alone – but it occurred to my thoughts, what call, what occasion, much less what necessity, I was in to go and dip my hands in blood – to attack people who had neither done nor intended me any wrong, who, as to me, were innocent, and whose barbarous customs were their own disaster, being in them a token indeed of God's having left them, with the other nations of that part of the world, to such stupidity and to such inhuman courses; but did not call me to take upon me to be a judge of their actions, much less an executioner of His justice; that whenever He thought fit He would take the cause into His own hands, and by, national vengeance, punish them for national crimes, but that, in the meantime, it was none of my business – that it was true, Friday might justify it, because he was a declared enemy, and in a state of war with those very particular people, and it was lawful for him to attack them; but I could not say the same with respect to me. These things were so warmly pressed upon my thoughts all the way as I went, that I resolved I would only go place myself near them, that I might oversee their barbarous feast, and that I would act then as God should direct; but that, unless something offered that was more a call to me than yet I knew of, I would not meddle with them.

With this resolution I entered the wood, and with all possible wariness and silence (Friday following close at my heels), I marched till I came to the skirt of the wood, on the side which was next to them – only that one corner of the wood lay between me and them – here I called softly to Friday, showing him a great tree, which was just at the corner of the wood; I bade him go to the tree, and bring me word if he could see there plainly what they were doing; he did so, and came immediately back to me, and told me that they might be plainly viewed there; that they were all about the fire, eating the flesh of one of their prisoners; and that another lay bound upon the sand, a little from them, whom he said they would kill next, and which fired the very soul within me. He told me it was not one of their nation, but one of the bearded men whom he had told me of, who came to their country in the boat. I was filled with horror at the very naming the white bearded-man, and, going to the tree, I saw plainly by my glass, a white man, who lay upon the beach of the sea, with his hands and his feet tied with flags, or things like rushes; and that he was a European, and had clothes on.

There was another tree, and a little thicket beyond it, about fifty yards nearer to them than the place where I was, which, by going a little way about, I saw I might come at undiscovered, and that then I should be within half shot of them; so I withheld my passion, though I was indeed enraged to the highest degree, and going back about twenty paces, I got behind some bushes, which held all the way till I came to the other tree, and then I came to a little rising ground, which gave me a full view of them at the distance of about eighty yards.

I had now not a moment to lose; for nineteen of the dreadful wretches sat upon the ground all close huddled together, and had just sent the other two to butcher the poor Christian, and bring him, perhaps, limb by limb, to their fire; and they were stooped down to untie the hands at his feet. I turned to Friday. "Now, Friday," said I, "do as I bid thee." Friday said he would. "Then, Friday," said I, "do exactly as you see me do; fail in nothing." So I set down one of the muskets and the fowling-piece upon the ground and Friday did the like by his; and with the other musket I took my aim at the savages, bidding him do the like. Then, asking him if he was ready, he said, "Yes." "Then fire at them," said I; and the same moment I fired also.

Friday took his aim so much better than I, that on the side that he shot he killed two of them, and wounded three more; and on my side, I killed one and wounded two. They were, you may be sure, in a dreadful consternation; and all of them who were not hurt, jumped up upon their feet immediately, but did not know which way to run, or which way to look; for they knew not from whence their destruction came. Friday kept his eyes close upon me, that, as I had bid him, he might observe what I did: so as soon as the first shot was made, I threw down the piece, and took up the fowling-piece, and Friday did the like; he sees me cock and present – he did the same again. "Are you ready, Friday?" said I. "Yes," says he. "Let fly, then," said I, "in the name of God;" and with that I fired again among the amazed wretches, and so did Friday, and as our pieces were now loaded with what I called swan shot, or small pistol bullets, we found only two drop; but so many were wounded, that they ran about yelling and screaming like mad creatures, all bloody, and miserably wounded most of them; whereof three more fell quickly after, though not quite dead.

'Now, Friday,' said I, laying down the discharged pieces, and taking up the musket, which was yet loaded, "follow me," said I – which he did with a deal of courage, upon which I rushed out of the wood and showed myself, and Friday close at my foot: as soon as I perceived they saw me, I shouted as loud as I could, and bade Friday do so too: and running as fast as I could, which, by the way, was not very fast, being loaded with arms as I was, I made directly towards the poor victim, who was, as I said, lying upon the beach or shore, between the place where they sat and the sea; the two butchers who were just going to work with him, had left him at the surprise of our first fire, and fled in a terrible fright to the sea-side, and had jumped into a canoe, and three more of the rest made the same way. I turned to Friday, and bade him step forwards, and fire at them; he understood me immediately, and, running about forty yards to be near them, he shot at them, and I thought he had killed them all; for I saw them all fall on a heap into the boat – though I saw two of them get up again quickly – however, he killed two of them, and wounded the third, so that he lay down in the bottom of the boat as if he had been dead.

While my man Friday fired at them, I pulled out my knife, and cut the flags that bound the poor victim; and loosing his hands and feet, I lifted him up, and asked him, in the Portuguese tongue, what he was? He answered, in Latin, *Christianus;* but was so weak and faint that he could scarce stand or speak. I took my bottle out of my pocket, and gave it him, making signs that he should drink, which he did; and I gave him a piece of bread, which he ate: then I asked him what countryman he was? and he said "Espagnole";

and being a little recovered, let me know, by all the signs he could possibly make, how much he was in my debt for his deliverance. "Seignor," said I, with as much Spanish as I could make up, "we will talk afterwards, but we must fight now: if you have any strength left, take this pistol and sword, and lay about you:" he took them very thankfully, and no sooner had he arms in his hands, but, as if they had put new vigour into them, he flew upon his murderers like a fury, and had cut two of them in pieces in an instant; for the truth is, as the whole was a surprise to them, so the poor creatures were so much frightened with the noise of our pieces, that they fell down for mere amazement and fear, and had no more power to attempt their own escape, than their flesh had to resist our shot – and that was the case of those five that Friday shot in the boat; for as three of them fell with the hurt they received, so the other two fell with the fright.

I kept my piece in my hand still, without firing, being willing to keep my charge ready, because I had given the Spaniard my pistol and sword; so I called to Friday, and bade him run up to the tree from whence we first fired, and fetch the arms which lay there, that had been discharged, which he did with great swiftness; and then, giving him my musket, I sat down myself to load all the rest again, and bade them come to me when they wanted. While I was loading those pieces, there happened a fierce engagement between the Spaniard and one of the savages, who made at him with one of their great wooden swords, the same weapon that was to have killed him before, if I had not prevented it: the Spaniard, who was as bold and as brave as could be imagined, though weak, had fought this Indian a good while, and had cut him two great wounds on his head; but the savage being a stout, lusty fellow, closing in with him, had thrown him down (being faint), and was wringing my sword out his hand, when the Spaniard, though undermost, wisely quitting his sword, drew the pistol from his girdle, shot the savage through the body, and killed him upon the spot, before I, who was running to help, could come near him.

Friday being now left at his liberty, pursued the flying wretches with no weapon in his hand but his hatchet; and with that he despatched those three, who, as I said before, were wounded at first, and fallen, and all the rest he could come up with; and the Spaniard coming to me for a gun, I gave him one of the fowling-pieces, with which he pursued two of the savages, and wounded them both; but, as he was not able to run, they both got from him into the wood, where Friday pursued them, and killed one of them; but the other was too nimble for him; and, though he was wounded, yet he plunged into the sea, and swam with all his might off to those who were left in the canoe; which three in the canoe, with one wounded, who we knew not whether he died or no, were all that escaped our hands of one-and-twenty. The account of the rest is as follows: –

Three killed at our first shot from the tree; two killed at the next shot; two killed by Friday in the boat; two killed by Friday, of those at first wounded; one killed by Friday in the wood; three killed by the Spaniard; four killed, being found dropped here and there, of the wounds, or killed by Friday in his chase of them; four escaped in the boat, whereof one was wounded, if not dead – twenty-one in all.

Those that were in the canoe worked hard to get out of gunshot; and, though Friday made two or three shots at them, I did not find that he hit any of them. Friday would have fain had me take one of their canoes, and pursue them; and, indeed, I was very anxious about their escape, lest, carrying the news home to their people, they should come back, perhaps, with two or three hundred of their canoes, and devour us by mere multitudes; so I consented to pursue them by sea; and, running to one of their canoes, I jumped in, and bade Friday follow me; but, when I was in the canoe, I was surprised to find another poor creature lie there alive, bound hand and foot, as the Spaniard was, for the slaughter, and almost dead with fear, not knowing what the matter was; for he had not been able to look up over the side of the boat: he was tied so hard, neck and heels, and had been tied so long, that he had really little life in him.

I immediately cut the twisted flags, or rushes, which they had bound him with, and would have helped him up; but he could not stand or speak, but groaned most piteously, believing, it seems, still that he was only unbound in order to be killed.

When Friday came to him, I bade him speak to him, and tell him of his deliverance; and, puling out my bottle, made him give the poor wretch a dram, which, with the news of his being delivered, revived him, and he sat up in the boat; but, when Friday came to hear him speak, and looked in his face, it would have moved any one to tears to have seen how Friday kissed him, embraced him, hugged him, cried, laughed, hallooed, jumped about, danced, sang, then cried again, wrung his hands, beat his own face and head, and then sang and jumped about again like a distracted creature. It was a good while before I could make him speak to me, or tell me what was the matter; but when he came a little to himself, he told me that it was his father.

It was not easy for me to express how it moved me, to see what ecstasy and filial affection had worked in this poor savage, at the sight of his father, and of his being delivered from death; nor indeed can I describe half the extravagances of his affection after this; for he went into the boat and out of the boat a great many times; when he went in to him, he would sit down by him, open his breast, and hold his father's head close to his bosom, half an hour together, to nourish it, then he took his arms and ankles, which were numbed and stiff with the binding, and chafed and rubbed them with his hands; and I, perceiving what the case was, gave him some rum out of my bottle to rub them with, which did them a great deal of good.

This action put an end to our pursuit of the canoe with the other savages, who were now gotten almost out of sight, and it was happy for us that we did not, for it blew so hard within two hours after, and before they could be gotten a quarter of their way, and continued blowing so hard all night, and that from the north-west, which was against them, that I could not suppose their boat could live, or that they ever reached to their own coast.

But to return to Friday. He was so busy about his father that I could not find in my heart to take him off for some time, but after I thought he could leave him a little, I called him to me, and he came jumping and laughing, and pleased to the highest extreme. Then I asked him if he had given his father any bread? He shook his head, and said, "None: ugly dog eat all up self." So I gave him a cake of bread out of a little pouch I carried on purpose. I also gave him a dram for himself, but he would not taste it, but carried it to his father. I had in my pocket, also, two or three bunches of my raisins, so I gave him a handful of them for his father. He had no sooner given his father these raisins, but I saw him come out of the boat, and run away as if he had been bewitched. He ran at such a rate – for he was the swiftest fellow of his feet that ever I saw – I say, he ran at such a rate, that he was out of sight, as it were, in an instant; and though I called, and hallooed too, after him, it was all one: away he went, and in a quarter of an hour I saw him come back again, though not so fast as he went, and as he came nearer, I found his pace was slacker, because he had something in his hand.

When he came up to me, I found he had been quite home for an earthen jug, or pot, to bring his father some fresh water, and that he had got two more cakes, or loaves of bread. The bread he gave me, but the water he carried to his father: however, as I was very thirsty too, I took a little sup of it. This water revived his father more than all the rum or spirits I had given him, for he was just fainting with thirst.

When his father had drunk, I called him to know if there was any water left. He said, "Yes"; and I bade him give it to the poor Spaniard, who was in as much want of it as his father; and I sent one of the cakes that Friday brought to the Spaniard too, who was indeed very weak, and was reposing himself upon a green place, under the shade of a tree, and whose limbs were also very stiff, and very much swelled with the rude bandage he had been tied with. When I saw that upon Friday's coming to him with the water, he sat up and drank, and took the bread, and began to eat, I went to him, and gave him a handful of raisins: he looked up in my face with all the tokens of gratitude and thankfulness that could appear in any countenance; but was so weak, notwithstanding he had so exerted himself in the fight, that he could not stand upon his feet: he tried to do it two or three times, but really was not able, his ankles were so swelled and so painful to him; so I bade him sit still, and caused Friday to rub his ankles, and bathe them with rum, as he had done his father's.

I observed the poor affectionate creature, every two minutes, or perhaps less, all the while he was here, turned his head about, to see if his father was in the same place and posture as he left him sitting; and at last he found he was not to be seen: at which he started up, and, without speaking a word, flew with that swiftness to him, that one could scarce perceive his feet to touch the ground as he went; but when he came, he only found he had laid himself down to ease his limbs; so Friday came back to me presently, and I then spoke to the Spaniard to let Friday help him up, if he could, and lead him to the boat, and then he should carry him to our dwelling, where I would take care of him; but Friday, a lusty young fellow, took the Spaniard quite up upon his back, and carried him away to the boat, and set him down softly upon the side or gunnel of the canoe, with his feet in the inside of it, and then lifted him quite in, and set him close to his father, and presently stepping out again, launched the boat off, and paddled it along the shore faster than I could walk, though the wind blew pretty hard too: so he brought them safe into our creek; and leaving them in the boat, runs away to fetch the other canoe. As he passed me, I spoke to him, and asked him whither he went? He told me, "Go fetch more boat"; so away he went, like the wind; for sure never man or horse ran like him, and he had the other canoe in the creek almost as soon as I got to it by land; so he wafted me over, and went then to help our new guests out of the boat, which he did, but they were neither of them able to walk; so that poor Friday knew not what to do.

To remedy this, I went to work in my thought, and calling to Friday to bid them sit down on the bank while he came to me, I soon made a kind of hand-barrow to lay them on, and Friday and I carried them up both together upon it between us: but when we got them to the outside of our wall or fortification, we were at a worse loss than before, for it was impossible to get them over, and I was resolved not to break it down: so I set to work again; and Friday and I, in about two hours' time, made a very handsome tent, covered with old sails, and above that with boughs of trees, being in the space without our outward fence, and between that and the grove of young wood which I had planted: and here we made two beds of such things as I had; namely, of good rice straw, with blankets laid upon it to lie on, and another to cover them on each bed.

My island was now peopled, and I thought myself very rich in subjects; and it was a merry reflection which I frequently made, how like a king I looked: first of all, the whole country was my own mere property, so that I had an undoubted right of dominion: secondly, my people were perfectly subjected; I was absolute lord and law-giver; they all owed their lives to me, and were ready to lay down their lives, if there had been occasion for it, for me; it was remarkable too, I had but three subjects, and they were of three different religions. My man Friday was a Protestant, his father a Pagan and a cannibal, and the Spaniard was a Papist: however, I allowed liberty of conscience throughout my dominions; but this by the way.

As soon as I had secured my two weak, rescued prisoners, and given them shelter, and a place to rest them upon, I began to think of making some provision for them; and the first thing I did, I ordered Friday to take a yearling goat, betwixt a kid and a goat, out of my particular flock, to be killed: then I cut off the hind quarter, and chopping it into small pieces, I set Friday to work to boiling and stewing, and made them a very good dish, I assure you, of flesh and broth, having put some barley and rice also into the broth; and as I cooked it without doors (for I made no fire within my inner wall), so I carried it all into the new tent; and having set a table there for them, I sat down and ate my dinner also with them: and, as well as I could, cheered them and encouraged them, Friday being my interpreter, especially to his father, and indeed to the Spaniard too; for the Spaniard spoke the language of the savages pretty well.

After we had dined, or rather supped, I ordered Friday to take one of the canoes, and go and fetch our muskets and other fire-arms, which, for want of time, we had left upon the place of battle; and the next day I ordered him to go and bury the dead bodies of the savages, which lay open to the sun, and would presently be offensive; and I also ordered him to bury the horrid remains of their barbarous feast, which I knew were pretty much, and which I could not think of doing myself; nay, I could not bear to see them, if I went that way: all which he punctually performed, and defaced the very appearance of the savages being there; so that when I went again, I could scarce know where it was, otherwise than by the corner of the wood pointing to the place.

I then began to enter into a little conversation with my two new subjects; and first, I set Friday to inquire of his father what he thought of the escape of the savages in that canoe? and whither we might expect a return of them with a power too great for us to resist? His first opinion was, that the savages in the boat never could live out the storm which blew that night they went off, but must of necessity be drowned or driven south to those other shores, where they were as sure to be devoured as they were to be drowned if they were cast away; but as to what they would do if they came safe on shore, he said he knew not; but it was his opinion, that they were so dreadfully frighted with the manner of being attacked, the noise and the fire, that he believed they would tell their people they were all killed by thunder and lightning, and not by the hand of man; and that the two which appeared (namely, Friday and I) were two heavenly spirits or furies come down to destroy them, and not men with weapons. This, he said, he knew, because he heard them all cry out so in their language to one another; for it was impossible for them to conceive that a man should dart fire, and speak thunder, and kill at a distance, without lifting up the hand, as was done now. And this old savage was in the right; for, as I understood since, by other hands, the savages of that part never attempted to go over to the island afterwards. They were so terrified with the accounts given by these four men (for it seems they did escape the sea), that they believed, whoever went to that enchanted island would be destroyed with fire from the gods.

This, however, I knew not, and therefore was under continual apprehensions for a good while, and kept always upon my guard; I and all my army; for, as there were now four of us, I would have ventured upon a hundred of them fairly in the open field at any time.

In a little time, however, no more canoes appearing, the fear of their coming wore off; and I began to take my former thoughts of a voyage to the main into consideration, being likewise assured by Friday's father, that I might depend upon good usage from their nation on his account, if I would go.

CHAPTER 17

I learn of more Spaniards among the
Savages – The Spaniard and Friday's Father
sail to the Continent – an English ship off
the Island – Boat comes on shore with
three Prisoners – Discover myself to the
Prisoners – Secure the Mutineers

But my thoughts were a little suspended, when I had a serious
discourse with the Spaniard, and when I understood that there
were sixteen more of his countrymen and Portuguese, who, having
been cast away, and made their escape to that side, lived there at
peace indeed with the savages, but were sore put to it for necessaries, and indeed for life; I asked him all the particulars of their
voyage, and found they were a Spanish ship, bound from the Rio
de la Plata to the Havanna, being directed to leave their loading
there, which was chiefly hides and silver, and to bring back what
European goods they could meet with there; that they had five
Portuguese seamen on board, whom they took out of another wreck;
that five of their own men were drowned when first the ship was
lost; and that these escaped through infinite dangers and hazards,
and arrived almost starved on the cannibal coast, where they
expected to have been devoured every moment.

He told me they had some arms with them, but they were
perfectly useless; for that they had neither powder nor ball, the
washing of the sea having spoiled all their powder, but a little which
they used at their first landing to provide themselves some food.

I asked him what he thought would become of them there;
and if they had formed no design of making any escape? He said
they had had many consultations about it; but that, having neither

vessel nor tools to build one, nor provisions of any kind, their counsels always ended in tears and despair.

I asked him how he thought they would receive a proposal from me, which might tend towards an escape; and whether, if they were all here, it might not be done? I told him with freedom, I feared mostly their treachery and ill usage of me, if I put my life in their hands; for that gratitude was no inherent virtue in the nature of man; nor did men always square their dealings by the obligations they had received, so much as they did by the advantages they expected. I told him, it would be very hard that I should be the instrument of their deliverance, and that they should afterwards make me their prisoner in New Spain, where an Englishman was certain to be made a sacrifice, what necessity, or what accident soever, brought him thither; and that I had rather be devoured alive, than fall into the merciless claws of the priests, and be carried into the Inquisition. I added, that otherwise, I was persuaded if they were all here we might, with so many hands, build a bark large enough to carry us all away, either to the Brazils southward, or to the islands or Spanish coast northward: but that if in requital they should, when I had put weapons into their hands, carry me by force among their own people, I might be ill used for my kindness to them, and make my case worse than it was before.

He answered, with a great deal of candour and ingenuity, that their condition was so miserable, and that they were so sensible of it, that he believed they would abhor the thought of using any man unkindly that should contribute to their deliverance; and that if I pleased, he would go to them with the old man, and discourse with them about it, and return again, and bring me their answer: that he would make conditions with them, upon their solemn oath, that they would be absolutely under my leading, as their commander and captain; and that they should swear upon the holy Sacraments and Gospel to be true to me, and go to such Christian country as I should agree to, and no other; and to be directed wholly and absolutely by my orders, till they were landed safely in such country as I intended; and that he would bring a contract from them under their hands for that purpose.

Then he told me, he would first swear to me himself, that he would never stir from me as long as he lived, till I gave him order; and that he would take my side to the last drop of blood, if there should happen the least breach of faith among his countrymen.

He told me, they were all of them very civil, honest men, and they were under the greatest distress imaginable, having neither weapons nor clothes, nor any food, but at the mercy and discretion of the savages – out of all hopes of ever returning to their own country; and that he was sure, if I would undertake their relief, they would live and die by me,

Upon these assurances, I resolved to venture to relieve them, if possible, and to send the old savage and this Spaniard over to them to treat: but when he had gotten all things in readiness to go, the Spaniard himself started an objection, which had so much prudence in it on one hand, and so much sincerity on the other hand, that I could not but be very well satisfied in it; and, by his advice, put off the deliverance of his comrades for at least half a year. The case was this: –

He had been with us now about a month, during which time I had let him see in what manner I had provided, with the assistance of Providence, for my support; and he saw evidently what stock of corn and rice I had laid up: which, as it was more than sufficient for myself, so it was not sufficient, at least, without good husbandry, for my family, now it was increased to number four: but much less would it be sufficient if his countrymen, who were, as he said, fourteen still alive, should come over; and least of all would it be sufficient to victual our vessel, if we should build one, for a voyage to any one of the Christian colonies of America. So he told me, he thought it would be more advisable to let him and the other two dig and cultivate some more land, as much as I could spare seed to sow; and that we should wait another harvest, that we might have a supply of corn for his countrymen when they should come; for want might be a temptation to them to disagree, or not to think themselves delivered, otherwise than out of one difficulty into another. "You know," says he, "the children of Israel, though they rejoiced at first at their being delivered out of Egypt, yet rebelled even against God himself, that delivered them, when they came to want bread in the wilderness."

His caution was so seasonable, and his advice so good, that I could not but be very well pleased with his proposal, as well as I was satisfied with his fidelity. So we fell to digging, all four of us, as well as the wooden tools we were furnished with permitted; and, in about a month's time, by the end of which it was such time, we had gotten as much land cured and trimmed up as we sowed twenty-two bushels of barley on, and sixteen jars of rice, which was, in short, all the seed we had to spare; nor indeed did we leave ourselves barley sufficient for our own food for the six months that we had to expect our crop, that is to say, reckoning from the time we set our seed aside for sowing; for it is not to be supposed it is six months in the ground in that country.

Having now society enough, and our number being sufficient to put us out of fear of the savages, if they had come, unless their number had been very great, we went freely all over the island, wherever we found occasion; and as here we had our escape or deliverance upon our thoughts, it was impossible, at least for me, to have the means of it out of mind. To this purpose, I marked out several trees which I thought fit for our work, and I set Friday and his father to cutting them down; and then I caused the Spaniard, to whom I imparted my thoughts on that affair, to oversee and direct their work: I showed them with what indefatigable pains I had hewed a large tree into single planks, and I caused them to do the like, till they had made about a dozen large planks of good oak, near two feet broad, thirty-five feet long, and from two inches to four inches thick: what prodigious labour it took up, any one may imagine.

At the same time, I contrived to increase my little flock of tame goats as much as I could: and to this purpose I made Friday and the Spaniard to go out one day, and myself with Friday the next day, for we took our turns; and by this means we got about twenty young kids to breed up with the rest; for whenever we shot the dam, we saved the kids, and added them to our flock: but, above all, the season for curing the grapes coming on, I caused such a prodigious quantity to be hung up in the sun, that I believe, had we been at Alicant, where the raisins of the sun are cured, we should have filled sixty or eighty barrels; and these, with our bread, were a great part of our food, and very good living too, I assure you; for it is an exceedingly nourishing food.

It was now harvest, and our crop in good order; it was not the most plentiful increase I had seen in the island; but, however, it was enough to answer our end, for from twenty-two bushels of barley, we brought in and thrashed out above two hundred and twenty bushels, and the like in proportion of the rice, which was store enough for our food to the next harvest, though all the sixteen Spaniards had been on shore with me; or, if we had been ready for a voyage, it would very plentifully have victualled our ship, to have carried us to any part of the world, that is to say, of America. When we had thus housed and secured our magazine of corn, we fell to work to make more wicker-work, namely, great baskets, in which

DANIEL DEFOE

we kept it; and the Spaniard was very handy and dexterous at this part, and often blamed me that I did not make some things for defence, of this kind of work; but I saw no need of it. And now, having a full supply of food for all the guests expected, I gave the Spaniard leave to go over to the main, to see what he could do with those he left behind him there: I gave him a strict charge in writing not to bring any man with him who would not first swear, in the presence of himself and of the old savage, that he would no way injure, fight with, or attack the person he should find in the island, who was so kind to send for them, in order to their deliverance; but that they would stand by and defend him against all such attempts; and, wherever they went, would be entirely under, and subjected to his command; and that this should be put in writing, and signed with their hands: how we were to have this done, when I knew they had neither pen nor ink, that, indeed, was a question which we never asked.

Under these instructions, the Spaniard and the old savage (the father of Friday) went away in one of the canoes, which they might be said to come in, or rather were brought in, when they came as prisoners to be devoured by the savages.

I gave each of them a musket with a firelock on it, and about eight charges of powder and ball, charging them to be very good husbands of both, and not to use either of them, but upon urgent occasions.

This was a cheerful work, being the first measures used by me in view of my deliverance for now twenty-seven years and some days. I gave them provisions of bread, and of dried grapes, sufficient for themselves for many days, and sufficient for their countrymen for about eight days' time; and, wishing them a good voyage, I let them go, agreeing with them about a signal they should hang out at their return, by which I should know them again, when they came back at a distance, before they came on shore.

They went away with a fair gale on the day that the moon was at full – by my account in the month of October – but as for the exact reckoning of days, after I had once lost it, I could never recover it again; nor had I kept the number of years so punctually as to be sure that I was right, though, as it proved when I afterwards examined my account, I found I had kept a true reckoning of years.

It was no less than eight days I waited for them, when a strange and unforeseen accident intervened, of which the like has not, perhaps, been heard of in history. I was fast asleep in my hutch one morning, when my man Friday came running in to me, and called aloud, "Master, master, they are come, they are come!"

I jumped up, and, regardless of danger, I went out as soon as I could get my clothes on, through my little grove – which, by the way, was by this time grown to be a very thick wood – I say, regardless of danger, I went without my arms, which was not my custom to do; but I was surprised, when, turning my eyes to the sea, I presently saw a boat at about a league and a half's distance, standing in for shore, with a shoulder-of-mutton sail, as they call it, and the wind blowing pretty fair to bring them in. Also I observed presently, that they did not come from that side which the shore lay on, but from the southernmost end of the island. Upon this I called Friday in, and bade him lie close, for these were not the people we looked for, and that we did not know yet whether they were friends or enemies.

In the next place, I went in to fetch my perspective glass, to see what I could make of them; and, having taken the ladder out, I climbed up to the top of the hill, as I used to do when I was apprehensive of any thing, and to take my view the plainer without being discovered.

I had scarce set my foot on the hill, when my eye plainly discovered a ship lying at an anchor, at about two leagues and a half's distance from me, south-south-east, but not above a league and a half from the shore. By my observation it appeared plainly to be an English ship, and the boat appeared to be an English long-boat.

I cannot express the confusion I was in, though the joy of seeing a ship, and one which I had reason to believe was manned by my own countrymen, and consequently friends, was such as I cannot describe; but yet I had some secret doubts hung about me, I cannot tell from whence they came, bidding me keep upon my guard. In the first place, it occurred to me to consider what business an English ship could have in that part of the world; since it was not the way to or from any part of the world where the English had any traffic, and I knew there had been no storms to drive them in there, as in distress; and that if they were really English, it was most probable that they were here upon no good design; and that I had better continue as I was, than fall into the hands of thieves and murderers.

Let no man despise the secret hints and notices of danger which sometimes are given him, when he may think there is no possibility of its being real. That such hints and notices are given us, I believe few that have made any observation of things can deny; that they are certain discoveries of an invisible world, and a converse of spirits, we cannot doubt; and if the tendency of them seems to be to warn us of danger, why should we not suppose they are from some friendly agent (whether supreme, or inferior and subordinate is not the question), and they are given for our good?

The present question abundantly confirms me in the justice of this reasoning; for had I not been made cautious by this secret admonition, come from whence it will, I had been undone inevitably, and in a far worse condition than before, as you will see presently.

I had not kept myself long in this posture, but I saw the boat draw near the shore, as if they looked for a creek to thrust in at for the convenience of landing; however, as they did not come quite far enough, they did not see the little inlet where I formerly landed my rafts, but ran their boat on shore upon the beach, at about half a mile from me, which was very happy for me; for otherwise they would have landed just, as I may say, at my door, and would have soon beaten me out of my castle, and, perhaps, have plundered me of all I had.

When they were on shore, I was fully satisfied they were Englishmen, at least, most of them; one or two I thought were Dutch, but it did not prove so. There were, in all, eleven men, whereof three of them I found were unarmed and (as I thought) bound, and when the first four or five of them were jumped on shore they took those three out of the boat as prisoners. One of the three I could perceive using the most passionate gestures of entreaty, affliction, and despair, even to a kind of extravagance; the other two, I could perceive, lifted up their hands sometimes, and appeared concerned indeed, but not to such a degree as the first.

I was perfectly confounded at the sight, and knew not what the meaning of it should be; Friday called out to me, in English, as well as he could, "Oh, master! you see English mans eat prisoners as well as savage man's;" "Why," said I, "Friday, do you think they are going to eat them then? "Yes," says Friday, "they will eat them." "No, no," said I, "Friday; I am afraid they will murder them indeed; but you may be sure they will not eat them."

All this while I had no thought of what the matter really was, but stood trembling with the horror of the sight, expecting every moment when the three prisoners should be killed; nay, once I saw one of the villains lift up his arm with a great cutlass (as the seamen

call it) or sword, to strike one of the poor men; and I expected to
see him fall every moment, at which all the blood in my body seemed
to run chill in my veins.

I wished heartily now for our Spaniard, and the savage that
was gone with him; or that I had any way to have come undiscovered within shot of them, that I might have rescued the three
men; for I saw no fire-arms they had among them; but it fell out
to my mind another way.

After I had observed the outrageous usage of the three men
by the insolent seamen, I observed the fellows run scattering about
the land, as if they wanted to see the country. I observed also, that
the three other men had liberty to go where they pleased; but they
sat down all three upon the ground very pensive, and looked like
men in despair.

This put me in mind of the first time when I came on shore,
and began to look about me: how I gave myself over for lost, how
wildly I looked round me, what dreadful apprehensions I had, and
how I lodged in the tree all night for fear of being devoured by wild
beasts.

As I knew nothing that night of the supply I was to receive
by the providential driving of the ship nearer the land by the storms
and tides, by which I have since been so long nourished and
supported; so these three poor desolate men knew nothing how
certain of deliverance and supply they were, how near it was to
them, and how effectually and really they were in a condition of
safety, at the same time they thought themselves lost, and their case
desperate.

So little do we see before us in the world, and so much reason
have we to depend cheerfully upon the great Maker of the world,
that He does not leave His creatures so absolutely destitute, but
that in the worst circumstances they have always something to be
thankful for, and sometimes are nearer their deliverance than they
imagine – nay, are even brought to their deliverance by the means
by which they seem to be brought to their destruction.

It was just at the top of high water when these people came
on shore, and while partly they stood parleying with the prisoners
they brought, and partly while they rambled about to see what kind
of place they were in, they had carelessly stayed till the tide was
spent, and the water was ebbed considerably away, leaving their
boat aground.

They had left two men in the boat, who, as I found afterwards, having drunk a little too much brandy, fell asleep; however, one of them wakened sooner than the other, and finding the boat too fast aground for him to stir it, hallooed for the rest who were straggling about, upon which they all soon came to the boat; but it was past all their strength to launch her, the boat being very heavy, and the shore on that side being a soft oozy sand, almost like a quicksand.

In this condition, like true seamen, who are, perhaps, the least of all mankind given to forethought, they gave it over, and away they strolled about the country again; and I heard one of them say aloud to another (calling them off from the boat), "Why, let her alone, Jack, can't ye? she'll float next tide." By which I was fully confirmed in the main inquiry, of what countrymen they were.

All this while I kept myself close, not once daring to stir out of my castle, any farther than to my place of observation, near the top of the hill; and very glad I was to think how well it was fortified. I knew it was no less than ten hours before the boat could be on float again, and by that time it would be dark and I might be more at liberty to see their motions, and to hear their discourse, if they had any.

In the meantime, I fitted myself up for a battle, as before, though with more caution, knowing I had to do with another kind of enemy than I had at first; I ordered Friday also, whom I had made an excellent marksman with his gun, to load himself with arms – I took myself two fowling-pieces and I gave him three muskets. My figure, indeed, was very fierce: I had my formidable goat-skin coat on, with the great cap I mentioned, a naked sword, two pistols in my belt, and a gun upon each shoulder.

It was my design, as I said above, not to have made any attempt till it was dark; but about two o'clock, being the heat of the day, I found that, in short, they were all gone straggling into the woods, and, as I thought, were all laid down to sleep. The three poor distressed men, too anxious for their condition to get any sleep, were, however, set down under the shelter of a great tree, at about a quarter of a mile from me, and, as I thought, out of sight of any of the rest.

Upon this I resolved to discover myself to them, and learn something of their condition. Immediately I marched in the figure above, my man Friday at a good distance behind me, as formidable for his arms as I, but not making quite so staring a spectre-like figure as I did.

I came as near them undiscovered as I could, and then, before any of them saw me, I called aloud to them, in Spanish, "What are ye, gentlemen?"

They started up at the noise, but were ten times more confounded when they saw me, and the uncouth figure that I made – they made no answer at all, but I thought I perceived them just going to fly from me, when I spoke to them in English: "Gentlemen," said I, "do not be surprised at me; perhaps you may have a friend near you, when you did not expect it." "He must be sent directly from Heaven, then," said one of them, very gravely, to me, pulling off his hat at the same time, "for our condition is past the help of man." "All help is from Heaven, sir!" said I; "but can you put a stranger in the way how to help you, for you seem to me to be in great distress? I saw you when you landed; and when you seemed to make application to the brutes that came with you, I saw one of them lift up his sword to kill you."

The poor man, with tears running down his face, and trembling, looking like one astonished, returned. "Am I talking to God or man? Is it a real man or an angel!" "Be in no fear about that, sir," said I: "if God had sent an angel to relieve you, he would have come better clothed, and better armed after another manner than you see me in. Pray, lay aside your fears: I am a man, – an Englishman, and disposed to assist you; you see I have one servant only – we have arms and ammunition; tell us freely, can we serve you? What is your case?"

"Our case," said he, "sir, is too long to tell you while our murderers are so near; but, in short, sir, I was commander of that ship; my men having mutinied against me, they have been hardly prevailed on not to murder me, and at last they have set me on shore in this desolate place, with those two men with me, one my mate, the other a passenger, where we expected to perish, believing the place to be uninhabited, and know not yet what to think of it."

"Where are those brutes, your enemies?" said I; "do you know where they are gone?" "There they are, sir," said he, pointing to a thicket of trees; "my heart trembles for fear they have seen us, and heard you speak; if they have, they will certainly murder us all,"

"Have they any fire-arms?" said I. He answered, "They had only two pieces, and one which they left in the boat." "Well, then," said I, "leave the rest to me: I see they are asleep; it is an easy thing to kill them all, but shall we rather take them prisoners?" He told me there were two desperate villains among them, that it was scarce safe to show any mercy to; but if they were secured, he believed all the rest would return to their duty: I asked him which they were? He told me he could not at that distance describe them; but he would obey my orders in anything I would direct. "Well," said I, "let us retreat out of their view or hearing, lest they awake, and we will resolve further;" so they willingly went back with me, till the woods covered us from them.

"Look you, sir," said I, "if I venture upon your deliverance, are you willing to make two conditions with me?" He anticipated my proposals by telling me, that both he and the ship, if recovered, should be wholly directed and commanded by me in everything; and if the ship was not recovered, he would live and die with me in what part of the world soever I would send him; and the two other men said the same.

"Well," said I, "my conditions are but two: First, that while you stay on this island with me, you will not pretend to any authority here; and if I put arms into your hands, you will upon all occasions give them up to me and do no prejudice to me or mine, upon this island, and in the meantime to be governed by orders. Second, that if the ship is, or may be recovered, you will carry me and my man to England, passage free."

He gave me all the assurance that the invention or faith of a man could devise, that he would comply with these most reasonable demands; and besides would owe his life to me, and acknowledge it upon all occasions as long as he lived.

"Well, then," said I, "here are three muskets for you, with powder and ball; tell me next what you think is proper to be done." He showed all the testimony of his gratitude that he was able, but offered to be wholly guided by me; I told him I thought it was hard venturing anything, but the best method I could think of was, to fire upon them at once as they lay; and if any were not killed at the first volley, and offered to submit, we might save them, and so put it wholly upon God's providence to direct the shot.

He said, very modestly, that he was loath to kill them if he could help it; but that those two were incorrigible villains, and had been the authors of all the mutiny in the ship, and, if they escaped, we should be undone still; for they would go on board, and bring the whole ship's company and destroy us all. "Well, then," said I, "necessity legitimates my advice; for it is the only way to save our lives." However, seeing him still cautious of shedding blood, I told him they should go themselves, and manage as they found convenient.

In the middle of this discourse, we heard some of them awake, and soon after we saw two of them on their feet. I asked him if either of them were the men who he had said were the heads of the mutiny? He said, "No." "Well, then," said I, "you may let them escape, and Providence seems to have wakened them on purpose to save themselves. Now," said I, "if the rest escape you, it is your fault."

Animated with this, he took the musket I had given him in his hand, and pistol in his belt, and his two comrades with him, with each man a piece in his hand; the two men who were with him going first, made some noise, at which one of the seamen, who was awake, turned about, and, seeing them coming, cried out to the rest; but it was too late then, for the moment he cried out they fired, I mean the two men, the captain wisely reserving his own piece: they had so well aimed their shot at the men they knew, that one of them was killed on the spot and the other very much wounded; but not being dead, he started up on his feet and called eagerly for help to the other: but the captain stepping to him, told him it was too late to cry for help, he should call upon God to forgive his villainy; and with that word knocked him down with the stock of his musket, so that he never spoke more: there were three more in the company, and one of them was also slightly wounded. By this time I was come; and when they saw their danger, and it was in vain to resist, they begged for mercy. The captain told them he would spare their lives, if they would give him any assurance of their abhorrence of the treachery they had been guilty of, and would swear to be faithful to him in recovering the ship, and afterwards in carrying her back to Jamaica, from whence they came. They gave him all the protestations of their sincerity that could be desired, and he was willing to believe them, and spare their lives, which I was not against; only I obliged him to keep them bound, hand and foot, while they were upon the island.

While this was doing, I sent Friday with the captain's mate to the boat with orders to secure her, and bring away the oars and sail, which they did; and by-and-by, three straggling men, that were (happily for them) parted from the rest, came back upon hearing the guns fired; and seeing their captain, who before was their prisoner, now their conqueror, they submitted to be bound also – and so our victory was complete.

It now remained that the captain and I should inquire into one another's circumstances, I began first, and told him my whole history, which he heard with an attention even to amazement, and particularly at the wonderful manner of my being furnished with provisions and ammunition; and, indeed, as my whole story is a collection of wonders, it affected him deeply: but when he reflected from thence upon himself, and how I seemed to have been preserved there on purpose to save his life, the tears ran down his face, and he could not speak a word more.

After this communication was at an end, I carried him and his two men into my apartments, leading them in just where I came out, namely, at the top of the house; where I refreshed them with such provisions as I had, and showed them all the contrivances I had made during my long, long inhabiting that place.

All I showed them, all I said to them, was perfectly amazing; but, above all, the captain admired my fortification; and how perfectly I had concealed my retreat with a grove of trees, which, having now been planted near twenty years, and the trees growing much faster than in England, was become a little wood, and so thick that it was impassable in any part of it, but at that one side where I had reserved my little winding passage into it; this I told him was my castle and my residence; but that I had a seat in the country, as most princes have, whither I could retreat upon occasion, and I would show him that too another time; but at present our business was to consider how to recover the ship. He agreed with me as to that, but told me he was perfectly at a loss what measures to take; for that there were still six-and-twenty hands on board, who, having entered into a cursed conspiracy, by which they had all forfeited their lives to the law, would be hardened in it now by desperation; and would carry it on, knowing that, if they were reduced, they should be brought to the gallows as soon as they came to England, or to any of the English colonies; and that therefore there would be no attacking them with so small a number as we were.

I mused for some time upon what he had said, and found it was a very rational conclusion, and that therefore something was to be resolved on very speedily, as well to draw the men on board into some snare for their surprise, as to prevent their landing upon us, and destroying us. Upon this, it presently occurred to me, that in a little while the ship's crew, wondering what was become of their comrades, and of the boat, would certainly come on shore in their other boat to seek for them; and that then perhaps they might come armed, and be too strong for us: this he allowed was rational.

Upon this, I told him the first thing we had to do was to stave the boat, which lay upon the beach, so that they might not carry her off; and taking everything out of her, leave her so far useless as not to be fit to swim; accordingly, we went on board, took the arms which were left on board out of her, and whatever else we found there – which was a bottle of brandy and another of rum, a few biscuit cakes, a horn of powder, and a great lump of sugar in a piece of canvas – the sugar was five or six pounds; all of which was very welcome to me, especially the brandy and sugar, of which I had had none left for many years.

When we had carried all these things on shore (the oars, mast, sail, and rudder of the boat were carried before, as above), we knocked a great hole in her bottom, that if they had come strong enough to master us, yet they could not carry off the boat. Indeed, it was not much in my thoughts, that we could be capable to recover the ship; but my view was, that if they went away without the boat, I did not much question to make her fit again to carry us away to the Leeward Islands, and call upon our friends the Spaniards in my way, for I had them still in my thoughts.

CHAPTER 18

Ship signals for her Boat – Receives no
answer – Sends another – We secure this
Boat's Crew, and recover the Ship

While we were thus preparing our designs, and had first by main
strength heaved the boat up upon the beach, so high that the tide
would not float her off at high water mark, and, besides, had broken
a hole in her bottom too big to be quickly stopped, and were sat
down musing what we should do, we heard the ship fire a gun, and
saw her make a waft with her ancient, as a signal for the boat to
come on board; but no boat stirred; and they fired several times,
making other signals for the boat.

At last, when all their signals and firings proved fruitless, and
they found the boat did not stir, we saw them (by the help of our
glasses) hoist another boat out, and row towards the shore; and we
found, as they approached, that there were no less than ten men in
her, and that they had fire-arms with them.

As the ship lay almost two leagues from the shore, we had a
full view of them as they came, and a plain sight of the men, even
of their faces; because the tide having set them a little to the east
of the other boat, they rowed up under shore, to come to the same
place where the other had landed, and where the boat lay.

By this means, I say, we had a full view of them, and the
captain knew the persons and characters of all the men in the boat:
of whom he said that there were three very honest fellows, who,
he was sure, were led into this conspiracy by the rest, being over-
powered and frightened; but that for the boatswain, who, it seems,
was the chief officer among them, and all the rest, they were as
outrageous as any of the ship's crew; and were, no doubt, made

desperate in their new enterprise; and terribly apprehensive he was that they would be too powerful for us.

I smiled at him, and told him, that men in our circumstances were past the operations of fear: that seeing almost every condition that could be was better than that we were supposed to be in, we ought to expect that the consequences, whether death or life, would be sure to be a deliverance: I asked him, what he thought of the circumstances of my life, and whether a deliverance were not worth venturing for? "And where, sir," said I, "is your belief of my being preserved here on purpose to save your life, which elevated you a little while ago? For my part," said I, "there seems to be only one thing amiss in all the prospect of it." "What's that?" says he. "Why," said I, "'tis that, as you say, there are three or four honest fellows among them, which should be spared; had they been all of the wicked part of the crew, I should have thought God's providence had singled them out to deliver them into your hands: for, depend upon it, every man of them that comes ashore are our own, and shall die or live, as they behave to us."

As I spoke this with a raised voice and cheerful countenance, I found it greatly encouraged him; so we set vigorously to our business. We had, upon the first appearance of the boat's coming from the ship, considered of separating our prisoners, and had indeed secured them effectually.

Two of them, of whom the captain was less assured than ordinary, I sent with Friday, and one of the three (delivered men) to my cave, where they were remote enough, and out of danger of being heard or discovered, or of finding their way out of the woods, if they could have delivered themselves: here they left them bound, but gave them provisions, and promised them, if they continued there quietly, to give them their liberty in a day or two: but that if they attempted their escape, they should be put to death without mercy. They promised faithfully to bear their confinement with patience, and were very thankful that they had such good usage as to have provisions and a light left them; for Friday gave them candles (such as we made ourselves), for their comfort; and they did not know but that he stood sentinel over them at the entrance.

The other prisoners had better usage: two of them were kept pinioned indeed, because the captain was not free to trust them; but the other two were taken into my service upon their captain's recommendation, and upon their solemnly engaging to live and die with us; so, with them and the three honest men, we were seven men well armed; and I made no doubt we should be able to deal well enough with the ten that were a-coming, considering that the captain had said there were three or four honest men amongst them also.

As soon as they got to the place where their other boat lay, they ran their boat into the beach, and came all on shore, hauling the boat up after them, which I was glad to see; for I was afraid they would rather have left the boat at an anchor, some distance from the shore, with some hands in her to guard her; and so we should not be able to seize the boat.

Being on shore, the first thing they did, they ran all to the other boat; and it was easy to see they were under a great surprise to find her stripped, as above, of all that was in her, and a great hole in her bottom.

After they had mused awhile upon this, they set up two or three great shouts, hallooing with all their might to try if they could make their companions hear; but all was to no purpose: then they came all close in a ring, and fired a volley of their small-arms, which, indeed, we heard, and the echoes made the woods ring; but it was all one: those in the cave, we were sure, could not hear; and those in our keeping, though they heard it well enough, yet durst give no answer to them.

They were so astonished at the surprise of this, that, as they told us afterwards, they resolved to go all on board again to their ship, and let them know there that the men were all murdered, and the longboat staved; accordingly, they immediately launched the boat again, and got all of them on board.

The captain was terribly amazed, and even confounded at this, believing they would go on board the ship again, and set sail, giving their comrades up for lost, and so he should still lose the ship, which he was in hopes we should have recovered; but he was quickly as much frightened the other way.

They had not been long put off with the boat, but we perceived them all coming on shore again; but, with this new measure in their conduct, which, it seems, they consulted together upon, namely, to leave three men in the boat, and the rest to go on shore, and go up into the country to look for their fellows.

This was a great disappointment to us; for now we were at a loss what to do; for our seizing those seven men on shore would be no advantage to us if we let the boat escape, because they would then row away to the ship; and then the rest of them would be sure to weigh and set sail, and so our recovering the ship would be lost.

However, we had no remedy but to wait and see what the issue of things might present. The seven men came on shore, and the three who remained in the boat put her off to a good distance from the shore, and came to an anchor to wait for them; so that it was impossible for us to come at them in the boat.

Those that came on shore kept close together, marching towards the top of the little hill, under which my habitation lay; and we could see them plainly, though they could not perceive us; we could have been very glad they would have come nearer to us, so that we might have fired at them; or that they would have gone farther off, that we might have come abroad.

But when they were come to the brow of the hill, where they could see a great way in the valley and woods, which lay towards the north-east part, and where the island lay lowest, they shouted and hallooed till they were weary; and not caring, it seems, to venture far from the shore, nor far from one another, they sat down together under a tree to consider of it. Had they thought fit to have gone to sleep there, as the other party of them had done, they had done the job for us; but they were too full of apprehensions of danger to venture to go to sleep, though they could not tell what the danger was they had to fear neither.

The captain made a very just proposal to me upon this consultation of theirs, namely, that, perhaps, they would all fire a volley again to endeavour to make their fellows hear, and that we should all sally upon them just at the juncture when their pieces were all discharged, and they would certainly yield, and we should have them without bloodshed. I liked the proposal, provided it was done while we were near enough to come up to them before they could load their pieces again.

But this event did not happen, and we lay still a long time very irresolute what course to take; at length I told them there would be nothing to be done, in my opinion, till night; and then, if they did not return to the boat, perhaps we might find a way to get between them and the shore, and so might use some stratagem with them in the boat to get them on shore.

We waited a great while, though very impatient for their removing, and were very uneasy; when, after long consultations, we saw them start all up, and march down toward the sea; it seems they had such dreadful apprehensions upon them of the danger of the place, that they resolved to go on board the ship again, give their companions over for lost, and so go on with their intended voyage with the ship.

As soon as I perceived them go towards the shore, I imagined it to be, as it really was, that they had given over their search, and were for going back again; and the captain, as soon as I had told him my thoughts, was ready to sink at the apprehensions of it; but I presently thought of a stratagem to bring them back again, and which answered my end to a tittle.

I ordered Friday and the captain's mate to go over the little creek westward, towards the place where the savages came on shore when Friday was rescued; and as soon as they came to a little rising ground, at about half a mile's distance, I bade them halloo as loud as they could, and wait till they found the seamen heard them; that as soon as ever they heard the seamen answer them, they should return it again, and then keeping out of sight take a round, always answering when the others hallooed, to draw them as far into the island, and among the woods, as possible, and then wheel about again to me, by such ways as I directed.

They were just going into the boat when Friday and the mate hallooed, and they presently heard them, and answering, ran along the shore westward, towards the voice they heard, when they were presently stopped by the creek, where, the water being up, they could not get over, and called for the boat to come up and set them over, as indeed I expected.

When they had set themselves over, I observed that the boat being gone up a good way into the creek, and, as it were, in a harbour within the land, they took one of the three men out of her to go along with them, and left only two in the boat, having fastened her to the stump of a little tree on the shore.

This was what I wished for, and immediately leaving Friday and the captain's mate to their business, I took the rest with me, and crossing the creek out of their sight, we surprised the two men before they were aware, one of them lying on the shore, and the other being in the boat; the fellow on shore was between sleeping and waking, and, going to start up, the captain, who was foremost, ran in upon him and knocked him down, and then called out to him in the boat to yield, or he was a dead man.

There needed very few arguments to persuade a single man to yield, when he saw five men upon him, and his comrade knocked down: besides, this was, it seems, one of the three who were not so hearty in the mutiny as the rest of the crew, and therefore was easily persuaded not only to yield, but afterwards to join very sincerely with us.

In the meantime, Friday and the captain's mate so well managed their business with the rest, that they drew them by hallooing and answering, from one hill to another, and from one wood to another, till they not only heartily tired them, but left them where they were very sure they could not reach back to the boat before it was dark; and indeed, they were heartily tired themselves also by the time they came back to us.

We had nothing now to do but to watch for them in the dark, and to fall upon them, so as to make sure work with them.

It was several hours after Friday came back to me before they came back to their boat – and we could hear the foremost of them, long before they came quite up, calling to those behind to come along – and could also hear them answer, and complain how lame and tired they were, and not being able to come any faster, which was very welcome news to us.

At length they came up to the boat; but it is impossible to express their confusion when they found the boat fast aground in the creek, the tide ebbed out, and their two men gone: we could hear them call to one another in a most lamentable manner, telling one another they were gotten into an enchanted island; that either there were inhabitants in it, and they should all be murdered; or else there were devils or spirits in it, and they should be all carried away and devoured.

They hallooed again, and called their two comrades by their names a great many times, but no answer: after some time, we could see them, by the little light there was, run about wringing their hands, like men in despair; and that sometimes they would go and sit down in the boat to rest themselves, then come ashore, and walk about again, and so the same thing over again.

My men would fain have had me give them leave to fall upon them at once in the dark; but I was willing to take them at some advantage, so to spare them, and kill as few of them as I could; and especially I was unwilling to hazard the killing any of our men, knowing the other men were very well armed: I resolved to wait to see if they did not separate; and therefore, to make sure of them, I drew my ambuscade nearer, and ordered Friday and the captain to creep upon their hands and feet as close to the ground as they could, that they might not be discovered, and get as near them as they could possibly, before they offered to fire.

They had not been long in that posture, till the boatswain, who was the principal ringleader of the mutiny, and had now shown himself the most dejected and dispirited of all the rest, came walking towards them with two more of the crew; the captain was so eager, at having the principal rogue so much in his power, that he could hardly have patience to let him come so near as to be sure of him; for they only heard his tongue before; but when they came nearer, the captain and Friday, starting up on their feet, let fly at them.

The boatswain was killed upon the spot; the next man was shot in the body, and fell just by him, though he did not die till an hour or two after; and the third ran for it.

At the noise of the fire, I immediately advanced with my whole army, which was now eight men; namely, myself, generalissimo; Friday, my lieutenant-general; the captain and his two men, and the three prisoners of war, whom we had trusted with arms.

We came upon them indeed in the dark, so that they could not see our number; and I made the man they had left in the boat, who was now one of us, to call them by name, to try if I could bring them to a parley and so might perhaps reduce them to terms, which fell out just as we desired; for indeed it was easy to think, as their condition then was, they would be very willing to capitulate; so he calls out as loud as he could to one of them, "Tom Smith! Tom Smith! "Tom Smith answered immediately, "Who's that? Robinson? "For it seems he knew his voice. The other answered, "Ay, ay; for God's sake, Tom Smith, throw down your arms, and yield, or you are all dead men this moment."

"Who must we yield to? where are they?" says Smith again. "Here they are," says he; "here is our captain and fifty men with him, have been hunting you this two hours; the boatswain is killed, Will Fry is wounded, and I am a prisoner, and if you do not yield, you are all lost."

"Will they give us quarter, then?" says Tom Smith, "and we will yield." "I'll go and ask, if you promise to yield," says Robinson. So he asked the captain, and the captain himself then calls out, "You, Smith, you know my voice; if you lay down your arms imme- diately and submit, you shall have your lives, all but Will Atkins."

Upon this Will Atkins cried out, "For God's sake, captain, give me quarter! What have I done? They have all been as bad as I" (which, by the way, was not true either; for it seems this Will Atkins was the first man that laid hold of the captain when they first mutinied, and used him barbarously, in tying his hands and giving him injurious language). However, the captain told him he must lay down his arms at discretion, and trust to the governor's mercy, by which he meant me; for they all called me governor.

In a word, they all laid down their arms, and begged their lives; and I sent the man that had parleyed with them, and two more, who bound them all; and then my great army of fifty men, which, particularly with those three, were in all but eight, came up and seized upon them all, and upon their boat; only that I kept myself and one more out of sight, for reasons of state.

Our next work was to repair the boat, and to think of seizing the ship; and as for the captain, now he had leisure to parley with them, he expostulated with them upon the villainy of their practices with him, and at length, upon the further wickedness of their design; and how certainly it must bring them to misery and distress in the end, and perhaps to the gallows.

They all appeared very penitent, begged hard for their lives; as for that, he told them they were none of his prisoners, but the commander's of the island; that they thought they had set him ashore in a barren uninhabited island, but it had pleased God so to direct them, that the island was inhabited, and that the governor was an Englishman; that he might hang them all there, if he pleased; but as he had given them all quarter, he supposed he would send them to England, to be dealt with there as justice required, except Atkins, whom he was commanded by the governor to advise to prepare for death; for that he would be hanged in the morning.

Though this was all fiction of his own, yet it had its desired effect. Atkins fell upon his knees to beg the captain to intercede with the governor for his life; and all the rest begged of him, for God's sake, that they might not be sent to England.

It now occurred to me, that the time of our deliverance was come, and that it would be a most easy thing to bring these fellows in to be hearty in getting possession of the ship; so I retired in the dark from them, that they might not see what kind of a governor they had, and called the captain to me; when I called as at a good distance, one of the men was ordered to speak again, and say to the captain, "Captain, the commander calls for you;" and presently the captain replied, "Tell his Excellency I am just a-coming." This more perfectly amazed them; and they all believed that the commander was just by with his fifty men.

Upon the captain's coming to me, I told him my project for

seizing the ship, which he liked wonderfully well, and resolved to put it in execution the next morning.

But in order to execute it with more art, and to be secure of success, I told him we must divide the prisoners, and that he should go and take Atkins, and two more of the worst of them, and send them pinioned to the cave where the others lay; this was committed to Friday, and the two men who came on shore with the captain.

They conveyed them to the cave, as to a prison; and it was indeed a dismal place, especially to men in their condition.

The others I ordered to my bower, as I called it, of which I have given a full description; and as it was fenced in, and they pinioned, the place was secure enough, considering they were upon their behaviour.

To these in the morning I sent the captain, who was to enter into a parley with them; in a word, to try them, and tell me, whether he thought they might be trusted or no, to go on board, and surprise the ship. He talked to them of the injury done him, of the condition they were brought to; and that though the governor had given them quarter for their lives, as to the present action, yet that if they were sent to England, they would be all hanged in chains, to be sure; but that if they would join in such an attempt as to recover the ship, he would have the governor's engagement for their pardon.

Any one may guess how readily such a proposal would be accepted by men in their condition: they fell down on their knees to the captain, and promised, with the deepest imprecations, that they would be faithful to him to the last drop, and that they should owe their lives to him, and would go with him all over the world; that they would own him for a father to them as long as they lived.

"Well," says the captain, "I must go and tell the governor what you say, and see what I can do to bring him to consent to it." So he brought me an account of the temper he found them in; and that he verily believed they would be faithful.

However, that we might be very secure, I told him he should go back again, and choose out five of them, and tell them, that they should see that they did not want men; but he would take out those five to be his assistants, and that the governor would keep the other two, and the three that were sent prisoners to the castle (my cave), as hostages for the fidelity of those five; and that if they proved unfaithful in the execution, the five hostages should be hanged in chains alive upon the shore.

This looked severe, and convinced them that the governor was in earnest: however, they had no way left but to accept it; and it was now the business of the prisoners, as much as of the captain, to persuade the other five to do their duty.

Our strength was now thus ordered for the expedition: – 1. The captain, his mate, and passenger. 2. Then the two prisoners of the first gang, to whom, having their characters from the captain, I had given their liberty, and trusted them with arms. 3. The other two whom I kept till now in my bower pinioned, but, upon the captain's motion, had now been released. 4. These five released at last; so that they were twelve in all, besides five we kept prisoners in the cave for hostages.

I asked the captain if he was willing to venture with these hands on board the ship; for, as for me and my man Friday, I did not think it was proper for us to stir, having seven men left behind; and it was employment enough for us to keep them as under, and supply them with victuals.

As to the five in the cave, I resolved to keep them fast; but Friday went twice a-day to them, to supply them with necessaries; and I made the other two carry provisions to a certain distance, where Friday was to take it.

When I showed myself to the two hostages, it was with the captain, who told them I was the person the governor had ordered to look after them, and that it was the governor's pleasure that they should not stir anywhere but by my direction; that if they did, they should be fetched into the castle, and be laid in irons; so that as we never suffered them to see me as governor, so I now appeared as another person, and spoke of the governor, the garrison, the castle, and the like, upon all occasions.

The captain now had no difficulty before him, but to furnish his two boats, stop the breach of one, and man them: he made his passenger captain of one, with four other men, and himself and his mate and five more went in the other; and they contrived their business very well, for they came up to the ship about midnight. As soon as they came within call of the ship, he made Robinson hail them, and tell them he had brought off the men and the boat, but that it was a long time before they had found them, and the like, holding them in a chat till they came to the ship's side; when the captain and the mate, entering first with their arms, immediately knocked down the second mate and carpenter with the butt end of their muskets. Being very faithfully seconded by their men, they secured all the rest that were upon the main and quarter decks, and began to fasten the hatches to keep those down who were below; when the other boat and their men, entering at the fore-chains, secured the forecastle of the ship, and the scuttle, which went down into the cock-room, making three men they found there prisoners.

When this was done, and all safe upon the deck, the captain ordered the mate, with three men, to break into the round-house, where the new rebel captain lay, and, having taken the alarm, was gotten up, and, with two men and a boy, had gotten fire-arms in their hands; and when the mate with a crow split open the door, the new captain and his men fired boldly among them, and wounded the mate with a musket-ball, which broke his arm, and wounded two more of the men, but killed nobody.

The mate, calling for help, rushed, however, into the round-house, wounded as he was, and with his pistol shot the new captain through the head, the bullets entering at his mouth, and came out again behind one of his ears, so that he never spoke a word; upon which the rest yielded, and the ship was taken effectually without any more lives being lost. As soon as the ship was thus secured, the captain ordered seven guns to be fired, which was the signal agreed upon with me, to give me notice of his success; which, you may be sure, I was very glad to hear, having sat watching upon the shore for it till near two of the clock in the morning.

Having thus heard the signal plainly, I laid me down; and it having been a day of great fatigue to me, I slept very sound, till I was something surprised With the noise of a gun; and presently starting up, I heard a man call me by the name of "Governor, governor I" and presently I knew the captain's voice; when, climbing up to the top of the hill, there he stood, and pointing to the ship, he embraced me in his arms: "My dear friend and deliverer!" says he, "there's your ship, for she is all yours, and so are we, and all that belong to her." I cast my eyes to the ship, and there she rode within a little more than half a mile of the shore – for they had weighed her anchor as soon as they were masters of her – and the weather being fair, had brought her to an anchor just against the mouth of a little creek; and the tide being up, the captain had brought the pinnace in near the place where I first landed my rafts, and so landed just at my door.

I was, at first, ready to sink down with the surprise; for I saw my deliverance indeed visibly put into my hands, all things easy, and a large ship just ready to carry me away whither I pleased to go. At first, for some time, I was not able to answer one word; but as he had taken me in his arms, I held fast by him, or I should have fallen to the ground.

He perceived the surprise, and immediately pulled a bottle out of his pocket, and gave me a dram of cordial, which he had brought on purpose for me; after I drank it, I sat down upon the ground, and though it brought me to myself, yet it was a good while before I could speak a word to him.

All this while the poor man was in as great an ecstasy as I, only not under my surprise, as I was; and he said a thousand kind tender things to me, to compose and bring me to myself; but such was the flood of joy in my breast, that it put all my spirits into confusion – at last it broke into tears, and in a little while after I recovered my speech.

Then I took my turn, and embraced him as my deliverer; and we rejoiced together. I told him I looked upon him as a man sent from Heaven to deliver me, and that the whole transaction seemed to be a chain of wonders; that such things as these were the testimonies we had of a secret hand of Providence governing the world, and an evidence that the eyes of an infinite power could search into the remotest corner of the world, and send help to the miserable whenever He pleased.

I forgot not to lift up my heart in thankfulness to Heaven; and what heart could forbear to bless Him who had not only in a miraculous manner provided for one in such a wilderness, and in such a desolate condition, but from whom every deliverance must always be acknowledged to proceed?

When we had talked awhile, the captain told me, he had brought me some little refreshments, such as the ship afforded, and such as the wretches who had been so long his masters had not plundered him of. Upon this he called aloud to the boat, and bids his men bring the things ashore that were for the governor; and indeed it was a present as if I had been one, not that I was to be carried along with them, but as if I had been to dwell upon the island still, and they were to go without me.

First, he had brought me a case of bottles full of excellent cordial waters; six large bottles of Madeira wine, the bottles held two quarts a-piece; two pounds of excellent good tobacco, twelve good pieces of the ship's beef, and six pieces of pork, with a bag of peas, and about a hundred weight of biscuits.

He brought me also a box of sugar, a box of flour, a bag full of lemons, and two bottles of lime juice, and abundance of other things: but besides these, and what was a thousand times more useful to me, he brought me six clean shirts, six very good neckcloths, two pair of gloves, one pair of shoes, a hat, and one pair of stockings, and a very good suit of clothes of is own, which had been worn but very little. In a word, he clothed me from head to foot. It was a very kind and agreeable present, as any one may imagine, to one in my circumstances: but never was anything in the world of that kind so unpleasant, awkward, and uneasy, as it was to me to wear such clothes at their first putting on.

After these ceremonies passed, and after all his good things were brought into my little apartment, we began to consult what was to be done with the prisoners we had; for it was worth considering whether we might venture to take them away with us or no, especially two of them, whom we knew to be incorrigible and refractory to the last degree; and the captain said, he knew they were such rogues, that there was no obliging them; and if he did carry them away it must be in irons, as malefactors, to be delivered over to justice at the first English colony he could come at; and I found that the captain himself was very anxious about it.

Upon this, I told him, that, if he desired it, I durst undertake to bring the two men he spoke of to make it their own request that he should leave them upon the island. "I should be very glad of that," says the captain, "with all my heart.

"Well," said I, "I will send for them, and talk with them for you;" so I caused Friday and the two hostages – for they were now discharged, their comrades having performed their promise – I say, I caused them to go to the cave, and bring up the five men, pinioned as they were, to the bower, and keep them there till I came.

After some time, I came thither dressed in my new habit, and now I was called governor again. Being all met, and the captain with me, I caused the men to be brought before me, and I told them, I had had a full account of their villainous behaviour to the captain, and how they had run away with the ship, and were preparing to commit further robberies; but that Providence had ensnared them in their own ways, and that they were fallen into the pit which they had digged for others.

I let them know that by my direction the ship had been seized, that she lay now in the road, and they might see by-and-by, that their new captain had received the reward of his villainy; for that they might see him hanging at the yard-arm: that as to them, I wanted to know what they had to say, why I should not execute them as pirates taken in the fact, as by my commission they could not doubt I had authority to do.

One of them answered in the name of the rest, that they had nothing to say, but this, that when they were taken, the captain promised them their lives, and they humbly implored my mercy: but I told them I knew not what mercy to show them; for, as for myself, I had resolved to quit the island with all my men, and had taken passage with the captain to go for England: and, as for the captain, he could not carry them to England, other than as prisoners in irons to be tried for mutiny, and running away with the ship, the consequence of which, they must needs know, would be the gallows; so that I could not tell what was the best for them, unless they had a mind to take their fate in the island; if they desired that, I did not care, as I had liberty to leave it: I had some inclination to give them their lives, if they thought they could shift on shore. They seemed very thankful for it; said they would much rather venture to stay there, than to be carried to England to be hanged: so I left it on that issue.

However, the captain seemed to make some difficulty of it, as if he durst not leave them there: upon this, I seemed to be a little angry with the captain, and told him that they were my prisoners, not his; and that, seeing I had offered them so much favour, I would be as good as my word; and that if he did not think fit to consent to it, I would set them at liberty as I found them: and, if he did not like that, he might take them again if he could catch them.

Upon this, they appeared very thankful, and I accordingly set them at liberty, and bade them retire into the woods, to the place whence they came, and I would leave them some fire-arms, some ammunition, and some directions how they should live very well, if they thought fit.

Upon this, I prepared to go on board the ship, but told the captain that I would stay that night to prepare my things; and desired him to go on board in the meantime, and keep all right in the ship, and send the boat on shore the next day for me: ordering him, in the meantime, to cause the new captain, who was killed, to be hanged at the yard-arm, that these men might see him.

When the captain was gone, I sent for the men up to me to my apartment, and entered seriously into discourse with them of their circumstances. I told them, I thought they had made a right choice: that, if the captain carried them away, they would certainly be hanged; I showed them their captain hanging at the yard-arm of the ship, and told them they had nothing less to expect.

When they all declared their willingness to stay, I then told them I would let them into the story of my living there, and put them into the way of making it easy to them: accordingly, I gave them the whole history of the place, and of my coming to it; showed them my fortifications, the way I made my bread, planted my corn, cured my grapes: and, in a word, all that was necessary to make them easy. I told them the story of the sixteen Spaniards that were to be expected; for whom I left a letter, and made them promise to treat them in common with themselves.

I left them my fire-arms, namely, five muskets, three fowling-pieces, and three swords: I had about a barrel of powder left; for after the first year or two I used but little, and wasted none. I gave them a description of the way I managed the goats, and directions to milk and fatten them, to make both butter and cheese.

In a word, I gave them every part of my own story; and I told them I would prevail with the captain to leave them two barrels of gunpowder more, and some garden-seed, which I told them I would have been very glad of; also I gave them the bag of peas which the captain had brought me to eat, and bade them be sure to sow and increase them.

Having done all this, I left them the next day, and went on board the ship; we prepared immediately to sail, but did not weigh that night. The next morning early, two of the five men came swimming to the ship's side, and, making a most lamentable complaint of the other three, begged to be taken into the ship for God's sake, for they should be murdered; and begged the captain to take them on board, though he hanged them immediately,

Upon this the captain pretended to have no power without me; but, after some difficulty, and after their solemn promises of amendment, they were taken on board, and were, some time after, soundly whipped and pickled: after which they proved very honest and quiet fellows,

Some time after this, I went with the boat on shore, the tide being up, with the things promised to the men, to which the captain, at my intercession, caused their chests and clothes to be added, which they took, and were very thankful for: I also encouraged them, by telling them, that if it lay in my way to send a vessel to take them in, I would not forget them.

CHAPTER 19

I leave the Island, and arrive in England –
Go to Yorkshire, and find most of my Family
dead – Go to Lisbon respecting my Estate in
Brazil – Meet an old Friend – We set out for
England over land – Annoyed by Wolves on
the Road

When I took leave of this island, I carried on board for relics, the
great goat-skin cap I had made, my umbrella, and one of my parrots:
also, I forgot not to take the money I formerly mentioned, which
had lain by me so long useless that it was grown rusty, or tarnished,
and could hardly pass for silver, till it had been a little rubbed and
handled, and also the money I found in the wreck of the Spanish
ship.

And thus I left the island the 19th day of December, as I found
by the ship's account, in the year 1686, after I had been upon it
eight-and-twenty years, two months, and nineteen days: being delivered from the second captivity the same day of the month that I
first made my escape in the long-boat from among the Moors of
Sallee.

In this vessel, after a long voyage, I arrived in England the
11th of June, in the year 1687, having been thirty and five years
absent.

When I came to England, I was a perfect stranger to all the
world, as if I had never been known there: my benefactor, and
faithful steward, whom I had left in trust with my money, was alive,
but had had great misfortunes in the world, was become a widow
the second time, and very low in the world. I made her easy as to
what she owed me, assuring her I would give her no trouble; but,

on the contrary, in gratitude to her former care and faithfulness to me, I relieved her as my little stock would afford, which, at that time, would, indeed, allow me to do but little for her; but I assured her, I would never forget her former kindness to me; nor did I forget her when I had sufficient to help her, as shall be observed in its place.

I went down afterwards into Yorkshire, but my father was dead, and my mother and all the family extinct, except that I found two sisters, and two of the children of one of my brothers: and as I had been long ago given over for dead, there had been no provision made for me; so that, in a word, I found nothing to relieve or assist me, and that little money I had would not do much for me as to settling in the world.

I met with one piece of gratitude, indeed, which I did not expect; and this was, that the master of the ship whom I had so happily delivered, and by the same means saved the ship and cargo, having given a very handsome account to the owners of the manner how I had saved the lives of the men, and the ship, they invited me to meet them and some other merchants concerned, and altogether made me a very handsome compliment upon that subject, and a present of almost two hundred pounds sterling.

But after making several reflections upon the circumstances of my life, and how little way this would go towards me settling in the world, I resolved to go to Lisbon, and see if I might not come by some information of the state of my plantation in the Brazils, and what was become of my partner, who, I had reason to suppose, had some years now given me over for dead.

With this view I took shipping for Lisbon, where I arrived in April following, my man Friday accompanying me very honestly in all these ramblings, and proving a most faithful servant upon all occasions.

When I came to Lisbon, I found out, by inquiry, and to my particular satisfaction, my old friend the captain of the ship, who first took me up at sea off the shore of Africa: he was now grown old, and had left off the sea, having put his son, who was far from a young man, into his ship, and who still used the Brazil trade. The old man did not know me, and, indeed, I hardly knew him; but I soon brought myself to his remembrance when I told him who I was.

After some passionate expressions of our old acquaintance, I inquired, you may be sure, after my plantation and my partner. The old man told me he had not been in the Brazils for about nine years; but that he could assure me that, when he came away, my partner was living, but the trustees, whom I had joined with him to take cognisance of my part, were both dead; that, however, he believed that I would have a very good account of the improvement of the plantation, for that, upon the general belief of my being cast away and drowned, my trustees had given in the account of the produce of my part of the plantation to the procurator-fiscal, who had appropriated it, in case I never came to claim it, one-third to the king, and two-thirds to the monastery of St. Augustine, to be expended for the benefit of the poor, and for the conversion of the Indians to the Catholic faith: but that if I appeared, or any one for me, to claim the inheritance, it would be restored, only that the improvement, or annual production, being distributed to charitable uses, could not be restored; but he assured me that the steward of the king's revenue (from lands), and the provedore, or steward of the monastery, had taken great care all along that the incumbent, that is to say, my partner, gave every year a faithful account of the produce, of which they received duly my moiety.

I asked him if he knew to what height of improvement he had brought the plantation; and whether he thought it might be worth looking after; or whether on my going thither, I should meet with no obstruction to my possessing my just right in the moiety.

He told me, he could not tell exactly to what degree the plantation was improved; but this he knew, that my partner was growing exceedingly rich upon the enjoying but one-half of it: and that, to the best of his remembrance, he had heard that the king's third of my part, which was, it seems, granted away to some other monastery, or religious house, amounted to above two hundred moidores a-year; that, as to my being restored to a quiet possession of it, there was no question to be made of that, my partner being alive to witness my title, and my name being also enrolled in the register of the country. Also he told me, that the survivors of my trustees were very fair, honest people, and very wealthy; and he believed I would not only have their assistance for putting me in possession, but would find a very considerable sum of money in their hands for my account, being the produce of the farm while their fathers held the trust, and before it was given up, as above, which, as he remembered, was about twelve years.

I showed myself a little concerned and uneasy at this account, and inquired of the old captain how it came to pass, that the trustees should thus dispose of my effects, when he knew that I had made my will and had made him, the Portuguese captain, my universal heir, etc.

He told me that was true; but that, as there was no proof of my being dead, he could not act as executor until some certain account should come of my death; and that, besides, he was not willing to intermeddle with a thing so remote: that it was true he had registered my will and put in his claim; and could he have given any account of my being dead or alive, he would have acted by my procuration, and taken possession of the *ingeino* (so they called the sugar house), and had given his son, who was now at the Brazils, order to do it.

"But," says the old man, "I have one piece of news to tell you, which perhaps may not be so acceptable to you as the rest, that believing you were lost, and all the world believing so also, your partner and trustees did offer to account to me, in your name, for six or eight of the first years of profit, which I received; but there being at that time," says he, "great disbursements for increasing the works, building an *ingeino*, and buying slaves, it did not amount to near so much as afterwards it produced; "however," says the old man, "I shall give you a true account of what I have received in all, and how I have disposed of it."

After a few days' further conference with this ancient friend, he brought me an account of the six first years' income of my plantation, signed by my partner and the merchant-trustees, being always delivered in goods, namely, tobacco in roll, and sugar in chests, besides rum, molasses, etc., which is the consequence of a sugar-work; and I found by this account, that every year the income considerably increased: but, as above, the disbursement being large, the sum at first was small: however, the old man let me see that he was debtor to me four hundred and seventy moidores of gold, besides sixty chests of sugar, and fifteen double rolls of tobacco, which were lost in his ship, he having been shipwrecked coming home to Lisbon, about eleven years after my leaving the place.

The good man then began to complain of his misfortunes, and how he had been obliged to make use of my money to recover his losses, and buy him a share in a new ship. "However, my old friend," said he, "you shall not want a supply in your necessity; as soon as my son returns, you shall be fully satisfied."

Upon this he pulls out an old pouch, and gives me two hundred Portugal moidores in gold; and giving me the writings of his title to the ship which his son was gone to the Brazils in, of which he was a quarter part owner, and his son another, he puts them both in my hands for security of the rest.

I was too much moved with the honesty and kindness of the poor man, to be able to bear this; and remembering what he had done for me, how he had taken me up at sea, and how generously he had used me on all occasions, and particularly how sincere a friend he was now to me, I could hardly refrain weeping at what he said to me; therefore, first, I asked him if his circumstances admitted him to spare so much money at that time, and if it would not straiten him? He told me, he could not say but it might straiten him a little; but, however, it was my money, and I might want it more than he.

Everything the good man said was full of affection, and I could hardly refrain from tears while he spoke. In short, I took one hundred of the moidores, and called for a pen and ink to give him a receipt for them; then I returned him the rest, and told him, if ever I had possession of the plantation, I would return the other to him also, as indeed I afterwards did; and that, as to the bill of sale of his part in his son's ship, I would not take it by any means; but that if I wanted the money, I found he was honest enough to pay me, and if I did not, but came to receive what he gave me reason to expect, I would never have a penny more from him.

When this was past, the old man began to ask me, if he should put me on a method to make my claim to my plantation. I told him, I thought to go over to it myself. He said, I might do so if I pleased; but that if I did not, there were ways enough to secure my right, and immediately to appropriate the profits to my use; and as there were ships in the river of Lisbon, just ready to go away to Brazil, he made me enter my name in a public register, with this affidavit, affirming upon oath that I was alive, and that I was the same person who took up the land for the planting the said plantation at first.

This being regularly attested by notary, and a procuration affixed, he directed me to send it with a letter of his writing, to a merchant of his acquaintance at the place; and then proposed my staying with him till an account came of the return.

Never anything was more honourable than the proceedings upon this procuration; for in less than seven months, I received a large packet from the survivors of my trustees, the merchants, on whose account I went to sea, in which were the following particular letters and papers enclosed: –

First, There was the account current of the produce of my farm, or plantation, from the year when their fathers had balanced with my old Portugal captain, being for six years; the balance appeared to be one thousand one hundred and seventy-four moidores in my favour.

Secondly, There was the account of four years more while they kept the effects in their hands, before the government claimed the administration as being the effects of a person not to be found, which they call civil death; and the balance of this, the value of the plantation increasing, amounted to three thousand two hundred and forty-one moidores.

Thirdly, There was the prior of the Augustine's account, who had received the profits for about fourteen years; but not being able to account for what was disposed to the hospital, very honestly declared he had eight hundred and seventy-two moidores not distributed, which he acknowledged to my account. As to the king's part, that refunded nothing.

There was also a letter of my partner's, congratulating me very affectionately upon my being alive; giving me an account how the estate was improved, and what it produced a-year, with a particular of the number of squares, or acres, that it contained; how planted, how many slaves there were upon it; and, making two-and-twenty crosses for blessings, told me he had said so many Ave Marias to thank the Blessed Virgin that I was alive; inviting me very passionately to come over and take possession of my own, and in the meantime to give him orders to whom he should deliver my effects, if I did not come myself; concluding with a hearty tender of his friendship, and that of his family; and sent me as a present, seven fine leopard skins, which he had, it seems, received from Africa by some other ship which he had sent thither; and who, it seems, had made a better voyage than I. He sent me also five chests of excellent sweetmeats, and a hundred pieces of gold uncoined, not quite so large as moidores.

By the same fleet my merchant-trustees shipped me twelve hundred chests of sugar, eight hundred rolls of tobacco, and the rest of the whole account in gold.

I might well say now, indeed, that the latter end of Job was better than the beginning. It is impossible to express the flutterings of my very heart, when I looked over these letters, and especially when I found all my wealth about me; for as the Brazil ships came all in fleets, the same ships which brought my letters brought my goods; and the effects were safe in the Tagus before the letter came to my hand. In a word, I turned pale, and grew sick; and had not the old man run and fetched me a cordial, I believe the sudden surprise of joy had overset nature, and I had died upon the spot.

Nay, after that, I continued very ill, and was so some hours, till a physician being sent for, and something of the real cause of my illness being known, he ordered me to be let blood, after which I had relief, and grew well; but I verily believe, if it had not been eased by the vent given in that manner to the spirits, I should have died.

I was now master, all on a sudden, of about fifty thousand pounds sterling in money, and had an estate as I might well call it, in the Brazils, of above a thousand pounds a-year, as sure as an estate of lands in England; and, in a word, I was in a condition which I scarce knew how to understand, or how to compose myself for the enjoyment of.

The first thing I did was to recompense my original benefactor, my good old captain, who had been first charitable to me in my distress, kind to me in the beginning, and honest to me at the end. I showed him all that was sent to me; I told him, that, next to the providence of Heaven, which disposes all things, it was owing to him; and that it now lay on me to reward him, which I would do an hundred fold. So I first returned to him the hundred moidores I had received of him; then I sent for a notary, and caused him to draw up a general release or discharge for the four hundred and seventy moidores, which he had acknowledged he owed me, in the fullest and firmest manner possible, after which I caused a procuration to be drawn, empowering him to be my receiver of the annual profits of my plantation, and appointing my partner to account to him and make the returns by the usual fleets to him in my name; and a clause in the end, being a grant of one hundred moidores a-year to him during his life, out of the effects; and fifty moidores a-year to his son after him, for his life. And thus I requited my old man.

I was now to consider which way to steer my course next, and what to do with the estate that Providence had thus put into my hands; and, indeed, I had more care upon my head now than I had in my silent state of life in the island, where I wanted nothing but what I had, and had nothing but what I wanted; whereas I had now a great charge upon me, and my business was how to secure it: I had never a cave to hide my money in, or a place where it might lie without lock or key, till it grew mouldy and tarnished before anybody would meddle with it. On the contrary, I knew not where to put it, or whom to trust with it; my old patron, the captain, indeed, was honest, and that was the only refuge I had.

In the next place, my interest in the Brazils seemed to summon me thither; but now I could not tell how to think of going thither till I had settled my affairs, and left my effects in some hands behind me. At first I thought of my old friend the widow, who, I knew, was honest, and would be just to me: but then, she was in years, and but poor, and for aught I knew, might be in debt; so that, in a word, I had no way but to go back to England myself, and take my effects with me.

I was some months, however, before I resolved upon this; and, therefore, as I had rewarded the old captain fully, and to satisfaction, who had been my former benefactor, so I began to think of my poor widow, whose husband had been my first benefactor, and she, while it was in her power, my faithful steward and instructor. So the first thing I did, I got a merchant in Lisbon to write to his correspondent in London, not only to pay a bill, but to go find her out, and carry her in money a hundred pounds from me, and to talk with her, and comfort her in her poverty, by telling her she should, if I lived, have a further supply. At the same time, I sent my two sisters in the country, each of them a hundred pounds, they being, though not in want, yet not in very good circumstances – one having been married, and left a widow; and the other having a husband not so kind to her as he should be.

But among all my relations or acquaintances, I could not yet pitch upon one to whom I durst commit the gross of my stock, that I might go away to the Brazils, and leave things safe behind me; and this greatly perplexed me.

I had once a mind to have gone to the Brazils, and have settled myself there, for I was, as it were, naturalised to the place; but I had some little scruple in my mind about religion, which insensibly drew me back, of which I shall say more presently. However, it was not religion that kept me from going thither for the present; and as I had made no scruple of being openly of the religion of the country, all the while I was among them, so neither did I yet; only that now and then, having of late thought more of it than formerly, when I began to think of living and dying among them, I began to regret my having professed myself a Papist, and thought it might not be the best religion to die in.

But, as I have said, this was not the main thing that kept me from going to the Brazils, but that really I did not know with whom to leave my effects behind me; so I resolved at last to go to England with them, where, if I arrived, I concluded I should make some acquaintance, or find some relations, that would be faithful to me; and accordingly I prepared to go for England with all my wealth.

In order to prepare things for my going home, I first (the Brazil fleet being just going away) resolved to give answers suitable to the just and faithful account of things I had from thence; and first, to the prior of St. Augustine I wrote a letter full of thanks for his just dealings, and the offer of the eight hundred and seventy-two moidores, which were undisposed of, which I desired might be given, five hundred to the monastery, and three hundred and seventy-two to the poor, as the prior should direct, desiring the good padre's prayers for me, and the like.

I wrote next a letter of thanks to my two trustees, with all the acknowledgment that so much justice and honesty called for; as for sending them any present, they were far above having any occasion for it.

Lastly, I wrote to my partner, acknowledging his industry in the improving the plantation, and his integrity in increasing the stock of the works; giving him instructions for his future government of my part according to the powers I had left with my old patron, to whom I desired him to send whatever became due to me, till he should hear from me more particularly; assuring him, that it was my intention, not only to come to him, but to settle myself there for the remainder of my life. To this I added a very handsome present of some Italian silks for his wife and two daughters – for such the captain's son informed me he had – with two pieces of fine English broad-cloth, the best I could get in Lisbon, five pieces of black baize, and some Flanders lace of a good value.

Having thus settled my affairs, sold my cargo, and turned all my effects into good bills of exchange, my next difficulty was, which way to go to England. I had been accustomed enough to the sea, and yet I had a strange aversion to go to England by sea at that time: and though I could give no reason for it, yet the difficulty increased upon me so much, that though I had once shipped my baggage in order to go, yet I altered my mind, and that not once, but two or three times.

It is true, I had been very unfortunate by sea, and this might be one of the reasons. But let no man slight the strong impulses of

DANIEL DEFOE

his own thoughts in cases of such moment. Two of the ships which
I had singled out to go in – I mean more particularly singled out
than any other, that is to say, so as in one of them to put my things
on board, and in the other to have agreed with the captain – I say,
two of the ships miscarried, namely, one was taken by the Algerines,
and the other was cast away on the Start near Torbay, and all the
people drowned except three; so that, in either of these vessels, I
had been made miserable, and in which most, it was hard to say.

Having been thus harassed in my thoughts, my old pilot, to
whom I communicated everything, pressed me earnestly not to go
by sea; but either to go by land to the Groyne, and cross over the
Bay of Biscay to Rochelle, from whence it was but an easy and safe
journey by land to Paris, and so to Calais and Dover; or to go up to
Madrid, and so all the way by land through France.

In a word, I was so prepossessed against my going by sea at
all, except from Calais to Dover, that I resolved to travel all the way
by land; which, as I was not in haste, and did not value the charge,
was by much the pleasanter way; and to make it more so, my old
captain brought an English gentleman, the son of a merchant in
Lisbon, who was willing to travel with me; after which, we picked
up two who were English, and merchants also, and two young
Portuguese gentlemen, the last going to Paris only: so that we were
in all six of us, and five servants, the two merchants and the two
Portuguese contenting themselves with one servant between two,
to save the charge, and as for me, I got an English sailor to travel
with me as a servant, besides my man Friday, who was too much a
stranger to be capable of supplying the place of a servant upon the
road.

In this manner I set out from Lisbon: and our company being
all very well mounted and armed, we made a little troop, whereof
they did me the honour to call me captain, as well because I was
the oldest man, as because I had two servants, and indeed was the
original of the whole journey.

As I have troubled you with none of my sea journals, so shall
I trouble you with none of my land journals. But some adventures
that happened to us in this tedious and difficult journey I must not
omit.

When we came to Madrid, we being all of us strangers to
Spain, were willing to stay some time to see the court of Spain,
and to see what was worth observing; but it being the latter part
of the summer, we hastened away and set out from Madrid about

the middle of October. But when we came to the edge of Navarre, we were alarmed, at several towns on the way, with an account that so much snow was fallen on the French side of the mountains, that several travellers were obliged to come back to Pampeluna, after having attempted, at an extreme hazard, to pass on.

When we came to Pampeluna itself, we found it so indeed; and to me, that had been always used to a hot climate, and indeed to countries where we could scarce bear any clothes on, the cold was insufferable; nor, indeed, was it more painful than it was surprising; to come but ten days before out of Old Castile, where the weather was not only warm, but very hot, and immediately to feel a wind from the Pyrenean mountains, so very keen, so severely cold, as to be intolerable, and to endanger benumbing and perishing of our fingers and toes, was very strange.

Poor Friday was really frighted when he saw the mountains all covered with snow, and felt cold weather, which he had never seen or felt before in his life.

To mend the matter, after we came to Pampeluna, it continued snowing with so much violence, and so long, that the people said winter was come before its time; and the roads, which were difficult before, were now quite impassable: in a word, the snow lay in some places too thick for us to travel; and being not hard frozen, as is the case in northern countries, there was no going without being in danger of being buried alive every step. We stayed no less than twenty days at Pampeluna; when (seeing the winter coming on, and no likelihood of its being better, for it was the severest winter all over Europe that had been known in many years) I proposed that we should all go away to Fontarabia, and there take shipping for Bordeaux, which was a very little voyage.

But while we were considering this, there came in four French gentlemen, who having been stopped on the French side of the passes, as we were on the Spanish, had found out a guide, who, traversing the country near the head of Languedoc, had brought them over the mountains by such ways, that they were not much incommoded with the snow; and where they met with snow in any quantity, they said it was frozen hard enough to bear them and their horses.

We sent for this guide, who told us he would undertake to carry us the same way with no hazard from the snow, provided we were armed sufficiently to protect us from wild beasts: for, he said, upon these great snows, it was frequent for some wolves to show

DANIEL DEFOE

themselves at the foot of the mountains, being made ravenous for want of food, the ground being covered with snow.

We told him we were well enough prepared for such creatures as they were, if he would ensure us from a kind of two-legged wolves, which we were told we were in most danger from, especially on the French side of the mountains.

He satisfied us there was no danger of that kind in the way that we were to go; so we readily agreed to follow him; as did also twelve other gentlemen, with their servants, some French, some Spanish, who, as I said, had attempted to go, and were obliged to come back again.

Accordingly, we all set out from Pampeluna, with our guide, on the 15th of November; and indeed I was surprised when, instead of going forward, he came directly back with us, on the same road that we came from Madrid, about twenty miles; when, having passed two rivers and come into the plain country, we found ourselves in a warm climate again, where the country was pleasant and no snow to be seen; but on a sudden, turning to the left, he approached the mountains another way; and though, it is true, the hills and the precipices looked dreadfully, yet he made so many tours, such meanders, and led us by such winding ways, we insensibly passed the height of the mountains, without being much encumbered with the snow; and all on a sudden he showed us the pleasant fruitful provinces of Languedoc and Gascoigne, all green and flourishing; though indeed they were at a great distance, and we had some rough way to pass yet.

We were a little uneasy, however, when we found it snowed one whole day and a night, so fast that we could not travel; but he bade us be easy, we should soon be past it all. We found, indeed, that we began to descend every day, and to come more north than before; and so, depending upon our guide, we went on.

It was about two hours before night when our guide, being something before us, and not just in sight, out rushed three monstrous wolves, and after them a bear, out of a hollow way adjoining to a thick wood. Two of the wolves flew upon the guide, and had he been half a mile before us, he had been devoured indeed, before we could have helped him; one of them fastened upon his horse, and the other attacked the man with that violence, that he had not time, or not presence of mind enough, to draw his pistol, but hallooed and cried out to us most lustily. My man Friday being next to me, I bade him ride up, and see what was the matter.

As soon as Friday came in sight of the man, he hallooed as loud as the other, "Oh, master! oh; master!" – but, like a bold fellow, rode directly up to the man, and with his pistol shot the wolf that attacked him in the head.

It was happy for the poor man that it was my man Friday; for he, having been used to that kind of creature in his country, had no fear upon him, but went close up to him and shot him as above; whereas any of us would have fired at a farther distance, and perhaps either missed the wolf, or endangered shooting the man.

But it was enough to have terrified a bolder man than I, and indeed it alarmed all our company, when, with the noise of Friday's pistol we heard on both sides the dismalest howlings of wolves, and the noise redoubled by the echo of the mountains, that it was to us as if there had been a prodigious multitude of them; and perhaps, indeed, there was not such a few as that we had no cause of apprehension.

However, as Friday had killed this wolf, the other, that had fastened upon the horse, left him immediately and fled, having happily fastened upon his head, where the bosses of the bridle had stuck in his teeth, so that he had not done him much hurt: the man, indeed, was most hurt; for the raging creature had bit him twice, once on the arm, and the other time a little above his knee; and he was just as it were tumbling down by the disorder of the horse when Friday came up and shot the wolf.

It is easy to suppose, that at the noise of Friday's pistol we all mended our pace, and rode up as fast as the way (which was very difficult) would give us leave to see what was the matter. As soon as we came clear of the trees which blinded us before, we saw plainly what had been the case, and how Friday had disengaged the poor guide; though we did not presently discern what kind of creature it was he had killed.

CHAPTER 20

Battle betwixt Friday and a Bear – Terrible
Fight with Wolves – Arrive in England
safely, and settle there, and marry

But never was a fight managed so hardily, and in such a surprising
manner, as that which followed between Friday and the bear, which
gave us all (though at first we were surprised and afraid for him)
the greatest diversion imaginable. As the bear is a heavy, clumsy
creature, and does not gallop as the wolf does, which is swift and
light, so he has two particular qualities, which generally are the rule
of his actions; first, as to men, who are not his proper prey – I say,
not his proper prey, because, though I can't say what excessive
hunger might do, which was now their case, the ground being all
covered with snow; yet as to men, he does not usually attempt them,
unless they first attack him; on the contrary, if you meet him in the
woods, if you don't meddle with him, he won't meddle with you:
yet then you must take care to be very civil to him, and give him
the road, for he is a very nice gentleman; he won't go a step out of
the way for a prince – nay, if you are afraid, your best way
is to look another way, and keep going on; for sometimes, if you
stop, and stand still, and look steadfastly at him, he takes it for an
affront, and if you throw or toss anything at him, and it hits him,
though it were but a bit of stick as big as your finger, he takes it
for an affront, and sets all other business aside to pursue his revenge;
for he will have satisfaction in point of honour, and this is his first
quality: the next is, that if he be once affronted, he will never leave
you, night or day, till he has his revenge, but follow at a good round
rate till he overtakes you. My man Friday had delivered our guide,
and when we came up to him, he was helping him off from his

horse; for the man was both hurt and frighted, and indeed the last more than the first; when, on a sudden, we espied the bear come out of the wood, and a very monstrous one it was, the biggest by far that ever I saw. We were all a little surprised when we saw him; but when Friday saw him, it was easy to see joy and courage in the fellow's countenance: "Oh! Oh! Oh!" says Friday, three times, pointing to him, "Oh, master! you give me te leave, me shakee te hand with him, me makee you good laugh."

I was surprised to see the fellow so pleased: "You fool you," said I, "he will eat you up!" "Eatee me up! eatee me up!" says Friday twice over again; "me eatee him up; me make you good laugh; you all stay here, me show you good laugh." So down he sits, and gets his boots off in a moment, and put on a pair of pumps (as we call the flat shoes they wear), and which he had in his pocket, and gives my other servant his horse, and with his gun away he flew, swift like the wind.

The bear was walking softly on, and offered to meddle with nobody, till Friday, coming pretty near, calls to him, as if the bear could understand him: "Hark ye! hark ye!" says Friday, "me speakee wit you." We followed at a distance: for now being come down to the Gascoigne side of the mountains, we were entered a vast great forest, where the country was plain, and pretty open, though many trees in it scattered here and there.

Friday, who had, as we say, the heels of the bear, came up with him quickly, and takes up a great stone, and throws it at him, and hit him just on the head, but did him no more harm than if he had thrown it against a wall: but it answered Friday's end; for the rogue was so void of fear, that he did it purely to make the bear follow him, and show us some laugh, as he called it.

As soon as the bear felt the stone, and saw him, he turns about, and comes after him, taking devilish long strides, and shuffling along at a strange rate, so as he would put a horse to a middling gallop. Away runs Friday, and takes his course as if he ran towards us for help; so we all resolved to fire at once upon the bear, and deliver my man, though I was angry at him heartily for bringing the bear back upon us, when he was going about his business another way, and especially I was angry that he had turned the bear upon us, and then run away; and I called out, "You dog," said I, "is this your making us laugh? Come away, and take your horse, that we may shoot the creature." He hears me, and cries out, "No shoot, no shoot, stand still, you get much laugh:" and as the nimble creature ran two feet for the beast's one, he turned on a sudden on one side of us, and seeing a great oak tree fit for his purpose, he beckoned us to follow, and, doubling his pace, he gets nimbly up the tree, laying his gun down upon the ground, at about five or six yards from the bottom of the tree.

The bear soon came to the tree, and we followed at a distance. The first thing he did, he stopped at the gun, smelled to it, but let it lie, and up he scrambles into the tree, climbing like a cat, though so monstrous heavy. I was amazed at the folly, as I thought it, of my man, and could not for my life see anything to laugh at yet till, seeing the bear get up the tree, we all rode nearer to him.

When we came to the tree, there was Friday got out to the small of a large limb of the tree, and the bear got about half-way to him. As soon as the bear got out to that part where the limb of the tree was weaker, "Ha," says he to us, "now you see me teachee the bear dance;" so he falls a-jumping and shaking the bough, at which the bear began to totter, but stood still, and began to look behind him, to see how he should get back: then, indeed, we did laugh heartily. But Friday had not done with him by a great deal: when he sees him stand still, he calls out to him again, as if he had supposed the bear could speak English, "What! you come no farther? Pray you come farther." So he left jumping and shaking the bough: and the bear, just as if he understood what he said, did come a little farther; then he fell a-jumping again, and the bear stopped again.

We thought now was a good time to knock him on the head, and called to Friday to stand still, and we would shoot the bear; but he cried out earnestly, "Oh, pray! oh, pray! no shoot, me shoot by and then" – he would have said by-and-by. However, to shorten the story, Friday danced so much, and the bear stood so ticklish, that we had laughing enough, indeed, but still could not imagine what the fellow would do: for first we thought he depended upon shaking the bear off, and we found the bear was too cunning for that too; for he would not get out far enough to be thrown down, but clings fast with his great broad claws and feet, so that we could not imagine what would be end of it, and where the jest would be at last.

But Friday put us out of doubt quickly; for, seeing the bear cling fast to the bough, and that he would not be persuaded to come any farther, "Well, well," said Friday, "you no come farther, me go, me go; you no come to me, me come to you;" and upon this he goes out to the smallest end of the bough, where it would bend with his weight, and gently lets himself down by it, sliding down the bough till he came near enough to jump down on his feet; and away he ran to his gun, takes it up, and stands still.

"Well," said I to him, "Friday, what will you do now? Why don't you shoot him?" "No shoot," says Friday, "no yet; me shoot now me no kill; me stay, give you one more laugh." And, indeed, so he did, as you will see presently; for when the bear saw his enemy gone, he comes back from the bough where he stood, but did it mighty leisurely, looking behind him every step, and coming backward till he got into the body of the tree; then, with the same hinder end foremost, he came down the tree, grasping it with his claws, and moving one foot at a time, very leisurely. At this juncture, and just before he could put his hind feet upon the ground, Friday stepped close to him, clapped the muzzle of his piece into his ear, and shot him as dead as a stone.

Then the rogue turned about to see if we did not laugh; and when he saw we were pleased by our looks, he falls a-laughing himself very loud – "So we kill bear in my country," says Friday. "So you kill them?" said I; "why, you have no guns. "No," says he, "no guns, but shoot great much long arrow."

This was, indeed, a good diversion to us: but we were still in a wild place, and our guide very much hurt, and what to do we hardly knew: the howling of wolves ran much in my head; and indeed, except the noise I once heard on the shore of Africa, of which I have said something already, I never heard anything that filled me with so much horror.

These things, and the approach of night, called us off, or else, as Friday would have had us, we should certainly have taken the skin of this monstrous creature off, which was worth saving; but we had three leagues to go, and our guide hastened us; so we left him, and went forward on our journey.

The ground was still covered with snow, though not so deep and dangerous as on the mountains; and the ravenous creatures, as we heard afterwards, were come down into the forest and plain country, pressed by hunger, to seek for food, and had done a great deal of mischief in the villages, where they surprised the country people, killed a great many of their sheep and horses, and some people too.

We had one dangerous place to pass, of which our guide told us, if there were any more wolves in the country, we should find them there; and this was a small plain, surrounded with woods on every side, and a long narrow defile or lane, which we were to pass to get through the wood, and then we should come to the village where we were to lodge.

It was within half an hour of sunset when we entered the first wood, and a little after sunset when we came into the plain. We met with nothing in the first wood, except that in a little plain within the wood which was not above two furlongs over, we saw five great wolves cross the road, full speed one after another, as if they had been in chase of some prey, and had it in view: they took no notice of us, and were gone and out of sight in a few moments.

Upon this our guide, who, by the way, was a wretched faint-hearted fellow, bade us keep in a ready posture; for he believed there were more wolves a-coming.

We kept our arms ready, and our eyes about us; but we saw no more wolves till we came through that wood, which was near half a league, and entered the plain: as soon as we came into the plain, we had occasion enough to look about us. The first object we met with was a dead horse, that is to say, a poor horse which the wolves had killed, and at least a dozen of them at work; we could not say, eating of him, but picking of his bones rather; for they had eaten up all the flesh before.

We did not think fit to disturb them at their feast, neither did they take much notice of us. Friday would have let fly at them, but I would not suffer him by any means; for I found we were like to have more business upon our hands than we were aware of. We were not gone half over the plain, but we began to hear the wolves howl in the woods, on our left, in a frightful manner; and presently after we saw about a hundred coming on directly towards us, all in a body, and most of them in a line, as regularly as an army, drawn up by experienced officers. I scarce knew in what manner to receive them; but found to draw ourselves in a close line was the only way – so we formed in a moment; but that we might not have too much interval, I ordered, that only every other man should fire; and that the others, who had not fired, should stand ready to give them a second volley immediately, if they continued to advance upon us; and that then those who had fired at first, should not pretend to load their fusils again, but stand ready, with every one a pistol, for we were all armed with a fusil and a pair of pistols each man; so we were, by this method, able to fire six volleys, half of us at a time; however, at present we had no necessity, for upon firing the first volley, the enemy made a full stop, being terrified, as well with the noise as with the fire; four of them being shot in the head, dropped; several others were wounded, and went bleeding off, as we could see by the snow. I found they stopped, but did not immediately retreat; whereupon, remembering that I had been told that the fiercest creatures were terrified at the voice of a man, I caused all our company to halloo as loud as we could, and I found the notion not altogether mistaken; for upon our shout, they began to retire and turn about: then I ordered a second volley to be fired in their rear, which put them to the gallop, and away they went to the woods.

This gave us leisure to charge our pieces again, and that we might lose no time, we kept going; but we had but little more than loaded our fusils, and put ourselves into a readiness, when we heard a terrible noise in the same wood on our left, only that it was farther onward the same way we were to go.

The night was coming on, and it began to be dusky, which made it the worse on our side; but the noise increasing, we could easily perceive that it was the howling and yelling of those hellish creatures; and on a sudden, we perceived two or three troops of wolves on our left, one behind us, and one on our front, so that we seemed to be surrounded with them; however, as they did not fall upon us we kept our way forward, as fast as we could make our horses go, which, the way being very rough, was only a good large trot; and in this manner we only came in view of the entrance of the wood through which we were to pass, at the farther side of the plain; but we were greatly surprised, when, coming near the lane, or pass, we saw a confused number of wolves standing just at the entrance.

On a sudden, at another opening of the wood, we heard the noise of a gun; and looking that way, out rushed a horse, with a saddle and a bridle on him, flying like the wind, and sixteen or seventeen wolves after him full speed: indeed, the horse had the heels of them; but as we supposed that he could not hold it at that rate, we doubted not but they would get up with him at last – and no question but they did.

Here we had a most horrible sight; for riding up to the entrance where the horse came out, we found the carcase of another horse, and of two men, devoured by these ravenous creatures. One of them was no doubt the same whom we heard fire a gun, for there lay a gun just by him fired off; but as to the man, his head, and the upper part of his body, were eaten up.

This filled us with horror, and we knew not what course to take; but the creatures resolved us soon, for they gathered about us presently, in hopes of prey; and I verily believe there were three hundred of them. It happened very much to our advantage, that at the entrance into the wood, but a little way from it, there lay some large timber trees, which had been cut down the summer before, and I suppose lay there for carriage. I drew my little troop in among these trees, and placing ourselves in a line behind one long tree, I advised them all to alight, and, keeping that tree before us for a breastwork, to stand in a triangle, or three fronts, enclosing our horses in the centre.

We did so, and it was well we did; for never was a more furious charge than the creatures made upon us in this place; they came on us with a growling kind of a noise, and mounted the piece of timber (which, as I said, was our breastwork), as if they were only rushing upon their prey; and this fury of theirs, it seems, was principally occasioned by their seeing our horses behind us, which was the prey they aimed at. I ordered our men to fire as before, every man; and they took their aim so sure, that indeed they killed several of the wolves at the first volley; but there was a necessity to keep a continual firing, for they came on like devils, those behind pushing on those before.

When we had fired our second volley of fusils, we thought they stopped a little, and I hoped they would have gone off; but it was but a moment, for others came forward again, so we fired our volleys of pistols; and I believe in these four firings we killed seventeen or eighteen of them, and lamed twice as many, yet they came on again.

I was loath to spend our last shot too hastily; so I called my servant, not my man Friday, for he was better employed – for, with the greatest dexterity imaginable, he charged my fusil and his own while we were engaged – but, as I said, I called my other man, and giving him a horn of powder, I bade him lay a train all along the piece of timber, and let it be a large train; he did so, and had but time to get away, when the wolves came up to it, and some were got upon it; when I, snapping an uncharged pistol close to the powder, set it on fire; and those that were upon the timber were scorched with it, and six or seven of them fell, or rather jumped in among us, with the force and fright of the fire: we despatched these in an instant, and the rest were so frighted with the light, which the night, for now it was very dark, made more terrible, that they drew back a little.

Upon which I ordered our last pistols to be fired off in one volley, and after that we gave a shout: upon this, the wolves turned tail, and we sallied immediately upon near twenty lame ones, which we found struggling on the ground, and fell a-cutting them with our swords, which answered our expectation; for the crying and howling they made were better understood by their fellows, so that they fled and left us.

We had, first and last, killed about threescore of them; and had it been daylight, we had killed many more. The field of battle being thus cleared, we made forward again; for we had still near a league to go. We heard the ravenous creatures howl and yell in the woods, as we went several times, and sometimes we fancied we saw some of them, but the snow dazzling our eyes, we were not certain; so in about an hour more, we came to the town where we were to lodge, which we found in a terrible fright, and all in arms; for it seems that the night before, the wolves and some bears had broken into that village, and put them in a terrible fright; and they were obliged to keep guard night and day, but especially in the night, to preserve their cattle, and indeed their people.

The next morning our guide was so ill, and his limbs so swelled with the rankling of his two wounds, that he could go no farther; so we were obliged to take a new guide there and go to Tholouse, where we found a warm climate, a fruitful, pleasant country, and no snow, no wolves or anything like them; but when we told our story at Tholouse, they told us it was Nothing but what was ordinary in the great forest at the foot of the mountains; especially when the snow lay on the ground; but they inquired much what kind of a guide we had gotten, that would venture to bring us that way in such a severe season, and told us, it was very strange we were not all devoured. When we told them how we placed ourselves, and the horses in the middle, they blamed us exceedingly, and told us it was fifty to one but we had been all destroyed – for it was the sight of the horses that made the wolves so furious, seeing their prey – and that at other times they are really afraid of a gun: but they being exceedingly hungry, and raging on that account, the eagerness to come at the horses had made them senseless of danger, and that if we had not by the continued fire, and at last by the stratagem of the train of powder, mastered them, it had been great odds but that we had been torn to pieces; whereas, had we been content to have sat still on horseback, and fired as horsemen, they would not have taken the horses so much for their own when men were on their back as otherwise; and withal they told us, that at last, if we had stood altogether and left our horses, they would have been so eager to have devoured them, that we might have come off safe, especially having our fire-arms in our hands, and being so many in number.

For my part, I was never so sensible of danger in my life; for seeing above three hundred devils come roaring and open-mouthed to devour us, and having nothing to shelter us or retreat to, I gave myself over for lost, and as it was, I believe I shall never care to cross those mountains again; I think I would much rather go a thousand leagues by sea, though I were sure to meet with a storm once a-week. I have nothing uncommon to take notice of in my passage through France, nothing but what other travellers have given an account of with much more advantage than I can. I travelled from Tholouse to Paris, and without any considerable stay came to Calais, and landed safe at Dover the 14th of January, after having had a severe cold season to travel in.

I was now come to the centre of my travels, and had in a little time all my new-discovered estate safe about me, the bills of exchange which I brought with me having been very currently paid.

My principal guide and privy counsellor was my good ancient widow, who, in gratitude for the money I had sent her, thought no pains too much, or care too great, to employ for me; and I trusted her so entirely with everything, that I was perfectly easy as to the security of my effects; and indeed I was very happy from my beginning, and now to the end, in the unspotted integrity of this good gentle-woman.

And now I began to think of leaving my effects with this woman, and setting out for Lisbon, and so to the Brazils. But now another scruple came in the way, and that was religion; for as I had entertained some doubts about the Roman religion, even while I was abroad, especially in my state of solitude, so I knew there was no going to the Brazils for me, much less going to settle there, unless I resolved to embrace the Roman Catholic religion, without any reserve; except, on the other hand, I resolved to be a sacrifice to my principles, be a martyr to religion, and die in the Inquisition: so I resolved to stay at home, and, if I could find means for it, to dispose of my plantation.

To this purpose I wrote to my old friend at Lisbon, who in return gave me notice, that he could easily dispose of it there; but that if I thought fit to give him leave to offer it in my name to the two merchants, the survivors of my trustees, who lived in the Brazils, who must fully understand the value of it, who lived just upon the spot, and whom I knew to be very rich, so that he believed they would be fond of buying it, he did not doubt but I should make four or five thousand pieces of eight the more of it.

Accordingly, I agreed, gave him orders to offer it to them, and he did so; and in about eight months more, the ship being then returned, he sent me an account, that they had accepted the offer, and had remitted thirty-three thousand pieces of eight to a correspondent of theirs at Lisbon to pay for it. In return, I signed the instrument of sale in the form which they sent from Lisbon, and sent it to my old man, who sent me the bills of exchange for thirty-three thousand pieces of eight for the estate; reserving the payment of one hundred moidores a-year to him (the old man) during his life, and fifty moidores afterwards to his son for his life, which I had promised them, and which the plantation was to make good as a rent-charge.

And thus I have given the first part of a life of fortune and adventure, a life of Providence's chequer-work, and of a variety which the world will seldom be able to show the like of, beginning foolishly, but closing much more happily than any part of it ever gave me leave so much as to hope for.

Any one would think, that in this state of complicated good fortune, I was past running any more hazards, and so indeed I had been, if other circumstances had concurred; but I was inured to a wandering life, had no family, nor any relations, nor, however rich, had I contracted much acquaintance; and though I had sold my estate in the Brazils, yet I could not keep that country out of my head, and had a great mind to be upon the wing again; especially I could not resist the strong inclination I had to see my island, and to know if the poor Spaniards were in being there; and how the rogues I left there had used them.

My true friend, the widow, earnestly dissuaded me from it, and so far prevailed with me, that almost for seven years she prevented my running abroad, during which time I took my two nephews, the children of one of my brothers, into my care; the eldest having something of his own, I bred up as a gentleman, and gave him a settlement of some addition to his estate, after my decease; the other I put out to a captain of a ship; and after five years, finding him a sensible, bold, enterprising young fellow, I put him into a good ship, and sent him to sea; and this young fellow afterwards drew me in, as old as I was, to further adventure myself.

In the meantime, I in part settled myself here; for, first of all, I married, and that not either to my disadvantage or dissatisfaction; and had three children, two sons and one daughter.

CLASSIC LITERATURE: WORDS AND PHRASES
adapted from the Collins English Dictionary

Accoucheur NOUN a male midwife or doctor ❏ *I think my sister must have had some general idea that I was a young offender whom an Accoucheur Policemen had taken up (on my birthday) and delivered over to her* (*Great Expectations* by Charles Dickens)

addled ADJ confused and unable to think properly ❏ *But she counted and counted till she got that addled* (*The Adventures of Huckleberry Finn* by Mark Twain)

admiration NOUN amazement or wonder ❏ *lifting up his hands and eyes by way of admiration* (*Gulliver's Travels* by Jonathan Swift)

afeard ADJ afeard means afraid ❏ *shake it – and don't be afeard* (*The Adventures of Huckleberry Finn* by Mark Twain)

affected VERB affected means followed ❏ *Hadst thou affected sweet divinity* (*Doctor Faustus 5.2* by Christopher Marlowe)

aground ADV when a boat runs aground, it touches the ground in a shallow part of the water and gets stuck ❏ *what kep' you? – boat get aground?* (*The Adventures of Huckleberry Finn* by Mark Twain)

ague NOUN a fever in which the patient has alternate hot and cold shivering fits ❏ *his exposure to the wet and cold had brought on fever and ague* (*Oliver Twist* by Charles Dickens)

alchemy ADJ false or worthless ❏ *all wealth alchemy* (*The Sun Rising* by John Donne)

all alike phrase the same all the time ❏ *Love, all alike* (*The Sun Rising* by John Donne)

alow and aloft phrase alow means in the lower part or bottom, and aloft means on the top, so alow and aloft means on the top and in the bottom or throughout ❏ *Someone's turned the chest out alow and aloft* (*Treasure Island* by Robert Louis Stevenson)

ambuscade NOUN ambuscade is not a proper word. Tom means an ambush, which is when a group of people attack their enemies, after hiding and waiting for them ❏ *and so we would lie in ambuscade, as he called it* (*The Adventures of Huckleberry Finn* by Mark Twain)

amiable ADJ likeable or pleasant ❏ *Such amiable qualities must speak for themselves* (*Pride and Prejudice* by Jane Austen)

amulet NOUN an amulet is a charm thought to drive away evil spirits. ❏ *uttered phrases at once occult and familiar, like the amulet worn on the heart* (*Silas Marner* by George Eliot)

amusement NOUN here amusement means a strange and disturbing puzzle ❏ *this was an amusement the other way* (*Robinson Crusoe* by Daniel Defoe)

ancient NOUN an ancient was the flag displayed on a ship to show which country it belongs to. It is also called the ensign ❏ *her ancient and pendants out* (*Robinson Crusoe* by Daniel Defoe)

antic ADJ here antic means horrible or grotesque ❏ *armed and dressed after a very antic manner* (*Gulliver's Travels* by Jonathan Swift)

antics NOUN antics is an old word meaning clowns, or people who do silly things to make other people laugh ❏ *And point like antics at his triple crown* (*Doctor Faustus 3.2* by Christopher Marlowe)

appanage NOUN an appanage is a living allowance ❏ *As if loveliness were not the special prerogative of woman*

DANIEL DEFOE

– *her legitimate appanage and heritage!* (*Jane Eyre* by Charlotte Brontë)

appended VERB appended means attached or added to ❑ *and these words appended* (*Treasure Island* by Robert Louis Stevenson)

approver NOUN an approver is someone who gives evidence against someone he used to work with ❑ *Mr. Noah Claypole: receiving a free pardon from the Crown in consequence of being admitted approver against Fagin* (*Oliver Twist* by Charles Dickens)

areas NOUN the areas is the space, below street level, in front of the basement of a house ❑ *The Dodger had a vicious propensity, too, of pulling the caps from the heads of small boys and tossing them down areas* (*Oliver Twist* by Charles Dickens)

argument NOUN theme or important idea or subject which runs through a piece of writing ❑ *Thrice needful to the argument which now* (*The Prelude* by William Wordsworth)

artificially ADJ artfully or cleverly ❑ *and he with a sharp flint sharpened very artificially* (*Gulliver's Travels* by Jonathan Swift)

artist NOUN here artist means a skilled workman ❑ *This man was a most ingenious artist* (*Gulliver's Travels* by Jonathan Swift)

assizes NOUN assizes were regular court sessions which a visiting judge was in charge of ❑ *you shall hang at the next assizes* (*Treasure Island* by Robert Louis Stevenson)

attraction NOUN gravitation, or Newton's theory of gravitation ❑ *he predicted the same fate to attraction* (*Gulliver's Travels* by Jonathan Swift)

aver VERB to aver is to claim something strongly ❑ *for Jem Rodney, the mole catcher, averred that one evening as he was returning homeward* (*Silas Marner* by George Eliot)

baby NOUN here baby means doll, which is a child's toy that looks like a small person ❑ *and skilful dressing her baby* (*Gulliver's Travels* by Jonathan Swift)

bagatelle NOUN bagatelle is a game rather like billiards and pool ❑ *Breakfast had been ordered at a pleasant little tavern, a mile or so away upon the rising ground beyond the green; and there was a bagatelle board in the room, in case we should desire to unbend our minds after the solemnity.* (*Great Expectations* by Charles Dickens)

bah EXCLAM Bah is an exclamation of frustration or anger ❑ *"Bah," said Scrooge.* (*A Christmas Carol* by Charles Dickens)

bairn NOUN a northern word for child ❑ *Who has taught you those fine words, my bairn?* (*Wuthering Heights* by Emily Brontë)

bait VERB to bait means to stop on a journey to take refreshment ❑ *So, when they stopped to bait the horse, and ate and drank and enjoyed themselves, I could touch nothing that they touched, but kept my fast unbroken.* (*David Copperfield* by Charles Dickens)

balustrade NOUN a balustrade is a row of vertical columns that form railings ❑ *but I mean to say you might have got a hearse up that staircase, and taken it broadwise, with the splinter-bar towards the wall, and the door towards the balustrades: and done it easy* (*A Christmas Carol* by Charles Dickens)

bandbox NOUN a large lightweight box for carrying bonnets or hats ❑ *I am glad I bought my bonnet, if it is only for the fun of having another bandbox* (*Pride and Prejudice* by Jane Austen)

barren NOUN a barren here is a stretch or expanse of barren land ❑ *a line of upright stones, continued the length of the barren* (*Wuthering Heights* by Emily Brontë)

basin NOUN a basin was a cup without a handle ❑ *who is drinking his tea* *out of a basin (Wuthering Heights* by Emily Brontë)

battalia NOUN the order of battle ❑ *till I saw part of his army in battalia (Gulliver's Travels* by Jonathan Swift)

battery NOUN a Battery is a fort or a place where guns are positioned ❑ *You bring the lot to me, at that old Battery over yonder* (*Great Expectations* by Charles Dickens)

battledore and shuttlecock NOUN The game battledore and shuttle-cock was an early version of the game now known as badminton. The aim of the early game was simply to keep the shuttlecock from hitting the ground. ❑ *Battledore and shuttlecock's a werry good game vhen you an't the shuttlecock and two lawyers the battledores, in which case it gets too excitin' to be pleasant (Pickwick Papers* by Charles Dickens)

beadle NOUN a beadle was a local official who had power over the poor ❑ *But these impertinences were speedily checked by the evidence of the surgeon, and the testimony of the beadle (Oliver Twist* by Charles Dickens)

bearings NOUN the bearings of a place are the measurements or direc-tions that are used to find or locate it ❑ *the bearings of the island (Treasure Island* by Robert Louis Stevenson)

beaufet NOUN a beaufet was a sideboard ❑ *and sweet-cake from the beaufet (Emma* by Jane Austen)

beck NOUN a beck is a small stream ❑ *a beck which follows the bend of the glen (Wuthering Heights* by Emily Brontë)

bedight VERB decorated ❑ *and bedight with Christmas holly stuck into the top. (A Christmas Carol* by Charles Dickens)

Bedlam NOUN Bedlam was a lunatic asylum in London which had statues carved by Caius Gabriel Cibber at its

entrance ❑ *Bedlam, and those carved maniacs at the gates (The Prelude* by William Wordsworth)

beeves NOUN oxen or castrated bulls which are animals used for pulling vehicles or carrying things ❑ *to deliver in every morning six beeves (Gulliver's Travels* by Jonathan Swift)

begot VERB created or caused ❑ *Begot in thee (On His Mistress* by John Donne)

behoof NOUN behoof means benefit ❑ *"Yes, young man," said he, releasing the handle of the article in question, retiring a step or two from my table, and speaking for the behoof of the landlord and waiter at the door (Great Expectations* by Charles Dickens)

berth NOUN a berth is a bed on a boat ❑ *this is the berth for me (Treasure Island* by Robert Louis Stevenson)

bevers NOUN a bever was a snack, or small portion of food, eaten between main meals ❑ *that buys me thirty meals a day and ten bevers (Doctor Faustus 2.1* by Christopher Marlowe)

bilge water NOUN the bilge is the widest part of a ship's bottom, and the bilge water is the dirty water that collects there ❑ *no gush of bilge-water had turned it to fetid puddle (Jane Eyre* by Charlotte Brontë)

bills NOUN bills is an old term meaning prescription. A prescription is the piece of paper on which your doctor writes an order for medicine and which you give to a chemist to get the medicine ❑ *Are not thy bills hung up as monuments (Doctor Faustus 1.1* by Christopher Marlowe)

black cap NOUN a judge wore a black cap when he was about to sentence a prisoner to death ❑ *The judge assumed the black cap, and the prisoner still stood with the same air and gesture. (Oliver Twist* by Charles Dickens)

boot-jack NOUN a wooden device to help take boots off ❏ *The speaker appeared to throw a boot-jack, or some such article, at the person he addressed* (*Oliver Twist* by Charles Dickens)

booty NOUN booty means treasure or prizes ❏ *would be inclined to give up their booty in payment of the dead man's debts* (*Treasure Island* by Robert Louis Stevenson)

Bow Street runner PHRASE Bow Street runners were the first British police force, set up by the author Henry Fielding in the eighteenth century ❏ *as would have convinced a judge or a Bow Street runner* (*Treasure Island* by Robert Louis Stevenson)

brawn NOUN brawn is a dish of meat which is set in jelly ❏ *Heaped up upon the floor, to form a kind of throne, were turkeys, geese, game, poultry, brawn, great joints of meat, sucking-pigs* (*A Christmas Carol* by Charles Dickens)

bray VERB when a donkey brays, it makes a loud, harsh sound ❏ *and she doesn't bray like a jackass* (*The Adventures of Huckleberry Finn* by Mark Twain)

break VERB in order to train a horse you first have to break it ❏*"If a high-mettled creature like this," said he, "can't be broken by fair means, she will never be good for anything"* (*Black Beauty* by Anna Sewell)

bullyragging VERB bullyragging is an old word which means bullying. To bullyrag someone is to threaten or force someone to do something they don't want to do ❏ *and a lot of loafers bullyragging him for sport* (*The Adventures of Huckleberry Finn* by Mark Twain)

but PREP except for (this) ❏ *but this, all pleasures fancies be* (*The Good-Morrow* by John Donne)

by hand PHRASE by hand was a common expression of the time meaning that baby had been fed either using a spoon or a bottle rather than by breast-feeding ❏ *My sister, Mrs. Joe Gargery, was more than twenty years older than I, and had established a great reputation with herself . . . because she had bought me up 'by hand'* (*Great Expectations* by Charles Dickens)

bye-spots NOUN bye-spots are lonely places ❏ *and bye-spots of tales rich with indigenous produce* (*The Prelude* by William Wordsworth)

calico NOUN calico is plain white fabric made from cotton ❏ *There was two old dirty calico dresses* (*The Adventures of Huckleberry Finn* by Mark Twain)

camp-fever NOUN camp-fever was another word for the disease typhus ❏ *during a severe camp-fever* (*Emma* by Jane Austen)

cant NOUN cant is insincere or empty talk ❏ *"Man," said the Ghost, "if man you be in heart, not adamant, forbear that wicked cant until you have discovered What the surplus is, and Where it is."* (*A Christmas Carol* by Charles Dickens)

canty ADJ canty means lively, full of life ❏ *My mother lived til eighty, a canty dame to the last* (*Wuthering Heights* by Emily Brontë)

canvas VERB to canvas is to discuss ❏ *We think so very differently on this point Mr Knightley, that there can be no use in canvassing it* (*Emma* by Jane Austen)

capital ADJ capital means excellent or extremely good ❏ *for it's capital, so shady, light, and big* (*Little Women* by Louisa May Alcott)

capstan NOUN a capstan is a device used on a ship to lift sails and anchors ❏ *capstans going, ships going out to sea, and unintelligible sea creatures roaring curses over the bulwarks at respondent lightermen* (*Great Expectations* by Charles Dickens)

case-bottle NOUN a square bottle designed to fit with others into a case ❏ *The spirit being set before him in a huge case-bottle, which had originally come out of some* *ship's locker (The Old Curiosity Shop* by Charles Dickens)

casement NOUN casement is a word meaning window. The teacher in Nicholas Nickleby misspells window showing what a bad teacher he is ❑ *W-i-n, win, d-e-r, der, winder, a casement.'* (*Nicholas Nickleby* by Charles Dickens)

cataleptic ADJ a cataleptic fit is one in which the victim goes into a trancelike state and remains still for a long time ❑ *It was at this point in their history that Silas's cataleptic fit occurred during the prayer-meeting* (*Silas Marner* by George Eliot)

cauldron NOUN a cauldron is a large cooking pot made of metal ❑ *stirring a large cauldron which seemed to be full of soup* (*Alice's Adventures in Wonderland* by Lewis Carroll)

cephalic ADJ cephalic means to do with the head ❑ *with ink composed of a cephalic tincture* (*Gulliver's Travels* by Jonathan Swift)

chaise and four NOUN a closed four-wheel carriage pulled by four horses ❑ *he came down on Monday in a chaise and four to see the place* (*Pride and Prejudice* by Jane Austen)

chamberlain NOUN the main servant in a household ❑ *In those times a bed was always to be got there at any hour of the night, and the chamberlain, letting me in at his ready wicket, lighted the candle next in order on his shelf* (*Great Expectations* by Charles Dickens)

characters NOUN distinguishing marks ❑ *Impressed upon all forms the characters* (*The Prelude* by William Wordsworth)

chary ADJ cautious ❑ *I should have been chary of discussing my guardian too freely even with her* (*Great Expectations* by Charles Dickens)

cherishes VERB here cherishes means cheers or brightens ❑ *some philosophic song of Truth that cherishes our daily life* (*The Prelude* by William Wordsworth)

chickens' meat PHRASE chickens' meat is an old term which means chickens' feed or food ❑ *I had shook a bag of chickens' meat out in that place* (*Robinson Crusoe* by Daniel Defoe)

chimeras NOUN a chimera is an unrealistic idea or a wish which is unlikely to be fulfilled ❑ *with many other wild impossible chimeras* (*Gulliver's Travels* by Jonathan Swift)

chines NOUN chine is a cut of meat that includes part or all of the backbone of the animal ❑ *and they found hams and chines uncut* (*Silas Marner* by George Eliot)

chits NOUN chits is a slang word which means girls ❑ *I hate affected, niminy-piminy chits!* (*Little Women* by Louisa May Alcott)

chopped VERB chopped means come suddenly or accidentally ❑ *if I had chopped upon them* (*Robinson Crusoe* by Daniel Defoe)

chute NOUN a narrow channel ❑ *One morning about day-break, I found a canoe and crossed over a chute to the main shore* (*The Adventures of Huckleberry Finn* by Mark Twain)

circumspection NOUN careful observation of events and circumstances; caution ❑ *I honour your circumspection* (*Pride and Prejudice* by Jane Austen)

clambered VERB clambered means to climb somewhere with difficulty, usually using your hands and your feet ❑ *he clambered up and down stairs* (*Treasure Island* by Robert Louis Stevenson)

clime NOUN climate ❑ *no season knows nor clime* (*The Sun Rising* by John Donne)

clinched VERB clenched ❑ *the tops whereof I could but just reach with my fist clinched* (*Gulliver's Travels* by Jonathan Swift)

close chair NOUN a close chair is a sedan chair, which is a covered chair which has room for one person. The sedan chair is carried on two poles by two men, one in front and one behind ❑ *persuaded even the Empress herself to let me hold her in her close chair* (*Gulliver's Travels* by Jonathan Swift)

clown NOUN clown here means peasant or person who lives off the land ❑ *In ancient days by emperor and clown* (*Ode on a Nightingale* by John Keats)

coalheaver NOUN a coalheaver loaded coal onto ships using a spade ❑ *Good, strong, wholesome medicine, as was given with great success to two Irish labourers and a coalheaver* (*Oliver Twist* by Charles Dickens)

coal-whippers NOUN men who worked at docks using machines to load coal onto ships ❑ *here, were colliers by the score and score, with the coal-whippers plunging off stages on deck* (*Great Expectations* by Charles Dickens)

cobweb NOUN a cobweb is the net which a spider makes for catching insects ❑ *the walls and ceilings were all hung round with cobwebs* (*Gulliver's Travels* by Jonathan Swift)

coddling VERB coddling means to treat someone too kindly or protect them too much ❑ *and I've been coddling the fellow as if I'd been his grandmother* (*Little Women* by Louisa May Alcott)

coil NOUN coil means noise or fuss or disturbance ❑ *What a coil is there?* (*Doctor Faustus 4.7* by Christopher Marlowe)

collared VERB to collar something is a slang term which means to capture. In this sentence, it means he stole it [the money] ❑ *he collared it* (*The Adventures of Huckleberry Finn* by Mark Twain)

colling VERB colling is an old word which means to embrace and kiss ❑ *and no clasping and colling at all*

(*Tess of the D'Urbervilles* by Thomas Hardy)

colloquies NOUN colloquy is a formal conversation or dialogue ❑ *Such colloquies have occupied many a pair of pale-faced weavers* (*Silas Marner* by George Eliot)

comfit NOUN sugar-covered pieces of fruit or nut eaten as sweets ❑ *and pulled out a box of comfits* (*Alice's Adventures in Wonderland* by Lewis Carroll)

coming out VERB when a girl came out in society it meant she was of marriageable age. In order to 'come out' girls were expecting to attend balls and other parties during a season ❑ *The younger girls formed hopes of coming out a year or two sooner than they might otherwise have done* (*Pride and Prejudice* by Jane Austen)

commit VERB commit means arrest or stop ❑ *Commit the rascals* (*Doctor Faustus 4.7* by Christopher Marlowe)

commodious ADJ commodious means convenient ❑ *the most commodious and effectual ways* (*Gulliver's Travels* by Jonathan Swift)

commons NOUN commons is an old term meaning food shared with others ❑ *his pauper assistants ranged themselves behind him; the gruel was served out; and a long grace was said over the short commons.* (*Oliver Twist* by Charles Dickens)

complacency NOUN here complacency means a desire to please others. Today complacency means feeling pleased with oneself without good reason. ❑ *Twas thy power that raised the first complacency in me* (*The Prelude* by William Wordsworth)

complaisance NOUN complaisance was eagerness to please ❑ *we cannot wonder at his complaisance* (*Pride and Prejudice* by Jane Austen)

complaisant ADJ complaisant means polite ❑ *extremely cheerful and* complaisant to their guest (*Gulliver's Travels* by Jonathan Swift)

conning VERB conning means learning by heart ❑ *Or conning more* (*The Prelude* by William Wordsworth)

consequent NOUN consequence ❑ *as avarice is the necessary consequent of old age* (*Gulliver's Travels* by Jonathan Swift)

consorts NOUN concerts ❑ *The King, who delighted in music, had frequent consorts at Court* (*Gulliver's Travels* by Jonathan Swift)

conversible ADJ conversible meant easy to talk to, companionable ❑ *He can be a conversible companion* (*Pride and Prejudice* by Jane Austen)

copper NOUN a copper is a large pot that can be heated directly over a fire ❑ *He gazed in stupefied astonishment on the small rebel for some seconds, and then clung for support to the copper* (*Oliver Twist* by Charles Dickens)

copper-stick NOUN a copper-stick is the long piece of wood used to stir washing in the copper (or boiler) which was usually the biggest cooking pot in the house ❑ *It was Christmas Eve, and I had to stir the pudding for next day, with a copper-stick, from seven to eight by the Dutch clock* (*Great Expectations* by Charles Dickens)

counting-house NOUN a counting house is a place where accountants work ❑ *Once upon a time – of all the good days in the year, on Christmas Eve – old Scrooge sat busy in his countinghouse* (*A Christmas Carol* by Charles Dickens)

courtier NOUN a courtier is someone who attends the king or queen – a member of the court ❑ *next the ten courtiers;* (*Alice's Adventures in Wonderland* by Lewis Carroll)

covies NOUN covies were flocks of partridges ❑ *and will save all of the*

best covies for you (*Pride and Prejudice* by Jane Austen)

cowed VERB cowed means frightened or intimidated ❑ *it cowed me more than the pain* (*Treasure Island* by Robert Louis Stevenson)

cozened VERB cozened means tricked or deceived ❑ *Do you remember, sir, how you cozened me* (*Doctor Faustus 4.7* by Christopher Marlowe)

cravats NOUN a cravat is a folded cloth that a man wears wrapped around his neck as a decorative item of clothing ❑ *we'd a' slept in our cravats to-night* (*The Adventures of Huckleberry Finn* by Mark Twain)

crock and dirt PHRASE crock and dirt is an old expression meaning soot and dirt ❑ *and the mare catching cold at the door, and the boy grimed with crock and dirt* (*Great Expectations* by Charles Dickens)

crockery NOUN here crockery means pottery ❑ *By one of the parrots was a cat made of crockery* (*The Adventures of Huckleberry Finn* by Mark Twain)

crooked sixpence PHRASE it was considered unlucky to have a bent sixpence ❑ *You've got the beauty, you see, and I've got the luck, so you must keep me by you for your crooked sixpence* (*Silas Marner* by George Eliot)

croquet NOUN croquet is a traditional English summer game in which players try to hit wooden balls through hoops ❑ *and once she remembered trying to box her own ears for having cheated herself in a game of croquet* (*Alice's Adventures in Wonderland* by Lewis Carroll)

cross PREP across ❑ *The two great streets, which run cross and divide it into four quarters* (Gulliver's Travels by Jonathan Swift)

culpable ADJ if you are culpable for something it means you are to blame ❑ *deep are the sorrows that spring from false ideas for which no man is culpable.* (*Silas Marner* by George Eliot)

cultured ADJ cultivated ❑ *Nor less when spring had warmed the cultured Vale* (*The Prelude* by William Wordsworth)

cupidity NOUN cupidity is greed ❑ *These people hated me with the hatred of cupidity and disappointment.* (*Great Expectations* by Charles Dickens)

curricle NOUN an open two-wheeled carriage with one seat for the driver and space for a single passenger ❑ *and they saw a lady and a gentleman in a curricle* (*Pride and Prejudice* by Jane Austen)

cynosure NOUN a cynosure is something that strongly attracts attention or admiration ❑ *Then I thought of Eliza and Georgiana; I beheld one the cynosure of a ballroom, the other the inmate of a convent cell* (*Jane Eyre* by Charlotte Brontë)

dalliance NOUN someone's dalliance with something is a brief involvement with it ❑ *nor sporting in the dalliance of love* (*Doctor Faustus Chorus* by Christopher Marlowe)

darkling ADV darkling is an archaic way of saying in the dark ❑ *Darkling I listen* (*Ode on a Nightingale* by John Keats)

delf-case NOUN a sideboard for holding dishes and crockery ❑ *at the pewter dishes and delf-case* (*Wuthering Heights* by Emily Brontë)

determined ◼1 VERB here determined means ended ❑ *and be out of vogue when that was determined* (*Gulliver's Travels* by Jonathan Swift) ◼2 VERB determined can mean to have been learned or found especially by investigation or experience ❑ *All the sensitive feelings it wounded so cruelly, all the shame and misery it kept alive within my breast, became more poignant as I thought of this; and I determined that the life was unendurable* (*David Copperfield* by Charles Dickens)

Deuce NOUN a slang term for the Devil ❑ *Ah, I dare say I did. Deuce take me, he added suddenly, I know I did. I find I am not quite unscrewed yet.* (*Great Expectations* by Charles Dickens)

diabolical ADJ diabolical means devilish or evil ❑ *and with a thousand diabolical expressions* (*Treasure Island* by Robert Louis Stevenson)

direction NOUN here direction means address ❑ *Elizabeth was not surprised at it, as Jane had written the direction remarkably ill* (*Pride and Prejudice* by Jane Austen)

discover VERB to make known or announce ❑ *the Emperor would discover the secret while I was out of his power* (*Gulliver's Travels* by Jonathan Swift)

dissemble VERB hide or conceal ❑ *Dissemble nothing* (*On His Mistress* by John Donne)

dissolve VERB dissolve here means to release from life, to die ❑ *Fade far away, dissolve, and quite forget* (*Ode on a Nightingale* by John Keats)

distrain VERB to distrain is to seize the property of someone who is in debt in compensation for the money owed ❑ *for he's threatening to distrain for it* (*Silas Marner* by George Eliot)

Divan NOUN a Divan was originally a Turkish council of state – the name was transferred to the couches they sat on and is used to mean this in English ❑ *Mr Brass applauded this picture very much, and the bed being soft and comfortable, Mr Quilp determined to use it, both as a sleeping place by night and as a kind of Divan by day.* (*The Old Curiosity Shop* by Charles Dickens)

divorcement NOUN separation ❑ *By all pains which want and divorcement hath* (*On His Mistress* by John Donne)

dog in the manger, PHRASE this phrase describes someone who prevents you from enjoying something that they themselves have no need for

You are a dog in the manger, Cathy, and desire no one to be loved but yourself (Wuthering Heights by Emily Brontë)

dolorifuge NOUN dolorifuge is a word which Thomas Hardy invented. It means pain-killer or comfort ❑ *as a species of dolorifuge (Tess of the D'Urbervilles* by Thomas Hardy)

dome NOUN building ❑ *that river and that mouldering dome (The Prelude* by William Wordsworth)

domestic PHRASE here domestic means a person's management of the house ❑ *to give some account of my domestic (Gulliver's Travels* by Jonathan Swift)

dunce NOUN a dunce is another word for idiot ❑ *Do you take me for a dunce? Go on? (Alice's Adventures in Wonderland* by Lewis Carroll)

Ecod EXCLAM a slang exclamation meaning 'oh God!' ❑ *"Ecod," replied Wemmick, shaking his head, "that's not my trade." (Great Expectations* by Charles Dickens)

egg-hot NOUN an egg-hot (see also 'flip' and 'negus') was a hot drink made from beer and eggs, sweetened with nutmeg ❑ *She fainted when she saw me return, and made a little jug of egg-hot afterwards to console us while we talked it over. (David Copperfield* by Charles Dickens)

encores NOUN an encore is a short extra performance at the end of a longer one, which the entertainer gives because the audience has enthusiastically asked for it ❑ *we want a little something to answer encores with, anyway (The Adventures of Huckleberry Finn* by Mark Twain)

equipage NOUN an elegant and impressive carriage ❑ *and besides, the equipage did not answer to any of their neighbours (Pride and Prejudice* by Jane Austen)

exordium NOUN an exordium is the opening part of a speech ❑ *"Now, Handel," as if it were the grave*

beginning of a portentous business exordium, he had suddenly given up that tone (Great Expectations* by Charles Dickens)

expect VERB here expect means to wait for ❑ *to expect his farther commands (Gulliver's Travels* by Jonathan Swift)

familiars NOUN familiars means spirits or devils who come to someone when they are called ❑ *I'll turn all the lice about thee into familiars (Doctor Faustus 1.4* by Christopher Marlowe)

fantods NOUN a fantod is a person who fidgets or can't stop moving nervously ❑ *It most give me the fantods (The Adventures of Huckleberry Finn* by Mark Twain)

farthing NOUN a farthing is an old unit of British currency which was worth a quarter of a penny ❑ *Not a farthing less. A great many back-payments are included in it, I assure you. (A Christmas Carol* by Charles Dickens)

farthingale NOUN a hoop worn under a skirt to extend it ❑ *A bell with an old voice – which I dare say in its time had often said to the house, Here is the green farthingale (Great Expectations* by Charles Dickens)

favours NOUN here favours is an old word which means ribbons ❑ *A group of humble mourners entered the gate: wearing white favours (Oliver Twist* by Charles Dickens)

feigned VERB pretend or pretending ❑ *not my feigned page (On His Mistress* by John Donne)

fence ❶ NOUN a fence is someone who receives and sells stolen goods ❑ *What are you up to? Ill-treating the boys, you covetous, avaricious, in-sa-ti-a-ble old fence? (Oliver Twist* by Charles Dickens) ❷ NOUN defence or protection ❑ *but honesty hath no fence against superior cunning (Gulliver's Travels* by Jonathan Swift)

fess ADJ fess is an old word which means pleased or proud ❑ *You'll be* *fess enough, my poppet* (*Tess of the D'Urbervilles* by Thomas Hardy)

fettered ADJ fettered means bound in chains or chained ❏ *"You are fettered," said Scrooge, trembling. "Tell me why?"* (*A Christmas Carol* by Charles Dickens)

fidges VERB fidges means fidgets, which is to keep moving your hands slightly because you are nervous or excited ❏ *Look, Jim, how my fingers fidges* (*Treasure Island* by Robert Louis Stevenson)

finger-post NOUN a finger-post is a sign-post showing the direction to different places ❏ *"The gallows," continued Fagin, "the gallows, my dear, is an ugly finger-post, which points out a very short and sharp turning that has stopped many a bold fellow's career on the broad highway."* (*Oliver Twist* by Charles Dickens)

fire-irons NOUN fire-irons are tools kept by the side of the fire to either cook with or look after the fire ❏ *the fire-irons came first* (*Alice's Adventures in Wonderland* by Lewis Carroll)

fire-plug NOUN a fire-plug is another word for a fire hydrant ❏ *The pony looked with great attention into a fire-plug, which was near him, and appeared to be quite absorbed in contemplating it* (*The Old Curiosity Shop* by Charles Dickens)

flank NOUN flank is the side of an animal ❏ *And all her silken flanks with garlands dressed* (*Ode on a Grecian Urn* by John Keats)

flip NOUN a flip is a drink made from warmed ale, sugar, spice and beaten egg ❏ *The events of the day, in combination with the twins, if not with the flip, had made Mrs. Micawber hysterical, and she shed tears as she replied* (*David Copperfield* by Charles Dickens)

flit VERB flit means to move quickly ❏ *and if he had meant to flit to Thrushcross Grange* (*Wuthering Heights* by Emily Brontë)

floorcloth NOUN a floorcloth was a hard-wearing piece of canvas used instead of carpet ❏ *This avenging phantom was ordered to be on duty at eight on Tuesday morning in the hall (it was two feet square, as charged for floorcloth)* (*Great Expectations* by Charles Dickens)

fly-driver NOUN a fly-driver is a carriage drawn by a single horse ❏ *The fly-drivers, among whom I inquired next, were equally jocose and equally disrespectful* (*David Copperfield* by Charles Dickens)

fob NOUN a small pocket in which a watch is kept ❏ *"Certain," replied the man, drawing a gold watch from his fob* (*Oliver Twist* by Charles Dickens)

folly NOUN folly means foolishness or stupidity ❏ *the folly of beginning a work* (*Robinson Crusoe* by Daniel Defoe)

fond ADJ fond means foolish ❏ *Fond worldling* (*Doctor Faustus 5.2* by Christopher Marlowe)

fondness NOUN silly or foolish affection ❏ *They have no fondness for their colts or foals* (*Gulliver's Travels* by Jonathan Swift)

for his fancy PHRASE for his fancy means for his liking or as he wanted ❏ *and as I did not obey quick enough for his fancy* (*Treasure Island* by Robert Louis Stevenson)

forlorn ADJ lost or very upset ❏ *you are from that day forlorn* (*Gulliver's Travels* by Jonathan Swift)

foster-sister NOUN a foster-sister was someone brought up by the same nurse or in the same household ❏ *I had been his foster-sister* (*Wuthering Heights* by Emily Brontë)

fox-fire NOUN fox-fire is a weak glow that is given off by decaying, rotten wood ❏ *what we must have was a lot of them rotten chunks that's called fox-fire* (*The Adventures of Huckleberry Finn* by Mark Twain)

frozen sea PHRASE the Arctic Ocean ❏ *into the frozen sea* (*Gulliver's Travels* by Jonathan Swift)

gainsay VERB to gainsay something is to say it isn't true or to deny it ❏ *"So she had," cried Scrooge. "You're right. I'll not gainsay it, Spirit. God forbid!" (A Christmas Carol* by Charles Dickens)

gaiters NOUN gaiters were leggings made of a cloth or piece of leather which covered the leg from the knee to the ankle ❏ *Mr Knightley was hard at work upon the lower buttons of his thick leather gaiters (Emma* by Jane Austen)

galluses NOUN galluses is an old spelling of gallows, and here means suspenders. Suspenders are straps worn over someone's shoulders and fastened to their trousers to prevent the trousers falling down ❏ *and home-knit galluses (The Adventures of Huckleberry Finn* by Mark Twain)

galoot NOUN a sailor but also a clumsy person ❏ *and maybe a galoot on it chopping (The Adventures of Huckleberry Finn* by Mark Twain)

gayest ADJ gayest means the most lively and bright or merry ❏ *Beth played her gayest march (Little Women* by Louisa May Alcott)

gem NOUN here gem means jewellery ❏ *the mountain shook off turf and flower, had only heath for raiment and crag for gem (Jane Eyre* by Charlotte Brontë)

giddy ADJ giddy means dizzy ❏ *and I wish you wouldn't keep appearing and vanishing so suddenly; you make one quite giddy. (Alice's Adventures in Wonderland* by Lewis Carroll)

gig NOUN a light two-wheeled carriage ❏ *when a gig drove up to the garden gate: out of which there jumped a fat gentleman (Oliver Twist* by Charles Dickens)

gladsome ADJ gladsome is an old word meaning glad or happy ❏ *Nobody ever stopped him in the street to say, with gladsome looks (A Christmas Carol* by Charles Dickens)

glen NOUN a glen is a small valley; the word is used commonly in Scotland ❏ *a beck which follows the bend of the glen (Wuthering Heights* by Emily Brontë)

gravelled VERB gravelled is an old term which means to baffle or defeat someone ❏ *Gravelled the pastors of the German Church (Doctor Faustus 1.1* by Christopher Marlowe)

grinder NOUN a grinder was a private tutor ❏ *but that when he had had the happiness of marrying Mrs Pocket very early in his life, he had impaired his prospects and taken up the calling of a Grinder (Great Expectations* by Charles Dickens)

gruel NOUN gruel is a thin, watery cornmeal or oatmeal soup ❏ *and the little saucepan of gruel (Scrooge had a cold in his head) upon the hob. (A Christmas Carol* by Charles Dickens)

guinea, half a NOUN a half guinea was ten shillings and sixpence ❏ *but lay out half a guinea at Ford's (Emma* by Jane Austen)

gull VERB gull is an old term which means to fool or deceive someone ❏ *Hush, I'll gull him supernaturally (Doctor Faustus 3.4* by Christopher Marlowe)

gunnel NOUN the gunnel, or gunwhale, is the upper edge of a boat's side ❏ *But he put his foot on the gunnel and rocked her (The Adventures of Huckleberry Finn* by Mark Twain)

gunwale NOUN the side of a ship ❏ *He dipped his hand in the water over the boat's gunwale (Great Expectations* by Charles Dickens)

Gytrash NOUN a Gytrash is an omen of misfortune to the superstitious, usually taking the form of a hound ❏ *I remembered certain of Bessie's tales, wherein figured a North-of-England spirit, called a 'Gytrash' (Jane Eyre* by Charlotte Brontë)

hackney-cabriolet NOUN a two-wheeled carriage with four seats for hire and pulled by a horse ❑ *A hackney-cabriolet was in waiting; with the same vehemence which she had exhibited in addressing Oliver, the girl pulled him in with her, and drew the curtains close.* (*Oliver Twist* by Charles Dickens)

hackney-coach NOUN a four-wheeled horse-drawn vehicle for hire ❑ *The twilight was beginning to close in, when Mr. Brownlow alighted from a hackney-coach at his own door, and knocked softly.* (*Oliver Twist* by Charles Dickens)

haggler NOUN a haggler is someone who travels from place to place selling small goods and items ❑ *when I be plain Jack Durbeyfield, the haggler* (*Tess of the D'Urbervilles* by Thomas Hardy)

halter NOUN a halter is a rope or strap used to lead an animal or to tie it up ❑ *I had of course long been used to a halter and a headstall* (*Black Beauty* by Anna Sewell)

hamlet NOUN a hamlet is a small village or a group of houses in the countryside ❑ *down from the hamlet* (*Treasure Island* by Robert Louis Stevenson)

hand-barrow NOUN a hand-barrow is a device for carrying heavy objects. It is like a wheelbarrow except that it has handles, rather than wheels, for moving the barrow ❑ *his sea chest following behind him in a hand-barrow* (*Treasure Island* by Robert Louis Stevenson)

handspike NOUN a handspike was a stick which was used as a lever ❑ *a bit of stick like a handspike* (*Treasure Island* by Robert Louis Stevenson)

haply ADV haply means by chance or perhaps ❑ *And haply the Queen-Moon is on her throne* (*Ode on a Nightingale* by John Keats)

harem NOUN the harem was the part of the house where the women lived ❑ *mostly they hang round the harem* (*The Adventures of Huckleberry Finn* by Mark Twain)

hautboys NOUN hautboys are oboes ❑ sausages and puddings resembling flutes and hautboys (*Gulliver's Travels* by Jonathan Swift)

hawker NOUN a hawker is someone who sells goods to people as he travels rather than from a fixed place like a shop ❑ *to buy some stockings from a hawker* (*Treasure Island* by Robert Louis Stevenson)

hawser NOUN a hawser is a rope used to tie up or tow a ship or boat ❑ *Again among the tiers of shipping, in and out, avoiding rusty chain-cables, frayed hempen hawsers* (*Great Expectations* by Charles Dickens)

headstall NOUN the headstall is the part of the bridle or halter that goes around a horse's head ❑ *I had of course long been used to a halter and a headstall* (*Black Beauty* by Anna Sewell)

hearken VERB hearken means to listen ❑ *though we sometimes stopped to lay hold of each other and hearken* (*Treasure Island* by Robert Louis Stevenson)

heartless ADJ here heartless means without heart or dejected ❑ *I am not heartless* (*The Prelude* by William Wordsworth)

hebdomadal ADJ hebdomadal means weekly ❑ *It was the hebdomadal treat to which we all looked forward from Sabbath to Sabbath* (*Jane Eyre* by Charlotte Brontë)

highwaymen NOUN highwaymen were people who stopped travellers and robbed them ❑ *We are highwaymen* (*The Adventures of Huckleberry Finn* by Mark Twain)

hinds NOUN hinds means farm hands, or people who work on a farm ❑ *He called his hinds about him* (*Gulliver's Travels* by Jonathan Swift)

histrionic ADJ if you refer to someone's behaviour as histrionic, you are being critical of it because it is dramatic and exaggerated

❑ But the histrionic muse is the darling (*The Adventures of Huckleberry Finn* by Mark Twain)

hogs NOUN hogs is another word for pigs ❑ *Tom called the hogs 'ingots'* (*The Adventures of Huckleberry Finn* by Mark Twain)

horrors NOUN the horrors are a fit, called delirium tremens, which is caused by drinking too much alcohol ❑ *I'll have the horrors* (*Treasure Island* by Robert Louis Stevenson)

huffy ADJ huffy means to be obviously annoyed or offended about something ❑ *They will feel that more than angry speeches or huffy actions* (*Little Women* by Louisa May Alcott)

hulks NOUN hulks were prison ships ❑ *The miserable companion of thieves and ruffians, the fallen outcast of low haunts, the associate of the scourings of the jails and hulks* (*Oliver Twist* by Charles Dickens)

humbug NOUN humbug means nonsense or rubbish ❑ *"Bah," said Scrooge. "Humbug!"* (*A Christmas Carol* by Charles Dickens)

humours NOUN it was believed that there were four fluids in the body called humours which decided the temperament of a person depending on how much of each fluid was present ❑ *other peccant humours* (*Gulliver's Travels* by Jonathan Swift)

husbandry NOUN husbandry is farming animals ❑ *bad husbandry were plentifully anointing their wheels* (*Silas Marner* by George Eliot)

huswife NOUN a huswife was a small sewing kit ❑ *but I had put my huswife on it* (*Emma* by Jane Austen)

ideal ADJ ideal in this context means imaginary ❑ *I discovered the yell was not ideal* (*Wuthering Heights* by Emily Brontë)

If our two PHRASE if both our ❑ *If*

our two loves be one (*The Good-Morrow* by John Donne)

ignis-fatuus NOUN ignis-fatuus is the light given out by burning marsh gases, which lead careless travellers into danger ❑ *it is madness in all women to let a secret love kindle within them, which, if unreturned and unknown, must devour the life that feeds it; and, if discovered and responded to, must lead ignis-fatuus-like, into miry wilds whence there is no extrication.* (*Jane Eyre* by Charlotte Brontë)

imaginations NOUN here imaginations means schemes or plans ❑ *soon drove out those imaginations* (*Gulliver's Travels* by Jonathan Swift)

impressible ADJ impressible means open or impressionable ❑ *for Marner had one of those impressible, self-doubting natures* (*Silas Marner* by George Eliot)

in good intelligence PHRASE friendly with each other ❑ *that these two persons were in good intelligence with each other* (*Gulliver's Travels* by Jonathan Swift)

inanity NOUN inanity is sillyness or dull stupidity ❑ *Do we not wile away moments of inanity* (*Silas Marner* by George Eliot)

incivility NOUN incivility means rudeness or impoliteness ❑ *if it's only for a piece of incivility like to-night's* (*Treasure Island* by Robert Louis Stevenson)

indigenae NOUN indigenae means natives or people from that area ❑ *an exotic that the surly indigenae will not recognise for kin* (*Wuthering Heights* by Emily Brontë)

indocible ADJ unteachable ❑ *so they were the most restive and indocible* (*Gulliver's Travels* by Jonathan Swift)

ingenuity NOUN inventiveness ❑ *entreated me to give him something as an encouragement to ingenuity* (*Gulliver's Travels* by Jonathan Swift)

DANIEL DEFOE

ingots NOUN an ingot is a lump of a valuable metal like gold, usually shaped like a brick ❑ *Tom called the hogs 'ingots' (The Adventures of Huckleberry Finn by Mark Twain)*

inkstand NOUN an inkstand is a pot which was put on a desk to contain either ink or pencils and pens ❑ *throwing an inkstand at the Lizard as she spoke (Alice's Adventures in Wonderland by Lewis Carroll)*

inordinate ADJ without order. Today inordinate means 'excessive'. ❑ *Though yet untutored and inordinate (The Prelude by William Wordsworth)*

intellectuals NOUN here intellectuals means the minds (of the workmen) ❑ *those instructions they give being too refined for the intellectuals of their workmen (Gulliver's Travels by Jonathan Swift)*

interview NOUN meeting ❑ *By our first strange and fatal interview (On His Mistress by John Donne)*

jacks NOUN jacks are rods for turning a spit over a fire ❑ *It was a small bit of pork suspended from the kettle hanger by a string passed through a large door key, in a way known to primitive housekeepers unpossessed of jacks (Silas Marner by George Eliot)*

jews-harp NOUN a jews-harp is a small, metal, musical instrument that is played by the mouth ❑ *A jews-harp's plenty good enough for a rat (The Adventures of Huckleberry Finn by Mark Twain)*

jorum NOUN a large bowl ❑ *while Miss Skiffins brewed such a jorum of tea, that the pig in the back premises became strongly excited (Great Expectations by Charles Dickens)*

jostled VERB jostled means bumped or pushed by someone or some people ❑ *being jostled himself into the kennel (Gulliver's Travels by Jonathan Swift)*

keepsake NOUN a keepsake is a gift which reminds someone of an

event or of the person who gave it to them. ❑ *books and ornaments they had in their boudoirs at home: keepsakes that different relations had presented to them (Jane Eyre by Charlotte Brontë)*

kenned VERB kenned means knew ❑ *though little kenned the lamplighter that he had any company but Christmas! (A Christmas Carol by Charles Dickens)*

kennel NOUN kennel means gutter, which is the edge of a road next to the pavement, where rain water collects and flows away ❑ *being jostled himself into the kennel (Gulliver's Travels by Jonathan Swift)*

knock-knee ADJ knock-knee means slanted, at an angle. ❑ *LOT 1 was marked in whitewashed knock-knee letters on the brewhouse (Great Expectations by Charles Dickens)*

ladylike ADJ to be ladylike is to behave in a polite, dignified and graceful way ❑ *No, winking isn't ladylike (Little Women by Louisa May Alcott)*

lapse NOUN flow ❑ *Stealing with silent lapse to join the brook (The Prelude by William Wordsworth)*

larry NOUN larry is an old word which means commotion or noisy celebration ❑ *That was all a part of the larry! (Tess of the D'Urbervilles by Thomas Hardy)*

laths NOUN laths are strips of wood ❑ *The panels shrunk, the windows cracked; fragments of plaster fell out of the ceiling, and the naked laths were shown instead (A Christmas Carol by Charles Dickens)*

leer NOUN a leer is an unpleasant smile ❑ *with a kind of leer (Treasure Island by Robert Louis Stevenson)*

lenitives NOUN these are different kinds of drugs or medicines: lenitives and palliatives were pain relievers; aperitives were laxatives; abstersives caused vomiting; corrosives destroyed human tissue; restringents caused constipation; cephalalgics stopped headaches;

276

icterics were used as medicine for jaundice; apophlegmatics were cough medicine, and acoustics were cures for the loss of hearing ❑ *lenitives, aperitives, abstersives, corrosives, restringents, palliatives, laxatives, cephalalgics, icterics, apophlegmatics, acoustics* (*Gulliver's Travels* by Jonathan Swift)

lest CONJ in case. If you do something lest something (usually) unpleasant happens you do it to try to prevent it happening ❑ *She went in without knocking, and hurried upstairs, in great fear lest she should meet the real Mary Ann* (*Alice's Adventures in Wonderland* by Lewis Carroll)

levee NOUN a levee is an old term for a meeting held in the morning, shortly after the person holding the meeting has got out of bed ❑ *I used to attend the King's levee once or twice a week* (*Gulliver's Travels* by Jonathan Swift)

life-preserver NOUN a club which had lead inside it to make it heavier and therefore more dangerous ❑ *and with no more suspicious articles displayed to view than two or three heavy bludgeons which stood in a corner, and a 'life-preserver' that hung over the chimney-piece.* (*Oliver Twist* by Charles Dickens)

lighterman NOUN a lighterman is another word for sailor ❑ *in and out, hammers going in ship-builders' yards, saws going at timber, clashing engines going at things unknown, pumps going in leaky ships, capstans going, ships going out to sea, and unintelligible sea creatures roaring curses over the bulwarks at respondent lightermen* (*Great Expectations* by Charles Dickens)

livery NOUN servants often wore a uniform known as a livery ❑ *suddenly a footman in livery came running out of the wood* (*Alice's Adventures in Wonderland* by Lewis Carroll)

livid ADJ livid means pale or ash coloured. Livid also means very angry ❑ *a dirty, livid white* (*Treasure Island* by Robert Louis Stevenson)

lottery-tickets NOUN a popular card game ❑ *and Mrs. Philips protested that they would have a nice comfortable noisy game of lottery tickets* (*Pride and Prejudice* by Jane Austen)

lower and upper world PHRASE the earth and the heavens are the lower and upper worlds ❑ *the changes in the lower and upper world* (*Gulliver's Travels* by Jonathan Swift)

lustres NOUN lustres are chandeliers. A chandelier is a large, decorative frame which holds light bulbs or candles and hangs from the ceiling ❑ *the lustres, lights, the carving and the guilding* (*The Prelude* by William Wordsworth)

lynched VERB killed without a criminal trial by a crowd of people ❑ *He'll never know how nigh he come to getting lynched* (*The Adventures of Huckleberry Finn* by Mark Twain)

malingering VERB if someone is malingering they are pretending to be ill to avoid working ❑ *And you stand there malingering* (*Treasure Island* by Robert Louis Stevenson)

managing PHRASE treating with consideration ❑ *to think the honour of my own kind not worth managing* (*Gulliver's Travels* by Jonathan Swift)

manhood PHRASE manhood means human nature ❑ *concerning the nature of manhood* (*Gulliver's Travels* by Jonathan Swift)

man-trap NOUN a man-trap is a set of steel jaws that snap shut when trodden on and trap a person's leg ❑ *"Don't go to him," I called out of the window, "he's an assassin! A man-trap!"* (*Oliver Twist* by Charles Dickens)

maps NOUN charts of the night sky ❑ *Let maps to others, worlds on worlds have shown* (*The Good-Morrow* by John Donne)

mark VERB look at or notice ❑ Mark but this flea, and mark in this (*The Flea* by John Donne)

maroons NOUN A maroon is someone who has been left in a place which it is difficult for them to escape from, like a small island ❑ *if schooners, islands, and maroons* (*Treasure Island* by Robert Louis Stevenson)

mast NOUN here mast means the fruit of forest trees ❑ *a quantity of acorns, dates, chestnuts, and other mast* (*Gulliver's Travels* by Jonathan Swift)

mate VERB defeat ❑ *Where Mars did mate the warlike Carthigens* (*Doctor Faustus Chorus* by Christopher Marlowe)

mealy ADJ Mealy when used to describe a face meant palid, pale or colourless ❑ *I only know two sorts of boys. Mealy boys, and beef-faced boys* (*Oliver Twist* by Charles Dickens)

middling ADJ fairly or moderately ❑ *she worked me middling hard for about an hour* (*The Adventures of Huckleberry Finn* by Mark Twain)

mill NOUN a mill, or treadmill, was a device for hard labour or punishment in prison ❑ *Was you never on the mill?* (*Oliver Twist* by Charles Dickens)

milliner's shop NOUN a milliner's sold fabrics, clothing, lace and accessories; as time went on they specialized more and more in hats ❑ *to pay their duty to their aunt and to a milliner's shop just over the way* (*Pride and Prejudice* by Jane Austen)

minching un' munching PHRASE how people in the north of England used to describe the way people from the south speak ❑ *Minching un' munching!* (*Wuthering Heights* by Emily Brontë)

mine NOUN gold ❑ *Whether both th'Indias of spice and mine* (*The Sun Rising* by John Donne)

mire NOUN mud ❑ *Tis my fate to be always ground into the mire under* the iron heel of oppression (*The Adventures of Huckleberry Finn* by Mark Twain)

miscellany NOUN a miscellany is a collection of many different kinds of things ❑ *under that, the miscellany began* (*Treasure Island* by Robert Louis Stevenson)

mistarshers NOUN mistarshers means moustache, which is the hair that grows on a man's upper lip ❑ *when he put his hand up to his mistarshers* (*Tess of the D'Urbervilles* by Thomas Hardy)

morrow NOUN here good-morrow means tomorrow and a new and better life ❑ *And now good-morrow to our waking souls* (*The Good-Morrow* by John Donne)

mortification NOUN mortification is an old word for gangrene which is when part of the body decays or 'dies' because of disease ❑ *Yes, it was a mortification – that was it* (*The Adventures of Huckleberry Finn* by Mark Twain)

mought PARTICIPLE mought is an old spelling of might ❑ *what you mought call me? You mought call me captain* (*Treasure Island* by Robert Louis Stevenson)

move VERB move me not means do not make me angry ❑ *Move me not, Faustus* (*Doctor Faustus 2.1* by Christopher Marlowe)

muffin-cap NOUN a muffin cap is a flat cap made from wool ❑ *the old one, remained stationary in the muffin-cap and leathers* (*Oliver Twist* by Charles Dickens)

mulatter NOUN a mulatter was another word for mulatto, which is a person with parents who are from different races ❑ *a mulatter, most as white as a white man* (*The Adventures of Huckleberry Finn* by Mark Twain)

mummery NOUN mummery is an old word that meant meaningless (or pretentious) ceremony ❑ *When they were all gone, and when Trabb and his men – but not his boy: I* looked for him – had crammed their mummery into bags, and were gone too, the house felt wholesomer. (*Great Expectations* by Charles Dickens)

nap NOUN the nap is the woolly surface on a new item of clothing. Here the surface has been worn away so it looks bare ❏ *like an old hat with the nap rubbed off* (*The Adventures of Huckleberry Finn* by Mark Twain)

natural ❶ NOUN a natural is a person born with learning difficulties ❏ *though he had been left to his particular care by their deceased father, who thought him almost a natural.* (*David Copperfield* by Charles Dickens) ❷ ADJ natural meant illegitimate ❏ *Harriet Smith was the natural daughter of somebody* (*Emma* by Jane Austen)

navigator NOUN a navigator was originally someone employed to dig canals. It is the origin of the word 'navvy' meaning a labourer ❏ *She ascertained from me in a few words what it was all about, comforted Dora, and gradually convinced her that I was not a labourer – from my manner of stating the case I believe Dora concluded that I was a navigator, and went balancing myself up and down a plank all day with a wheelbarrow – and so brought us together in peace.* (*David Copperfield* by Charles Dickens)

necromancy NOUN necromancy means a kind of magic where the magician speaks to spirits or ghosts to find out what will happen in the future ❏ *He surfeits upon cursed necromancy* (*Doctor Faustus chorus* by Christopher Marlowe)

negus NOUN a negus is a hot drink made from sweetened wine and water ❏ *He sat placidly perusing the newspaper, with his little head on one side, and a glass of warm sherry negus at his elbow.* (*David Copperfield* by Charles Dickens)

nice ADJ discriminating. Able to make good judgements or choices ❏

consequently a claim to be nice (*Emma* by Jane Austen)

nigh ADV nigh means near ❏ *He'll never know how nigh he come to getting lynched* (*The Adventures of Huckleberry Finn* by Mark Twain)

nimbleness NOUN nimbleness means being able to move very quickly or skillfully ❏ *and with incredible accuracy and nimbleness* (*Treasure Island* by Robert Louis Stevenson)

noggin NOUN a noggin is a small mug or a wooden cup ❏ *you'll bring me one noggin of rum* (*Treasure Island* by Robert Louis Stevenson)

none ADJ neither ❏ *none can die* (*The Good-Morrow* by John Donne)

notices NOUN observations ❏ *Arch are his notices* (*The Prelude* by William Wordsworth)

occiput NOUN occiput means the back of the head ❏ *saw off the occiput of each couple* (*Gulliver's Travels* by Jonathan Swift)

officiously ADJ kindly ❏ *the governess who attended Glumdalclitch very officiously lifted me up* (*Gulliver's Travels* by Jonathan Swift)

old salt PHRASE old salt is a slang term for an experienced sailor ❏ *a 'true sea-dog', and a 'real old salt'* (*Treasure Island* by Robert Louis Stevenson)

or ere PHRASE before ❏ *or ere the Hall was built* (*The Prelude* by William Wordsworth)

ostler NOUN one who looks after horses at an inn ❏ *The bill paid, and the waiter remembered, and the ostler not forgotten, and the chambermaid taken into consideration* (*Great Expectations* by Charles Dickens)

ostry NOUN an ostry is an old word for a pub or hotel ❏ *lest I send you into the ostry with a vengeance* (*Doctor Faustus 2.2* by Christopher Marlowe)

outrunning the constable PHRASE outrunning the constable meant spending more than you earn ❏ *but I shall by this means be able to* check your bills and to pull you up if I find you outrunning the constable. (*Great Expectations* by Charles Dickens)

over ADJ across ❑ *It is in length six yards, and in the thickest part at least three yards over* (*Gulliver's Travels* by Jonathan Swift)

over the broomstick PHRASE this is a phrase meaning 'getting married without a formal ceremony' ❑ *They both led tramping lives, and this woman in Gerrard-street here, had been married very young, over the broomstick (as we say), to a tramping man, and was a perfect fury in point of jealousy.* (*Great Expectations* by Charles Dickens)

own VERB own means to admit or to acknowledge ❑ *It's my old girl that advises. She has the head. But I never own to it before her. Discipline must be maintained* (*Bleak House* by Charles Dickens)

page NOUN here page means a boy employed to run errands ❑ *not my feigned page* (*On His Mistress* by John Donne)

paid pretty dear PHRASE paid pretty dear means paid a high price or suffered quite a lot ❑ *I paid pretty dear for my monthly fourpenny piece* (*Treasure Island* by Robert Louis Stevenson)

pannikins NOUN pannikins were small tin cups ❑ *of lifting light glasses and cups to his lips, as if they were clumsy pannikins* (*Great Expectations* by Charles Dickens)

pards NOUN pards are leopards ❑ *Not charioted by Bacchus and his pards* (*Ode on a Nightingale* by John Keats)

parlour boarder NOUN a pupil who lived with the family ❑ *and somebody had lately raised her from the condition of scholar to parlour boarder* (*Emma* by Jane Austen)

particular, a London PHRASE London in Victorian times and up to the 1950s was famous for having very dense fog – which was a combination of real fog and the

smog of pollution from factories ❑ *This is a London particular . . . A fog, miss'* (*Bleak House* by Charles Dickens)

patten NOUN pattens were wooden soles which were fixed to shoes by straps to protect the shoes in wet weather ❑ *carrying a basket like the Great Seal of England in plaited straw, a pair of pattens, a spare shawl, and an umbrella, though it was a fine bright day* (*Great Expectations* by Charles Dickens)

paviour NOUN a paviour was a labourer who worked on the street pavement ❑ *the paviour his pickaxe* (*Oliver Twist* by Charles Dickens)

peccant ADJ peccant means unhealthy ❑ *other peccant humours* (*Gulliver's Travels* by Jonathan Swift)

penetralium NOUN penetralium is a word used to describe the inner rooms of the house ❑ *and I had no desire to aggravate his impatience previous to inspecting the penetralium* (*Wuthering Heights* by Emily Brontë)

pensive ADV pensive means deep in thought or thinking seriously about something ❑ *and she was leaning pensive on a tomb-stone on her right elbow* (*The Adventures of Huckleberry Finn* by Mark Twain)

penury NOUN penury is the state of being extremely poor ❑ *Distress, if not penury, loomed in the distance* (*Tess of the D'Urbervilles* by Thomas Hardy)

perspective NOUN telescope ❑ *a pocket perspective* (*Gulliver's Travels* by Jonathan Swift)

phaeton NOUN a phaeton was an open carriage for four people ❑ *often condescends to drive by my humble abode in her little phaeton and ponies* (*Pride and Prejudice* by Jane Austen)

phantasm NOUN a phantasm is an illusion, something that is not real. It is sometimes used to mean ghost ❑ *Experience had bred no fancies in* him that could raise the phantasm of appetite (*Silas Marner* by George Eliot)

physic NOUN here physic means medicine ❑ *there I studied physic two years and seven months* (*Gulliver's Travels* by Jonathan Swift)

pinioned VERB to pinion is to hold both arms so that a person cannot move them ❑ *But the relentless Ghost pinioned him in both his arms, and forced him to observe what happened next.* (*A Christmas Carol* by Charles Dickens)

piquet NOUN piquet was a popular card game in the C18th ❑ *Mr Hurst and Mr Bingley were at piquet* (*Pride and Prejudice* by Jane Austen)

plaister NOUN a plaister is a piece of cloth on which an apothecary (or pharmacist) would spread ointment. The cloth is then applied to wounds or bruises to treat them ❑ *Then, she gave the knife a final smart wipe on the edge of the plaister, and then sawed a very thick round off the loaf: which she finally, before separating from the loaf, hewed into two halves, of which Joe got one, and I the other.* (*Great Expectations* by Charles Dickens)

plantations NOUN here plantations means colonies, which are countries controlled by a more powerful country ❑ *besides our plantations in America* (*Gulliver's Travels* by Jonathan Swift)

plastic ADV here plastic is an old term meaning shaping or a power that was forming ❑ *A plastic power abode with me* (*The Prelude* by William Wordsworth)

players NOUN actors ❑ *of players which upon the world's stage be* (*On His Mistress* by John Donne)

plump ADV all at once, suddenly ❑ *But it took a bit of time to get it well round, the change come so uncommon plump, didn't it?* (*Great Expectations* by Charles Dickens)

plundered VERB to plunder is to rob or steal from ❑ *These crosses stand*

for the names of ships or towns that they sank or plundered (*Treasure Island* by Robert Louis Stevenson)

pommel ❶ VERB to pommel someone is to hit them repeatedly with your fists ❑ *hug him round the neck, pommel his back, and kick his legs in irrepressible affection!* (*A Christmas Carol* by Charles Dickens) ❷ NOUN a pommel is the part of a saddle that rises up at the front ❑ *He had his gun across his pommel* (*The Adventures of Huckleberry Finn* by Mark Twain)

poor's rates NOUN poor's rates were property taxes which were used to support the poor ❑ *"Oh!" replied the undertaker; "why, you know, Mr. Bumble, I pay a good deal towards the poor's rates."* (*Oliver Twist* by Charles Dickens)

popular ADJ popular means ruled by the people, or Republican, rather than ruled by a monarch ❑ *With those of Greece compared and popular Rome* (*The Prelude* by William Wordsworth)

porringer NOUN a porringer is a small bowl ❑ *Of this festive composition each boy had one porringer, and no more* (*Oliver Twist* by Charles Dickens)

postboy NOUN a postboy was the driver of a horse-drawn carriage ❑ *He spoke to a postboy who was dozing under the gateway* (*Oliver Twist* by Charles Dickens)

post-chaise NOUN a fast carriage for two or four passengers ❑ *Looking round, he saw that it was a post-chaise, driven at great speed* (*Oliver Twist* by Charles Dickens)

postern NOUN a small gate usually at the back of a building ❑ *The little servant happening to be entering the fortress with two hot rolls, I passed through the postern and crossed the drawbridge, in her company* (*Great Expectations* by Charles Dickens)

pottle NOUN a pottle was a small basket ❑ *He had a paper-bag under each arm and a pottle of*

DANIEL DEFOE

strawberries in one hand . . . (Great Expectations by Charles Dickens)

pounce NOUN pounce is a fine powder used to prevent ink spreading on untreated paper ❑ *in that grim atmosphere of pounce and parchment, red-tape, dusty wafers, ink-jars, brief and draft paper, law reports, writs, declarations, and bills of costs (David Copperfield* by Charles Dickens)

pox NOUN pox means sexually transmitted diseases like syphilis ❑ *how the pox in all its consequences and denominations (Gulliver's Travels* by Jonathan Swift)

prelibation NOUN prelibation means a foretaste of or an example of something to come ❑ *A prelibation to the mower's scythe (The Prelude* by William Wordsworth)

prentice NOUN an apprentice ❑ *and Joe, sitting on an old gun, had told me that when I was 'prentice to him regularly bound, we would have such Larks there! (Great Expectations* by Charles Dickens)

presently ADV immediately ❑ *I presently knew what they meant (Gulliver's Travels* by Jonathan Swift)

pumpion NOUN pumpkin ❑ *for it was almost as large as a small pumpion (Gulliver's Travels* by Jonathan Swift)

punctual ADJ kept in one place ❑ *was not a punctual presence, but a spirit (The Prelude* by William Wordsworth)

quadrille ■ NOUN a quadrille is a dance invented in France which is usually performed by four couples ❑ *However, Mr Swiveller had Miss Sophy's hand for the first quadrille (country-dances being low, were utterly proscribed) (The Old Curiosity Shop* by Charles Dickens) ■ NOUN quadrille was a card game for four people ❑ *to make up her pool of quadrille in the evening (Pride and Prejudice* by Jane Austen)

quality NOUN gentry or upper-class people ❑ *if you are with the quality*

(The Adventures of Huckleberry Finn by Mark Twain)

quick parts PHRASE quick-witted ❑ *Mr Bennet was so odd a mixture of quick parts (Pride and Prejudice* by Jane Austen)

quid NOUN a quid is something chewed or kept in the mouth, like a piece of tobacco ❑ *rolling his quid (Treasure Island* by Robert Louis Stevenson)

quit VERB quit means to avenge or to make even ❑ *But Faustus's death shall quit my infamy (Doctor Faustus 4.3* by Christopher Marlowe)

rags NOUN divisions ❑ *Nor hours, days, months, which are the rags of time (The Sun Rising* by John Donne)

raiment NOUN raiment means clothing ❑ *the mountain shook off turf and flower, had only heath for raiment and crag for gem (Jane Eyre* by Charlotte Brontë)

rain cats and dogs PHRASE an expression meaning rain heavily. The origin of the expression is unclear ❑ *But it'll perhaps rain cats and dogs to-morrow (Silas Marner* by George Eliot)

raised Cain PHRASE raised Cain means caused a lot of trouble. Cain is a character in the Bible who killed his brother Abel ❑ *and every time he got drunk he raised Cain around town (The Adventures of Huckleberry Finn* by Mark Twain)

rambling ADJ rambling means confused and not very clear ❑ *my head began to be filled very early with rambling thoughts (Robinson Crusoe* by Daniel Defoe)

raree-show NOUN a raree-show is an old term for a peep-show or a fairground entertainment ❑ *A raree-show is here, with children gathered round (The Prelude* by William Wordsworth)

recusants NOUN people who resisted authority ❑ *hardy recusants (The Prelude* by William Wordsworth)

282

redounding VERB eddying. An eddy is a movement in water or air which goes round and round instead of flowing in one direction ❏ *mists and steam-like fogs redounding everywhere* (*The Prelude* by William Wordsworth)

redundant ADJ here redundant means overflowing but Wordsworth also uses it to mean excessively large or too big ❏ *A tempest, a redundant energy* (*The Prelude* by William Wordsworth)

reflex NOUN reflex is a shortened version of reflexion, which is an alternative spelling of reflection ❏ *To cut across the reflex of a star* (*The Prelude* by William Wordsworth)

Reformatory NOUN a prison for young offenders/criminals ❏ *Even when I was taken to have a new suit of clothes, the tailor had orders to make them like a kind of Reformatory, and on no account to let me have the free use of my limbs.* (*Great Expectations* by Charles Dickens)

remorse NOUN pity or compassion ❏ *by that remorse* (*On His Mistress* by John Donne)

render VERB in this context render means give. ❏ *and Sarah could render no reason that would be sanctioned by the feeling of the community.* (*Silas Marner* by George Eliot)

repeater NOUN a repeater was a watch that chimed the last hour when a button was pressed – as a result it was useful in the dark ❏ *And his watch is a gold repeater, and worth a hundred pound if it's worth a penny.* (*Great Expectations* by Charles Dickens)

repugnance NOUN repugnance means a strong dislike of something or someone ❏ *overcoming a strong repugnance* (*Treasure Island* by Robert Louis Stevenson)

reverence NOUN reverence means bow. When you bow to someone, you briefly bend your body towards them as a formal way of showing them respect ❏ *made my reverence* (*Gulliver's Travels* by Jonathan Swift)

reverie NOUN a reverie is a day dream ❏ *I can guess the subject of your reverie* (*Pride and Prejudice* by Jane Austen)

revival NOUN a religious meeting held in public ❏ *well I'd ben a-running' a little temperance revival thar' bout a week* (*The Adventures of Huckleberry Finn* by Mark Twain)

revolt VERB revolt means turn back or stop your present course of action and go back to what you were doing before ❏ *Revolt, or I'll in piecemeal tear thy flesh* (*Doctor Faustus 5.1* by Christopher Marlowe)

rheumatics/rheumatism NOUN rheumatics [rheumatism] is an illness that makes your joints or muscles stiff and painful ❏ *a new cure for the rheumatics* (*Treasure Island* by Robert Louis Stevenson)

riddance NOUN riddance is usually used in the form good riddance which you say when you are pleased that something has gone or been left behind ❏ *I'd better go into the house, and die and be a riddance* (*David Copperfield* by Charles Dickens)

rimy ADJ rimy is an ADJECTIVE which means covered in ice or frost ❏ *It was a rimy morning, and very damp* (*Great Expectations* by Charles Dickens)

riper ADJ riper means more mature or older ❏ *At riper years to Wittenberg he went* (*Doctor Faustus chorus* by Christopher Marlowe)

rubber NOUN a set of games in whist or backgammon ❏ *her father was sure of his rubber* (*Emma* by Jane Austen)

ruffian NOUN a ruffian is a person who behaves violently ❏ *and when the ruffian had told him* (*Treasure Island* by Robert Louis Stevenson)

sadness NOUN sadness is an old term meaning seriousness ❏ *But I* *prithee tell me, in good sadness* (*Doctor Faustus* 2.2 by Christopher Marlowe)

sailed before the mast PHRASE this phrase meant someone who did not look like a sailor ❑ *he had none of the appearance of a man that sailed before the mast* (*Treasure Island* by Robert Louis Stevenson)

scabbard NOUN a scabbard is the covering for a sword or dagger ❑ *Girded round its middle was an antique scabbard; but no sword was in it, and the ancient sheath was eaten up with rust* (*A Christmas Carol* by Charles Dickens)

schooners NOUN A schooner is a fast, medium-sized sailing ship ❑ *if schooners, islands, and maroons* (*Treasure Island* by Robert Louis Stevenson)

science NOUN learning or knowledge ❑ *Even Science, too, at hand* (*The Prelude* by William Wordsworth)

scrouge VERB to scrouge means to squeeze or to crowd ❑ *to scrouge in and get a sight* (*The Adventures of Huckleberry Finn* by Mark Twain)

scrutore NOUN a scrutore, or escritoire, was a writing table ❑ *set me gently on my feet upon the scrutore* (*Gulliver's Travels* by Jonathan Swift)

scutcheon/escutcheon NOUN an escutcheon is a shield with a coat of arms, or the symbols of a family name, engraved on it ❑ *On the scutcheon we'll have a bend* (*The Adventures of Huckleberry Finn* by Mark Twain)

sea-dog PHRASE sea-dog is a slang term for an experienced sailor or pirate ❑ *a 'true sea-dog', and a 'real old salt,'* (*Treasure Island* by Robert Louis Stevenson)

see the lions PHRASE to see the lions was to go and see the sights of London. Originally the phrase referred to the menagerie in the Tower of London and later in Regent's Park ❑ *We will go and see the lions for an hour or two*

– it's something to have a fresh fellow like you to show them to, Copperfield (*David Copperfield* by Charles Dickens)

self-conceit NOUN self-conceit is an old term which means having too high an opinion of oneself, or deceiving yourself ❑ *Till swollen with cunning, of a self-conceit* (*Doctor Faustus chorus* by Christopher Marlowe)

seneschal NOUN a steward ❑ *where a grey-headed seneschal sings a funny chorus in a funnier body of vassals* (*Oliver Twist* by Charles Dickens)

sensible ADJ if you were sensible of something you were aware or conscious of something ❑ *If my children are silly I must hope to be always sensible of it* (*Pride and Prejudice* by Jane Austen)

sessions NOUN court cases were heard at specific times of the year called sessions ❑ *He lay in prison very ill, during the whole interval between his committal for trial, and the coming round of the Sessions.* (*Great Expectations* by Charles Dickens)

shabby ADJ shabby places look old and in bad condition ❑ *a little bit of a shabby village named Pikesville* (*The Adventures of Huckleberry Finn* by Mark Twain)

shay-cart NOUN a shay-cart was a small cart drawn by one horse ❑ *"I were at the Bargemen t'other night, Pip;" whenever he subsided into affection, he called me Pip, and whenever he relapsed into politeness he called me Sir; "when there come up in his shay-cart Pumblechook."* (*Great Expectations* by Charles Dickens)

shilling NOUN a shilling is an old unit of currency. There were twenty shillings in every British pound ❑ *"Ten shillings too much," said the gentleman in the white waistcoat.* (*Oliver Twist* by Charles Dickens)

shines NOUN tricks or games ❑ *well, it would make a cow laugh to see the* *shines that old idiot cut* (*The Adventures of Huckleberry Finn* by Mark Twain)

shirking VERB shirking means not doing what you are meant to be doing, or evading your duties ❑ *some of you shirking lubbers* (*Treasure Island* by Robert Louis Stevenson)

shiver my timbers PHRASE shiver my timbers is an expression which was used by sailors and pirates to express surprise ❑ *why, shiver my timbers, if I hadn't forgotten my score!* (*Treasure Island* by Robert Louis Stevenson)

shoe-roses NOUN shoe-roses were roses made from ribbons which were stuck on to shoes as decoration ❑ *the very shoe-roses for Netherfield were got by proxy* (*Pride and Prejudice* by Jane Austen)

singular ADJ singular means very great and remarkable or strange ❑ *"Singular dream," he says* (*The Adventures of Huckleberry Finn* by Mark Twain)

sire NOUN sire is an old word which means lord or master or elder ❑ *She also defied her sire* (*Little Women* by Louisa May Alcott)

sixpence NOUN a sixpence was half of a shilling ❑ *if she had only a shilling in the world, she would be very lilkely to give away sixpence of it* (*Emma* by Jane Austen)

slavey NOUN the word slavey was used when there was only one servant in a house or boarding-house – so she had to perform all the duties of a larger staff ❑ *Two distinct knocks, sir, will produce the slavey at any time* (*The Old Curiosity Shop* by Charles Dickens)

slender ADJ weak ❑ *In slender accents of sweet verse* (*The Prelude* by William Wordsworth)

slop-shops NOUN slop-shops were shops where cheap ready-made clothes were sold. They mainly sold clothes to sailors ❑ *Accordingly, I took the jacket off, that I might*

learn to do without it; and carrying it under my arm, began a tour of inspection of the various slop-shops. (*David Copperfield* by Charles Dickens)

sluggard NOUN a lazy person ❑ *"Stand up and repeat 'Tis the voice of the sluggard,'"* said the Gryphon. (*Alice's Adventures in Wonderland* by Lewis Carroll)

smallpox NOUN smallpox is a serious infectious disease ❑ *by telling the men we had smallpox aboard* (*The Adventures of Huckleberry Finn* by Mark Twain)

smalls NOUN smalls are short trousers ❑ *It is difficult for a large-headed, small-eyed youth, of lumbering make and heavy countenance, to look dignified under any circumstances; but it is more especially so, when superadded to these personal attractions are a red nose and yellow smalls* (*Oliver Twist* by Charles Dickens)

sneeze-box NOUN a box for snuff was called a sneeze-box because sniffing snuff makes the user sneeze ❑ *To think of Jack Dawkins — lummy Jack — the Dodger — the Artful Dodger — going abroad for a common twopenny halfpenny sneeze-box!* (*Oliver Twist* by Charles Dickens)

snorted VERB slept ❑ *Or snorted we in the Seven Sleepers' den?* (*The Good-Morrow* by John Donne)

snuff NOUN snuff is tobacco in powder form which is taken by sniffing ❑ *as he thrust his thumb and forefinger into the proffered snuff-box of the undertaker: which was an ingenious little model of a patent coffin.* (*Oliver Twist* by Charles Dickens)

soliloquized VERB to soliloquize is when an actor in a play speaks to himself or herself rather than to another actor ❑ *"A new servitude! There is something in that," I soliloquized (mentally, be it understood; I did not talk aloud)* (*Jane Eyre* by Charlotte Brontë)

285

sough NOUN a sough is a drain or a ditch ❑ *as you may have noticed the sough that runs from the marshes* (*Wuthering Heights* by Emily Brontë)

spirits NOUN a spirit is the nonphysical part of a person which is believed to remain alive after their death ❑ *that I might raise up spirits when I please* (*Doctor Faustus 1.5* by Christopher Marlowe)

spleen **1** NOUN here spleen means a type of sadness or depression which was thought to only affect the wealthy ❑ *yet here I could plainly discover the true seeds of spleen* (*Gulliver's Travels* by Jonathan Swift) **2** NOUN irritability and low spirits ❑ *Adieu to disappointment and spleen* (*Pride and Prejudice* by Jane Austen)

spondulicks NOUN spondulicks is a slang word which means money ❑ *not for all his spondulicks and as much more on top of it* (*The Adventures of Huckleberry Finn* by Mark Twain)

stalled of VERB to be stalled of something is to be bored with it ❑ *I'm stalled of doing naught* (*Wuthering Heights* by Emily Brontë)

stanchion NOUN a stanchion is a pole or bar that stands upright and is used as a buidling support ❑ *and slid down a stanchion* (*The Adventures of Huckleberry Finn* by Mark Twain)

stang NOUN stang is another word for pole which was an old measurement ❑ *These fields were intermingled with woods of half a stang* (*Gulliver's Travels* by Jonathan Swift)

starlings NOUN a starling is a wall built around the pillars that support a bridge to protect the pillars ❑ *There were states of the tide when, having been down the river, I could not get back through the eddy-chafed arches and starlings of old London Bridge* (*Great Expectations* by Charles Dickens)

startings NOUN twitching or night-time movements of the body ❑ *with midnight's startings* (*On His Mistress* by John Donne)

stomacher NOUN a panel at the front of a dress ❑ *but send her aunt the pattern of a stomacher* (*Emma* by Jane Austen)

stoop VERB swoop ❑ *Once a kite hovering over the garden made a swoop at me* (*Gulliver's Travels* by Jonathan Swift)

succedaneum NOUN a succedaneum is a substitute ❑ *But as a succedaneum* (*The Prelude* by William Wordsworth)

suet NOUN a hard animal fat used in cooking ❑ *and your jaws are too weak For anything tougher than suet* (*Alice's Adventures in Wonderland* by Lewis Carroll)

sultry ADJ sultry weather is hot and damp. Here sultry means unpleasant or risky ❑ *for it was getting pretty sultry for us* (*The Adventures of Huckleberry Finn* by Mark Twain)

summerset NOUN summerset is an old spelling of somersault. If someone does a somersault, they turn over completely in the air ❑ *I have seen him do the summerset* (*Gulliver's Travels* by Jonathan Swift)

supper NOUN supper was a light meal taken late in the evening. The main meal was dinner which was eaten at four or five in the afternoon ❑ *and the supper table was all set out* (*Emma* by Jane Austen)

surfeits VERB to surfeit in something is to have far too much of it, or to overindulge in it to an unhealthy degree ❑ *He surfeits upon cursed necromancy* (*Doctor Faustus chorus* by Christopher Marlowe)

surtout NOUN a surtout is a long close-fitting overcoat ❑ *He wore a long black surtout reaching nearly to his ankles* (*The Old Curiosity Shop* by Charles Dickens)

swath NOUN swath is the width of corn cut by a scythe ❑ *while thy* *hook Spares the next swath* (*Ode to Autumn* by John Keats)

sylvan ADJ sylvan means belonging to the woods ❑ *Sylvan historian* (*Ode on a Grecian Urn* by John Keats)

taction NOUN taction means touch. This means that the people had to be touched on the mouth or the ears to get their attention ❑ *without being roused by some external taction upon the organs of speech and hearing* (*Gulliver's Travels* by Jonathan Swift)

Tag and Rag and Bobtail PHRASE the riff-raff, or lower classes. Used in an insulting way ❑ *"No," said he; "not till it got about that there was no protection on the premises, and it come to be considered dangerous, with convicts and Tag and Rag and Bobtail going up and down."* (*Great Expectations* by Charles Dickens)

tallow NOUN tallow is hard animal fat that is used to make candles and soap ❑ *and a lot of tallow candles* (*The Adventures of Huckleberry Finn* by Mark Twain)

tan VERB to tan means to beat or whip ❑ *and if I catch you about that school I'll tan you good* (*The Adventures of Huckleberry Finn* by Mark Twain)

tanyard NOUN the tanyard is part of a tannery, which is a place where leather is made from animal skins ❑ *hid in the old tanyard* (*The Adventures of Huckleberry Finn* by Mark Twain)

tarry ADJ tarry means the colour of tar or black ❑ *his tarry pig-tail* (*Treasure Island* by Robert Louis Stevenson)

thereof PHRASE from there ❑ *By all desires which thereof did ensue* (*On His Mistress* by John Donne)

thick with, be PHRASE if you are 'thick with someone' you are very close, sharing secrets – it is often used to describe people who are planning something secret ❑ *Hasn't he been thick with Mr*

Heathcliff lately? (*Wuthering Heights* by Emily Brontë)

thimble NOUN a thimble is a small cover used to protect the finger while sewing ❑ *The paper had been sealed in several places by a thimble* (*Treasure Island* by Robert Louis Stevenson)

thirtover ADJ thirtover is an old word which means obstinate or that someone is very determined to do want they want and can not be persuaded to do something in another way ❑ *I have been living on in a thirtover, lackadaisical way* (*Tess of the D'Urbervilles* by Thomas Hardy)

timbrel NOUN timbrel is a tambourine ❑ *What pipes and timbrels?* (*Ode on a Grecian Urn* by John Keats)

tin NOUN tin is slang for money/cash ❑ *Then the plain question is, an't it a pity that this state of things should continue, and how much better would it be for the old gentleman to hand over a reasonable amount of tin, and make it all right and comfortable* (*The Old Curiosity Shop* by Charles Dickens)

tincture NOUN a tincture is a medicine made with alcohol and a small amount of a drug ❑ *with ink composed of a cephalic tincture* (*Gulliver's Travels* by Jonathan Swift)

tithe NOUN a tithe is a tax paid to the church ❑ *and held farms which, speaking from a spiritual point of view, paid highly-desirable tithes* (*Silas Marner* by George Eliot)

towardly ADJ a towardly child is dutiful or obedient ❑ *and a towardly child* (*Gulliver's Travels* by Jonathan Swift)

toys NOUN trifles are things which are considered to have little importance, value, or significance ❑ *purchase my life from them bysome bracelets, glass rings, and other toys* (*Gulliver's Travels* by Jonathan Swift)

tract NOUN a tract is a religious pamphlet or leaflet ❑ *and Joe*

Harper got a hymn-book and a tract (*The Adventures of Huckleberry Finn* by Mark Twain)

train-oil NOUN train-oil is oil from whale blubber ❑ *The train-oil and gunpowder were shoved out of sight in a minute* (*Wuthering Heights* by Emily Brontë)

tribulation NOUN tribulation means the suffering or difficulty you experience in a particular situation ❑ *Amy was learning this distinction through much tribulation* (*Little Women* by Louisa May Alcott)

trivet NOUN a trivet is a three-legged stand for resting a pot or kettle ❑ *a pocket-knife in his right; and a pewter pot on the trivet* (*Oliver Twist* by Charles Dickens)

trot line NOUN a trot line is a fishing line to which a row of smaller fishing lines are attached ❑ *when he got along I was hard at it taking up a trot line* (*The Adventures of Huckleberry Finn* by Mark Twain)

troth NOUN oath or pledge ❑ *I wonder, by my troth* (*The Good-Morrow* by John Donne)

truckle NOUN a truckle bedstead is a bed that is on wheels and can be slid under another bed to save space ❑ *It rose under my hand, and the door yielded. Looking in, I saw a lighted candle on a table, a bench, and a mattress on a truckle bedstead.* (*Great Expectations* by Charles Dickens)

trump NOUN a trump is a good, reliable person wo can be trusted ❑ *This lad Hawkins is a trump, I perceive* (Treasure Island by Robert Louis Stevenson)

tucker NOUN a tucker is a frilly lace collar which is worn around the neck ❑ *Whereat Scrooge's niece's sister the plump one with the lace tucker: not the one with the roses blushed.* (*A Christmas Carol* by Charles Dickens)

tureen NOUN a large bowl with a lid from which soup or vegetables are served ❑ *Waiting in a hot tureen!* (*Alice's Adventures in Wonderland* by Lewis Carroll)

turnkey NOUN a prison officer; jailer ❑ *As we came out of the prison through the lodge, I found that the great importance of my guardian was appreciated by the turnkeys, no less than by those whom they held in charge.* (*Great Expectations* by Charles Dickens)

turnpike NOUN the upkeep of many roads of the time was paid for by tolls (fees) collected at posts along the road. There was a gate to prevent people travelling further along the road until the toll had been paid. ❑ *Traddles, whom I have taken up by appointment at the turnpike, presents a dazzling combination of cream colour and light blue; and both he and Mr. Dick have a general effect about them of being all gloves.* (*David Copperfield* by Charles Dickens)

twas PHRASE it was ❑ *twas but a dream of thee* (*The Good-Morrow* by John Donne)

tyrannized VERB tyrannized means bullied or forced to do things against their will ❑ *for people would soon cease coming there to be tyrannized over and put down* (*Treasure Island* by Robert Louis Stevenson)

'un NOUN 'un is a slang term for one – usually used to refer to a person ❑ *She's been thinking the old 'un* (*David Copperfield* by Charles Dickens)

undistinguished ADJ undiscriminating or incapable of making a distinction between good and bad things ❑ *their undistinguished appetite to devour everything* (*Gulliver's Travels* by Jonathan Swift)

use NOUN habit ❑ *Though use make you apt to kill me* (*The Flea* by John Donne)

vacant ADJ vacant usually means empty, but here Wordsworth uses it to mean carefree ❑ *To vacant musing, unreproved neglect* (*The Prelude* by William Wordsworth)

valetudinarian NOUN one too concerned with his or her own health. ❑ *for having been a valetudinarian all his life* (*Emma* by Jane Austen)

vamp VERB vamp means to walk or tramp to somewhere ❑ *Well, vamp on to Marlott, will 'ee* (*Tess of the D'Urbervilles* by Thomas Hardy)

vapours NOUN the vapours is an old term which means unpleasant and strange thoughts, which make the person feel nervous and unhappy ❑ *and my head was full of vapours* (*Robinson Crusoe* by Daniel Defoe)

vegetables NOUN here vegetables means plants ❑ *the other vegetables are in the same proportion* (*Gulliver's Travels* by Jonathan Swift)

venturesome ADJ if you are venturesome you are willing to take risks ❑ *he must be either hopelessly stupid or a venturesome fool* (*Wuthering Heights* by Emily Brontë)

verily ADJ verily means really or truly ❑ *though I believe verily* (*Robinson Crusoe* by Daniel Defoe)

vicinage NOUN vicinage is an area or the residents of an area ❑ *and to his thought the whole vicinage was haunted by her.* (*Silas Marner* by George Eliot)

victuals NOUN victuals means food ❑ *grumble a little over the victuals* (*The Adventures of Huckleberry Finn* by Mark Twain)

vintage NOUN vintage in this context means wine ❑ *Oh, for a draught of vintage!* (*Ode on a Nightingale* by John Keats)

virtual ADJ here virtual means powerful or strong ❑ *had virtual faith* (*The Prelude* by William Wordsworth)

vittles NOUN vittles is a slang word which means food ❑ *There never was such a woman for givin' away vittles and drink* (*Little Women* by Louisa May Alcott)

voided straight PHRASE voided straight is an old expression which means emptied immediately ❑ *see the rooms be voided straight* (*Doctor Faustus 4.1* by Christopher Marlowe)

wainscot NOUN wainscot is wood panel lining in a room so wainscoted means a room lined with wooden panels ❑ *in the dark wainscoted parlor* (*Silas Marner* by George Eliot)

walking the plank PHRASE walking the plank is a punishment in which a prisoner would be made to walk along a plank on the side of the ship and fall into the sea, where they would be abandoned ❑ *about hanging, and walking the plank* (*Treasure Island* by Robert Louis Stevenson)

want VERB want means to be lacking or short of ❑ *The next thing wanted was to get the picture framed* (*Emma* by Jane Austen)

wanting ADJ wanting means lacking or missing ❑ *wanting two fingers of the left hand* (*Treasure Island* by Robert Louis Stevenson)

wanting, I was not PHRASE I was not wanting means I did not fail ❑ *I was not wanting to lay a foundation of religious knowledge in his mind* (*Robinson Crusoe* by Daniel Defoe)

ward NOUN a ward is, usually, a child who has been put under the protection of the court or a guardian for his or her protection ❑ *I call the Wards in Jarndyce. The are caged up with all the others.* (*Bleak House* by Charles Dickens)

waylay VERB to waylay someone is to lie in wait for them or to intercept them ❑ *I must go up the road and waylay him* (*The Adventures of Huckleberry Finn* by Mark Twain)

weazen NOUN weazen is a slang word for throat. It actually means shrivelled ❑ *You with a uncle too! Why, I knowed you at Gargery's when you was so small a wolf that I could have took your weazen betwixt this finger and thumb and chucked* *you away dead* (*Great Expectations* by Charles Dickens)

wery ❶ ADV very ❑ *Be wery careful o' vidders all your life* (*Pickwick Papers* by Charles Dickens) ❷ *See* wibrated

wherry NOUN wherry is a small swift rowing boat for one person ❑ *It was flood tide when Daniel Quilp sat himself down in the wherry to cross to the opposite shore.* (*The Old Curiosity Shop* by Charles Dickens)

whether PREP whether means which of the two in this example ❑ *we came in full view of a great island or continent (for we knew not whether)* (*Gulliver's Travels* by Jonathan Swift)

whetstone NOUN a whetstone is a stone used to sharpen knives and other tools ❑ *I dropped pap's whetstone there too* (*The Adventures of Huckleberry Finn* by Mark Twain)

wibrated VERB in Dickens's use of the English language 'w' often replaces 'v' when he is reporting speech. So here 'wibrated' means 'vibrated'. In Pickwick Papers a judge asks Sam Weller (who constantly confuses the two letters) 'Do you spell it with a 'v' or a 'w'?' to which Weller replies 'That depends upon the taste and fancy of the speller, my Lord' ❑ *There are strings . . . in the human heart that had better not be wibrated* (*Barnaby Rudge* by Charles Dickens)

wicket NOUN a wicket is a little door in a larger entrance ❑ *Having rested here, for a minute or so, to collect a good burst of sobs and an imposing show of tears and terror, he knocked loudly at the wicket;* (*Oliver Twist* by Charles Dickens)

without CONJ without means unless ❑ *You don't know about me, without you have read a book by the name of The Adventures of Tom Sawyer* (*The Adventures of Huckleberry Finn* by Mark Twain)

wittles ❶ NOUN vittles is a slang word which means food ❑ *I live on broken wittles – and I sleep on the coals* (*David Copperfield* by Charles Dickens) ❷ *See* wibrated

woo VERB courts or forms a proper relationship with ❑ *before it woo* (*The Flea* by John Donne)

words, to have PHRASE if you have words with someone you have a disagreement or an argument ❑ *I do not want to have words with a young thing like you.* (*Black Beauty* by Emily Brontë)

workhouse NOUN workhouses were places where the homeless were given food and a place to live in return for doing very hard work ❑ *And the Union workhouses? demanded Scrooge. Are they still in operation?* (*A Christmas Carol* by Charles Dickens)

yawl NOUN a yawl is a small boat kept on a bigger boat for short trips. Yawl is also the name for a small fishing boat ❑ *She sent out her yawl, and we went aboard* (*The Adventures of Huckleberry Finn* by Mark Twain)

yeomanry NOUN the yeomanry was a collective term for the middle classes involved in agriculture ❑ *The yeomanry are precisely the order of people with whom I feel I can have nothing to do* (*Emma* by Jane Austen)

yonder ADV yonder means over there ❑ *all in the same second we seem to hear low voices in yonder!* (*The Adventures of Huckleberry Finn* by Mark Twain)